THE LOST KINGDOM

RIFT
BOOK 2

CHRIS FRITSCHI

The Lost Kingdom
by
Chris Fritschi

Copyright © 2022 by Christopher Fritschi. All rights reserved. This book or parts thereof may not be reproduced in any form, stored in any retrieval system, or transmitted in any form by any means—electronic, mechanical, photocopy, recording, or otherwise—without prior written permission of the publisher, except as provided by United States of America copyright law.

V4

ISBN:
ISBN-13:

Click or visit
chrisfritschi.com

CONTENTS

Disclaimer   v
Acknowledgments   ix

1. Phantom   1
2. Damning Evidence   12
3. If Not For Friends   27
4. Keys Port   44
5. The Cave   55
6. Deadly Maze   67
7. Gamion   80
8. The Wiltsen   94
9. O'Shef Vale   108
10. Hide   121
11. Change In Plans   136
12. Limborn   152
13. A Little Practice   164
14. Crossing the Shade   176
15. Teck City   191
16. Family   204
17. The Bounty Agent   213
18. Just Out of Reach   226
19. Monsters   240
20. Stitchers   253
21. Jail   266
22. Traitor   279
23. The Graveyard   292
24. Hunted   307
25. Outsiders   322
26. Plans Within Plans   335
27. Stone And Steel   349
28. A Clash of Mages   362
29. One Loose Thread   377
30. Meet me in my Reader Group   381
31. Your Review Helps   382

The Rift Series	383
Other Books From Chris	385
About the Author	387

DISCLAIMER

This is a work of fiction. Names, characters, businesses, places, events and incidents are either the products of the author's imagination or used in a fictitious manner. Any resemblance to actual persons, living or dead, or actual events is purely coincidental.

To my wife.

ACKNOWLEDGMENTS

The pages of his book are the result of all the people who gave their input, guidance, and knowledge. Thank you all.

A special thanks to those special souls for sharing your knowledge and experience.

- The Rift -
Edger City
Refinery
Small
Town Diner
Destroyed
Harvestor
Salta Dyrin
Stitcher
Bar
Freedom
Clan
Suhun City
The Graveyard
100 200 300 400 500

1

PHANTOM

The ground crunched under the hulking tracks of the huge squat machine as it lumbered over the blasted landscape.

Oily grey clouds, heavy and dense, had been spreading for days. They were growing thick and changing to an ugly burnt purple. Blooms of lightning sparked mutely, shrouded within the clouds.

The air felt tight and brittle as needles of electricity strobed within the boiling clouds.

Creatures and insects sensed the change in the air. They knew what was about to happen and fled beyond the reach of the approaching destruction. The only thing remaining was the Turbin Series Three harvester and the destruction was why it was here.

Thirty-eight miles away, Galin glanced up from the game on his Skypad. He briefly checked to see that nothing had changed on the harvester's status board. He shifted in his chair and went back to work on his high score.

The building was filled with the nonstop noise of forklifts and the *whirr* of heat exchangers. Voices echoed over the refinery's loudspeaker in the background as the other harvester pilots shouted in conversation from their stations over the noise.

Galin had learned to tune out the cacophony of racket years ago.

Sure, his last med-check had said the noise was damaging his hearing, but he shrugged it off.

'Sure, doctors are always gonna find something. Healthy people don't make them money.'

It didn't matter. His union guaranteed free medical. He could get hearing implants if he ever needed them.

Through the Skypad, he saw an indicator light change from white to orange on the board of his pilot station.

"Galin," said a voice over his shoulder. "Time to fire it up."

"Yeah, Twill," he grumbled. "I saw the light too. Don't you have something to do?"

Galin tapped on his panel, bringing up the real-time map of the storm's position. From the comfort of his station, miles away, the storm was nothing more than a digital blob on his screen, but Galin had seen the awesome power of these storms first-hand. It didn't matter how far away he was, it made him uneasy to think he lived on the same planet as something so powerful.

The harvester had been waiting, motionless and dormant for days, but with the first signs of static charge in the air, the small onboard management bot, nicknamed Hank, began bringing the inert beast to life.

The AHS22 operations bot ran through the start-up procedure, activating communications and linking the harvester to Galin's pilot station.

Inside the belly of the harvester, Galin's smiling face appeared on the screen.

"How ya doing, Hank?" asked Galin.

Hank had been built with only three fingers on each hand; it was all it needed to perform its job. It gave Galin a passable thumbs-up.

Galin's coffee cup stopped mid-way to his mouth, and he leaned in closer; his face filling the display.

"What the..." he said. "Hank. Look at me."

Hank obeyed and turned to face the screen.

To be accurate, Hank didn't have a face in the traditional sense. Two optics were mounted above a speaker and audio receptors. The large lenses gave it a cow-eyed appearance. Below that was an omni-directional auditory ring. All of this was attached to a flexible gooseneck that could tilt and swivel.

"Who did that?" Galin shouted, flushing red as he pushed away from his terminal.

The other pilots glanced over from their own stations, several of them smirking.

"What's all the excitement, guy?" Twill asked, coming over. The grin on his face hinted he already knew.

Fuming, Galin pointed at his screen.

Hank gazed patiently back. Draped on his metal frame was a t-shirt that said, 'I'm with stupid.'

The crowd around Galin erupted in laughter. He glared at Twill, who couldn't catch his breath.

"I'm telling you for the last time," Galin growled, "stop picking on Hank."

"It's just a bot," Twill said, wiping his streaming eyes.

"He's my..." Galin paused. He thought of Hank as a friend. Over his years of piloting harvesters, everyone else had continued to upgrade their bots but not Galin. He had grown attached to Hank. The only time the bot spoke was to provide system status, but he was a good listener. In his heart of hearts, Galin believed Hank liked him too.

"He's what?" Twill prodded with a grin. He could sense Galin was hiding something.

"My responsibility," Galin finished. "If that shirt jams up his works, I'll be the one that gets chewed out for it."

Twill didn't look convinced, but his smile faded when Galin leaned in close to underscore his seriousness. Everything about the look in his eyes said, 'You crossed the line.'

"Okay. I got it," Twill said.

Galin went back to his station without another look at his antagonist, who tried to laugh it off, but he had been put in his place and everyone knew it.

"All right, Hank," Galin said, checking his board. The readings showed the storm was building quickly. "Let's get ready for the show."

The Series Three onboard sensors scanned the surrounding landscape. Tall jagged Nightcrag mountains shouldered each other in the distance, marking the edge of the storm. The mountain range formed an impenetrable barrier which the storm never drifted beyond. The mountains were scorched and blasted from centuries of storms, but the scarred, raw rock was the only thing that defied the powerful lightning storms..

Adding to their ominous appearance were the sulfurous vapors and fiery glow from the volcanos scattered though out the long chain of mountains.

Glowing tendrils of orange-red molten rock trickled down into pools of lava where sluggish bubbles boiled to the top, bursting with a wet plop and flinging sizzling droplets into the air.

Few places were as foreboding and hellish as the Nightcrag mountain range.

Near by the Series Three, a flash of blinding purple light lanced down from the clouds, smashing into the ground. Clots of sizzling dirt blew out, producing a smoldering crater. The deafening crack of lightning created a shockwave that would throw a person off their feet. If they were too close, their lungs would be scorched by the super-heated air and die.

Hank checked the sensors and located the point of impact. The bot went through the tedious safety protocols of bringing the big harvester to life without complaint. Satisfied everything was working within tolerances, it flipped the final switches, sending power from the harvester's mini reactor to the four massive drive motors that powered its tracks.

The harvester rumbled over the cracked ground until it reached the crater, then ran a sensor check of the impact. The readings spiked into the green, indicating the lightning had successfully pierced through the surface layer and hit a layer of rare mineral deposit of Craynite.

The tremendous heat and electrical charge had reacted with the mineral, and in the split second of liquifying, its elemental structure had completely changed. The new element boiled to the surface where it cooled into a dark-purple crystalline material called Gramite.

This highly fissionable material was the primary energy source for the Teck.

Long lasting, clean, and naturally occurring, its discovery had replaced all other sources of energy within two generations.

The Gramite storm field was one of only five discovered on the Teck half of the planet. None of them had existed before the world had fractured. The event, known as the Rift, had changed many things. Some beneficial, others terrible.

Yet, in the face of this incredible source of energy, the Teck had kept their hate of the Creet and their magic at the forefront of their minds, over generations.

How the Creet had discovered magic was unknown and mostly rumors, but every Teck believed in their hearts that it was the Creet who had nearly destroyed the world after they discovered magic.

In the screen above Hank's head, Galin shook away the thought and turned his attention back to his bot.

Hank activated the harvester's forward mandibles. With a hum, the claws reached out and scooped up the Gramite, then retracted under a hatch in the belly of the harvester. Additional sensors confirmed the Gramite crystal was stable before opening the hatch.

The claws lifted it through the hatch into a small containment box, which sealed closed with a hiss of air. A conveyer moved the precious cargo to the rear of the harvester, into the shielded storage locker.

A green light confirmed the hatch was closed and the harvester was ready for the next deposit.

The bot didn't have to wait long. A searing bolt punched the ground, followed by three more in rapid succession.

"Did you see that?" Galin smiled, impressed. His tiny voice bounced off the walls of the harvester's cabin. "This is turning into a severe storm. That's money in the bank for the company, and a bonus for us."

The cabin vibrated as Hank pivoted the harvester to the nearest of the three strikes. The impact crater was still smoking when Hank rolled up and activated the scanner.

Galin's digital face frowned when the scanner showed it was empty. The bolt had hit an area devoid of Craynite.

"It happens," he said, trying to cheer up the bot. "Let's hit the next one."

Another bolt struck a mile away.

Hank pivoted the harvester and steered it to the far crater.

"It's going to be a busy day," smiled Galin.

After several hours, the storage locker was reaching capacity and the end of its shift. The sun had gone down, and the night sky gave the storm a perfect backdrop to display its true immensity. Powerful jagged bolts of purple lightning shattered the darkness, but Hank wasn't interested in the show. The harvesting settled into its usual rhythm and eventually Galin dozed off. As much as he liked Hank, the bot was not much for carrying a conversation.

Everything looked like it was going to be another tedious shift when a massive bolt slammed into the harvester. Monitors and controls went black, and all contact was lost with the harvester.

Flakes of shielding flew off, melting into droplets, but the Turbin

Series Three was designed with several layers of composite shielding for just such an event.

That would have been little comfort if a living person had been inside. The sound alone would have ruptured their eardrums, and the cavitation would have caused organ damage.

Galin was jarred awake by the angry buzz of system fault indicators.

He sat up, blinking in confusion. The first thing his eyes landed on was the systems display which was scrolling one error message after another.

The comms screen was a hissing snow storm of static.

"Hank?" he said, feeling the first butterflies of worry in his gut. "Hank, come in. You okay, buddy?"

Within the steel crypt of the Series Three, Hank brushed off the strike as a minor event and went about the task of bringing the giant machine back online.

With all of its systems down, the windowless harvester was blind to the outside world. Which is why, neither Hank nor Galin saw the monstrous silhouette approaching, backlit by the lightning.

Nothing on Galin's board was responding, and Hank wasn't answering his calls. He jabbed the keyboard, issuing commands to the system, but it had zero effect.

His eyes anxiously searched his console for any sign of activity. It had never taken this long.

Twill looked up as Galin rushed past him.

"Late for a date?" Till teased, but Galin never looked back as he headed for his service truck.

He jumped in and pressed the accelerator before he switched the truck on. Halfway across the work-yard, he remembered his lights and slapped at the button. The gates of the yard blurred past him as he glanced at his Skypad on the seat next to him.

The thing skittered frustratingly as he tried to hit the uplink option and kept missing.

Swearing an oath, he finally landed his finger on the right button, connecting him to his pilot station.

"I'm coming, Hank," he said.

Outside the inert harvester, lightning vanished and the blackness of night returned, masking the giant as it closed the distance to the harvester.

Hank brought up the last of the operational sensors and set to the task of checking all the systems, starting with the storage locker.

The harvester's storage locker had been engineered with a ridiculous amount of redundant systems and for good reason. If a lightning bolt were to hit even one of the sealed containers holding a crystal, it would set off an instantaneous and unimaginable fusion reaction. A nanosecond later, everything in a ten mile radius would be vaporized.

The systems check came back green across the board. Hank switched the harvester back to operational status, and the cabin was filled with the blare of the proximity alarm.

None of this made sense to Hank. How could this be happening when the harvester wasn't moving, but his display showed something of titanic size nearly on top of him.

Hank threw full power to the harvester's four drives. Its treads chewed up the ground, trying to avoid the impact, but the big machine was too slow.

Hank was flung against the wall as something slammed into the harvester's side. Critical systems began blinking red, and above the wail of alarms, Hank heard the shriek of twisting steel.

The bot anchored itself to the superstructure as the great machine shuddered.

Outside, the giant grabbed one of the harvester's huge tracks and ripped it away. The drive wheel began smoking, melting bearings as it spun out of control.

For the first time in its existence, Hank was overloaded by the avalanche of things happening, many of which were beyond its programming.

It throttled back the stream of error data and searched for the highest priority to deal with first.

The harvester registered several critical failures and fired off an automated distress signal, first starting with its pilot, Galin, then up the chain of command to everyone who should know that millions of dollars' worth of machine was about to turn into scrap.

The harvester's reactor failsafe system went into action, shutting down the core and plunging the interior of the harvester into complete darkness.

Outside, the giant raised a hand high above its head and formed its fingers into a wedge. With all its might, it speared the top of the harvester.

The big machine's reinforced shielding was meant to withstand lightning strikes, not tons of focused steel. The giant's blow tore through the thick skin of the harvester. Then, with a yank, it tore a ragged hole into the machine's side.

Hank turned to see what was happening as another stab of lightning backlit the giant, partially blinding its optics. What little was documented among the static filled recording appeared to be an enormous head peering back at Hank.

The giant took hold of the harvester's shell and peeled it back. Power cables arced and crackled, filling the Series Three with smoke.

Heedless of the harvester's death throes, the giant ripped away the shell until the storage locker was exposed. The safety latches, holding the locker in place, snapped like dried twigs as the giant carefully worked it loose. It was clear it understood what was inside.

Propping the harvester up on its left side, the giant examined the locker until it was satisfied it hadn't suffered any breaches.

Behind it, headlights appeared in the distance, approaching fast. Galin was grinding the accelerator pedal into the floor, trying to squeeze every last drop of power the engine could give.

His Skypad showed the harvester was still a ways off, but he could see the red emergency strobe mounted on the top of its hull.

The giant let go of the harvester, which groaned as it slammed back down, the superstructure breaking under its own weight.

Galin couldn't understand what he was seeing. At first, he thought there was a huge black shadow on the side of the Series Three, but shadows shouldn't block the beam of the strobe light.

Then the shadow stood up and up... and up. Galin crushed the brakes. The front of the truck nosed down as the tires ripped gouges in cracked ground, fighting for traction. The steering wheel spun, breaking his grip, and the truck slewed sideways. Mindless that the truck was dangerously close to rolling, Galin stuck his head out the window, looking up as the giant's eyes rose above him.

Thick billows of dust swallowed the truck as it came to a stop, blinding him from the towering creature. He slapped at the handle and wrestled the door open in a mad scramble to get outside the dust.

He franticly turned one way and another, looking for the creature, but the night had swallowed it up. Through the soles of his boots, he felt the ground tremble with each step as it strode away.

The storm had passed, leaving only the brooding rumble of the receding clouds and the labored hum of his truck as Galin stood there dumbstruck.

Hank!

Carefully avoiding the maze of jagged wreckage, he worked his way into the harvester.

"Hank!" he called, poking his head through the gaping hole. He panned his light over the tangled mess. "Where are you, buddy? Talk to me. Please."

Junk rattled as a three fingered hand pushed into view and gave him a thumbs-up. Galin laughed with relief, grateful his friend was alive.

He spent the rest of the night digging out his bot.

A response crew wouldn't be sent until they were certain the storm was completely over. When they arrived with the sun, they stood slack-jawed at the sight of the gutted harvester.

As Galin tried to explain what he'd seen – or thought he's seen the others traded looks of fear mingled awe.

Nobody wanted to be around if the monstrosity decided to visit the refinery plant.

More than a few were thinking about how much vacation time they had accrued and how it might be a good idea to collect on it, starting today.

2

DAMNING EVIDENCE

"It's not going to happen," Brell snapped; her voice echoing around the ancient chamber. She got to her feet, something she instantly regretted, feeling every bruise, cut, and injury.

"What are we going to do about that?" Kase asked, changing the subject.

He nodded to the wrecked remains of the robot, Billy.

"I'm not touching that thing," Brell said, looking around the chamber. "Seems fitting to just leave it here. We killed off that evil witch thing. That psycho scrap pile can take its place."

"The witch thing was a wraith," he said. "We didn't kill it. Only a very powerful mage could do that. We sent it back to…"

"Please," Brell said, holding out her hand to stop him. "Do not tell me you believe in that 'plane of existence' gibberish."

"You saw it!" Kase said, getting to his feet with a groan. "The ground opened under its feet. There was a whole different world through that hole."

"I saw something," she conceded, "but I can't say what it was."

"It's called magic," he said.

They were standing in the main chamber of the Temple of Blessed Light. That was how it was known to the residents of the city that had been built around it generations ago.

The founders had been drawn by the pillar of light emanating from the temple and had interpreted its annual appearance as a holy display.

Not everyone was as quick to agree.

Brookwal, the town's mage, had studied the carvings on the outer wall of the temple. They revealed this place was, in fact, a tomb created for the return of a mage. One who had chosen to twist natural magic into something dark and evil.

His name was Kregryn, and he had summoned a demon wraith to guard this chamber until he returned.

In all of his exploration of ancient places, Kase had never heard of the mage. But he had seen Kregryn's work, places he had prepared for a secret ritual.

Kase looked down at the relic that had been used to bind the wraith to this place. It was identical to the one his mother Sula had taken from a crumbling chamber under the ruins of a long abandoned city.

That very night, their camp had been attacked by raiders. They hadn't been interested in valuables. They'd been after Sula and the relic.

Even at twelve years old, Kase had been clever, and he'd used that cunning to trick most of the raiders into chasing a horse he'd made them believe was carrying the relic.

He'd thought he had rescued his mother, but that moment had been short lived. Other raiders had surprised him, knocking him unconscious. When Kase had eventually opened his eyes, his mother was gone.

He never saw her again.

Now, years later, he held a similar relic. The memories of that terrible night and his failure to save his mother came flooding back.

He squeezed the relic until his knuckles turned white, focusing his last eleven years of regret, sleepless nights, and bitter tears onto the carved stone.

Something deep stirred inside him.

A force of unspeakable power churned just beyond his beckoning thoughts as the desire for revenge took hold of him.

"Careful," Alwyn warned.

Kase blinked, coming out of his haze.

"You have to be mindful of yourself," Alwyn said. "Magic is much more intuitive than you understand. What you might think of as a harmless wish could be all the prompting magic needs to flow through you. Unprepared, it could overwhelm you like a flash flood. By the time you realized what was happening, it would be too late to control it."

"Sorry," Kase said. "Today's been…"

"Unconventional?" the mage offered.

"Yes." He smiled. "Nobody's going to believe we beat a wraith. It was…"

Kase's mouth clopped shut when he saw Brell staring at him like he was insane.

"Talking to your invisible friend?" she asked. "You know that makes you look crazy, right?"

"He's not invisible," Kase said, holding up his gloved hand.

"Oh, right," she said. "He lives in your glove. That makes it all better."

"It's a SpiritBridge," he insisted. "Alwyn lets me connect –"

"It's magic. It's unnatural and you shouldn't mess with it," she said.

"Are all Tecks like you?" Kase frowned.

"The good ones are," she said, holding out her hand. "Give me back my gun."

Kase handed her the wrecked weapon, which had finally stopped smoldering.

She turned it over in her hand, examining the cracked and charred casing.

"Speaking of scrap," she said, jamming it into her holster with a bitter sigh.

Kase felt oddly guilting for having broken it even though he had used it to save her life.

"It's not your fault," she said, reading his expression.

"Thanks," Kase said.

"Mostly," she added. "Let's get out of here. This place is oppressive."

"So soon?" he said. "It's amazing here. Look at the carvings. It must have been here for... I don't know, hundreds of years? I need to come back here with my journal and take notes." He snapped his fingers, and his eyebrows shot up. "You know, I think the runes on the monolith could be an unknown language. It might be the only example of its kind."

"Come back?" Brell said, incredulous. "We barely survived coming here the first time."

"But it's safe now," he said.

"Maybe not," Alwyn said. "There could be other traps."

"It was nice knowing you," she said. "I'm leaving."

Brell swept the floor with her eyes, making sure she hadn't dropped anything, and headed for the door.

Determined to stay, Kase watched as she reached the far end of the room, and the sudden sense of being alone bore down on him. It wasn't a feeling of loneliness but an impression that the chamber was watching him, judging how vulnerable he would be alone.

He could feel the grim mood of the place beginning to glare down on him. Suddenly, being here alone did not feel like such a good idea.

Brell disappeared around the corner, and Kase hurried to catch up.

The destruction of the wraith had broken several of the spells used to guard the tomb. The narrow hallway was as tight a squeeze as before, but the overwhelming fear that had swarmed their minds the first time through was gone.

Their spirits rose the moment they walked out the tomb door.

Stepping into the walled courtyard, they felt the gloom of the chamber fall away. The night air was cool and fresh, and they took deep breaths.

"Help me up," Brell said when they reached the wall. "I'll pull you up."

"How about I pull you up instead?" Kase said.

He felt Brell's eyes travel up and down his body as a smirk curled the corner of her mouth.

"I'm not strong enough?" he asked, bristling.

"I'm not in the mood to argue," she said and cupped her hands together.

He stepped into her hands, and Brell raised him up with surprising ease.

She's stronger than she looks.

He grabbed the top of the wall and quietly pulled himself up. From his perch, he looked around, checking the square was empty of people. He nodded, seeing they were alone.

Bracing himself, Kase reached down but was just short of her hand. He grunted as Brell jumped and grabbed his hand. She was heavier than he'd expected and nearly pulled him off the wall. He quickly anchored himself and pulled.

How much stuff is she carrying under her cloak?

He strained with the effort, but finally helped pull her to the top, where she clambered up next to him. Kase quickly adopted a casual grin as if hoisting her up had been easy.

"You need a minute?" She grinned, looking at his red, sweating face.

"For what?" he asked, waving her off.

The lattice of vines on the outside wall made it a simple task to scale down, and soon they were standing in the square.

"After I get my stuff from the inn, I'm going home," Brell said. "Thanks for, I don't know, helping out."

After their chance encounter at the Brood Moors battlefield, Kase had joined Brell in her hunt for Ethan Five Seven; an android embedded with a human's psychopathic personality. Their search for the serial killer had to wait until Brell returned to Teck and replace her gun.

"I meant what I said," he said. "I'm going with you to the Teck world."

Brell stopped and turned to him, her face stern.

"I meant what I said too." She frowned. "You're not coming. You don't belong there, *and* if anyone realizes I've smuggled a Creet across the Rift, take a wild guess at who would go to prison for the rest of her life."

"What about the blood debt?" he asked. "Just a moment," he said, counting on his fingers. "I saved your life three times. That's *three* blood debts. You're sworn to protect me, or is that more a guideline than a rule?"

"Hey," she growled. "Don't mock what you don't understand. Yes, I'm honor bound to keep you alive, but that doesn't mean I can't punch you in the face."

"I wasn't mocking," he protested. "In any case, I do understand. You should be mad at yourself, not me. I'm simply the one reminding you of your debt. You can't just up and go without me."

"I'll only be gone for a little while," Brell said, feeling too tired to argue.

"How long is a while?" Kase asked.

Brell didn't like being cornered, especially when she knew she was wrong.

"A month," she said, sounding like she was grinding stones with her teeth. "Do you think you can go that long without getting yourself killed?"

"It's hard to say," he said. "I've been known to have streaks of very poor judgement."

"What's the rush?" Brell asked as they headed down the street to their rented room.

"Rush?"

"Why are you in a hurry for me to come back?" she asked, studying him with a sidelong look.

Kase didn't have an answer, at least not one she would accept. From their time together, it was clear Brell wasn't the 'friends' type. In fact, she wasn't a lot of types when it came to people.

He had the impression she was much more comfortable with people when they were at the other end of her gun.

As prickly as she was, Kase saw a better friend in her than in many of the ones he had back home.

She grabbed him roughly by the arm, jolting him out of his thoughts.

"What?" he blurted.

"Something's wrong," she whispered, pulling him out of the glow of the street light and into the shadows.

There was a crowd gathered outside the inn where they were renting a room. They could hear snatches of angry conversations and see scowling faces in the torchstones' light.

Brell glanced at Kase, who only shrugged.

"I didn't do anything," he said.

She was about to speak when a tall, hard-looking man in uniform appeared from the inn's doorway. The crowd went quiet, looking up at him in anticipation as he set his jaw.

He dramatically raised his hand, and the crowd gasped. From it dangled a bright green ribbon.

"That belongs to my Arlens!" a woman cried.

The crowd boiled with shock and anger. Kase squeezed Brell's arm and pulled her deeper into the shadows.

"I saw that ribbon mixed in with Billy's trinkets," he hissed. The color drained from his face as a new realization dawned on him. "Now I understand why he was so proud of them. Those were trophies from his kills."

"Bots don't keep trophies," Brell said.

"They're not supposed to kill either," he said.

The man in uniform stepped out of the way as the innkeeper took his place and spoke to the mob.

"I didn't know any of this was going on under my roof. I thought they were good people," she said to the crowd, her face streaked with tears. "Killers!" she barked; her face suddenly tight with anger. "My inn, our city, has been defiled by killers."

"They murdered my little girl," a woman said, grabbing the ribbon out of the man's hand and waving it over her head.

"Now hold on, folks," the man said. "We haven't found her yet. We might still find her alive."

"I wish that were true," Kase said. "I told you when we first found Billy we should have destroyed that bot."

"Find the strangers!" someone in the crowd shouted.

"As police chief, I'll say what we do," the man said, but he had already lost control of the crowd, and his words fell on deaf ears.

The people were yelling for "justice," but what they genuinely wanted was blood.

"They ain't left," someone said. "Their horses are still in the stable."

"Get back there and lock the stable doors," someone yelled. "Everyone else, spread out and find them. Gather your neighbors to help."

"Careful," the innkeeper cried. "They're killers."

"That's just great," Brell said as people raised knives, cleavers, and clubs above their heads.

"Come on," Kase said, having seen enough.

"Where...?" Brell started, but Kase had already left the doorway. She slipped out of the shadows and quickly caught up to him as he turned onto another street.

"The city's surrounded by mountains," Kase said, thinking out loud. "The only way out is through the front gate."

"If we run right now, we might make it there before they close it," she said.

"There's people everywhere," he said. "We aren't going to make it there without crossing paths with a mob. They'll shout for help as soon as they see us."

"Anyone gets in the way," Brell started, putting her hand on her gun. Then she remembered it was wrecked and swore under her breath.

"We're trapped," she said. "What about hiding out at your guild?"

"The thieves guild?" he scoffed. "After what happened at New Runefal, they're as eager to kill us as these folks. We should go back to the chamber and hide..."

"Is there something seriously wrong with your head?" she hissed. "I'm not going inside that tomb again."

"The wraith is gone," he said.

"Tell me it's one hundred percent safe inside there," she said. "Go on, say it."

Kase hesitated, thinking it over.

"That's what I thought," she said. "It's not an option."

Both of them knew it was useless to explain that Billy, the bot, was responsible for killing the girl. They'd be condemned just for having brought the bot into the city. Brell would be revealed as a Teck, and even if the good people of the Blessing Light accepted their story, Brell would be executed or handed over to the authorities.

The only choice was to escape.

They hurried away from the inn, finding a neighborhood that hadn't been roused by shouts of the angry mob.

Lights from torchstones lit up the far street as one of the search groups passed by.

"We're running out of time," Kase said as they saw lights coming on in the homes around them.

They ducked into an alcove as the sound of running feet came stamping up behind them.

"Murderers are in the city!" a man cried, running by. "Turn out! Help find them before they kill again."

Kase and Brell moved all the way back into the alcove. They squeezed into the dark pocket, surrounded on three sides by high cold walls. Their only protection was the fragile darkness.

"What did you do?" a voice croaked near their heads.

They spun, startled, but couldn't' see through the deep shadows.

"Over here," the voice said, and something small jabbed Kase in the cheek. He could just make out a small shape clinging to the side of the wall.

"Frog?" Kase asked.

"Gumplin, if it's all the same to you," the frog said.

It was the same frog they had seen on the desk of the town's mage, Brookwal. He was the one who had told them the truth behind the large temple.

They stared, at a loss for words at the implausibility of their situation, topped off with a stone frog.

"Brookwal heard there was a commotion and sent me to see if you'd gotten yourselves killed," Gumplin said.

"That was thoughtful," Brell quipped.

"It was a likely conclusion," the frog said, "since you treated the very real possibility of facing a wraith as lightly as haggling the corner baker. An alternate outcome was not likely."

Brell grumbled something, but Kase ignored it.

"Everyone thinks we killed a little girl, but it wasn't us," Kase said. "I swear it."

Gumplin eyed them closely, a croak rumbling deep inside his chest. "The alternative also seems unlikely," the frog said. "Follow me."

The frog walked along the face of the wall, to the back of the alcove, its stone feet lightly clicking as it went. It turned, climbed up and over the rear wall, and disappeared from sight.

Kase and Brell looked at the impassable wall, not sure what was supposed to happen next.

"That was helpful," Brell said. "How long do you think it'll take before that surly bookend realizes we can't climb walls?"

They heard the subtle sound of crunching, like grains of sand being rubbed underfoot. A puff of cool night air washed over them as the wall swung open.

Behind them, the sound of voices grew louder from the street. A pool of light grew as a mob approached, searching the street.

Kase and Brell hurriedly moved past the open wall, which then sighed closed behind them.

Gumplin looked down on them with his ever-present disgruntled expression as he clung to the side of the building.

"Stay to this narrow alley until you reach a sewer grate" it said.

"Another sewer," Brell said.

"Turn right," Gumplin said. "Then right again. Keep going until you reach a dead end. Move quietly. Do not stop for anything."

"What do we do at the dead end?" Kase asked.

"Wait, of course," Gumplin said, turning away.

They watched the stone frog climb up until it disappeared into the dark.

Their gazes shifted to the dim passage ahead.

"Move quietly," Gumplin's voice repeated, just above a whisper from far off. "And no light. There are things here you do not want to awaken."

Kase glanced at Brell's heavy square toe boots, then at his own soft leather ones.

"Don't worry about me," Brell said, drawing a wicked looking knife out. "If something wakes up, I'll put it back to sleep."

Kase hadn't seen this knife before. Even in the weak light of the alley, the edge looked so sharp it gave him chills.

He took out his assassin's dagger and softly crept forward.

The night was cold, chilled by the air coming off the snow covered mountains ringing most of the city. Patches of thin dirty ice as brittle as dead leaves formed over the scummy water and reflected the dull cast of the sky above.

The menace in Gumplin's warning grew in Kase's mind. Places like this were a playground for his imagination, which wasted no time devising ever more terrifying images of what *things* might be lurking around them.

The smallest sound began to put them on edge.

Brell's boot scraped against something underfoot, drawing a string of whispered swearing from her. They stopped, listening for the faintest sign that the noise had drawn attention.

All was still.

Ahead, Kase saw the sewer grate, but his stomach clenched when it appeared they were coming to a dead end.

His head filled with doubt and worry.

Did I miss the grate on the right? Should we turn around? Why am I leading in the first place?

It wasn't until they reached the grate that Kase realized the shadows had been playing tricks on him. The alleyway branched off to the left and right. The tension squeezing his chest was broken, and he could breathe again.

He glanced up, noticing the peculiarly high walls around them. Surely, he would have seen these tall buildings from the street, but he hadn't.

And why aren't there any windows?

He leaned in closer, thinking the stonework looked very old and crudely fashioned.

There was no doubting their surroundings were solid, but he suspected they were walking through a place that didn't exist in the world he knew.

He couldn't see it with his eyes, but his senses told him everything was slightly skewed, just a hair off center, tilting ever so slightly this way and that.

If there were people beyond these walls, he imagined they would be as subtly misshapen as the rest of this place.

His thoughts were broken when he felt Brell close to his ear.

"What is it?" she whispered. "Why did you stop?"

Kase only shook his head in reply and turned, taking the right alley.

The light struggled to reach down to them, weakening until he could only see shadows within shadows. The walls stretched higher and closer together, squeezing the sky above to a fine thread until it was entirely gone and they were submerged in darkness.

Kase felt Brell's hand gently land on his shoulder. He was a blind guide leading the blind. He used his free hand to feel his way, gently skimming the surface of the wall. It was the only tangible thing that assured him there was still a world around him.

He felt Brell's hand gently tighten, betraying her own unease building.

He cursed the Gumplin as his nerves began to unravel.

What was that bloody frog thinking, sending us into this...

He winced as Brell's hand painfully squeezed him.

Hoping to calm her, he reached up to give her a reassuring pat.

His hand landed on something bony, gnarled, and inhuman.

The grip dug deeper into him.

A gasp jumped from his lungs, and he squeezed the enchanted dagger, vanishing from the spot and escaping the vice-like grip. He reappeared a few feet ahead. His heart pounded in his ears as he spun around, frantically digging a torchstone out of his pocket.

Light flared from his palm in the narrow confines as he held it up, revealing a ghastly, withered human face. It was suspended by eight rickety legs between the two walls. The creature keened in pain as its gnarled hands shielded its eyes from the light.

Kase instantly raised his hand to cast a push spell but stopped himself at the last moment. This thing had slipped in, between him and Brell. Casting the push spell would fling it into Brell's face.

A large hate-filled eye peeked out from under the monster's hand. It locked onto him right before charging, its legs stitching across the walls.

He thought to yank the thing past him, only to change his mind. *I can't lose sight of it.*

Once in the dark, the thing would have all the time it needed to scheme its next attack.

The creature was nearly on him. The idea of it skittering over his body sent a shiver of revulsion through him.

His mind desperately scrambled for what to do. He dared not cast push or pull. What was left?

Something in between.

He stuck out his glove, instantly feeling the surge of raw magic, like a huge wall of water, wanting to course though him all at once. He focused his willpower, harnessing only what he needed to cast.

The monster leapt at him.

"Off!" Kase said, verbalizing his intent.

Time slowed as he watched the hideous thing fly at him; its sharp, spindly legs twitching in the air.

His mind screamed at him to duck, run, or move, to do something, but don't just stand there.

He flinched, anticipating the feel of the disgusting thing smacking his face in the next second... Nothing.

His eyes opened, and he saw the monster suspended in air, crawling on something unseen.

He chuckled, realizing he had cast an invisible barrier or shield.

'Not bad for a beginner.'

One of the creature's spindly legs stabbed through the shield.

"For a beginner," Alwyn said. "It's a weak spell, and the vile thing will find a way through very soon."

'What do I do?'

"Kill it," Alwyn said. "What else?"

Kase stabbed at the thing with his dagger, but its point simply skipped across the magic shield.

The monster's needle-tipped leg flicked around, trying to reach him. He'd have to end the spell to stab it, but it would then be able to stab him.

Another leg speared through, this one dangerously close to his extended hand.

Kase stepped back and the monster moved with him.

Idiot, of course the shield moves with me.

He was thinking of turning and pinning the monster between the shield and the wall when a third leg jabbed through.

The spell was failing.

Kase tried to concentrate on his spell, hoping to strengthen the shield, but it wasn't working.

Another leg stabbed through next to his hand. The ugly face twisted with a smile, seeing Kase's hand was in reach.

Its leg lanced down, but the sharp point thumped harmlessly off the glove's armor. Angry, it attacked feverishly, stabbing again and again without effect.

Retrieved from the Brood Moor battlefield, this was a soldier's glove and made to protect its wearer.

The monster seemed to puzzle out the problem and spotted a place on the glove that was unprotected. The needle tip raised high.

Kase had to do something right now.

Suddenly, the shield shuddered, vibrating along his arm. Confusion turned to disgust as he watched the monster get split in two. Half its body slid off the shield and landed with a wet thud on the ground. The other half hung, suspended by the legs still stuck through the shield.

Kase pulled his hand back in revulsion, breaking the spell. The dissected corpse dropped to the ground with a sickening crunch.

His torchstone winked off the sharp blade of Brell's knife.

"You okay?" she asked, looking around for more threats.

"I'm... I'm all right," Kase said, not feeling all right in the least. "What happened to you?"

"One of those things led me down the other alley," she said.

"Gumplin said to take the right alley," he said.

"I know that," she snapped, "but in the dark, I felt a tug and thought it was you."

She looked meaningfully at the dead monster and Kase nodded.

"And I thought that was you," he said.

"I don't care what the fly-trap said," she said, switching on a light from her arm terminal. "I'm keeping this on the rest of the way."

"I won't argue with that," Kase said.

"And just for the record," she said, "that's one blood debt paid; two left."

"I'm not complaining." Kase chuckled.

Brell stepped over the gory lump, and they continued down the alley.

They heard a sound just beyond the reach of their light, but whatever it was had left them alone.

A short time later, they reached the dead end of the alley.

It wasn't long after that that they heard the gritty sound of the wall opening. Warm, welcoming light filled the alley, and they thankfully stepped though.

3

IF NOT FOR FRIENDS

Kase and Brell watched the wall close behind them, tense and unwilling to relax until the darkness of the alley shrank to a sliver. They finally breathed when the passage disappeared behind the sealed wall.

They glanced around, seeing they were standing in a pantry. Cured meats and dried herbs hung from the low rafters adding to the scent of aged wine mingled with savory, smoked beef. The pleasant aroma chased away their rattled nerves, filling their nostrils and whetting their appetites.

Brookwal stood in front of them, leaning on a simple cane of dark wood, his withered arm discreetly concealed within his robe.

"I am happy to see you," he said, the lines in his face crinkling with his smile. "Come. I have questions."

"Thank you for helping us," Kase said.

Brell only nodded, feeling reluctant about her level of gratitude after being lead into that alley.

They climbed the short stairs and walked through a door that opened into a modest kitchen. The simple room allowed for a squat stove beside a wooden carving board. Shelves beneath it were stacked with pans, pots, and skillets. A tall refrigerator stood in the other corner with a wide spotless white sink as its neighbor.

Through there, the mage led them into what was clearly the dining room.

Judging from the stacks of books taking up most of the table, Brookwal didn't entertain much, if at all.

Yet, there were two mugs of steaming something and plates with cuts of cheese, meats, some kind of cream sauce, and a rainbow of different fruits.

"For you, of course," Brookwal said, gesturing for them to sit down.

"Thank you." Kase smiled, sitting down.

Brell sat down with a sigh; happy to be off her feet.

"Thanks."

"You're welcome," Brookwal said with a grunt as he lowered himself into a seat.

"It's a bit last minute," Gumplin croaked, hopping out from between the stacks of books. "We weren't sure how many of you would..."

"Survive?" Brell said.

"I suppose," the frog said, "if you want to look at it that way."

"I can't think of a better word, can you?" Brell said.

"I did wonder, Gumplin" Brookwal said, "why, of all the secret passages, you chose that one?"

"One passage is the same as another," the stone frog said, looking directly at Brell, "to a *bookend*."

The heat drained from Brell's face, and Kase frowned at her. Brookwal cocked an eyebrow, glancing between the frog and Brell, sensing friction.

"Well," he said, drawing an end to whatever had happened between them. "Let's get to how you managed to get the town into an uproar."

"There were three of us when we came into the city," Kase said, glancing at Brell. "One was..."

"A robot," Brell said, "and my responsibly. I believed it was safe. I was wrong." She paused as she felt the weight of her choices building on her shoulders. "It killed a kid, and the police chief found the girl's hair ribbon in our room."

Brookwal frowned at the table. Taking a deep breath, he exhaled with a long sigh. His brow furrowed in thought. The frog shifted his front feet, glancing from the mage to Brell with its ever-present frown.

"Which makes you a Teck," the mage said finally.

"Yes."

"And you brought this... device with you to Creet?" Brookwal asked. His eyes settled on Brell, clear, strong, and unflinching, giving weight to his question.

"No," she replied. "We found it in the ruins of a dead city. I didn't know the bot was dangerous." Brell glanced at Kase before returning to Brookwal's gaze. "Another bot has come to the Creet world. A killer. I'm here to hunt it down and destroy it. After I've finished the job I'll return to my world."

"You are taking a large risk," Brookwal said. "Most people would happily hang you regardless of your purpose here."

"I understand," she said.

"I don't think you do," Brookwal said darkly. "This conversation would be very different if it wasn't for your friend." He nodded to Kase. "In case you had forgotten, the Teck are the enemy of this world... all of them. Had I known, I would have dealt with you myself."

The warmth of the room suddenly drained away. Kase sensed Brell tensing and felt a knot of dread in his stomach. He worries she would say something, making matters worse.

"But you're not," Kase blurted, hoping to defuse whatever Brell was preparing to do.

Brookwal and Brell stared at each other across the table for a long time before the mage looked away. "I'm not," he said, the hardness fading from his face. "Technology is a pursuit of the reckless and power hungry. Abominations, just like your robot, are the fruit it bears."

Kase winced. He could practically hear the verbal slap, but Brell remained outwardly stoic.

"I don't hold you directly responsible for the child's death," Brookwal said, "but your hands are not entirely without stain."

"Sir," Kase said, clearing his throat. "With all respect, you're misjudging her."

Gumplin gasped, open mouth, at the impertinence. "What nerve! The gall of –"

Brookwal waved his hand, bringing the frog's protest to an end.

"Brell would have destroyed Billy; that was the robot, if she'd had the smallest doubt it was dangerous," Kase said. "She is willingly taking her own life in her hands coming to Creet, but she's doing this because there's a bot roaming our world, killing our people. She's putting Creet lives before her own. That's as good a testament about her character as any."

Brookwal's chin lowered to his chest. The fingers of his good hand tapped absently on the table. Gumplin stuck out its chin, unwilling to look at Kase or Brell.

"It's difficult to argue with the boy," Alwyn said.

Kase started at the unexpected voice.

"I'm sure you speak from experience," said Brookwal.

'I forgot he can hear you. He can't, um, hear me, can he?'

"No," Alwyn said but nothing more.

"All right." Brookwal's shoulders slumped. "I'm tired. You two will stay here tonight."

"What's left of it," Gumplin added.

"Tomorrow we'll figure out how to get you out of the city," the mage said.

"Thank you," Brell and Kase said.

"What of the machine that killed the child?" Gumplin asked.

Kase threw the frog an annoyed glance. The prickly creature seemed determined to stoke Brookwal into a bad mood again.

"It's destroyed," Brell said.

"What if it's discovered?" the frog persisted, looking at Brookwal. "No doubt these two were seen at your door the day before. Someone will come here with questions for you."

"We left its remains in the heart of the tomb," Kase said.

"Then it's very unlikely anyone will discover it," Brookwal said. "At least not soon enough to make any difference. Now I am done. Gumplin, show them their rooms."

"All right," it croaked, disgruntled.

"And no more complaining," the mage continued. "Your opinion has been heard. That's sufficient."

The frog ground its stone lips together, saying nothing.

Brookwal left, leaning more heavily on his cane than before.

"All right you two," Gumplin said. "This way."

"If you don't mind," Kase said, "I'm starving. I'm going to have some of this first."

The frog's eyes widened at the impertinence.

"That's a great idea," she said, sitting down.

Gumplin's mouth opened and closed as it wrestled to contain its complaint. At a loss for words, it let out a discontented gravelly burble.

It felt like they'd just closed their eyes when Kase and Brell woke up to the sound of fists thumping on a distant door.

Squinting through red rimmed eyes, they peered out the window to see what the noise was about. Fifteen, perhaps twenty people stood at a neighbor's door across the street.

A woman answered, and a man from the group stuck out his chest importantly as he spoke to her.

There was no question about what was happening. The search for them had continued throughout the night.

"They're not giving up," Brell mumbled.

"I have to admire their persistence." Kase yawned.

"I don't," she said.

The woman shut the door, and the leader of the mob came to Brookwal's door. This time, instead of beating on the door as if trying to knock it down, the man gave it a respectful rap.

He stepped back and straightened his shirt and vest as he and the rest of them waited for someone to answer.

Kase and Brell backed away from the window, out of view. They could hear the murmur of voices below, then the sound of the door closing.

The mob moved to the next door, taking their prying eyes with them.

Brell groaned as she sat on her bed to pull on her boots.

"Did we even sleep?" she muttered.

"It's a new day, right?" Kase said, trying to lift their groggy spirits.

"Yeah. In the same dump," she said. "Trapped in the same city with the same psychos."

She snapped the last buckle on her boot and pulled on her cloak. Kase put on his glove, wiggling his fingers until it felt right. He didn't expect to be casting any magic anytime soon but wearing his spiritbridge would allow Alwyn and Brookwal to talk to each other.

Stepping outside their room, they were greeted with the smell of cooking from downstairs.

The carpet muffled the clomp of Brell's boots on the stairs, but it was a reminder that she was prickly company first thing in the morning.

Reaching the bottom floor, they turned toward the dining room. They passed the study; its doors were open and Brookwal was already at his desk.

"Good morning," Kase said.

The mage looked up and smiled, waving them in.

"Be there in a minute," Brell said and disappeared into the dining room.

"A rather short night," Brookwal said, "but I hope it helped. You're going to need your wits today."

Kase tried to keep his smile from cracking as he sat down across from the mage. It struck him as ironic that he had spent the last ten years cooped up in his town. He hadn't felt like he could have an adventure soon enough. Yet, after two days in this city, he had reached his fill and then some.

At least Brookwal appeared to be in a better mood. Kase hadn't been looking forward to mediating between Brell and the mage.

Brookwal glanced at Kase's spiritbridge before meeting his eyes. "How long have you had that?" he asked.

"A few weeks," Kase said.

"Are you serious about learning magic?" he asked. "Or do you wear it to impress your girl –"

"Friend," Kase said, glancing back at the hallway door. "She's my friend."

"Ah." He smiled. "How does your practice go?"

"Good," Kase said, sensing the mage was leading up to something. "Yes, good. A little tricky a couple of times…"

"Like when you nearly magicked yourself to death?" Brell said, settling into the chair next to him. "Is it okay if I eat in here?"

She displayed her plate of food, and Brookwal agreed with a wave. The smell reached Kase's nose, inspiring a grumble from his stomach, but he ignored it.

"You did what?" Brookwal said, raising his eyebrows.

"It was a hectic situation," Kase said. "I cast before I was prepared. The magic… got away from me."

Brookwal chuckled and sat back in his chair.

"You're never truly a mage," he said, "until you drop your guard at least once."

"I wouldn't be too quick to call him a mage," Alwyn said. "He's got a long way to go."

"You would know better than I," Brookwal said.

Brell wrinkled her nose, looking curiously between Kase and Brookwal. "Did I miss something?" she asked.

"He's talking to Alwyn," Kase said, gesturing with his gloved hand.

She stared at him with a wry look as she stuck a piece of toast into her mouth.

"Have you mastered the spells you've been taught?" Brookwal asked.

"Yes."

"He has not," Alwyn cut in. "He's a novice at best."

"What about the spell I cast last night?" Kase said defensively. "Nobody taught me that one. I created that shield spell on my own."

"Impressive," Brookwal said.

"It would have been if it had worked," Alwyn said.

'*Whose side are you on?*' Kase asked.

"There are no sides," Alwyn said. "Brookwal obviously wants to teach you a spell, and I'm trying to help him understand your limitations."

"He's right." Brookwal said.

"Uh huh," Brell mumbled, pretending to follow the conversation. "Listen to the glove."

"But what I have in mind is something very minor when it comes to casting," Brookwal said. "It will give you more variety. Help relieve the boredom."

Kase wanted a powerful spell. He felt he was ready, but that was an argument he knew he wouldn't win. Still, it was a new spell. It would do... for now.

"It's an illusion spell," Brookwal said. "Very simple to use, providing you keep a clear and focused mind."

Kase glanced at Brell, expecting another remark, but she was busying herself with breakfast.

"How do I cast it?" Kase asked.

"This type of spell relies on the imagination," Brookwal said. "Not something every mage has. You must be able to mentally visualize the thing you want to create. You must consider every aspect perfectly. Else, it will utterly fail."

Kase and Brell turned, hearing a knock on the study door, but the door was open and nobody was near it.

"That was the spell." Brookwal smiled.

"Oh," Kase said, wearing an unconvincing smile. "That's, uh..."

"Examine this," Brookwal said, handing Kase a document that appeared out of thin air.

The sheet had an official seal and ribbon attached in the corner.

"The bearer of this proclamation," Kase read, "has been granted free passage to all areas of the city. They are acting in the name of Chief Counsel Gumplin." Kase's eyebrows rose as he looked up at Brookwal. "The frog?"

"Look again." The mage nodded at the document. The seal suddenly vanished as well as the writing. "You can create small illusions, but they only last a few moments, depending on the caster, of course."

"That's great!" Brell said through a wad of food. "Whammy up a couple of those things, and we can walk out of here."

"Were it so simple," the mage said. "I don't know what the real counsel seal looks like. Anyone guarding the gate would know it's a fake. And I've never seen his signature. You can only create what you know."

"It's a fine spell," Alwyn agreed. "I think it'll be good training for you."

"All right," Kase said, warming to the idea. His imagination flipped through endless ways to practice it.

"Now listen very carefully and pay close attention. This is how you cast it."

Brookwal proceeded to teach Kase the steps necessary for casting the spell.

Brell was inwardly impressed. It was much more complex than she had first assumed. By the time the mage had finished his lesson, she was beginning to understand that magic was more of a discipline rather than simply waving your arms in the air.

"I think that's all," Brookwal said, seeing the fatigue on Kase's face. "Have something to eat. Afterward, we'll talk about how to get you out of the city."

Kase got up but paused when Brell stayed in her chair. "Aren't you coming?"

"I'd like her to stay," Brookwal said. "We got off on the wrong foot last night."

Kase hesitated, glancing doubtfully at Brell. He looked at her until she made eye contact with him. He hoped she understood his expression. *Don't insult the master mage.*

Brell sat chewing and smiling at Brookwal.

The mage followed Kase with his eyes until he left the room.

"I was wondering when we'd get around to this," Brell said. "Are you and I going to have a problem?"

Her smile became an icy mask, and although she appeared to be relaxed, she was slowly tensing, readying herself to move quickly.

"There will always be a problem while you are on Creet land," Brookwal said, but his tone lacked the acid he'd spoken with the night before. "The sooner you find and destroy the robot you're looking for, the better it will be for everyone involved. I am putting myself at risk in harboring you. If any of the townsfolk discover what you are, they'll have some very pointed questions for me. How is it that I, their master mage, did not know there was a Teck walking among us?"

"Everyone makes mistakes," Brell said. "But you're not going to report me."

"No," Brookwal said. "You are a necessary evil. You and your killing robot are from the same world. You have a better understanding of that thing than anyone here. That makes you the best solution for finding and destroying the machine as quickly as possible."

"That's the plan," Brell said, getting up.

"But when you're done, you leave our lands."

"I can't be away from this..." Brell paused, realizing the importance of choosing her next words carefully. "I'll be glad to get back home."

"Won't we all," Gumplin said, waddling into the study as she was leaving.

"Watch it, ashtray," Brell said under her breath as she passed the stone frog.

By the time Brookwal had called Kase and Brell back to his study, the sun had taken on the golden cast of late afternoon.

Gumplin reported that the search parties had thinned out but hadn't disappeared altogether. There were eyes watching for strangers from many windows.

"Is there a secret passage that leads out of the city?" Kase asked.

Gumplin pushed the stem of his pipe to the corner of his mouth and chuckled. "Good idea," it said.

"Don't be difficult," Brookwal said. He turned back to Kase and Brell. "None that I would recommend. There's two, but both are far more dangerous than the alley you took last night.

Kase's memory flashed back on the monster that had attacked him. He shook his head, clearing the image away.

"But the thought has sparked an idea," he said. "As the town mage, part of my duties include catching the odd monster that finds its way here. Most of the time, I destroy them outright, but I have free rein to do what I please...such as sharing them with my fellow mages. We are a curious lot and eager to stay current on all things monsters," Brookwal said. "Where they live. What they eat. Weaknesses, skills, and so on."

"The master will box you up," Gumplin said, "and send you through the city gate."

"It's that simple?" Kase said. "You pack us in a couple of boxes and ride us out of town?"

"Yes," the mage said. "The best plans are the simplest."

"Unless the guards want to inspect what's inside," Brell said. "Then we're conveniently packaged up, and all they have to do is dump us in jail."

"Risks abound around us," the mage said, "even when stepping out your own door. You never know what can happen."

"That's true," Brell said. "I don't know what will happen. Do you?"

Kase didn't like the way Brell had fixed her eyes on the mage. Even he didn't miss the accusation.

"You are free to attempt an escape without my help," Brookwal said, taking her pointed stare in stride.

"No need," Kase said, pushing back his chair as he stood up. "What do we do?"

"You'll start in the workshop," Brookwal said.

Two hours later, the mage's assistant climbed up onto the wagon's bench seat.

"I don't understand, master," he complained with a nasal whine. "A task like this is better suited for a common laborer. Isn't my time better spent learning from you?"

"And you are, Sernal. Today's lesson is about humility and obedience," Brookwal said. "I can't trust this task to a common laborer. It's a special favor for a fellow mage."

Sernal glanced at the two small crates in the rear of the wagon, sighing theatrically.

"Take the wagon out of the city until you reach the main road," the mage said. "Leave it there. Return on the pony and let me know when you're back."

Grumbling, the assistant looked back at the brown and white rippled pony.

"Leave everything?" he asked. "The horses too?"

"Yes," the mage said. "And be careful. These boxes contain sensitive samples. It would be... unfortunate for the one who provoked them."

Sernal's eyes grew wide as he looked at the crates again. There was unwanted curiosity in his gaze, and Brookwal suspected the eager assistant would want to see the creatures for himself.

"Would you like to see them?" the mage asked.

"Yes, master! It would be a rare pleasure.

"Of course." Brookwal stepped to the closest crate. "I should tell you, they're covered with eyes, which makes them particularly tricky. You must avoid eye contact at all costs; otherwise, they'll possess your mind." The mage chuckled as he reached for the lid. "Next thing you know, you're laughing insanely, watching yourself cutting your own throat."

Sernal's shoulders jerked and he paled, suddenly turning his back on the crates. "It's a long drive," he said, "and I don't want to keep your friend waiting. Perhaps next time."

"Are you sure?" the mage asked, putting his hand on the lid.

"Yes!" he yelped, covering his eyes.

"If you insist," the mage said, enjoying himself. "Be sure you give the same warning to the guards at the gate. Understand?"

"Yes sir." Sernal nodded.

"Right then." Brookwal pointed his cane down the street. "On your way."

Sernal twitched on the reigns and clicked at the two horses. They took up the strain and pulled the wagon away from the curb and down the street.

"Do you think it's a wise idea to trust Sernal with this task?" Gumplin asked.

"He carries my authority," he said. "A laborer could be easily intimidated."

"Hmmmm," the stone frog said thoughtfully. "You didn't answer my question."

"I know." The wagon disappeared around the corner.

Balled up inside the crates, Brell and Kase felt each jolt as the wagon rocked over the street. The boxes were very short, forcing Kase's knees against his chest. The confined space only allowed for the most shallow of breaths.

Brookwal had designed the crates to appear so small a grown adult was unlikely to fit inside. Anything larger would have attracted undo suspicion.

If they wanted to reach freedom, they had to endure a near suffocating, dark, hot, and claustrophobic ride.

Brell could feel her spine painfully rubbing on the hard wood. Muscles everywhere were twitching and cramping.

She squirmed, hoping for relief, but only made it worse when her hip suddenly knotted, forcing her to gasp in pain. She fought back her instinct to explode free of the box. With huge effort, she was able to move her hand enough to push a knuckle into the muscle.

The eternity of this new hell seemed to draw out for hours, but it had only been fifteen minutes.

Sernal pulled up to the closed gate; two guards stepped into view. They eyed him, waiting for him to explain his purpose for leaving.

"Open the gate," Sernal said importantly. "I'm on mage business."

The older of the two guards didn't need to hear anything else and nodded as he put his hand on the lever to open the large doors.

"Just a minute," the younger guard said.

Sernal looked down on the fresh faced guard, who was nearly swimming in his uniform.

"We're looking for two murderers," he said, eyeing the crates meaningfully.

"Give it a rest, Cyren," the older guard said. "We don't trifle with mage business."

"The killers could be anywhere," Cyren said. "My mom said the entire town is being turned upside down. Nobody found nothing. And it just so happens that the mage wants to send *two* crates out of the city?"

"Why do you have to make everything a chore?" the other guard grumbled. "All right. We'll do it by the book. I've had rashes less irritating than you." The old guard stepped up to the side of the wagon. He straightened his shoulders and adopted the ridged stance of professionalism. "By order of the city council," he said, "nobody can leave the city without a letter of permission. Do you have that document in your possession?"

"Uh… no," Sernal said, suddenly feeling much less in charge.

"Then we must inspect your wagon and all of its contents."

A smile curled the corners of Cyren's mouth.

The older guard bent over and peered under the flat-bed wagon. He stood up and surveyed the crates, then turned to Sernal. "Done," the guard said. "No signs of killers anywhere. On your way."

"What about *inside* the crates?" Cyren prompted.

Brell and Kase could hear the conversation going on outside. The mage's plan hadn't accounted for an overzealous guard. If Cyren kept up his nagging, the next sound would be a crowbar prying open a crate.

Kase turned his head to drain the pools of sweat from his eyes as he raced to think of a way to stop the guards.

"You can't open that!" Sernal said. "Are you stupid?"

That was the wrong thing to say to any guard, including lazy ones.

"Well, since you put it like that," the older guard said, "we wouldn't want to do anything *stupid*, like not doing our jobs."

"There's dangerous monsters in there." Sernal gasped.

The older guard paused as a look of doubt clouded his face. He glanced at Sernal as he tried to think of a way out of this situation. "I think we better leave these alone," he said. "Mage business takes special protocol."

"What protocol?" Cyren asked, looking at the guard, unconvinced.

"It just does," he snapped.

Cyren wasn't going to be dissuaded and took out his knife. "Hide if you want," he said. "I'm doing my duty."

Kase was wheezing for air when he saw the tip of the guard's knife slip under his lid. He had to do something, but what would make the guard stop? An idea bloomed in his mind.

He slowed his breath and followed the steps Brookwal had taught him earlier this morning. *Attention to detail. Clarity of mind. Imagine the illusion as if it were real.*

Cyren gripped the handle of his knife and began prying. Suddenly, a large spindly spider leg sprang out from under the crate lid and swiped at him.

Both guards jumped back with a yelp as the bony appendage raked the air, looking for the intruder.

"Let him out," Cyren cried. "Open the door!"

The older guard was already at the lever. The tall thick doors groaned on their hinges as they laboriously swung open.

Cyren clutched his spear with shaking hands, his terror stricken eyes willing the gate to open faster.

With a heave, the gate opened wide enough to let the cart through.

"Go!" the guards ordered.

Sernal flicked the reins and drove out with the guards practically pushing the cart with their spears.

Behind him, he heard a squawk and the clank and rattle of armor as the old guard smacked Cyren, knocking his helmet onto the street.

"Next time I tell you not to mess with mage business," he growled, "you'll listen."

Occupied with urging the horses into a trot, Sernal luckily didn't see the spidery leg vanish into thin air. But any shred of curiosity he'd had about the crates before was long gone. The sooner he put this wagon behind him, the better.

He gave the reins another snap, hurrying on the horses, who picked up speed.

For the occupants of the cramped boxes, the next twenty minutes were punishing. The wagon amplified every rut and stone it ran over, brutally knocking Kase and Brell around. The air in their cramped confines tasted like they'd breathed it in a hundred times before, complete with a generous helping of road dust. The dust and sweat formed a thin layer of mud on their skin, yet their mouths were as dry as bleached bones.

A few minutes later, Brell reached her physical and mental limit. She was getting out of the box, Sernal or not. She braced her knees against the lid and was about to push it open when the wagon stopped. Wonderful, glorious stillness.

She almost cried with relief. Kase must have been as fed up as her because she could hear the squeal of the nails in his crate as he pushed against the lid.

Sernal's back was to the cart when he heard it too. *The thing is getting loose!*

His fingers attacked the knot, untying the pony from the back of the wagon. He threw himself onto its back, wheeled the pony around, and spurred it into an instant run. The sound of its galloping hooves quickly faded.

Brell and Kase bullied their way out of the crates and collapsed onto the bed of the wagon. Panting, wet with sweat and mud, they basked in the fresh air. Every breath was glorious.

"I'll take on an entire town of angry mobs before I do that again," Brell said. "I don't care how many bodies I have to walk over."

Kase laughed, languishing in the luxury of stretching out his arms and legs.

After they had recovered, they sat up and took in their surroundings. The setting sun painted the sky with vibrant oranges and purples. The jagged mountain range, surrounding the distant city were backlit, making them resemble dark bony fingers. Around them was an open landscape and a single road winding out from horizon to horizon.

"Well?" Brell asked, looking at Kase for a direction.

"That way," he said, thumbing behind them. "But first." He reached under the bench seat and pulled out a large cloth bundle.

He unrolled it, revealing a generous supply of food and all their personal items from their hotel room.

"How did he get his hands on our stuff?" she asked, arching an eyebrow.

A silly grin spread over Kase's face, making Brell groan.

"Magic," he said.

"Sorry I asked."

4

KEYS PORT

Kase's eyes brightened with anticipation as he and Brell cleared the edge of the forest, and the gates of Keys Port came into view.

Home!

The weeks of travel had gone by without incident, but the miles had been long, made longer still by having to avoid towns and cities.

Both had agreed they would accept roughing it in the wilderness and reduce the risk of someone identifying Brell as a Teck.

"That's McLennon's." pointed Kase. "He owns the inn. There's always strange…" He caught Brell's sidelong glance at him. "Different types of people there. It's a good place to stay."

"Meaning what?" she asked. "Are you saying I shouldn't go into your town?"

Both of them were tired and saddle weary. Kase didn't take offense, but it did make him think about how he'd explain her presence.

"No," he said. "My uncle has enough room for you, but he's pretty hard-headed, and once he's got something in his mind, he doesn't let go easily."

"It can't be easy," Brell said, "living with someone like that."

"Yes." Kase, catching a snort of laughter before it got away from him. "Luckily, you are more flexible than he is."

"It's important to keep an open mind," Brell said.

"And maybe carry a smaller chip on your shoulder."

"It's not a chip when you know you're better than everyone else,."

"Better how?"

"You want me to go through the entire list again," she asked, "or just the high points?"

"Since you're so much better," he said, "then you shouldn't have any trouble being civil. Surely, someone from an advanced civilization can do that."

"Yes," Brell said. "At least you admitted my civilization is more advanced." She smiled with a satisfied look as they steered their horses toward the front gate.

The two guards perked up as they approached and put on their best stern looks.

"Welcome to Keys Port," one of the guards said. "State your business."

"Tule," Kase said. "It's me."

The guards peered closer until they recognized Kase under all the road dust and shaggy hair.

"Hamerson?" Tule smiled. "We was wondering if we'd see you again. You look like you've seen some things."

"And then some," Kase said. He noticed the other guard studying at Brell. "This is Brell. I can vouch for her."

"Fair enough," Tule said.

"I'll find you at McLennon's some time," Kase said. "I'll tell you about my trip."

"If you're buying, I'll be there." Tule chuckled.

The other guard gave a distracted smile as he ran his eyes up and down Brell's clothing. "Where are you from?" he asked.

"Guys," Kase said, shifting in his saddle with a grimace. "I'd really like to get out of this saddle and clean up."

"Sure, sure," Tule said. "Go on."

He waved them through as the other guard kept staring at her.

"You don't have to get your nose out of joint every time a stranger comes through," Tule scolded. "They're fine."

"I won't apologize for caring about who comes into my city," said the other guard.

Passing through the gate, Brell took her time to scan the town. Kase led them down the main street under the glances of hopeful merchants. Some recognized Kase and waved, while others saw them as potential customers and invited them to check out their products.

They followed the border of the town square until they stopped at the Regent's house.

Horses and riders were both grateful for the rest as Kase and Brell climbed down from their saddles.

"I just came up with another reason why life's better in Teck," Brell said, massaging blood circulation back into her rear. "No horses."

She followed him as he walked around to the front porch of the tall house.

Kase slapped his clothes, kicking up clouds of dust, before going inside. The ocean breeze whisked it away as Brell followed his example, amused by the plumes of dust.

"I can't remember the last time I was this dirty," she said.

"Kase?"

They looked at the top of the porch, seeing a gruff-faced man looking at them with a smile of relief.

"Uncle." Kase smiled, climbing the stairs.

His uncle was taken completely by surprise when Kase wrapped his arms around him in a hug.

"Uh..." the uncle stammered. "It's good to see you too." He returned the hug, tentatively patting Kase's back. "I was worried about you," he said. "I was expecting you back weeks ago."

"So was I," Kase said. "But the trip didn't go the way I planned."

"Who's this?" he asked, looking over Kase's shoulder.

"Brell," Kase answered simply. "She's a friend."

The uncle gave her a quick look but took in a lot. There was a hint of recognition in his face, but of what he didn't say.

"Retired military," she said, sticking out her hand.

"I thought I saw something familiar about you," he said, smiling as he shook her hand. "You two look like you need a shower and a meal," he continued, gesturing them inside.

"That would be very welcome, sir," Brell said.

The uncle nodded, appreciating the show of respect and the company of someone with a shared experience.

"You can call me Obern," he said.

They stepped into the foyer, where hallways led off to the study, library, visiting room, and kitchen.

A modestly wide stairway circled to the second floor, which held the bedrooms.

"Janis!" the uncle called.

A clatter of metal rang down the hall.

"Yes?" a voice called from the kitchen.

"Three for dinner if it doesn't disrupt your cooking," he called in an effortlessly clear voice.

"Consider it done," Janis answered.

More clattering was followed by the patter of feet growing louder.

"Is that master Kase?" she said, coming into the foyer.

Her head barely reaching Kase's shoulder, the small woman beamed at Kase with shining eyes of orange. The blue flecks in her eyes seemed to brighten as she looked at him.

"Ah, look at you! You look like a pile of old clothes grew eyes," she said, insisting on helping him out of his coat.

"This is Brell," Kase said as soon as he escaped her fussing.

Janis greeted her with a broad smile and bright eyes. She was tiny and quick to smile, but there was nothing frail about the woman. Brell saw there was a core of steel in her, which most likely came in handy around Kase's uncle.

"Janis traveled with me during my campaigns," Obern said. "She was my personal nurse."

"Nurse-maid was more like it, the way he fussed over the slightest bullet wound," quipped Janis.

"She ran many a field hospital," he said with obvious pride. "But we can trade war stories over dinner."

"Thank you for your hospitality," Brell said.

Kase looked at her, open mouthed, wondering who this person was. It certainly wasn't the opinionated, gruff bounty hunter he had been traveling with.

"Come on, miss," said Janis, already heading for the stairs. "I'll show you your room. And while you're in this house," she said with a stern nod to Kase, "you can expect complete privacy."

His protest died on his lips. There was nothing he could say that Janis would believe. As far as Janis was concerned, men were at their best when kept at a respectable distance.

Obern put a friendly hand on Kase's shoulder and looked meaningfully at him. "I'm very glad you're back," he said.

The sincerity in his eyes wasn't lost on Kase. His uncle was talking to him like an adult, and it made him wonder how different he must look compared to when he'd left.

"I'm glad to be back," Kase said. "At least for a while."

His uncle's smile faltered, but he propped it back up.

"Brell gave up something to help me," he said. "She didn't have to, but now she needs my help. It wouldn't be right to turn my back on her."

The uncle looked deep into Kase's eyes for a moment. His gaze softened and he gave his shoulder a squeeze. "You've grown some while you were on the road," he said. "I should have let you go sooner."

"No," Kase said. "You were right to keep me as long as you did. A younger version of myself would have been made a fool and probably not lived to make it back home. My father would be proud of how you raised me."

The uncle's eyes moistened, but he pretended to cough before his emotions betrayed him. "Go on," he said, with a slap on the shoulder. "Get yourself cleaned up, and you can tell me about your journey over a good meal, eh?"

They parted, his uncle going outside and Kase climbing the stairs to his room.

He was overcome with a strange feeling of nostalgia as he neared his bedroom door.

The house hadn't changed. It was the same familiar place he'd always known (and somethings hated), but he was seeing it through different eyes.

Before it had an air of power over him. It was home – shelter and cage. Some days, it had been oppressive and there'd been nothing he'd wanted more than to leap out of his bedroom window and fly away.

The hold it had had on him was gone now. Walking into his room was the strangest thing of it all. Everything was as he'd left it: the rumpled bed, the books scattered on his desk, the maps on the wall.

It feels like someone else's room. I wasn't gone that long, was I? Why does it feel so different?

In a sense, it was like the house was holding up a younger version of himself. It brought back a memory of something his father had told him.

He had been watching him shaving in the mirror. To that younger Kase, his father's arms had been like a bear's, big and powerful. His hands were thick and strong. Those hands would swallow Kase's hand whole, and when he'd lifted him up, there was no safer place in the world.

He'd playfully splashed water on his face, rinsing off the last remnants of shaving cream. He'd caught himself in the mirror and went quiet. It was as though he hadn't seen himself in a very long time and was transfixed by what he saw.

His broad chest showed the signs of many battles. Streaks of pale skin highlighted his scars. Here and there, his muscle was cratered from a bullet wounds.

He leaned in, looking at the crows-feet in the corners of his eyes, the creases in his forehead, and the wisps of gray already frosting his temples.

He'd briefly glanced at Kase before returning to the mirror. His chest rose and fell with a melancholy sigh, before the smile eventually returned.

"The road ages you," he'd said simply. "Be sure you pick the right one to travel. You don't want to look at the marks it leaves with any regrets."

No regrets, thought Kase, looking at his room.

He slid the backpack off his shoulder. It landed with a puff of dust and sagged over.

That bag.

He remembered how excited he'd been to get to the Brood Moors and fill it. He hadn't known his three companions would be dead by the time it was full.

Yes. There're regrets. Maybe the road we get isn't by choice.

His thoughts were broken as he heard the familiar clomp of Brell's boots walking past his door. His stomach, which didn't concern itself with sentimentality, growled loudly, objecting from neglect.

In the short time since they'd arrived, Janis had done an astonishing job of laying out the table with enough food to fill them up three times over.

"Don't be shy," she said to Brell as she laid another platter down.

Brell did a double take, thinking Janis was talking to someone else since her plate was nearly filled to the edges.

Kase had hardly looked up since sitting down and was putting a sizable dent into his own helpings.

Between mouthfuls, Kase told his uncle about the events of his travels, careful to omit details that would lead to uncomfortable questions.

"A titan whale?" his uncle said. "You're the first person I know to have seen one up close."

"Maybe too close." Kase laughed. "I didn't know the ocean could hide something that big."

"How did you and Brell meet?" Obern asked.

Furtive glances passed between them, but neither were quick to answer. Kase bought himself a little time to think up a story by putting a large chunk of steak into his mouth. He nodded as he chewed, gesturing that he'd get to that story once he gnawed his way through the meat.

Brell was silent and deflected the uncle's glance with a smile.

"After," Kase said, pushing his food into one cheek, "my boat was destroyed by pirates…"

"Pirates?" The uncle frowned. "In our waters?"

"We were three days sailing from here," Kase said.

"Close enough. That's something I'll have to address. They're getting too bold. So you met after the pirates," he prompted.

Kase was aware that his uncle wasn't just making general conversation. He had questions in his mind about Brell.

"I met up with a group of refugees," Kase said. "Their village had been attacked by a monster." That was as close as he wanted to get to the details of that story. Any generic monster would suit the story. There was no need to reveal it was a murderous robot. "Brell was traveling with them," Kase said.

"How interesting," the uncle said lightly. "Funny how chance throws people together, eh?"

Brell interjected before Obern could bring up another question. "How did you come to be regent here?" she asked.

"Ah yes," he said. "My brother left to find his wife, Kase's mother. You told her all of this, didn't you?"

Kase nodded but gestured 'a little' with his finger and thumb.

"My brother asked me to look after Kase while he was gone," said Obern, with a glance at Kase. "I don't think either of us imagined it would be this many years. At any rate, the people of this city appreciated my military experience and knew I could maintain order, which I can tell you, can be challenging when you have strangers of all sorts passing through your port. But we've hardly given you a chance to talk. You said you were in the military? Where did you serve?"

The fork between Kase's plate and mouth slowed to a crawl as he glanced at Brell, wondering if this was when his uncle would catch her in a lie.

"Rift security," she said without hesitation. "I was stationed at Dogwood base."

"I don't know it," the uncle said.

"We never had any interaction with the Teck," she said. "It was mostly the edgers that kept us busy."

"I hear they're a rough lot," he said.

"They've almost become their own society," she said. "There used to be only shanty towns where they'd set up to mine the Rift and then move on. But they've put down permanent roots, building cities and operating out of there."

"I have a lot of friends who are still in the army," the uncle said. "Anyone from the Iron Rams outfit ever pass your way?"

"You mean Iron Goats?" Brell chuckled.

Obern's eyebrows shot up and he laughed. "I'll take that as a yes," he said.

"Only by reputation, sir." She smiled.

The uncle prodded his food around his plate, chuckling to himself. "Kase tells me you'll be leaving soon," he said.

"I have some unfinished business to take care of."

"What would that be?" Obern asked with a disarming smile. "If you don't mind my asking."

She looked at him, knowing what he meant, but tilted her head, feigning confusion.

"I couldn't help but notice your clothing," he said. "Armored boots, fighting knife at the hip, another under your cloak, and your belt looks more tactical than utilitarian."

Brell had noticed the way the uncle had sized her up when they'd first arrived. She'd seen him mentally ticking check marks each time he saw something uncommon about her, the same way she'd done, determining if he was friend or foe.

She might've hoped he wouldn't force the subject, but she knew he wasn't the sort to shy away from confrontations, whether causing them or being pulled into them. "I hunt monsters," she said directly.

"Hmmm, which explains why you were traveling with the refugees." He nodded. "You were gathering information about it."

"Yes, sir," she said. "As you know, the more you know about your enemy, their habits, weaknesses, and how they think, the better chance for success."

"Spoken like a true soldier." He smiled. "I miss those days. It's a strange thing, how uncomplicated the battlefield is. Even facing an enemy of thousands, it is so less complex than a single day of running this city."

"We can depend on the rules of battle," she said. "They don't change. They aren't fickle. There's no need to consider diplomacy. It's failed. That's why we're there."

The uncle nodded, vigorously jabbing his fork in her direction.

"Well said!" he agreed. "I must remember that."

Janis came into the room, looking both annoyed and apologetic. "Sorry, sir," she said, glancing over her shoulder. "There's a problem between the baker and weaver... again."

"There," the uncle said. "You see? You can't even pick your battles. All my time is used managing the battles of others."

He pushed back his chair, standing up as he wiped his mouth with his napkin. "I enjoyed our conversation," he said and left for the front door, with Janis following behind.

Kase gazed at Brell with admiration.

"What?" Brell said, taking another bite off her fork.

"I've never seen my uncle warm to anyone as quickly as you," he said. "You really know all the right things to say."

"There's a framed plaque with his regimental colors in the study," she said, tapping her arm terminal. "I looked up its history."

Kase smiled at first, but then it faded as he looked around the room, wondering what else she might have *looked up*.

"Feeling a little exposed?" She smirked.

"Don't do that here, all right?" he said. He made it sound like a request, but his eyes told her he wasn't asking.

"I'm not spying on you," she said.

Kase only grunted in reply. He had never thought about Brell's ability to find information about everything she looked at. Following on the heels of that was *who* she might share that information with.

"We're friends, right?" he asked.

Brell shrugged her shoulders noncommittally.

"The things you've seen," he said. "What you've learned about us... Creets. That information could be used against us if the wrong people got it."

"Wrong people?" she asked, putting down her fork.

"Yes," Kase said, putting down his. "People with power or access to those who have it. People who don't like Creets."

"I told you when we first met that I'm not a spy," she said, her brows furrowing.

"I'm not saying you are," Kase said, wanting to keep that raw nerve from flaring into an argument. "But if someone else…"

"The wrong someone?" she added.

"Exactly." He nodded. "If they saw what you saw –"

"One," Brell said, holding up a finger. "Nobody touches my terminal. Two, it's got four layers of encryption, which means nobody touches my terminal. Three. The only reason I'm here is to melt that evil rust bucket, Ethan Five Seven." She looked across the table, her eyes never wavering. "Get it through your head. I'm no danger to you."

He pondered her words for a moment before nodding, and the tension drained from the room.

"I know," he said, nodding some more. "I'm still learning about what you can do with your tech. Each time I see something new… It's unnerving."

"That's how I feel about your magic," she said.

"I didn't know that," Kase said. "That is, I know you don't like it, but –"

"Think about it from my perspective," she said. "Tech needs programming, hardware, and a power source. You don't need anything. You can make things out of thin air. That's powerful and a little frightening."

Kase hadn't thought of it that way. Up until now, he had considered technology much more powerful than magic, but Brell was right. He didn't need anything… Well, that wasn't entirely true. He couldn't do any of it without his spiritbridge.

He hadn't been born with a connection to magic the way a natural was. His glove – or more accurately, Alwyn's essence housed within the glove acted as a bridge to magic. It was beginning to make more sense why the Teck world was so mistrustful of the Creet.

"I'm stuffed," Brell said, pushing back from the table. "That's the best meal I've had in months. It wouldn't hurt to walk it off."

"And I can show you around town."

Brell rolled her eyes but said nothing.

5

THE CAVE

"Besides," Kase continued, "I have to complete my contract and drop the backpack off at McLennon's."

Brell got up, picking up her plate as Janis came in.

"No." She frowned, looking like she was about to give Brell's hand a slap. "I'll clear up. I like things done in a certain way."

Brell dutifully put down the plate. Janis smiled, satisfied order had been restored to the house.

"A pretty girl like you should be out collecting boyfriends," she said.

Brell and Kase snickered at the thought.

"Oh, I'm sorry," Janis said. "Are you two..."

"No," Kase said, his face flushing.

"Him?" Brell said with a laugh.

Janis looked between them before shrugging and set about collecting plates.

Kase went upstairs to get the backpack, while Brell walked out to the front porch, still chuckling.

She sat on the steps with an unobstructed view of the town square. It was well kept with small gardens on each side. White stones bordered the square, which was lined with sandstone.

People walked by on their way to who knew where.

Brell wondered what it must be like to live in a place like this. *Peaceful. Boring.*

"What did you mean by *him?*" Kase asked, coming out with the pack slung over a shoulder.

Brell looked up as he stopped next to her. Her lips formed a subtle smile that softened her strong features.

"Why do you care?" she asked.

Kase's eyebrows went up, realizing what she was implying.

"I don't," he said, shifting on his feet. "Not personally. But if there was someone who was like me."

Brell groaned good naturedly as Kase embellished.

"You know, clever," he said. "Good looking. Not too much. Handsome but humble. And smart."

"Let me know when you get to the part where they look like you," she said, standing up.

His mouth gaped open and she laughed out loud, something he rarely saw. He was surprised at how much it changed the way she looked. Her rough edges dropped away, revealing a different person inside. Kase ignored the jab and laughed with her.

She followed him as he stepped off the porch and led her to the main street. Along the way, he pointed out the various points of interest, which, in Brell's opinion, were few and far in between.

"No matter how many times I see it," she said, nodding to the blacksmith's shop, "I can't believe that's how you fabricate metal."

"Oh, no," Kase said. "He mostly does repairs or makes hand tools. Cooking knives, skillets, things for the farmers."

"That's what fabricate means." She grinned.

"Okay, you can stop now," Kase said. "I know what it means. I meant, we do have factories that make steel and other metals."

"You wouldn't know it by looking around here," she said.

"It's expensive to ship it all the way here. It makes the cost higher, and this town isn't a thriving metropolis. Cities and towns closer to the factories get most of it. We do fine using what we have."

"But you have trains," she said. "After all these years, it doesn't make sense that they can't supply you with better materials to construct buildings."

"You're the first person I've talked to that even brought this up," Kase said. "I guess the people here are happy with what they already have. Are the Teck?"

Brell didn't have any more questions. She didn't exactly avoid looking at Kase, but he thought it was amusing that she suddenly found so many other things to occupy her interest.

He assumed, rightly so, he'd given her something to ponder about her own culture.

The doors of the main gate were wide open, which was customary for this time of day. The two guards had easy duty, and their only interest was knowing who was entering the city.

Both of them acknowledged Kase with a nod and a good word, but Brell was met with sidelong glances. Kase had gotten used to her and often overlooked the impression she made.

Her grey cloak was cut in a style foreign to them. Hidden under it was her tactical belt and holster, arm terminal, and of course her armored chest plate. Her boots were armored with the same dull gray plating as her chest piece, which gave her a military appearance.

She flicked her dark hair out of her face so the guards could see she wasn't shy about looking back at them.

Altogether, her outfit made her stand out in Keys Port, and honestly, just about everywhere else.

The guards watched them until they nearly reached the inn before losing interest.

"I didn't know you were the bar type." Brell smiled as they stepped up to the door.

"It's an inn," Kase corrected, then paused and added, "Slash tavern."

"Bar. Tavern. What's the difference?"

"Taverns are friendlier," he said, opening the door.

"That's what I need," Brell said, following him inside. "More friends."

They entered a large hall dotted with several tables. Light streamed in the generous windows as someone sat on the edge of the stage, tuning their guitar.

Unlike the evenings, when the tavern was at its busiest, most of the tables were empty.

Hearing the clatter of bottles, Kase and Brell looked across the room, where someone was rummaging behind the bar.

"Hallo!" Kase called as they crossed the floor.

A head popped up from behind the bar, covered with a mop of dirty blond hair. His hazel eyes went wide with delight when they landed on Kase.

"You're not dead!" he cried, breaking into a broad smile.

"Good to see you too, Doiel." Kase grinned.

Doiel came around the bar and practically ran into Kase, wrapping him in a rough hug.

"I didn't know I was missed so much," Kase grunted.

"Huh?" Doiel said, letting go. "Oh, yeah. Sure. Of course I missed you. But even better you just made me eighty coins."

"What?"

"When we learned you had left for the Brood Moors, all of us got together and put money into a collection."

"In case I didn't come back?" he asked. "But my uncle's got money."

"It wasn't as much a collection as it was a pool," Doiel said.

"You guys were betting that I'd die?" Kase frowned.

"No!" Doiel said. "No. No. Well, some did, but not me. I knew you'd come through."

"Thanks for the vote of confidence."

"Of course," said Doiel, smacking Kase on the arm. "I'm your friend. Hey," he said, eyeing him up and down. "You're not missing anything, are you? You still have all your fingers, toes, and uh..." He leaned in, giving Kase a conspiratorial nudge with his elbow. "All your vitals?"

"Yes," Kase said, holding up his hands.

"I knew you'd come through for me!" Doiel grinned. "You're the best friend anyone could ask for."

"If only you could say the same thing," Brell murmured under her breath.

"Where's McLennon?" Kase said, less and less happy with the reunion.

"In the back," he said, his good mood unspoiled by Kase's frown. "I'll get him for you, buddy. Mr. McLennon!" he shouted. "Someone here to see you. We'll catch up tonight. Drinks are on me." He looked at Brell as if she had just appeared and gave her a quick nod. "Her too if you want."

"What's all the shouting?" boomed a voice.

The double doors in the back of the room parted, and McLennon strode in, his dark eyes fixing on the troublesome Doiel.

"I told ya..." McLennon began. Then he saw Kase, and his face brightened. "Ha, ha, ha. Bless me! You're a sight for sore eyes."

The big man crossed the distance to Kase and engulfed him in his massive arms. Brell grinned, seeing Kase's face squashed against the innkeeper's broad chest as he was lifted off his feet.

McLennon stepped back, clasping Kase's shoulders in his meaty hands.

"Let's have a look at ya." He chuckled. "You've been places; that's clear enough."

"That's true," Kase said, grateful the feeling was returning to his face. "This is my friend, Brell," he said, seeing the innkeeper glance at her.

"Nice to meet you, Miss Brell," he said, sticking out his hand. She took it, and her whole body wobbled as he shook her hand. "Any friend of Kase's is welcome here."

"Just Brell," she said. "Thank you. You have a nice ba... tavern."

"I do what I can with what I got." McLennon cast a dark glance at the grinning Doiel. "Boy. There's plenty to do before tonight's crowd," he growled. "Find something."

Doiel started, his smile vanishing, and he dashed back to the bar, where he disappeared among the clattering of bottles.

"Now then, what can I get for you?" McLennon turned back to Kase with a broad smile.

"You remember the last night I was here?" Kase asked after a careful glance around the room.

"Sure," the innkeeper said. His smile quickly melted into a frown when he remembered the sinister stranger asking for Kase. He'd had a killer's languid manner and a smile that never reached his eyes. "Oh... I haven't seen him since then," he said, glancing furtively around the room. "He sent a message for you. I was to keep it until you showed up."

He turned and disappeared into the back room, returning with a simple envelope. "I hoped that night was the last time you'd have dealings with the man," McLennon said, handing Kase the envelope. "I've seen enough of the world to know you want to stay away from someone like that."

"I agree," Kase said, tapping the parcel. "Whatever's inside this should be the end of it."

"Then I'll leave you to it," the innkeeper said. "Nice to meet you, Miss..."

"Brell is fine," she said. "You too."

With the message in hand, they left the tavern and went outside.

"The looks on your faces..." Brell said. "That guy really made an impression on you."

"His name is Qynn," he said. "He called himself a smuggler, but I think it's more likely he's an assassin."

"Well," she said, looking at the envelope, "what's your killer got to say?"

Kase slid his thumb under the flap and tore it open. Inside, he found a handwritten note. "It's instructions about where to leave the relics," Kase said. "When he picks them up, he'll leave my payment."

"Just like that?" Brell said. "Leave them and trust he'll pay you? That doesn't sound sketchy at all."

"Whatever that means, I agree," Kase said, "but I don't have a lot of options."

"Where are you supposed to leave it?" she asked.

"There's a cave," he said, reading the note.

"That right there," she said, tapping the note. "That's what sketchy means."

"It's under the cliffs outside town," he said. "I'm supposed to follow them until I find a hidden door."

"This just keeps getting better."

"I've explored everywhere," Kase said. "I've never seen a cave."

"When do we go?" she asked.

Kase glanced at her, surprised she was including herself in something potentially dangerous.

"Of course I'm going," she scoffed. "Remember?"

The blood debt. How could I forget?

"We should wait until my uncle leaves for his office," Kase said. "He'll be there for hours, working on the day's ledgers and documents."

Kase and Brell occupied themselves, watching the manor house from a discreet vantage point across the town square while they waited until his uncle left for his office across the town square.

"That's it," Kase said, standing up. "By the time we reach the house, he'll be up to his eyes in paperwork."

The sun was past its zenith, and it promised to be a clear night. Kase hoped they'd be back long before sunset. He was excited to find the unexplored cave. His thrill for adventure couldn't wait to discover what was inside.

They entered his home, and Brell waited downstairs while Kase went to his room and got the bag.

"Is everything you promised in the bag?" Brell asked.

"Yes," Kase said, hefting it.

Brell noticed he was wearing his assassin's dagger. "It's going to be that kind of night?" she asked.

Kase chuckled. "I hope not," he said, remembering Qynn and his shiny knife.

They retraced their steps to the front gate and turned off the road before reaching the tavern.

Following the instructions, they crossed the wide field until they reached the edge of the forest. From there, they turned again, toward the cliffs, following a well-worn path. They stopped for a moment at Chopper's Stone. A local landmark, it was a large boulder with a straight cleft in the top of it. The story was a giant tried to win a bet by chopping the stone in half. The giant almost succeeded, but his blade broke before the stone did. The giant left in defeat and was never seen again.

"This way," Kase said, pointing off the path.

"What's this way?"

"Nothing," he said. "I've been through here more times than I can count. That's what's strange."

"This is beginning to feel a lot like an ambush," she said.

She reached under her cloak, behind her back, and loosened her curved knife.

Kase glanced around the shadowy woods, remembering Qynn's invisible pet lizard.

There was no path, only layer after layer of forest.

The thick forest ended abruptly, opening into a pasture of tall grass. Brell nudged him as he looked at the note.

"We're not going in there," Brell said flatly. It wasn't a question.

Not far away was a dilapidated old house. It looked like a converted barn with a second floor added on. At one time, it must have been an impressive building, but generations of neglect had taken its toll.

The roof sagged under the burden of age. The decorative windows were empty black holes, the colorful glass, victims of children's stones.

Brell stared at it, searching the windows for an ashen face leering back at her. There were only empty sockets – tatters of curtains curling in the breeze.

"It's the Cullon Manor," Kase said. "Nobody lives there."

"Since when?"

"Ever," Kase said. "At least, no one's lived there since I was born."

"Have you ever been inside?"

"No." He chuckled, shaking his head. "Gamion told me to never go in there. If he said that, it must be a bad place."

"Who?"

"A friend of mine," he said. "He's the town mage."

"The instructions talk about a cave below the cliffs, right?" she said.

Kase blinked, breaking the hold the house had on his gaze. "Yes," he said, rereading the note. "But we keep walking toward the house."

Reluctantly, they began crossing the pasture, the sinister house looming nearer.

The closer they got, the more they began to doubt they were going the right way.

"Does the note say anything else?" Brell asked.

"No, only that we'll know it when we see it."

"I really hate clues like that," she said, speaking from experience.

With his next step, Kase yelped, disappearing beneath the tall grass.

"What happened?" Brell asked, scanning for him.

"I'm all right," he said. "It just surprised me. I stepped into a gully. I think this is the way down to the shore."

"Where are you?" she called.

His hand appeared above the grass, and she followed it until she stepped into the shallow ravine.

There was a clear path that carved through the pasture and sloped away towards the ocean cliffs.

Kase turned and followed the gully with Brell behind him. The land ended abruptly with a sharp drop to the surf far below.

Brell looked at Kase expectantly as he searched the instructions how to get down there.

"Did you forget the rope?" she asked.

"This doesn't say anything about needing it," said Kase.

He glanced from the cliff to the note and back.

"Look around," he said. "There's nothing to tie a rope too even if we had one."

Brell was about to say something when Kase held up his hand. "I got it," he said, and laid down on his belly. He scooted up to the edge and looked over.

"I thought so," said Kase, waving Brell over.

Together they stuck their heads out, and spotted a series of toe holds carved out of the face of the cliff.

"I'm sure those are perfectly safe," she said. "You go first."

The wind whipped and pulled at them as they clung to the side of

63

the cliff. The toe holds were solid and well made, but the height and sheer drop drained them of any confidence.

Kase hugged the wall, his eyes straight ahead, inches from the bare rock.

He heard Brell above him suddenly laugh, and in spite of knowing better, he looked up at her.

"What?" he asked, trying to keep the tremble out of his voice.

"What kind of idiots keep ending up in situations like this?" she called down.

Kase's mind flipped through all of the dangers they'd experienced during their travels, bringing him to the vision of the two of them clinging to this cliff with only shallow holes in the rock to keep them from plunging to their deaths.

He suddenly saw the absurdity of it and started to laugh with her. The wind howled around their ears in protest, but they didn't feel it. The laughter was like a cleansing tonic, washing away the fear that had nearly frozen them in place.

Slowly, carefully, they made their way down until, at last, their feet touched the rocky shore.

They took a moment, each working the stiffness out of their hands.

"I've never been here before," Kase said.

He looked around with growing excitement.

The pebbles crunched under his boots as he looked up at the cliff wall, moving side to side.

"See how this part of the cliff face is recessed?" he said. "It naturally formed in a way that nothing casts a shadow on it. There's no contrast. Looking at it from any angle... it blends in making it impossible to see it from the sea"

"Riveting," Brell said, picking errant blades of grass off her pants.

"Or was it formed this way from the Rift?" Kase said. "You know it changed entire geographies changed."

"You might want to wrap up your lecture because I think the tide's coming in," she said.

Kase glanced down and noticed the water had crept closer.

He stepped deeper into the recess and saw the opening of the cave.

They traded glances and walked in.

Kase took out his torchstone, and Brell turned on her light. He ran his hand over the cave wall and nudged the stones underfoot.

"The walls are smooth," he said.

"Great," Brell mumbled.

"Notice the rocks? They don't have rough edges," he said, lowering his torchstone to the cave floor.

"I get it. They're smooth because the ocean comes in at high tide," she said. "Are you always like this in new places?"

"Aren't you?" he asked.

"I'm a goal driven girl," she answered. "Get in. Do the job. Get out. Simple and no fuss."

"Look at that!" he said, pointing to carvings on the wall.

As they moved deeper into the cave, they began seeing sets of markings. Each of them were different from the others. They were a mix of symbols, pictograms, and letters.

"I bet these are pirate glyphs," he said. "Each one written in a code only the captain and a trusted few of his crew would know how to read. Instructions to find the treasure they buried somewhere in the cave."

"Caves," Brell said. "Plural."

Kase looked ahead and saw it split into three tunnels.

"How deep does this go?" he wondered aloud. "I've heard about sea caves being dug out from years of erosion. Over time, they can reach for miles."

"In that case, let's leave the sightseeing for another time," she said. "I don't feel like spending the night in here. What's the note say?"

Kase scanned Qynn's note. "We take the right tunnel."

Staying to the right, they trudged deeper into the tunnel. The dry air was cold and tasted of dust. The tunnel walls became rough with chisel marks gouged into the rock. This part of the tunnel was manmade.

Farther on, Brell turned and shined her light back where they had come. "The tunnel is curving to the right."

"And sloping up," Kase added.

"Does the note tell you how we're supposed to find a hidden door?"

"I'm looking for another pirate glyph."

They had only gone a short way before Kase stopped and held his torchstone close to the wall. "I think this is it." He looked between the note and the glyph. "Yes, this is it," he said, nodding.

The glyph was in the shape of a large diamond. Following its border were letters – some upside down, others sideways, and others elongated. At the bottom of the diamond was a crudely scratched out stick figure of a woman.

Following the instructions, Kase traced his finger over the stretched 'Y', sideways 'S', and 'G'. Then he touched the four points of the diamond, starting at the bottom, then left, top, and right.

"That's it," he said, stepping back.

They listened and watched.

"Nothing's happening," said Brell, scanning up and down the tunnel.

"It might have," he said, "and we just didn't see it."

He stepped up to the tunnel wall, to the left of the glyph, and tentatively put his hands on it. He felt the cool rough stone but nothing more. Brell did the same on the right.

"Are we looking for a switch?" she asked, feeling along the wall.

"I don't know," Kase said. "Look for..."

"I found something," Brell called. "Or more accurately, nothing."

Kase looked over and saw Brell's arms had disappeared into the wall up to her elbows.

"Good work," he said.

"It's what I do." She smiled.

6

DEADLY MAZE

He watched Brell as she felt around, finding the edges of the hidden opening. The portal was wide enough for a single person and high enough, providing they stooped.

With a grin, Kase walked into the wall and disappeared.

Brell paused for a moment, weighing the risks that she had no idea what waited on the other side. Would it stop and she'd be fused into the rock? Once on the other side, could she find her way back? Was she walking into a bottomless pit?

"How's it look in there?" she called. She didn't hear anything. "Kase?"

And now he's in trouble, and I have to help him out of it.

She steadied herself and walked into the portal, not knowing what to expect.

She came out the other side and stifled a gag as the stale and musty air caught at the back of her throat.

She opened her eyes and saw Kase backlit by his torchstone. Boxes, books, bits of furniture, bundles of clothing, and unidentifiable junk were stacked from floor to ceiling. Each stack was tightly wedged between more stacks on either side, creating high long walls that stretched out in either direction. The walls were hardly wide enough for them to walk though single file.

Murky light revealed narrow passages disappearing far into the gloom.

Brell turned around, looking back from where she'd come in and saw a weathered old door. "This place is insane," she said.

"Shh!" Kase hissed sharply. He turned and looked at her. The light casting long shadows on his face made him look sallow and drawn. "Do you know where we are?" he whispered.

She shook her head, unwilling to make any noise.

"We're in the basement of Cullon Manor," he said.

"It's a trap" she said, looking for threats.

"No," he said. "It would have happened by now."

"We need to dump the bag and get out of here."

"Leave the bag with the old woman," he said, reading the instructions.

They moved cautiously down the passage, tense and ready for something to spring at them, but the dead stillness remained unbroken.

They reached an intersection, and Kase leaned forward, peeking around the corners. All he saw were empty passages similar to their own. Tightly bunched walls of sagging piles of junk reaching to the ceiling lead in both directions. The air was still and thick with specks of undisturbed dust hanging motionless in the air. Nothing moved in here.

"Which way?"

Kase shrugged. The only direction he was thinking of was the one leading back to the tunnel.

The stories of Cullon Manor were the bread and butter of children's nightmares in Keys Port. Even the adults had stories to tell. He'd heard a fair share of 'manor stories' but had considered them just gossip.

Since he'd been old enough to walk, Kase had spent his life crawling around creepy tombs, dark chambers, and ancient, long dead cities. He remembered impressing his friends by saying he had seen what real scary looked like.

This place moves to the top of the list.

There was an unnatural stillness to the place. A presence of awareness, waiting. He didn't want to move and draw its attention but knew he had no choice.

"All right," he said. "Here we go."

They headed forward, glancing down the paths that branched off. Some of the passages were blocked by tons of junk from a collapsed wall.

Coming to another intersection, they noticed one corridor was noticeably wider than the others.

The other paths splintered off in every direction, some turning sharply out of sight, others only deep enough to walk into before they came to a dead end.

"It all looks like one big deranged dream to me," Brell said. "You choose."

"That hallway is wider for a reason," he said. "We'll go that way."

"It feels like we've been walking for miles."

"It's this place," he said, glancing at the note. "I think..."

"That's it," she said. "Someone is definitely playing games with us."

To their left was another path, impossibly long. They had seen the old house from the field, and the corridor before them stretched ten times its length.

At the other end, they could just make out a tiny pale speck. Their instincts told them that was their destination.

Encouraged this could signal the end of their search, they headed down the corridor. Like everywhere else, the path was walled with stacks of moldy old junk. There were no side paths branching off this one. It was another sign that they were on the right track.

Eventually they were close enough to confirm their guess about the pale speck was right. Several paces ahead was the lone figure of an old woman.

She sat in a simple chair on a low pedestal. Her frail body leaned forward and she had her face in her hands, which were thin and gaunt.

"Did you notice she hasn't moved?" Brell asked.

"Yes," Kase said. "I think..." He took a few cautious steps closer until he could see her clearly, then stopped and put his hands on his hips. "It's a statue."

Brell moved up alongside him so she could study the figure in more detail. "It's been here a long time," she said.

Dust laid heavy on the old carving, like a winter's snow.

"No one else has," Kase said.

The statue was placed in the middle of a small amphitheater with thirty or more paths all converging like spokes on a wheel.

"There's no footprints on the floor," he said.

"We're here now," Brell said. "What now?"

"It says leave the bag next to the old woman," he said, reading the note. "Be warned. Do not talk to her." Kase puzzled over that last part. "What does that mean?"

"Just what it says," Brell said, wanting to get out of here. "Dump the bag and let's go."

Kase leaned closer, looking at the details of the statue.

"What are you doing?" she said, the tension growing in her voice. "This isn't the time to play archeologist."

"I might never get another chance to be here again," he said.

"And you might never get another chance to get out," she growled. "Leave the creepy statue alone and let's go."

"This could be a famous piece looted from a museum after the Rift," he said, leaning in even more. "The attention to detail is remarkable."

The quiet was shattered when Kase gasped and threw out his arms as he lost his balance, toppling toward the statue.

Brell's heart stopped; knowing she was, too far to stop to grab him

He was about to crash into the statue when he stopped in the middle of his fall.

"Just kidding." He chuckled, amused by the dread on her face.

"You think that was funny?" she seethed. "I've killed for less."

"You should have seen your face," chuckled Kase, mocking her expression.

"You are going to pay so much for that," she said, dripping with anger.

"I was just lightening the moment," he said, slipping the backpack off his shoulder. He propped the bag against the base of the statue a bit too hard. The woman started to fall over, rocking frighteningly on its pedestal. Kase's hands shot out to steady it until it settled back in place. "Whew," he said, patting the statue's head. "There you go."

"Kase!" Brell snapped.

His eyes flew open, realizing what he'd just done. "I was just being polite," he cried to whoever was listening.

He looked at Brell, who was crouched, glancing around them, ready for an attack.

The basement returned to its crypt-like silence. They paused breathlessly, turning away from the statue, searching the quiet for the slightest noise but nothing happened.

Kase shrugged, offering Brell a weak smile of apology.

"All you had to do was put down a bag," she rasped. "How hard is that?"

A creak behind them had them turning back around.

The old woman's withered stone face was looking at them. Her eyes were blank orbs, and her face wore a mournful expression heavy with sadness. She reached out her hands in supplication. "I'm so hungry," she said with a voice like dry bones scraping on stone. "So... very..." Her lips peeled back, ghastly stretching to her ears, exposing rows and rows of teeth. "*Very* hungry."

Fixated, Kase stared, motionless as the wizened statue stepped down from her chair and reached for him. Acting quickly, Brell grabbed Kase and yanked him back, putting herself between the statue and him. Her knife flashed into her hand as she lunged at the old woman, who sighed, amused at her next meal.

In an arc of glinting steel, Brell slashed the woman's arm, reversed the blade and whipped the knife across her throat.

Small chips of stone flicked off the statue, which paid no attention to the assault.

"Crap," Brell muttered. Turning, she pushed Kase ahead of her and ran.

Racing down the long corridor, Brell and Kase looked back. The bent old woman grunted and scampered far behind them.

"So hungry," she cried plaintively.

They tore around a corner. The torchstone's light bounced, casting leaping shadows ahead.

Somewhere behind them, one of the stacks toppled and crashed. Then another.

Brell looked behind her. The statue was gone.

"She's not there," she said. "Where is she?"

All around them, they heard the crash of junk falling over like ancient, dead trees.

Kase sped up, pulling Brell behind him. "She's circling around us," he said. "She's trying to block our way out."

They turned another corner, hearing creaking ahead. They stopped dead in their tracks as a pillar of junk toppling toward them.

They jumped back around the corner as hundreds of pounds of junk smashed into the floor around them. Choking clouds of thick dust billowed up, making it hard to see.

"We have to keep going." He coughed.

They threw themselves at the tangled pile on all fours, furiously scrambling over it.

Ahead, they could see the way was blocked, forcing them to take a turn. But which one?

They paused, each looking at the other for direction.

"Please feed me," rasped a leathery voice nearby.

They paled, realizing it was coming from the other side of one of the walls.

"Push!" Kase yelled.

They threw their bodies against the stacks. The wall of moldering, old junk crunched as it avalanched with a crash. They didn't know if they'd buried the old woman but didn't wait to find out.

An inhuman wail spewed into the air, filling their ears.

Beyond caring about their direction, they raced down paths, turning this way and that. Soon they were completely lost.

Kase abruptly stopped, holding up his hand to Brell, gesturing for silence.

They turned, listening, trying to hear over their own thudding heartbeats.

Their eyes met, searching for an answer neither of them had.

What do we do?

For all they knew they were traveling in circles.

"She's herding us," Brell said. "Keeping us chasing our tails."

"She's tiring us out," he said. "Then she'll wait for us to fall asleep."

"Easy pickings." Brell nodded.

"We're changing the game," Kase said. "We don't wait for her to find us. Let's bring her here. You chipped her with your knife."

"She's not indestructible," Brell said, a hint of a smile in her eyes. "Can you use your magic to throw her back?"

He frowned at the question. The last time Kase had cast with too much force the magic had nearly killed him. He was a little nervous about testing his limits again

"Throw her how far?" he asked.

Brell held up a small metallic gray cylinder. An orange stripe ringed the top and 'ZM2-5' was written underneath in fat block letters. It was meaningless to Kase, but the wicked grin on Brell's face made him want to back away from it.

"Just enough we don't get cooked."

Kase nodded without conviction. Casting under pressure, especially for a novice like him was dangerous, and the spell could be unreliable.

"Wait here," she said. "I'll draw her out. When she shows up, I'm going to stick this on her. Then you throw her away from us."

"I'm ready," he said.

Cautiously, Brell moved down the passage, careful not to make a sound.

Kase could feel his confidence in his spell shrinking as Brell moved further away. He waved for her to come closer, but she frowned and gestured she wouldn't.

She finally stopped, farther than he was comfortable with.

She gave him a thumbs up, and he nodded, signaling he was ready.

"Hey, plaster cast!" Brell yelled.

They heard the rustle of movement heading for them.

Brell thumbed the safety cap off the top of her grenade and

pressed the plunger. She felt it click under her thumb. The moment she released the plunger she would have a few short seconds before it exploded.

No going back now.

Kase watched her as she stared down the opposite corridor. She tensed, prepared to act as soon as the old woman came around the corner.

Suddenly, the wall between Kase and Brell exploded out as the old woman charged into view. Gaping in surprise, the pale hag turned toward Kase.

This isn't the plan.

"Here!" Brell shouted.

The woman turned, her face scowling, her mouth yawning open into a sea of teeth.

The plan had fallen apart.

The old woman scrabbled for Brell as Kase watched, a ball of ice writhing in his gut. He desperately grasped for something to do.

If he cast now, he'd throw the woman right into Brell. *Pull* and the monster would be on top of him.

Hurry, now. Do something NOW!

He saw Brell throw the cylinder, the top of it flashing red. It hit the woman, who paused in confusion.

The monster and Brell were too close. She'd never escape the blast of the grenade. She glanced at Kase; their eyes met. She was scared but resigned.

Brell dove to the ground, but he knew it wouldn't save her.

Cast!

Kase's body clenched as he channeled his focus into a tight beam of thought. Glaring at the woman, he opened himself to the swell of magic.

The spell violently gripped her, knocking off dust and flakes of stone. The old woman sensed her attacker and glowered at Kase.

Pull!

The monster was brutally yanked off her feet, and rocketed toward Kase.

Brell's mouth formed into an unheard protest.

The hag flailed and snarled as she streaked through the air.

Kase came out of his tunnel vision and suddenly realized the hurtling stone cannon ball was about to take off his head.

With a scream, he threw himself to the ground. Arms and legs scrambling, he madly crawled through the hole the monster had charged through.

The grenade exploded, sending a hail storm of wreckage and burning fragments whipping just above his head.

The world around him swam out of focus. He laid there knocked senseless as his mind slowly pieced together the last few seconds.

Brell's face swam in front of him out of the haze of floating cinders and swirling dust.

She was yelling something at him, but he only shook his head, bewildered.

She grabbed his arm and pulled him up.

He gazed around at the small fires and charred debris as she threw his arm over her shoulder and rushed into the smoke.

They pushed their way through the wall of acrid smoke, stinging their eyes and nostrils.

They couldn't see where they were going, but Brell kept yelling, smiling about something.

And then they broke out of the smoke. Glorious cold air washed over them.

Kase blinked the grit out of his eyes and saw they were back in the tunnel.

He sucked in the cold stale air like it was nectar.

"We're out?" he croaked.

"You got lucky," Brell growled. "You blew a hole through the tunnel wall."

"The monster?" he asked.

She patted him with her free hand, kicking up a plume of grit dust.

"You're wearing it." She grinned.

Kase's laugh turned into a hacking cough, and he wiped the snot from his nose.

"What happened to our plan?" she asked, propping him against the tunnel wall.

"I don't remember it including blowing yourself up," he said.

"Yeah," she chuckled. "I didn't see that coming."

"As soon as it turned for you, I knew what I had to do," he said.

"That was fast thinking."

He glanced at her out of the corner of his eye, wondering if she saw through his lie. In truth, he'd had no idea what he was doing until he'd done it.

Soon Kase's legs were sound enough to support him, and he pushed away from the wall.

"What was that thing you stuck to her?" he asked.

"A multi-force mini grenade," she said. "Two to five power."

"Was that a two?" he asked, impressed.

"In all the excitement," she said, "I might have switched it to five."

"I thought you didn't get rattled." Kase smirked.

"Don't start," she said.

They worked their way through the tunnel until they saw dim sunlight illuminating the walls ahead.

The air freshened, and stepping onto the open shore, they shared a sigh of relief, basking in the gusts of salty air.

"What do you think your smuggler friend is going to do about the mess we left back there?"

"I left him the bag," Kase said sharply. "He'll just have to dig for it."

Brell gazed out across the sparkling water, nodding in agreement.

The following morning, Kase examined his face in the mirror. All things considered, it wasn't as bad as he'd thought.

Cuts and scratches crisscrossed the left side of his face. One of his eyes was red and swollen, and his eyebrows were scorched.

He smiled at himself, appreciating the mementos of his adventure.

The night before, they had waited at the tavern until Kase had been sure his uncle had gone to bed. Then they'd patted themselves free from as much dust and dirt as they reasonably could before returning home.

Both of them were tired and had hardly exchanged a nod before heading to their rooms for the night.

Now the sun was up and Kase was freshly washed. His appetite had a keen edge, and he was eager to rummage through the kitchen for breakfast.

Walking into the dining room, he found Brell already there with a steaming cup of brew. Her plate was empty except for a few crumbs and a couple of bones picked clean.

"You missed your uncle," she said.

"Oh?" he asked, pausing at the kitchen door.

"He cares about you," she said. "He's kind of a worrier."

"He takes his promise seriously," he said. "I suppose I can't blame him. Keeping someone's family safe is a big responsibility."

He went into the kitchen, criss-crossing the room as he gathered a plate and utensils. Poking his head in the refrigerator, he browsed through the plates, bowls, and platters of leftovers.

He sat down at the table with a healthy sampling of everything.

Brell watched him from over the rim of her cup as she enjoyed the earthy aroma of her brew.

"So," she said, putting down the cup. There was a change in her tone that made Kase look up from his plate. "I have to go. It'll be a while before I'm back; restocking my gear, replacing the gun... you know, but it's not forever."

"That's all right," Kase said. "I did what I needed to complete my deal with Qynn. I can be packed in an hour."

A melancholy smile crossed her face as she swirled the remnants of her cup.

"I've thought about this a lot," she said. "Being on Teck, it's a bad idea."

"But I'm still going." He smiled, untroubled. "With everything that we've been through, how much worse could Teck be? We can handle whatever comes up."

"I don't want to burst your bubble," she said, "but there's no 'we.' Not in the Teck world. There's just you, a Creet, and that's only the beginning of your troubles. If they find out you're Creet *and* use magic... I can't begin to describe how screwed you are."

"But –"

She cut him off with her hand. "And if they connect me with you, I'd either spend the rest of my life in prison, or they'd execute me on the spot."

"We're not going to be there for more than a couple of days," Kase said, then grinned at her. "It takes at least a week before we usually get into trouble."

"*Anything* could happen," she said, her voice growing stern.

"Here's the plan," Kase said.

"No. There's no plan," she said, leaning over the table. "You're staying here and I'm going. If it's important to you, I'll let you know when I'm back, but when I do, I'm hunting down E57 alone."

Kase waved his hand dismissively, sweeping away her protest.

"All right. I'll go with you as far as the Rift," he said. "That will give you plenty of time to reconsider. Once you change your mind, bam, I'll be right there. No time wasted waiting for me to catch up. That's the best offer I can make, and," he said, holding up a finger for emphases, "it's pretty darned thoughtful of me."

"Is it?" Brell growled, not amused in the slightest.

"I'll continue to guide you while you're on Creet," he said, leaning back in his chair. "Help you navigate our numerous and complex customs, avoid unwanted attention because," he gestured to her appearance, "you're obviously a Teck. All of that, plus my sparkling companionship, free of charge."

"Obviously?" she asked. "Obviously, I'm Teck? What happened to me being a monster hunter?"

"Well..." he said, arching an eye at her. He popped a bite of chicken in his mouth, chewing loudly. "Look at you. You stand out like a ... something that stands out."

"How does your ego fit inside such a tiny pinhead?" she asked.

"Sometimes I amaze even myself." He grinned.

"But seriously," she said, her smile disappearing. "You're not going."

"All right," he said, looking calm. "Here's what's going to happen. I'll find my own way across. Do a little exploring on my own. No," he said, stopping her protest with an outstretched hand. "The pendulum swings both ways. You can do what you want. So can I."

"That's your way of saying you're going to be a constant pain in my butt until I give in," she said.

"I wouldn't use those exact words," he said.

"I would. Why is this so important to you?"

"Important?"

"Why are you so determined to go with..." She stopped, eyeing him as she sat back in her chair. "Kase. You aren't... I mean, you and me..."

"You and me, what?" he said, genuinely confused before he realized what she was inferring. "What?" he said, sitting up. "No. Are you kid..."

Brell's eyebrows rose, looking at him a bit taken aback.

"I didn't mean it like that," Kase stammered. "I mean, you're not my... not that you aren't whatever you are, which is fine, but..."

"You might want to quit before you hurt yourself." She grinned with little humor.

Kase sputtered to a stop and busied himself with rearranging the food on his plate. After a moment, he looked back at her.

"You're my friend, Brell," he said at last. "That means something important to me. There's nothing about us that should fit together, but we do. There's a reason we met. I couldn't tell you why, but I know it would be a mistake if we..."

"Broke up?" she teased.

"Parted ways." He smiled. "There's no harm in sticking together until we find out why."

7

GAMION

"Is this a good idea?" Brell asked.

"Gamion's one of the most interesting people you'll ever meet," Kase said.

Sun streamed through the green canopy of the forest, creating pillars of soft golden light. Steam rose from the damp soil where sunlight splashed onto the forest floor. The air was sweet with the scent of pine, and the woods echoed with the sounds of chatters and chirps.

Brell spotted a herd of deer foraging in the distance. One of them watched her with its large dark eyes, twitching its ears as it stood sentinel over the others.

"There it is," Kase said more to himself than to Brell.

She followed his gaze and looked up through the branches and saw a tower.

"Isn't that...?" she began.

"A lighthouse, yes," Kase said. "Amazing, isn't it?"

"Here?" she said, looking around the forest.

"The ocean was closer before the Rift."

"How does he feel about Tecks?" she asked.

Kase only shrugged which did little to calm Brell's doubts.

If this person was as powerful with magic as Kase had led her to believe, she could find herself in a dangerous situation. She hadn't fought a magic user before.

When in doubt, strike first, she thought.

That philosophy hadn't failed her in the past. At least she had a plan, which was better than letting random chance decide her future.

They came out of the woods, entering into a small pasture of grass and wildflowers.

"That's his house." Kase smiled, eager to see his friend again.

The door Gamion used for selling enchanted items, tools, cookery, and potions was closed, which was unusual for this time of day but not unheard of.

Kase's imagination pictured the mage busy devising a new spell, surrounded by bubbling pots and ancient tombs written in lost languages.

They followed the path around to the front of the house, where they saw the front door open – also not unheard of.

Brell did a quick look around their surroundings out of reflex as Kase walked up to the door and knocked.

"Gamion," he said. "It's Kase. Are you in there?"

He glanced at her and shrugged.

"He can be like this," he said. "There is always a hundred errands going on at once, and he doesn't have room in his head for things like closing doors or combing his beard.

This was beginning to feel like it was going to take longer than Kase had described. She lifted her face, enjoying the warmth of the sun on her face while he knocked again, this time louder, and called through the doorway.

He paused for a moment, listening but got no reply.

"What are you doing?" asked Brell, as Kase stepped inside. "Is it normal to invade other people's homes here?"

"Gamion knows me," he said. "All I'm doing is returning something I borrowed from him. Come on. You've never seen a place like this before."

Brell tilted her head, feeling awkward about being in a stranger's house, but Kase's matter-of-fact temper put her at ease.

Still, it would be interesting to learn more about Creet mages.

In the time since she had been in the Creet world, she had discovered there were a lot of things that contradicted what Tecks thought about their counterparts. There were still many things about the Creet culture that were backward to Brell. Their rejection of technology continued to baffle her. Their belief in magic was superstitious foolishness. She corrected herself. She had seen, first hand, that magic was controllable.

That didn't make it better. In fact, it made it worse.

Teck saw magic as an unstable force of immeasurable power, and the Creet were like children playing with fire.

Most Teck were convinced the Rift was caused because a Creet experiment with magic had gotten out of control.

Brell wasn't sure what she believed, but she kept her doubts to herself. Yet, since traveling with Kase, she had seen what magic was capable of. Maybe it was possible.

Even Kase had admitted to her how difficult it was for him to control his spells, and his were a beginner's level.

Even using the word *spell* made her fell silly.

She thought about the incident at New Runefal. Kase had flung four thieves across the street like they were paper dolls. If that was beginner magic, it was shocking to imagine what a fully fledged mage was capable of.

"What are you waiting for?" Kase asked, sticking his head out the door.

"Relax," she said and followed him inside.

He led her from the entryway and into the study.

The room was lit by a large window and bordered by cluttered bookcases on either side.

The center of the room was occupied by a stool and large table, which, like the bookcases, had little to no spare room.

The one piece of open furniture was an overstuffed red velvet chair.

Everywhere Brell looked, she saw baubles and trinkets, bottles and books. Pieces of strange skeletons were jumbled in with small chests and boxes.

"Kind of amazing, isn't it?" He grinned.

"If they handed out awards for hoarding, he'd get first place." She chuckled.

"I guess you could see it like that." Kase frowned, her joke lost on him. "But just look at this collection. It's fantastic."

"What does it all do?" she asked.

"I have no idea," Kase said, his eyes sparkling with wonder. "These things have come from all over the world. Who knows how many mages have been a part of their creation? Everything here has its own story to tell. Oh... hello."

"Who are you talking... gaaah!" Brell yelped. "That's an eye!"

Sitting on a bookshelf was a single glass eye. It turned to stare at Brell, who found it completely unsettling.

"That's just creepy," she said. "Why does it keep staring?"

"It's an eye." Kase smiled. "What's it supposed to do?"

"Blinking once in a while would help," she said.

"Blink with what?" he asked, chuckling with amusement.

"Uh... yeah," she said. "I see your point. Does it understand what we're saying? Can it hear?"

"Sure," he said, waving to the eye.

The eye turned toward him and jiggled slightly in reply.

"It can hear without ears," Brell scoffed, "but it can't blink. That's what's wrong with magic"

"Magic isn't about logic," he said. "It's an art. It's not rigid like science."

"And that doesn't bother you?" she said, folding her arms. "It's like running with a match through a dark room filled with barrels of gunpowder. You can't see what you're doing until you run into it. Sooner or later, that match is going to touch the wrong barrel."

"It's not that simple," he said. "Magic has its own rules. A reckless mage doesn't live very long. Consider it a self correcting problem."

"Uh huh," Brell said, distracted by the staring eye.

Kase began browsing a bookcase, wondering if there was anything new to the collection.

He stopped, glancing over his shoulder, then looked at Brell, who was casually taking in the strange surroundings.

"Did you hear something?" he asked.

"Nope."

He shrugged and turned back to the bookcase, but a moment later, he heard it again.

Concentrating, he worked out it was a voice. Whispering, coming from...

Somewhere.

Very faint, he heard the voice in his ears, but strangely also in his head. He turned his head this way and that, trying to locate where it was coming from.

The hallway.

A quick glance at Brell told him she hadn't heard it.

Kase speculated Gamion had discovered something mysterious and had brought it home.

Curiosity being a great weakness, Kase had to see what it was.

Not wanting to attract attention, Kase casually moved closer to the door opening into the hallway.

There it is again.

The words were both tantalizingly and frustratingly out of reach. He sensed more than heard the voice beckoning him.

Plaintive and weak. There was a sadness about the voice; the clearer he heard it, the heavier the despair. He stepped into the hall and paused, listening.

Please...

His eyes went wide as he clearly made out the word. The voice sounded so frail that even the act of speaking was a terrible burden.

Here... please.

It was coming from down the hall. Kase took a step, then hesitated. In all the years he had visited Gamion, the study was the only room he'd been invited to. It was comfortable and familiar, but now he felt like he was intruding.

This felt wrong. He looked back the way he'd come and considered turning around.

Rescue me... torment, the pain.

The breath hitched in Kase's chest. The anguish in the voice pierced him. Someone, something was suffering. The weight of their torment bore down on him.

He took a step, then another. The next thing he knew, he was standing at Gamion's kitchen.

His brow wrinkled as he scanned the room, confused. He didn't know what he had been expecting, but it wasn't this. It was entirely ordinary, which made it all the more peculiar.

Closer.

It beckoned him forward. No, beckoned wasn't the right word. The voice grew more urgent, insistent, but Kase didn't note the change.

A fuzzy dream-like aura had settled around him. He felt like his feet were moving of their own accord, as if he were watching himself in a dream. He didn't have to think about walking; they moved on their own.

He reached the other end of the kitchen, facing the wall. The strangeness of it broke him out of his haze, and he looked around.

To his left was a trap door, leading to the basement, he imagined. There was nothing strange or uncommon about it at first glance, except...

Why is it locked?

It was more than that. It was secured. The door was stout and reinforced with strong bands and hinges.

Are you there?

"I'm here," Kase said.

He raised his hand to his mouth, alarmed. The sound of his voice had startled him because it had spoken without conscious thought, as if someone else was speaking for him.

Apprehension trickled into his mind. A danger was stalking him, lurking at the edge of his perception, drawing him in.

I shouldn't be here.

Stay!

He rocked on his feet as the voice echoed through him with unexpected strength. It wasn't a plea. It was a demand.

Open the door. The door. Open it.

The voice became stronger, softly firm but irresistibly commanding. He bent down and wrapped his fingers around the heavy padlock.

Hungry anticipation radiated from the other side of the trapdoor. Someone else was controlling him, reeling him into the darkness that waited below.

"*Enough!*" a voice boomed.

Kase leapt back as if pushed. The kitchen was a jangle of noise, windows rattling and pots and pans clanging together.

Terrified and confused, he turned and saw Gamion in the doorway, brimming with rage.

"To my study!" he demanded.

His words pumped though Kase's limbs, driving him out of the room.

Fury burned in the mage's eyes, and he bristled with angry sparks of magic.

Kase flew out of the kitchen, shaken and pale beyond anything he had ever known.

Gamion glanced out of the corner of his eye, making sure the spell controlling the curious fool was broken.

He was thankful he had pulled back on his anger at the last instant and didn't blow Kase across the room with his *command* spell.

Seething, he strode to the trapdoor, looking down his nose on it with disgust.

It's just a matter of time, came a mocking voice into Gamion's mind.

His face twisted in revulsion, the trespassing presence leaving him feeling unclean.

"This is my fault," Gamion growled. "I let myself be lulled into thinking you had lost some of your strength. I showed you mercy where all you should know is suffering."

The mage closed his eyes and gave a brief twitch of his hand.

A wail of pain reverberated through his mind.

Stop. I'm begging you.

Gamion smiled as another scream of agony filled his head. He waved his hand. The sounds abruptly ended.

The mage took a deep breath, letting it out slowly. He ran his fingers through his long beard and smoothed the ruffles from his robes.

"That's better," he said.

The lines in his face softened, and the corners of his mouth curled with a hint of a smile. The shoulders under his robes dropped as he reverted to the small old mage everyone knew him as.

In the study, Brell started as Kase ran in shaking and white. He glanced back at the study doors with dread.

"What happened?" she asked.

Kase opened his mouth but only croaked something unintelligible.

Gamion walked into the study, catching Brell by surprise. She had not seen or heard anyone enter the house.

"Stop right there!" Brell said, reaching for her knife.

"Thank you, but I think I'll stop here instead," he said, crossing the room. "The floor is a bit wobbly there and it makes me dizzy."

He looked at Brell with mild amusement and shifted on his feet.

"Now then," began Gamion, his pale gold eyes sizing her up. "Hello. Who are you?"

Of all the horrors Brell had expected to come into view, this short grinning bearded old man hadn't even made the list.

"I'm, uh... Brell," she said.

"Very pleased to meet you," he said, reaching past a shaken Kase and offering her his hand.

"Sure," she said, taking it.

"Now then," he said, turning his attention to Kase. "You had no business snooping around my home. I expected better of you. Very disappointing."

Frowning, he stared expectantly at Kase for a long moment.

"Oh, my mistake," Gamion said, flicking the end of Kase's nose. "I forgot that part."

All the stiffness suddenly left Kase, as though he had been freed from a shell of ice.

"As I was saying," Gamion began.

"What happened?" Kase stammered, looking between Brell and the mage.

"You should be the one doing the explaining," Gamion said.

"I was here," Kase said. "But then I was in the kitchen because... uh..."

Kase's gaze flittered around the room as he tried to remember how he had ended up in the kitchen, but like waking from a nightmare, the memory of it had disappeared, leaving only rattled nerves in its wake.

"And then you were there," he continued, "and now I'm here."

"You're not making any sense." Brell frowned with concern. "What did you do?" she asked pointedly of Gamion.

"Am I not allowed to scold rude behavior in my own home?" Gamion said, unconcerned.

Kase looked deeply confused, which was secretly no surprise to the mage. Catching Kase off guard, Gamion had cast a spell on him, scattering his memory of the past few minutes. It was a delicate thing, that spell, and easy to resist if the person saw it coming and fought its affects.

It was also extremely unsettling to the recipient, much like shaking a snow globe, but Kase would recover in time.

Inwardly, Gamion was thankful that he hadn't been forced to use a stronger, more permanent spell. As much as he would regret it, he would do worse to keep the secret in his basement.

"I do apologize for shouting like that," Gamion said. "A mage's shout can be unnerving."

"I've never heard of that spell before," Kase said. He was quickly beginning to feel his normal self, and his jangled nerves had settled down.

"I imagine there's a fair number of things you have yet to discover." Gamion smiled. "You're a Teck," he said, turning his eyes on Brell.

She nodded, unsure of what to say. It felt like there were a dozen unfinished conversations spinning around her and she didn't know which one she was expected to join next.

"I've been there, you know," Gamion said. "Interesting place. Nice people. The air smells funny."

"Okay," Brell said, deciding the least confusing choice was to be agreeable.

"I didn't know that," Kase said.

"Well, of course not," Gamion said, looking exasperated. "I just told you. Never mind. Yes, I was there. A long time ago. I expect some things and people are not what they used to be."

His eyes lingered on Brell. She felt the sensation that he could see through her, and she resisted the urge to squirm.

"Why were you there?" Kase asked.

"Arbitrator business," said the mage.

"You were a judge?" Brell asked.

"Judge, jury, et cetera, et cetera," he said, looking bored and twirling his finger.

"Arbitrators are powerful mages," Kase said excitedly. "They keep peace in the region against monsters and any other magic-related bad guys."

"That sounds dangerous," Brell said. "Did you ever run into a mage more powerful than you?"

"Brell!" Kase objected.

"More powerful?" Gamion said, thinking to himself. "Yes, many times."

"You did?" Kase said, surprised. "But you're..."

"Still alive?" The mage chuckled. "The fight isn't always decided by the power of magic, Kase. You have to use your wits. Be devious. That's how I caught the rogue mage in your world."

"In Teck?" she said, unsettled. "I thought all of you, uh, your people were migrated out generations ago. If a Creet was found now, it would be all over the news."

He listened to her with a bemused smile and sat down in his over-stuffed chair.

"They don't want it to be public knowledge," Gamion said, "any more than the leaders here on Creet. Can you imagine the chaos? How would people know if they were looking at Creet or Teck?" He raised an eyebrow and cocked his head, looking at Brell, making her shift on her feet uncomfortably. "Suspicion and distrust would spring up like wild fire. People would imagine seeing Creets in every shadow, under every bed, using magic everywhere. No. It wouldn't do. Better to keep a blanket on it."

"Our officials knew you were there?" Brell asked, surprised.

"I should think so," he said. "They certainly knew enough to stay away and let me do my job. It's easier for everyone and avoids friction between our two worlds."

"What was your rogue mage doing?" she asked.

"Naz? Terrible things," Gamion said, leaning forward. "Terrible and dangerous things. He was a student of a dark mage. Like all their kind, they hunger for power and not to harness it for the betterment of others. Naz turned his attention to trying something new – melding dark magic with technology."

"Did he succeed?" Kase asked.

"When we caught him, he was close to discovering something," he said. "We'll never know since we destroyed all of his work. Everything."

Gamion's eyes drifted up to the ceiling as memories of that time came to his mind.

"What did you do with Naz?" Kase asked.

"He escaped, the coward," the mage said. "Naz had cultivated many followers to his warped thinking. He lured them with promises of passing his knowledge to them. He used the acolytes to great effect, using them to infiltrate places of influence and power. One of them was in my party." The mage's face darkened, and his salt and pepper eyebrows knitted together. "I insisted that I work alone, but the fools believed he was more powerful than me. Ha! Not an ounce of intelligence between them." He glowered over the memory, but the shadow cleared and he brightened again. "His apprentice sacrificed himself so Naz could escape."

"Did you hunt him down again?" Brell asked.

"No," Gamion said. "His own hubris did the job for me. Apparently, he returned to his ambition of dark magic and technology, this time with reckless urgency. By then, he knew well enough to fear me." The mage chuckled. "He lived long enough to see his creation turn on him and everyone around it. I heard the carnage was... impressive."

"What about the thing he created?" Brell asked. "Is it still loose in my world?"

"Oh, yes," Gamion said lightly. "I wouldn't worry about it."

"Really? Because it sounds like there is a lot to worry about," she said.

"Since this is the first time you've heard of it," he said, "it's likely the poor creature ran off to where it could be left alone."

He made sense, but it didn't entirely ease Brell's concerns. Something unnatural was running free on her world.

"He should have surrendered," Kase said.

"Better off dead," Gamion said, surprising Kase and Brell. "I've never known a dark mage to change. Once the tendrils of dark magic has taken over their minds, they'll go to their graves feeding the insatiable hunger to feel its power. But here I am running on about ancient history when you've got some stories of your own to tell."

He said the last while looking into Brell's eyes. Then he turned, giving Kase his full attention.

"How did your trip to the Brood Moors go? You're all in one piece, I'm happy to see. Although, you haven't come back entirely unmarked. And what's this? You're wearing a spiritbridge? Is there no end of surprises?"

Brell found an empty chair to sit in as Kase told him about everything that had happened.

Gamion listen attentively, yet when Kase omitted parts about Ethan Five Seven, the mage glanced at Brell. Somehow, he knew there were holes in the story.

When Kase finished, Gamion blinked at them in astonishment.

"A wraith?" he said, sitting up. "And you're here to tell about it? Extraordinary! You two make a formidable pair. Even I would think twice about taking on a creature like that. Kase, I have to say, and no offense meant, I would have wagered you'd have killed yourself with a spell by now."

"Well…" Brell began.

"Didn't I tell you," Kase said, quickly cutting in. "I was meant to be a mage."

"Well, yes." Gamion grinned, his gold eyes twinkling. "Let's not eat the apple before it's ripe."

"And I got this," Kase said, showing him the relic from the tomb. "Alwyn told me that forging this into my spiritbridge will make my spells more potent."

Gamion took the relic, examining it closely as he murmured to himself.

"It's a fine piece," he said, handing it back. "Your Alwyn is correct, if not a bit irresponsible. You're still quite new to casting spells, Kase. You, yourself, said you briefly lost control of the magic, and it nearly killed you."

"I didn't say that," Kase said.

"No?" asked the mage, glancing at Brell with surprise. "Regardless, I caution you to rethink your decision. You haven't had that piece examined. What is its history? Does it have an alliance? That sort of thing."

Kase looked at it, frowning as he considered Gamion's warning. He put it away with a wider perspective than when he'd taken it out.

"You'll need a spirit-forge to do it," said the mage.

"Do you know where I can find one?"

"A what?" Brell said.

"Creating a spiritbridge is a difficult, time consuming, and complex ritual," Gamion said.

"A ritual," she said, barely concealing her scoff.

"A procedure if that suits you better," the mage said, unperturbed. "It takes years to learn the necessary skills. The ones who are capable are far and few. Finding a forger is nearly as challenging as the rit... procedure. They're a secretive bunch and may create only two spiritbridges in their lifetime."

"I don't understand why they would spend so much of their lives learning to do something, then hide it," she said.

Gamion smiled, nodding to Kase.

"Imagine thousands of him walking around, able to cast spells." he grinned.

"Enough said." chuckled Brell.

"That's a little unfair," Kase said. "I think the world would be a better place if more people were like me. I'm honest…"

"Mostly," Gamion said.

"Fair," Kase continued undaunted. "Helpful, loyal."

"Then we can only curse the fates for blessing us with just one of you," Gamion said.

"I couldn't agree more." Kase grinned. "Life is unfair."

8

THE WILTSEN

Kase adjusted his pack and cinched down the strap, holding it secure to his saddle. He was excited about starting their journey to the Rift. He wanted to tell his friends where he was going. That would forever set his fame in stone among them, but of course, word would get back to his uncle. Perhaps he would set his fame in stone *after* he returned.

I might have proof too.

Brell had grudgingly agreed to let him come. She harbored concerns about him being in the Teck world. She secretly kept the option open of leaving him behind at the Rift.

Kase had already said his goodbyes to his uncle, who had warmly shaken Brell's hand. He'd given her a meaningful nod while giving Kase's back a sidelong glance. A silent request for her to look after him.

Understanding, she'd returned the gesture. Part of her had wanted to tell him that the Kase he knew was not the same one she had traveled with. Even if she had, it wouldn't have mattered. She'd experienced first-hand that people were slow to let go of their perceptions.

Hearing the creak of leather, she looked up as Kase climbed into his saddle. The horse nickered at the bit and flicked its ear with a wary look back at Kase until he settled into his seat.

It was her turn. Even after their long journey, she wasn't comfortable riding on something that possessed a will of its own.

"We're still friends, right?" she said, rubbing the horse's velvet nose.

Brell flinched when it unexpectedly blew in her face, its breath warm and seated with grass.

"See that?" Kase chuckled. "He likes you."

"Uh, okay," she said, feeling the urge to wash her face.

"Don't they resent being forced to carry people?" she asked.

"Some do," he answered, "but you rode him all the way here. He trusts you."

It had taken a while for Brell to get used to riding an animal, but she'd adapted...more or less.

She hadn't done any riding during their five days in town and some of her confidence had faded.

"It's all right," Kase said kindly. "Go on."

"I'm working up to it, okay?" she said, gripping the pommel.

The horse sensed her doubt and shifted, wondering if it wanted her on its back.

"Climb up like you belong there," Kase said.

Taking a quick breath, Brell stuck her boot into the stirrup and hopped up, smoothly swinging her other leg over and landing neatly in the saddle.

"Hey," she smiled, pleased with herself. "I still got it."

"It's like you've been riding your whole life." Kase grinned. "Ready?"

Brell nodded, giving the horse a gentle squeeze with her legs. It was all the prompting the animal needed. She turned the horse around until they were heading toward the city's main gate.

"How long this time?" one of the guards asked as they passed through.

"A week," said Kase, pulling a number out of the air.

"No longer if you can help it, all right?" the other guard asked.

Kase glanced at him curiously.

"I got eighty coin on you coming back in eight days," the guard said.

"I'm telling you, you're throwing your money away," the other one said.

They left the guards to debate among themselves and continued up the road, passing McLennon's tavern.

"Hey, Kase!" someone yelled.

He turned and saw Doiel charge out of the tavern doors and run up to him.

"Hold up," he said, waving a paper over his head.

"Hi, Doiel," Kase said.

"I'm glad I caught you," he said breathlessly.

"What's happened?" asked Kase looking concerned.

"We started another pool," he said. "The others won't like it, but I thought you might want to make a bet if you make it back."

"You guys are really funny," Kase said, not feeling very amused. "What are my odds?"

"Not good," Doiel said casually.

Kase motioned for the betting sheet, and Doiel handed the paper up to him. He examined the various bets people had made on him.

"Who bet three hundred coin that I die?" said Kase incredulous.

"Let me see." Doiel, holding out his hand. He scrunched up his face as he read through the troublingly long list.

"Oh, that's Fredrey," he said.

"I don't even know them!" he said.

"She's the new fortune teller," Doiel said. "She moved in while you were gone."

Kase glanced at Brell, who was pressing her lips together, snickering.

"You better hope she's got a lousy track record," she said.

Kase looked down at Doiel's smiling face.

"Thanks for the offer," Kase said, unsettled. "Maybe next time."

"Sure," Doiel said. "Sure. Well, have a great time out there."

He stepped back and gave a short wave before turning his attention to the paper.

Kase nudged his horse and they trotted away with Brell smirking beside him.

They followed the well-traveled road for another two days before coming to the Mata'Kai river. From there they would take a ferry to O'Shef Vale, a thriving port city.

The ferry was patiently rocking with the current when they arrived at the small docks.

They wouldn't need their horses for the next leg of their trip. Brell was surprised at the pang of regret when she handed over her horse at the dockside stables. She was going to miss it, but that was something she didn't want to share with Kase for fear he might tease her about it.

Riding horses was ridiculed by Tecks. They considered it backward, if not primitive. She was comfortable keeping secrets to herself and added this one to her list.

From the stables, they carried their packs up the ramp to the ferry's deck just as it blew the final whistle before departure.

Kase quickly stowed his belongings and hurried up to the observation deck just as they were casting off. A smile spread across his face as he watched the widening gap of water between the dock and the ferry.

Above him, the whistle gave a short blast as the deck crew secured the boarding ramp.

He felt the boat vibrate under his feet as the propellers began to spin. The water churned into a creamy froth as they moved out into the middle of the river.

This is it!

There was an undeniable sensation, a sort of crossing a border when he was separated from land. Even when it was within swimming distance.

Water was its own domain. It abided by rules that were foreign to land, just as the many of the creatures that lived above and below its surface did.

97

The Mata'Kai was one of the rivers that ran across the country. The waterway had been a main course used by large and small commerce. Before trains had taken over shouldering the big jobs, large barges had ruled the river, carrying tall stacks of steel and timber, feeding the need of growing cities.

From the upper deck, Kase enjoyed the view, gazing past the tamed pastures of farmland. He studied the lands beyond, where they turned feral and unbroken, running all the way to the hazy outlines of mountains.

He shook his head ironically with a smile.

I have never been there.

He scanned the left.

Or there. Or there.

It didn't matter which direction he looked in. It was unexplored.

I will though. I'll travel all of it.

The idea made him grin while he imagined the possibilities of what laid beyond his eyesight.

He stayed up there until the sun began to sink below the horizon. The chilled breeze made him shiver.

He went downstairs, into the common lounge and found Brell with her feet up on another chair.

"I was just thinking about grabbing dinner," she said. "You hungry?"

The thought of a warm meal sounded like just the thing.

"Let's go," he said.

During their passage, it wasn't long before each of them fell into a routine. After breakfast, they made several rounds, walking the deck before Brell went back to her room.

Tapping up the mysteries of the universe, Kase thought.

Her explanation was far less exotic.

She was trying to make arrangements in Teck for new and replacement gear. By settling the deals with her suppliers now, she could quickly return to the hunt for Ethan Five Seven.

But her supplier was being annoyingly and unexpectedly cagy. Something was going on, but they weren't saying.

With so much free time, Kase explored the ferry and befriended most of her crew.

The ship's engineer spent most of his time below deck in the engine room. He was always oiling or polishing something on the big machine.

He introduced himself as Clanten, and it took a few times for him to get Kase's name right due to his bad hearing.

He caught Kase glancing at his hand, which was missing a couple of fingers.

"I learned the hard way," Clanten said, wiggling his remaining digits, "a ship's engine ain't a play thing, but thank the fates I'm a quick learner, or there'd be nothing left for my wife to hang a ring on."

Clanten had been seeing to the needs of the ship's engine since he was a boy. He knew every inch of it and could, and did, happily explain not only how it worked but also where every part had been manufactured.

The engine was down in the belly of the ferry, below the waterline. Because of its weight, it made a perfect ballast, but that wasn't something you ever said around Clanten.

His beauty wasn't dead weight, and fair warning to anyone who said otherwise.

High above was the ferry's captain, who had his own stories to share and was pleased by the interest Kase showed in the boat.

The captain had been in the navy and used to patrol the coast, hunting pirates.

Captain Peralt did not understand how people could romanticize pirates.

"The first time you come face to face with one of those scoundrels," he said, "those illusions quickly fall by the wayside. They're a hard lot, crude, and only care about what makes them money. Life is cheap to them."

"I had a close call with a pirate ship not long ago," Kase said.

"Luckily, we slipped into a fog bank and reached shallow water, but they shot my small boat out from under me."

Kase suddenly remembered the boat he had *borrowed* when he, Gault, Dentword and Sallia had gone to the Brood Moors.

Oh no. I still owe Peakon a boat.

It had been his idea to steal it, fully expecting to bring it back. But that plan, like so many others during the journey, had unexpectedly changed.

He didn't know how much a boat like that cost, but he was sure it was a lot more than he had. He decided to keep an eye out on this trip for opportunities to make some money.

"You're lucky," the captain said. "If they had caught you, you'd either already be sold on the slave market, or your bones would be sitting at the bottom of the sea, picked clean by the fish."

"Slaves?" Kase asked, dumbfounded. "I thought that was ancient history."

"In this part of the world, yes." The captain chuckled coldly. "I've been from one end of the continent to the other. There are places where you would swear you were in another world, another time."

"I've never traveled that far," Kase said, feeling the wanderlust swelling in his chest. "What are the people like?"

"Some are just like you and me," the captain said. "Others? Very different. Some aren't even people."

"What are they?" Kase asked. His imagination was running wild with the possibilities.

"Not from this world," he said. "Maybe the offspring of a mage playing creator. Maybe they came through the Nac'Aura. I couldn't tell you."

"An entire civilization coming through the portal?" wondered Kase. "Have you seen it?"

"The Nac'Aura?" chuckled the captain. "No. I heard no one's seen it in hundreds of years. But if you're asking if it's possible for an entire population to appear through it, how can you say? It's a thing of magic, not bound by the laws of nature in this world." He tapped his fingers on the big ship's wheel in thought. "I don't pretend to be a scientist, so take what I say as one man's opinion, but when you consider how much our world changed since the Nac'Aura was created, I think things like size don't matter to it."

"I'm going to see those new places," Kase said. "Visit other civilizations."

"Don't wait too long," the captain said. "Some of those places might not be there, or something new might take their place."

Kase frowned, feeling confused.

"I don't understand," he said. "Are they dying out?"

The captain didn't answer, instead turning his attention to the river ahead. Kase watched as the bow drifted to the right, moving closer to the bank.

"That's the Wiltsen," the captain said, nodding to the left.

Kase looked but only saw water.

"You won't see her," he said, glancing at the clock above the windshield.

The way he looked at it gave Kase the impression there was an importance to the time. It was nearing half past five in the evening.

The captain's eyes flicked to the side, gauging the low sun before returning to the river ahead.

"We have time," the captain said.

Kase was sure the captain wasn't speaking to him, so didn't ask.

"She's under the water. A ferry like this one."

"How did she sink?" Kase asked.

He looked closely where the boat had gone down. He noticed subtle ripples and eddies and wondered if those were the telltale signs of its grave.

"The official captain's court said she hit a submerged boulder," he scoffed. "I can show you eight different charts of this river and none of them show a boulder there," he murmured hotly under his breath.

Kase thought it better not to interrupt and busied himself with looking at the dimming landscape.

"Boulders don't appear and disappear," the captain said.

"If it wasn't a boulder...?" Kase asked, feeling he'd been invited back into the conversation.

The captain's jaw clenched and pressed his lips, barring the words from escaping his mouth. He eyed Kase a moment, gauging the potential reaction from his audience.

"A shark," the captain said at last. "A bloody great shark."

Kase was filled with questions but wisely chose one that wouldn't give the captain cause to feel he was being mocked.

"The river's that deep?" he asked. "Deep enough to hide a big fish?"

"In some places, yes," said the captain. "There's been stories going back before I came here. Something that swims this river. Every few years, someone says they see something in the river. Big, gray green, rough scales, then it's gone in a wake of ripples."

"But a shark?" Kase asked.

"Mr. Clanten is friends with one of the divers that investigated the wreck. 'Weren't a boulder that sunk the Wiltsen,' the diver told him. 'Rocks don't leave teeth marks.'"

The captain checked the time again, then glanced out the windscreen at the receding site of the wreck.

It was more than Kase's curiosity could bear.

"Are we late for something?" he asked, suspecting tardiness had nothing to do with it.

"I don't like being here after it's dark," he said.

"Did someone die in the wreck?" Kase asked.

The captain was a mature, educated man. He didn't strike Kase as the kind of person who gave much to old wives' tales.

"Everyone died," the captain said, flatly.

Kase looked back at the site of the wreck. It was a short swim to the bank of the river.

Anyone could swim that far.

He imagined the water littered with the floating dead. It was a gruesome image, and he shook his head to free the scene from his mind.

"They never recovered any bodies," the captain said. "They checked the banks for miles. None of them were ever seen again."

The captain bit his lower lip and subtly shook his head, disagreeing with himself.

Kase puzzled over the captain's conflict. It was clear that what he said and thought were in disagreement.

"But they were," Kase said, "weren't they?"

The captain nodded, focusing his eyes on something unseen and far away, from another time.

"There's been talk," he said, "about these waters, at night. Ship's crew have seen people just under the surface of the water, their pale faces looking up at them as they followed beside the boat. Sometimes, only a lone soul circling, disappearing, then reappearing somewhere else alongside. Other times, the dark water was filled with pale glowing figures. They would motion for the captain to change his course, trying to lure him into the rocks or tree stumps, hoping to rip her belly out and sink her."

Kase stepped out onto the small wing of the bridge and looked over the side. His heart jumped into his throat when he saw something under the murky water, but in the same instant, he realized it was only the pale froth, thrown up by the bow wave. He looked again just to be sure in spite of himself.

Curiosity made him want to be part of the few who had seen the apparitions, but common sense questioned if the experience was worth the price of looking into those sallow, mournful faces. Would he resist their beckoning into that cold endless hell?

He shuddered, deciding the experience was not something he wanted to carry with him for the rest of his life and pushed himself away from the railing.

The captain glanced at him, his eyes crinkling in a humorless smile.

"You chose right," he said. "Living is enough of a burden. It doesn't make sense to double the load with dwelling on the dead as well."

One of the crew came in and opened the lanterns, turning on the torchstones inside and filling the bridge with light.

Looking around, he had a commanding view of the boat and saw the crew turning on the navigation lights.

"Right on time," the captain said, checking the overhead clock. "That will be Old Rick's Point."

Looking ahead, Kase saw an orange light in the distance.

"Is it dangerous running at night?" Kase asked.

"It can be," the captain said. "But the fenders around the hull are enchanted. If we get too close to a hazard, those fenders'll sound off good and loud. That takes some of the guesswork out of the job. I'd prefer to have a Jobsen river chart, but that kind of magic gets expensive. At least, that's what the river boat company says." He chuckled darkly to himself. "Not as expensive as losing an entire boat."

"I know a mage who enchants things," Kase said. "Maybe he would make one for you."

"Thank you for the offer," the captain said, "but I'll have to refuse. A chart like that is the next best thing to being able to see through the water. It shows you every mud bank, hazard, and shelf within a couple of miles. Jobsen's been used for years and never led a boat captain wrong. Believe me, I'm tempted to accept your offer, that is, if your mage were willing to do it, but it only takes one mistake, one time for the enchantment to miss a hazard…"

"I see what you mean," Kase said.

This threw a new light on Kase's perspective of magic. He'd grown up with it around him and had never really thought about what it took to enchant something. Gamion had told him how difficult it was, but Kase had been too starstruck with daydreams of someday casting his own spells that the old mage's words had been meaningless noise.

The reality was, enchanting an object demanded an extraordinary amount of forethought and intelligence. Most people wouldn't give a refrigerator a second look. It's a box that keeps things cold. Simple enough. But a mage had to impart just the right magic to keep food from spoiling or turning it into a block of ice. It had to obey the boundaries of the box. Imagine the chaos if a refrigerator didn't stop at the walls of its case. It just kept on refrigerating everything for miles around it. Or what if the freezer blast froze anything on contact? A person's hand could be instantly frozen.

It was considerations like this that made enchanting an object so intensely complex.

Yet, the numberless varieties of consequences did little to

discourage mages from practicing enchantments, and this, many believed, accounted for the steady population of monsters.

A horn echoed off the water from the far bank, bringing Kase out of his musings.

The captain enjoyed Kase's visits and was a tolerant man, too polite to say when Kase had overstayed his welcome, but he made it clear by his absence of conversation that the time had come.

In fact, it was later than Kase realized. He hurried into the galley to the rattle of pots being dried and stowed for the night as the cooks prepared to close for the night.

Kase was able to reluctantly coax them into one last plate of food but rushed through his meal under the annoyed sidelong glances and disgruntled mutterings of the galley staff.

His cheeks were stuffed with food, like a Cabbit storing seeds for the winter, and his plate was only half cleared when they turned off the lights.

The message was clear. *Go away.*

He and Brell had bought one of the cheapest cabins the boat had to offer. It looked more like a cupboard. Its only furniture was two bunks, one over the other, hugging the inside of the hull. They were long enough to stretch out in but with so little head room that they had to crawl in and out of them. Their gear gently swayed on the stowage hooks as Kase came in. Brell was already asleep, and he eased the small door closed.

There was only enough floor space for one person at a time, which required masterful timing to get in and out of their bunks.

He climbed up into his bunk and pulled the warm but scratchy blanket under his chin.

Closing his eyes, he settled down, lulled by the soft hush of water sliding by.

Kase's imagination was his tonic and curse. It could whisk him away to a distant land, richly fascinating with exciting cultures, spin stories of myth and lore out of thin air, and paint vivid landscapes of long abandoned cities with hidden secrets waiting for him to explore.

But it could also become macabre. Pretending to innocently lead him down a path of tempting mysteries, only to whisper in his ear about things hiding in the shadows, watching, stalking. Was that sound only the wind or caused by a careless monster?

Was that hushed rustling Brell rolling over in her sleep, or was something slithering across the floor? Had that shadow always been in the corner of the room, or was it new?

He was contently listing to the sound of the river flowing against the hull when fear whispered to him.

This bunk is so small. I can hardly move, it's so tight.

He ran his fingertips over the painted wood.

It's only a thin skin of wood keeping out cold black water. What if we hit a drifting log? It would punch into the cabin with no effort.

His imagination went into a full run.

It would pour in so fast.

He pictured himself and Brell squirming to climb out of their bunks as the water rose.

Fighting to open the door; the chill water climbing over our heads.

Kase opened his eyes and reluctantly looked at the hull planking as if it might bite him. He forced himself to be sensible and gently rapped on the wood. The feel of solid timbers instantly reassured him, chasing away his fears.

His breathing calmed and his eyes drooped while he shifted into a more comfortable position.

Feeling his imagination had been put back in its box, he closed his eyes and relaxed. Sleep wrapped its soft arms around him, and he let himself fall into it.

Somewhere around him, the ship softly creaked.

An image of one of the Wiltsen's dead passengers flashed into his mind. He saw them, waxy white faces, swimming alongside the boat, just on the other side of the hull from him. They were picking at the hull with the jagged tips of their bony fingers; as they dug a hole through the wood.

Kase's eyes flew open as he searched the cabin for the lone sound. He laid motionless in the dark, waiting. Needing to confirm it hadn't come from the hull next to his bed.

Did *it* know he had heard it? The quiet of the cabin drew out without another sound. Was it waiting until he wasn't listening?

Kase scowled, berating himself for acting like a child, giving in to every imaginary spook and specter his mind tossed at him.

He focused his thoughts on the journey ahead. He was going to see the Rift for the first time.

What was it like? Could the force holding the worlds apart be felt?

There were so many questions, it pushed out any more thoughts of monsters, and he fell into a deep sleep.

9
O'SHEF VALE

The city of O'Shef Vale was humming with activity as they neared the docks. A horn bellowed from the pier, and the ferry answered in reply. Its small horn sounded absurdly miniature in comparison as the boat steered toward its assigned place.

Crew stood at the bow and stern with thick ropes in hand as their counterparts waited on the dock, ready to catch and tie them off on the sturdy cleats that would hold them fast.

Kase and Brell leaned on the rail, taking in the span of the different shapes and sizes of boats tied along the expansive and crowded docks.

Throngs of travelers were boarding and departing up and down the ramps of the other boats. People hurriedly waded through the press of crowds while calling over their shoulders to their companions, trying to keep track of each other.

Cranes dipped and rose, snatching cargo from the ships' holds and filling up large flatbed wagons.

The ferry's engine rumbled as the captain reversed the propeller, slowing her approach.

Kase looked down, watching the hull, lined with a generous row of fenders to protect it, kiss the docks.

Ropes flew across to the waiting hands, and once secured, the ramp rolled into place.

The bustle of the docks was infectious and spilled onto the ferry as soon as the gate swung open. The ferry's deck was alive with the chatter of passengers maneuvering to be the next off, but Kase and Brell were content to wait.

Neither of them were interested in the push and jostle that eventually awaited them.

"The last time I was here," Kase said, "this place was a quarter of the size it is now."

He'd been returning from the trip where his mother had been taken. O'Shef Vale had felt very large and unfriendly to the ten year old boy. Then, as it was now, nobody had had time for a leisurely greeting.

"I am surprised you Creet have anything like this," Brell said.

"You expected a few of us squatting around a fire," smirked Kase, "banging two rocks together?"

"Pretty much."

Beyond the low terminals that lined the docks was another row of buildings. The scattered but orderly pillars of smoke made the train station easy to spot.

Beyond that, were huge humps of docked airships. Together, their backs looked like a school of giant whales.

To the right and further away, they could make out a busy latticework of masts, crossbeams, and red tipped funnels where ocean-going ships were adding to their share of travelers.

O'Shef Vale was a unique meeting of inland waterways and a large protected ocean bay.

Building a train station there made perfect sense and would manage passengers and freight. The weather was historically calm with rare exceptions, which made it the perfect port for airships.

All of this added to the influx of people and supplies which had grown and grown until the ports had taken over every other industry.

Stepping onto the dock, Brell stamped her feet with a smile.

"I like that," she said. "Solid ground."

They turned and melded into the crowds, steadily making their way to the central concourse.

"I like people," Kase said as they wove their way through the sea of bodies.

"I never would have guessed," Brell quipped. "I don't like them in big groups."

"How about individually?"

"Even less," she grumbled.

"I didn't know so many people could be in one place at one time," he grinned.

"It's the closest thing to what I'm used to on my side of the world," Brell said. "You could almost call it modern."

"It is modern," Kase said. "Just because something isn't made up of wires and..."

"Circuits,"

"And circuits," Kase said, "doesn't mean it's primitive."

"If you feel better thinking that, I won't burst your bubble."

The argument of magic verses technology had slowly evolved into a harmless rivalry, and they were content to let the conversation lose steam. A pitched battle of which was superior was a no-win situation. To admit the other was better was to admit their own way of life, culture, and beliefs were flawed. Neither of them were going to surrender ground on that hill.

Kase caught a hint of something cooking, and his mouth began watering. Across the concourse, he spotted a row of storefronts and guessed the scent was coming from there.

"Hungry?" he asked Brell.

"I might be."

The wide plaza allowed generous room for the people passing through, and Kase and Brell made it to the other side without bumping into anyone.

Closer now, they saw a bakery, a tavern, and a candy shop. They angled for the tavern, where the hostess steered them toward two seats at the counter.

They studied the menu, situated above a wide window looking into the kitchen.

"Anything to drink?" asked a tired looking waitress.

"Yesh," a voice called.

Two seats away, they saw a nicely dressed and obviously drunk man. His head wobbled like his neck had no bones as he tried to keep his eyes fixed on the waitress.

She rolled her eyes, ignoring him, and looked at Kase and Brell expectantly.

"Just a sandwich," Kase said. "The number three."

The waitress's sullen eyes shifted to Brell, who ordered the steak plate.

"Three and seven," she hollered through the window.

"As I was saying," began the drunk.

"I told you no more," the waitress said. "You can't even stand up."

The drunk recoiled, taking grave offense.

"You think so?" he said, putting his hands on the counter. "Watch this."

He lowered his foot, with intention of standing, but it swayed back and forth as if the floor was trying to dodge out of its way.

A smirk curled the waitress's mouth, and the drunk stuck his chin out defiantly.

He stepped off the stool and promptly collapsed to the floor.

"Ah ha!" said the drunk, holding up a finger. "You'll notice I landed on my back. Why? Because I chose to. A drunk couldn't have done that."

"Do you need help up?" Kase offered.

"No need," said the drunk, making a gesture with his hand.

Everyone started with alarm as a creature suddenly appeared next to him.

It looked like a thin bear with a dog's face and a human's hands. It glanced at Brell and Kase with its large soft eyes and gave them an embarrassed smile. It nodded apologetically to the people around it for its sudden appearance, then looked down on the drunk.

"Be a good fellow and help me up," he said, extending his hand to the creature.

It leaned down and wrapped its thick fingers around his hand before easing the man to his feet as easily as if picking up a flower petal.

"That stool is cursed," the drunk said, pointing an accusing finger at it. "See that it doesn't eject me again."

The creature propped the drunk up against the counter with one of its strong hands and sighed. It looked around the tavern dejectedly, wishing it had something genuinely useful to do.

"There's no magic allowed in here," the waitress said with an edge to her voice.

"Did I wake up in Teck this morning?" the drunk sneered. "You can't tell me where I can and can't use magic."

The waitress's expression became dark and menacing as she leaned across the counter and looked deeply into the drunk's eyes.

"I. Just. Did."

Suddenly, her eyes became bright, glowing green. Smoldering wisps of smoke snaked out of them, curling above her eyebrows.

The smiles froze on Kase and Brell, and they dared not do anything to risk her attention.

The drunk balked, his indignation suddenly evaporating.

"I won't take this abuse any longer. We're leaving," he said over his shoulder to the creature.

The waitress's lips pulled back in what might loosely be described as a smile. Her teeth were bright white and accented with sharp fangs.

The animal or whatever it was looped a powerful arm around the drunk's chest and picked him up without effort.

The waitress's face returned to normal as she watched the drunk leave and disappear in the crowd.

"Nothing worse than a drunk mage," the waitress grumbled, "am I right?"

Kase and Brell bobbed their heads in agreement when they heard applause coming from outside.

Craning their necks, they looked through the tavern door and saw a crowd of people forming, but for what, they couldn't tell.

"I'm going to see what I'm missing," Kase said.

Brell shrugged and followed.

"We'll be back," she said to the waitress.

They reached the outer ring of the crowd and saw a group of kids waving to everyone. They were wearing matching shirts and pants with a golden boot on their chests.

"What's going on?" Kase asked one of the onlookers.

"It's the Stompers," the man said. He must have thought that was explanation enough, which it clearly wasn't.

"Who?" said Kase.

"From New Vass," he said. "They're the defending Knottball champions."

"Knottball?" asked Brell.

"It's a rough game," Kase said. "Two teams on a long narrow field. A ball's put in the center and the teams fight to reach the other team's goal. I didn't know they let kids play it."

"Why not?" Brell asked, standing on the tips of her feet to get a better look at the kids.

"As I said, it's a rough game. There's no pads and only a couple of rules. Like, you can't use weapons or magic. Everything else is fair game."

She looked at the kids, none of them over eleven, as they waved and jutted out their jaws, smiling at their fans.

A gasp rippled through the crowd, and the guy near Kase swore under his breath.

Another group of children had just appeared from another walkway and onto the concourse.

"That's the Crush team," the fan said. "They're from Mesa River. Both teams are heading to the championship in Hatchis Glen."

People started shuffling, pushing themselves between the two teams, who had realized their arch rivals had appeared.

Many of the surrounding fans began looking worried, some even fearful and left.

"Where's everyone going?" asked Brell, exasperated.

"These kids hate each other," said the fan. "Things could get ugly."

"You're joking," Brell scoffed. "They're kids. If they act up, you take them by the ear and stick them in a corner."

"Not if you don't want the gurn kicked out of you."

She arched an eyebrow and looked more closely at the Stomper team. There wasn't a single cherubic face among them. Boys and girls alike, they had hard features and mean eyes. Their hands were small but strong and balled up into fists. The muscles in their necks went taunt as they searched the crowd for their rivals.

Brell had seen professional bare knuckle fighters who now looked soft compared to these children.

"I smell Mesa River trash," yelled one of the Stompers to the chuckles of his team.

"Try saying that to my face," a girl yelled from the other team.

"Without throwing up, looking at you?" the Stomper called.

The people, who Kase and Brell now realized was the teams' crew and management tried to form a human barrier, but the kids swarmed forward, squirming between legs and arms to reach their hated rivals.

The intensity chiseled on the children's faces was comical to Brell, and she chuckled in Kase's ear.

"It's so cute how they think they're ... Oh my gosh!" she blurted as the two waves of children clashed with unchecked but tiny violence.

Two boys made straight for a lone girl, who saw them coming. She shifted nervously on her feet, and her brow knitted in worry as she glanced around for someone to help her.

Everyone else was already occupied with their own fights, and she was alone.

The two boys smiled, seeing the same thing. They didn't maneuver or split up to flank her. She was easy prey.

"That's not happening," Brell said as she pushed past Kase to protect the girl. But she was too far away with too many people in the way to reach her in time.

The boys charged. At first, the girl hesitated, looking like she wanted to run, but it was all an act. She went into action, going straight at the boy on the left. She grabbed him by the shirt and head-butted him so hard Brell heard the *clok* from where she was standing.

The boy's eyes rolled up in his head, and he dropped like a sack of apples.

The other boy was surprised but not discouraged. He curled his fingers up into a tight little ball, and he swung, catching the girl square on the jaw. Her hair flared out like a cape as she spun from the impact.

Feeling a quick victory, the boy yanked her back around, ready for another strike. His fist sailed at her as she delivered a jarring kick to his belly amid the cheers of fans.

"She's the team's center guard," one said. "Nobody gets past her."

The boy's eyes bulged out as the air shot out of his lungs. Flushing red, he grabbed his stomach and fell over.

All spectators' eyes turned as someone screamed.

Kase and Brell stood with mouths agog as a man tried to fend off four kids from the Crush team.

"That's the defensive coach of the Stompers," the fan said.

Two of the kids wrapped themselves around the coach's leg, punching and biting him.

"This is insane." Brell grinned.

Whistles pealed above the chaos, snapping Brell and Kase out of the spectacle.

"I don't want to be here when the police start asking questions," she said.

She took Kase by the arm and guided him away from the crowd.

"The airship terminal is through there." She headed into the long breezeway with Kase along side, leaving the sounds of the mini riot fading behind.

The breezeway wound its way higher up until they reached the airship central hub. From there walkways branched out to the different airship terminals.

Brell went to the central desk for directions to their terminal while Kase wandered over to the large bay window looking out onto one of the docked airships.

The craft was enormous. Cabin windows lined each of the twenty decks that sat on a long smooth steel cigar-shaped platform.

Stubby wings were positioned on either side of the nose and tail of the balloon. On the underneath, near the back of the platform was a long fin with its own pair of small wings.

Kase looked at the thing, feeling his pulse quicken.

I'm going to be on that. Flying!

"Good news, bad news," Brell said, appearing besides him.

"That ship is fantastic," said Kase, gesturing out the window. "How long before we board?"

"Okay," Brell said, "make that one good news and two bad news. The good news is we can board now. The bad news is, one, that's not ours. Two, the police are questioning everyone going on our ship."

"Why?" Kase asked, glancing at the airship with disappointment.

"Nobody knows or is saying," she said. "Maybe because it's going to the Rift. Smuggling, escaping the law... Whatever the case, I'll never make it through that checkpoint."

She patted her cloak, gesturing to the damning evidence she carried.

"If you say I told you so," she growled, "I will hurt you."

"Why don't you dump all that stuff in a trash can?" he asked. "I mean, you're still dressed..." He caught sight of her glaring at him and paused. "Differently. That's not a crime."

"Do you have any idea how much this gear costs?"

"At least your arm terminal?" he said. "If they find that..."

"No," she said flatly. "That's not going to happen. We have to find another way to get on."

They looked out the window at the airship. Two large cables anchored it to a steel tower. A gantry extended from the top of the tower to the main deck of the ship where cargo and passengers boarded. Inside the tower was an elevator that carried people from the boarding gate to the observation and loading platform.

"Don't tell me you're thinking of climbing that tower" Kase said.

Brell didn't answer.

"Or we find another way to the Rift," he suggested.

"A boat will take too long," she said. "The guy who's getting us across the Rift isn't going to sit around and wait. He's got a small window of time to get to this side, connect with us, and get us back to the Teck side before anyone figures out what he's up to."

"Let's go to the terminal," said Kase. "Maybe we can figure something out."

Brell's face was lined with concern, but she agreed.

Being a bounty hunter brought with it an expansive list of dangers of varying degrees. She had gotten used to most of them, and the very bad ones, she chose not to think about. She had been doing this long enough to know that bounty hunters who lived in a constant state of dread more often died from heart attacks than from being killed by the criminals they hunted.

They reached the terminal, and Kase immediately saw the problem.

A line of impatient passengers meandered around the terminal as three police officers questioned each person before boarding.

They inspected everyone's baggage, looked under coats and cloaks, and most troubling of all, they paid special attention to the person's appearance, their way of speaking, and mannerisms.

"They're looking for Tecks," Kase said.

"I thought so to," Brell said. "I was hoping I was being paranoid."

"Your instincts were right," said Kase as they casually moved to the side of the room. "You don't think they're looking for you?"

"I've been careful to stay off the grid," she said, leaning against the wall. She pretended to look for something in her bag to explain why they hadn't joined the line.

"What's a grid?" Kase asked.

"Notice the third policemen?" she said. "He looks different from the other two."

Kase hadn't seen it before, but now that she'd called attention to it, he recognized why.

"It's a mage," he said. "Whatever is going on, it's serious."

Pretending to be in conversation, they thought about what they could do, but with every passing minute, they began to recognize they had little, or no options.

A commotion caught their attention, and they looked at the checkpoint. The police were smiling as they spoke with two men. From where they stood, Kase and Brell couldn't hear them, but oddly, the police didn't examine their bags.

In fact, the police waved the men through to board the ship.

Kase and Brell watched in confusion as one of the police quipped a joke to the two men. They turned, laughing, and waved before disappearing around the corner.

Kase saw it.

"They're soldiers," he said.

"How do you know?".

"He had a tattoo on his cheek," Kase said. "I wasn't sure at first, but it was a skeleton hand. My uncle served with soldiers who have the same tattoo."

"Fascinating," Brell said curling the corner of her mouth.

"That's how we get you past the checkpoint."

"I'm not tattooing my face," she hissed.

"Not permanently." Kase smiled.

"I'm tired and stressed," she said. "If you don't get to the point…"

"The illusion spell Brookwal taught me," Kase said. "I can use it to make it look like you have the same tattoo."

"You're not using magic on my face. What if you get it wrong? What if my head explodes or I grow a third eye?"

"I thought you had more faith in me," he said, slightly hurt.

"Yeah," she said. "When you're lighting a candle or doing one of your party tricks. Then I have tons of faith in you, but we're talking about my face. Get it?"

"All right," Kase said. "I'll do it on your bag. Just for practice."

"Okay." She angled in such a way that nobody could see what they were doing.

Kase pulled on his glove and fixed his fingers until it fit right.

"You're back," Alwyn said. "Has it been long?"

'I'm practicing casting an illusion of a tattoo.'

"Strange things, tattoos," Alwyn said. "I had one. It was of a cat I had once."

Kase turned his focus to the spell. He imagined the image of the skeletal hand. He concentrated on each bone, trying to remember how it looked.

"I made the mistake of enchanting it," Alwyn said. "The tattoo, I mean. It meowed all night."

'Shhhhhhh.'

"Oh, sorry. I forgot how hard the beginner spells are for you."

'Alwyn!'

The mage went silent, and Kase took a deep breath, collecting his focus.

Brell said nothing, knowing Kase needed concentration.

She was looking at her bag when a skeletal hand appeared on it.

Kase opened his eyes and saw the mark.

"What do you think?" he asked. He didn't believe he had to ask. It was perfect.

"Okay," she said. "That's pretty good."

"Pretty good?" he said, annoyed. "It's perfect. Do you feel better about doing this now?"

They glanced across the room, and the line was now decidedly smaller. In a few minutes, they would be the only ones left in the room, making themselves look painfully suspicious.

"Do it," she said.

"Not here," Kase said. "I don't want to risk being interrupted."

"Yeah," she said. "A botched spell on my face would be bad."

They left the terminal and walked a short distance to an alcove where a door lead into an employee's break room.

"Here," Kase said.

"Where do you need me?" asked Brell. "Standing? Sitting? Should we be by the window so you have better light?"

"Calm down," he said. "Have a seat."

Brell put down her bag and sat down. She put her hands on her thighs and turned the side of her face toward him.

"Like this?" she asked, the tension clear in her voice.

"That's fine," he said. "Now... just be still."

"Mmm hmmm," she said.

She watched him out of the corner of her eye as he began to slowly move his gloved hand near her face. His lips moved as he murmured something, and he closed his eyes.

Brell sat rigidly, hardly daring to breathe for fear of moving.

Suddenly, Kase sneezed, jerking his hand.

His eyes flew open and his face went pale.

"Oh no!" he groaned. "Oh no."

"What did you do?" gasped Brell, jumping to her feet.

"I'm so sorry," he said, holding his hand to his mouth. "Brell, I'm sooo..."

"I told you this would happen," she said, racing for the window. She turned her face, looking at her reflection with horror filled eyes.

Kase sputtered from a snicker into a laugh.

"You miserable sack of..." she seethed, realizing the joke.

"I'm sorry," he laughed. "I couldn't resist. There's nothing wrong with your face. The spell worked fine."

"Oh," she said, crossing the room toward him. "There's going to be something wrong with your face."

The flight hostess checked the clock and saw it was time to close the gates when two more people hurried into the terminal.

The police had been preparing to end their shift and sighed, resenting the late comers.

Brell walked up and the police recognized the tattoo on her cheek.

"A couple of your friends are already on board," one of them said, waving her through.

She only nodded and hurried up the hall to the waiting elevator.

"What happened to you?" the policemen asked, looking at Kase's black eye.

The other policemen took his bag and rummaged through it half-heartedly.

"I lost a bet," said Kase.

"Must have been some bet," the policeman said, handing back his bag.

"It was worth it," grinned Kase as they waved him through.

10

HIDE

Wind whipped around Kase as he stood at the end of the gantry, marveling at the airship floating majestically before him.

Unlike the one he had gazed at in the terminal, this ship was smaller. It only had five decks, and if you asked anyone else, they'd tell you it was kind of a piece of junk, but to Kase it was gorgeous.

"Hey!" the ship's steward called. "We got a schedule to keep, and we're already behind."

"Oh," Kase said, coming out of his revelry. "Sorry."

He glanced down as he walked along the gantry and instantly regretted it.

He didn't have a fear of heights except for when it was warranted; this time it was. The gantry was made of panels of steel mesh but built to be light and to allow the constant gusts of wind to flow easily around and through it.

It felt very fragile, and he could see right through it to the ground far below.

Looking down, the ground seemed to fall away. The further it went, the more it narrowed to a point. Beads of cold sweat speckled Kase's face, and he forced himself to look ahead.

He caught the steward smirking at him but said nothing and

wiped his face as he gratefully came aboard.

The gantry swung away, and the steward closed the hatch, spinning a wheel that latched it securely in place.

Kase entered the ship's main lobby, where Brell was waiting for him. She was looking at her tattoo in a piece of tarnished brass.

"How long is this going to last?" she asked.

"I don't know," Kase said. "It's the first time I've done it. A couple of hours, I think."

Inwardly, he wondered if it would last much longer, maybe even years.

No. Brookwal said illusions don't last more than a few hours at the most.

"How long is this going to last?" he asked, pointing to his black eye.

"I'm sorry about that," she said, looking at her scuffed knuckles. "I might have overreacted."

"You're not sure?" he said.

"Welcome aboard the Rift Eagle," a voice said over the loud speaker. "I am Captain Pullmic and will be commanding the ship during our flight to the Rift. It should be smooth sailing with calm winds and pleasant weather. If you have any questions, the ship's crew will be happy to help. Enjoy your trip."

"I'm going to drop off my gear," Brell said.

On one of the lobby walls was a map of the ship, each deck with numbered rooms, the dining room, bridge, and lounge.

"That's me," Brell said, pointing to a square on the bottom deck.

"It looks small,"

"Because it's made for one person," she said, cocking her eyebrow.

"Where's my room?" he asked.

"You didn't reserve one?" she asked, her eyebrows arching in surprise.

"Me? I thought... you bought the tickets," Kase stammered. "You didn't get me a room?"

He started to panic when Brell grinned, enjoying a little payback.

"Oh, I see. The eye wasn't enough? You had to make me worry?"

"Yeah," she smiled. "That sounds about right."

"You're kind of a bully," he said. "You know that?"

"That's true too," she said, looking for the hallway leading to their rooms.

They walked down the carpeted hallway, occasionally pressing themselves against the wall to make room for passengers going the other way.

"That's yours," Brell said, gesturing to a cabin door.

The number forty-three was engraved on a small plaque on the door.

It opened to a very small cabin slightly larger than the one on the ferry. Inside was an upholstered seat and small table. The bed folded down from the wall above the seat. Behind a narrow door was the bathroom with a miniature sink, shower, and toilet.

Everything looked a bit worn and dated, but he understood they were flying on a working ship and not a pleasure cruise.

Kase put his bag down on the seat and looked out the porthole. He craned his head and saw the cityscape of O'Shef Vale shrinking in the distance.

He stepped back into the hallway and knocked on Brell's door. He heard a muffled groan on the other side before she opened it and stared at him.

"Isn't this amazing?" He grinned.

"No," she said flatly. "It wasn't amazing the first time I flew on this tub when I came here, and it's not amazing now."

Kase tilted his head, feeling perplexed.

"What's wrong?"

"Nothing," she said.

"Something is," he said, not taking the hint. "You're being you but double."

She looked at him in a way that made it clear to anyone else that she wasn't interested in pursuing the conversation, but it only made Kase more curious.

After it became obvious he wasn't leaving, she slumped against the door with a drawn out sigh.

"And you're being you," she said. "I get it. This is all new, and you're having an adventure, but I'm not. I'm going back to my world.

That means I have people I have to answer to. I was hired to take on a bounty I haven't caught."

"That's not your fault," he said.

"I've worked hard to make my reputation," she said. "There's other hunters who have been waiting for me to make a mistake so they can get ahead of me. That means bounty agents might start looking at other hunters to get the jobs done before they consider me. I'll have to drop my rates..." She sighed again and looked at Kase with a pained expression. "Do you understand?"

"Yeah," he said, feeling bad for her. "I'm sorry."

"It's not your fault," she said.

"You wouldn't be going home if I didn't break your gun," he said.

She nodded. "Okay. It's your fault."

She smiled at him good naturedly. "But you saved my life," she said. "I'll take the busted gun any day."

"They don't have to know," he said.

Brell's eyebrows knitted as she searched his face for understanding.

"You're going back for a new gun..."

"Guns," she corrected. "Big ones."

"That's all you need," he continued. "Nothing says you have to report to your... uh..."

"Bounty agent," she said, a smile spreading to her eyes. "That might work. Broon is one of the top agents. He's got a lot of eyes and ears in a lot of cities. It's why he's the first to know when a bounty comes up. It might be tricky avoiding his people, but it's not impossible."

"It sounds like the competition between bounty agents gets hot."

"And ugly," she said. "There have been wars, but that was years ago."

"There's got to be other agents eager to have you working for them," Kase said. "Maybe they'd even secretly help you if you agreed to do some jobs for them."

"Caxor has been hounding me for years to work for him," she said with growing enthusiasm. "He would jump at the chance to get me."

"There you are," Kase said, spreading his hands. "Problem

solved."

Brell went quiet, thinking through the details of how she would do it.

"You can thank me now." Kase grinned.

"You did good," she said, coming out of her thoughts.

"And...?" prompted Kase.

Brell frowned at him, pressing her lips together as he waited patiently.

"Thank you," she grumbled.

"Was that so hard?"

"Don't be so smug."

"It's one of my more charming traits," he said.

Brell went back in her room to think through her new plan, and Kase left to explore this ship.

He discovered that most of the passengers were Edgers mining the Rift. When the world had fractured in half, it had exposed hard to reach deposits of ores and minerals, some of which had never been known of before.

It took a special breed of person to dig deep mines to reach valuable and much needed ores. Edgers were the same. Going over the edge of the world and scaling its raw face was not for the soft skinned and faint hearted.

The dangers they faced bound the Edgers into a tight community. Being an Edger was its own credentials and instantly earned you a welcome by others of your kind even if they'd never met you before.

Kase's curiosity of other people and cultures naturally drew him to find out more about them, but he was an outsider and no one had any interest in sharing their time with him.

He shrugged off their rejection without insult. There was an entire ship to explore, and he wasted no time doing it.

Unlike cruise airships, this was a working ship for working people. The traditional sense of customer service did not exist on the Rift Eagle.

Most of the crew hardly acknowledged Kase's questions and made a point of ignoring him as they busied themselves with their rounds.

Undaunted, he headed for the one place he was guaranteed to find someone happy to talk to him.

"What the gurn are you doing in my engine room?" scowled the dirt smudged face of the engineer.

"I wanted to admire the heart of the ship," Kase said, scanning the gleaming machinery.

"Is that so?" the man asked, his grim expression fading.

"It's my first time on an airship," Kase said. "I'll bet there's nothing on the ground or water that compares to an engine like this."

"You couldn't be more right," the engineer agreed.

"Kase," he said, extending his hand.

"Logi," the engineer said, shaking it.

Kase unconsciously glanced at Logi's hand, noting he had all his fingers.

"What would you like to know?"

"I don't know where to begin." Kase chuckled.

He looked down the expanse of the engine room, seeing hunks of machinery, each connected to the next with stout cables and driveshafts.

"Follow me," he said, with a wide grin.

Before long, the engineer was giving Kase the grand tour. Four huge turbines powered the main propeller. Smaller engines were used for the maneuvering propellers that Logi called fans.

"If push comes to shove," he said, "I can get her up to sixty-four knots. Faster if the wind's behind me."

Kase's head was so filled with facts and dimensions he had run out of ways to express his admiration and only nodded with a look of wonderment.

"Underneath us is what keeps us afloat," Logi said, stomping his boot on the floor.

"That's the platform I saw from the boarding tower?" Kase said. "What's in it?"

"That I can't tell you," Logi said, waving his hand. "Magic-made gas is all I know. But I can tell you how it works."

He walked Kase over to a bank of wheels, each with its own gauge above it.

"The platform, as you call it, is made up of compartments filled with gas. Each one of these controls a plunger in one of those compartments. Turning the wheel one way lowers the plunger. When the gas gets squeezed, it loses its lift and the ship sinks a little. Raise the plunger and the gas expands and lift increases."

Kase hadn't heard of gas being able to do that before, but alchemists were constantly experimenting with elements, discovering and creating new things.

"Hey," Logi said, glancing around to make sure they were alone. "Want to see something really special?"

Kase's wide grin was all the answer the engineer needed.

He led him over to the middle of the engine room and took a coat, work belts, gloves and helmets off a hanger rack. He handed them to Kase and took others for himself.

Kase pulled on the heavy coat, quickly feeling too warm.

"Here," said Logi, handing him goggles.

He put them on and looked up in time to see the engineer handing him a rifle.

"What's this?" he asked.

"That's a Falmas Fifty-Eight," Logi said. "Just in case."

Kase began to wonder what he was getting himself into.

"In case of what?" he asked, but his words were drowned out when Logi knelt down and opened a hatch in the floor. Instantly, the room was filled with the roar of wind. Kase looked down and saw wide open, empty air. Far, far below was a smudge of blue ocean between the wisps of cloud.

Kase gasped as Logi grabbed the edge of the hatch and nimbly lowered himself through it.

He grinned up at him with a broad smile as the wind whipped his hair around. He looked like a mad scientist.

"Follow me," Logi said and disappeared from view.

Kase swore under his breath, feeling his feet rooted to the deck. "You're out of your mind," he whispered to himself.

Logi's face reappeared in the hatch. Looking up at him, he waved him down.

"Hand me the gun," he shouted over the rush of wind.

Kase handed it down, and Logi slung it over his shoulder.

"Come on," Logi said. "When you lower yourself down, feel for the ladder with your foot."

Everything in Kase's head told him this was a terrible idea, but a part of him had to see what was down there.

He sat down and swung his feet over the edge of the hatch. A cloud of butterflies buzzed in his stomach. He gripped the edge of the hatch and forced himself to take a breath.

If I fall, I'm going to have a long time to regret this before I hit.

He looked down, searching for the ladder but seeing only miles of empty air under his dangling feet.

He jolted when Logi's hand appeared and grabbed his ankle. He realized the engineer was guiding his foot to the ladder. Feeling a sliver of confidence, Kase wiggled off the edge and lowered himself through the hatch.

He felt Logi's hand pull his foot to a ladder rung, and relief spread through him. As he came down, he saw the maintenance ladder in front of him and tightly grabbed it.

Kase scanned around, seeing the ladder lead to a platform. Logi was already half way down.

If he can do it...

Kase grabbed the next rung, then the next and kept going until he saw he was just above the platform.

Coming down the last few rungs, Logi gave him a solid pat on the shoulder.

"You got spice, boy," he shouted over the noise. "Not many will come down here. Me? I love it."

He opened his arms expansively and gazed outward.

The view was both terrifying and magnificent. They stood on a platform attached just above the bottom tip of the large rudder under the airship.

Behind them spun a giant propeller that powered the ship.

It was close enough that if Kase stretched out his arm, he could touch it. Each time a blade spun past them, the air made a loud *whop* sound.

Logi snapped a safety cable around Kase, making him feel better about his precarious situation.

He looked out into a great blue sky. Mountainous clouds drifted by and below like majestic silent animals roving a limitless plain.

Below, the blue ocean sparkled, rippling with threads of white as winds blew, frothing the tips of the waves.

Gazing up, he followed the sleek lines of the gleaming rudder, a great shinning shark fin, as the airship floated impossibly above.

From his vantage point, he could see the superstructure that supported the airship's main deck. Under its edge, he saw several smaller versions of the large gas cylinder that the ship rested on.

"What are those?" he asked.

Logi craned his head and looked up. "Life boats. They got a bit of gas in them to drift to the ground."

"How about that," Kase said.

Up until now he'd never considered the airship could fall out of the air, but now that he had... He quickly shut out the images popping into his mind.

"I suppose they're handy," Logi said. "As long as the ship's not in a free fall. Chances are, you'd get swept into the air, and the ship would drop away beneath you. Good bye, ship. Good bye, life boat. Hello, long drop."

"That doesn't bother you?" Kase asked.

"When it's your time," Logi said, "it won't matter if you're on solid ground, snuggled up in bed, or hundreds of feet in the air. Your time is your time."

"What's the rifle for?" asked Kase, changing the subject.

"Sea bats," said Logi, taking it off his shoulder.

"Bats? Up here?"

"Big ones too," said Logi. "That's why I got this lever action bolt thrower."

He worked the lever under the rifle, aimed it, and pulled the trigger.

With a crack, a bolt of twisting lightning flashed out. They watch the bolt as it sizzled away into the distance.

"That's got to hurt," chuckled Kase.

"Nah, a single bolt like that will just annoy a bat."

Kase blinked in surprise. The bolt looked like it would do a lot of damage. He certainly didn't want to be on the receiving end of one.

"How big are the bats?"

"About twice your size," Logi said. "They ride the thermals and hide inside the clouds. When they spy a meal, they swoop down. By the time you know what's happening, they already got their claws in you."

"Do they attack ships?" Kase asked, scanning the nearby clouds with concern.

"No," he said. "Sometimes, they get tired and hang on the rigging. One or two isn't a problem, but a flock of them will knock you out of the air. Want to try it?" he asked, offering the rifle to Kase.

"Thanks," he said, taking the gun.

His uncle had a couple of guns from his time in the army and had collected a few since then. He had taken Kase shooting and, according to his uncle, Kase was a fair marksmen.

"Each time you work the lever without shooting it, it generates a stronger bolt," Logi said.

"What's the most you ever levered it?"

"Twelve," the engineer said, grimacing. "That was about seven too many. My eyebrows didn't grow back for a year."

Kase ignored the temptation to see what a big bolt looked like and only pumped the lever once. He aimed toward the open sky and squeezed the trigger, just the way his uncle had taught him.

CRACK!

Bright light flared in front of his face, and he felt tiny needles prickle his face. A bolt of lightning lanced away, leaving tendrils of sparks trailing behind.

"Want to see if I can attract some bats?" Logi asked. "A single bolt won't hurt them any, but you have to be careful. Sometimes, you get one that decides it wants revenge."

He imagined himself suspended by a pair of taloned feet, being swept away and watching the airship shrinking in the distance.

"Maybe some other time," Logi said, seeing the expression on Kase's face. "Anyway, I've been having trouble with the secondary bearings. They probably need greasing."

He unhooked Kase and gestured to the ladder.

Kase hadn't realized how cold his hands were. The heavy coat with the fur lining and high collar had kept the rest of him nicely warm.

He scaled up the ladder and pulled himself through the hatch, followed by Logi.

"Thanks for the tour."

"Glad for the company," said Logi, holding out his hand.

Leaving the engine room, Kase couldn't help but notice how much quieter it was inside. Warmer too.

He made his way back to his room and took out his journal.

He took his time writing down his experience, what Logi told him about how the engine and gearing of the rudders worked, along with dozens of other notations.

By the time he finished, there were stars outside his porthole and his stomach was making it clear it was being neglected.

He came out of his room, and throwing caution to the wind, he knocked on Brell's door.

"Good timing," she said, opening the door.

"You're in a good mood," he said.

"I had time to think through your idea," she said. "I know an agent I can contact when we reach Teck."

"Can you trust him?" Kase asked.

Brell scoffed. "A bounty agent? They're essentially a licensed criminal. But if working with me pays better than ratting me out, it'll be okay."

"Sounds like a colorful bunch of people." Kase smiled. "Dinner?"

"Yes."

Dinner was simple but flavorful and they could get as many helpings as they wanted. One helping was enough for Kase, and he was feeling pleasantly full after cleaning off his plate, but Brell went back for seconds.

He looked at her with an amused smile as she sat down with her second full helping. She could eat him under the table.

Where does she put it all?

As she ate, he told her about exploring the airship and meeting Logi. He described how the ship operated and the large engines powering the huge propeller.

"This thing runs on whale spit?" she said, smirking.

"It's not whale spit," Kase said, offended. "It goes through an alchemy refining process. Mages were able to create a process where it separates the impurities. Then they…"

In truth, Kase didn't know what they did, but Brell's scoffing annoyed him. He wasn't about to let her think the Creet were scientifically inferior to the Teck.

"The alchemist enriches it," Kase said, making it up as he went. "Magic changes its properties and it becomes an exceptional source of fuel. It powers any kind of engine, including trains and ships."

"And it's made from whale spit," Brell said.

"What do you use for energy?" Kase asked. "Your own sense of self-satisfaction?"

Brell took out her pistol and pressed open a small catch. She continued to work on it for a few moments until the gun came apart. She tapped part of it on the table, and a small disk fell out.

"That," she said.

Kase went to pick it up but stopped, glancing at her for direction.

"It's safe." she said.

He picked it up and examined it. The disk was about the size of his thumbnail and as thick as two coins. It was semi-transparent with a burnt purple color. He rubbed his thumb over it, feeling the smooth surface but noticed a small piece had chipped off.

"This powers your gun?" he asked, fascinated.

"It used to before it burned out," she said. "It's called Gramite. We use crystals like that to power everything on Teck."

"I've never seen anything like it," he said. "Where do you get them?"

"Storm fields," she said. "I don't know the history, how they were discovered, whatever. I just use them. What I know is that after the Rift, super storms started forming. These are violent and powerful lightning storms, but they only happen in specific locations. Part of what makes them different is the purple lightning."

"Like this?" Kase said, holding up the disk.

"Yeah," she said. "They're dangerous and unpredictable. You do not want to get caught in one. That's why everyone avoided them at first because, you know, the dying part. Eventually, someone built an armored car strong enough to withstand a few lightning strikes and drove into the field to see what was going on. What they found were small craters with purple crystals in each one. They discovered that under the surface was a layer of something or other. I don't know the technical name, but it looks like course sand. When the lightning hit it, it liquified the sand, changing its structure and reformed it into a super charged crystal. Everyone got excited once they figured out how to harness the energy it produced, and bam, we had a new source of power."

"That's incredible," Kase said. "These storm fields must be rare. I've never heard of them in our world."

"They only form over deposits of Craynite," she said. "There aren't very many of them. And that's kind of a problem. Some countries have them and others don't. Haves and have nots."

"Sounds like what wars start over," he said.

"More than a few," Brell said, taking another bite of food. "A couple of the fields were destroyed. The crystals are volatile in their natural form. One country decided if the other guy didn't want to share, then nobody would have them. They set off a bomb on the field. Poof."

"No more field?"

"Oh yes." Brell chuckled. "No more field. No more anything for twenty square miles. Just a big hole. That shook up a lot of people. It's probably what brought everyone to the peace table. Losing an energy source like that was just stupid. So everyone made agreements to play nice and share. Since then it's been mostly quiet."

"There's always someone who wants to fight," Kase said. "My uncle told me that a lot."

"He's right."

He handed her the disk, and she put it back in the pistol and reassembled it.

After she was finished eating, they walked outside onto the bow observation deck. Fins placed around the base of the deck reflected the winds up and away, leaving only an occasional gentle breeze.

The deck was lit in the glow of Hyra's white moonlight. Anoux was just peeking over the horizon. Her unmistakable pale silver, blue cast and great size earned her the role of the big sister of the three moons.

Feeling nicely full, Kase and Brell leaned on the railing, enjoying the crisp air.

"Do you mind if I ask you something?"

"Even when I do, it doesn't stop you." Brell chuckled.

"How did you end up being a bounty hunter?"

"I have a knack for it," she said. "I just got out... from my last job. I looked around a bit. Went on some interviews. But when I saw rows and rows of people sitting in little boxes... That little space was their whole world for eight hours a day."

"I can't picture you doing that," Kase said.

"Me neither," she said. "The idea of it made my palms sweat. I looked for something outdoors. Construction, hunting guide, even a farm."

"You on a farm?" he said. "I didn't think you and nature mixed."

"I ran into an old friend of mine," she said, ignoring him. "I hadn't seen him in a long time, but he looked good, you know? Happy. Okay, not ecstatic, but he was doing something that he felt good about."

"Bounty hunting," Kase said. "That I can see you doing."

"What does that mean?" Brell asked, giving him a sidelong glance.

"You're resourceful," Kase said. "Smart. I think you thrive on challenges."

"Oh," Brell said, expecting him to tease her. "Thanks. My first contract was easy enough. I had a partner at the time showing me the ropes. Agents began to see I had a talent for the work and started sending me meatier contacts. Better payouts."

"But more dangerous?"

"Yes." Brell smiled. "I got knocked around a few times. I bit off more than I could chew with a couple of the contracts."

"But that didn't stop you?"

"Once," she said, suddenly looking somber. "I went after a stitcher…"

"A what?" he asked.

"Someone who self-augments their body with tech,"

"You're saying people put that stuff in their body?" he said, screwing up his face in disgust. "That's unnatural."

"Don't judge what you don't know," she said. "You've been secluded in your town half your life. You don't even know about your own world, let alone mine."

"That's true," Kase said, realizing he had hit a nerve. "I didn't mean to offend you."

"I don't have anything to be offended about," she said sharply.

An awkward quiet hung in the air for several moments.

"You went after the stitcher?" he asked.

Brell shifted on her feet. Kase assumed she was deciding if she wanted to continue the story.

"The information I had on her was sketchy," she said. "The bounty agent didn't do their homework. They just wanted the fat reward money. So they threw a bunch of junk on the stitcher's profile; I don't know, hoping some of it was right. The end result was me walking into a situation I wasn't ready for."

"Sounds like it didn't go your way," Kase said.

Brell chuckled darkly. "You could say that," she said. "I stopped taking contracts after that. I had plenty of time to think about it, but after I picked myself up, I knew it was what I really wanted to do. But I had to be a lot smarter. I only dealt with agents who had good…" She laughed. "As good a reputation as you can have for that kind of work."

"And you have been doing it ever since?" he asked.

"It keeps me busy," she said.

11

CHANGE IN PLANS

Kase woke up to the sound of hurried knocking on his door.

He squinted at the sunlight streaming through the porthole as he threw back the bed covers and got up, ignoring the gritty floor under his bare feet.

"Com..." He croaked, cleared his throat, and tried again. "Give me a minute."

His clothes from the day before were on the floor and the quickest at hand. He gave his shirt a sniff.

It will do.

Pants and shirt on, he opened the door, finding Brell looking impatient.

"We stopped," she said.

"Huh?" asked Kase, glancing at the porthole.

"Stopped," she repeated. "Not moving. Motionless."

"All right," he said, groggily waving her off. "Did we break down?"

"No," she said. "Look outside."

He shuffled to the porthole, and shielding the glare with his hand, he saw another airship approaching.

"Huh," said Kase, who couldn't think of anything else to say. He didn't see why he should care, but Brell did.

"I heard they're going to dock with us," she said.

"Uh huh," he grunted, looking at the airship again. "It's early and I just woke up. I promise I'll be a lot more interested after I've had breakfast."

"There might be a Teck bounty hunter onboard," she said.

"Where'd you get that idea?" Kase asked, trying to wrangle his hair into place with his fingers. "Nobody knows you're here except me."

"And the Edger who's going to smuggle us across the Rift," she scowled.

"Because...?" He stared. "Oh, the reward."

"Right," Brell said. "Let's get to the observation deck before they arrive. I want to see if I'm right."

"Then what?" he asked, searching for a sock.

"If I am..." She smiled, grimly. "This boat's going to have one less Teck bounty hunter by the time we reach our destination."

Kase shoved his hands into his pockets as they stood on the upper deck. The chill air dashed away his lingering cobwebs of sleep but also woke up his appetite.

The cold brought out a rosy color on Brell's nose and cheeks, but she was too focused on the approaching airship to notice the sharp temperature.

The new airship was smaller and sleekly made with a single deck for its passengers. As it neared, it rose above them and turned until it was parallel.

Kase and Brell watched a hatch open and a rope was lowered. There was something hanging from the end of it, and they quickly realized it was a person with a black hood over their head.

Three of the Rift Eagle's crew came out on deck and grabbed the person's legs, guiding them down. One of the crew unhooked the rope and signaled to the smaller ship. The rope quickly receded back through the hatch.

Two of the crew caught the hooded figure as they stumbled and righted them.

"His hands are tied," Brell said.

Looking up, they saw a rope ladder come out of the same hatch. A lone cloaked figure stood on the bottom rung and leaned out, keeping the prisoner in sight.

Wind buffeted the figure on the ladder and blew back their hood. Long red hair streamed out, whipping in the wind.

"I think you were right," Kase said. "She's wearing armor like yours but no gun. I don't see any tech on them."

"She's Creet," Brell said. "She hunts Tecks."

"But she's not here for you."

"No, she's already got her prisoner."

"How many Teck are running around in my world?" He frowned.

"No idea," she said, watching everything the hunter did.

The woman stepped off the ladder as the Rift Eagle's captain strode up to her.

His jaw was set, and he set his stern eyes on her. With a jerk of his head, he told her to follow him inside.

The prisoner cocked their head, listening to the short conversation, then twitched as the hunter took them roughly by the arm.

The prisoner must have said something because the hunter leaned closer to hear them over the noise. Suddenly, the prisoner lunged, head-butting the hunter hard. She stumbled back but quickly recovered.

"That had to hurt," Kase said, sucking in a sharp breath through his teeth.

"Here it comes," Brell said as they watched the hunter wind up and slug the prisoner in the gut.

The hooded figure doubled over, and the hunter grabbed their arm and roughly led the staggering prisoner inside.

Brell and Kase left the railing and hurried inside where they could look down on the lower deck from the open atrium above.

"This is not a prison barge," the captain protested.

"I know, Captain," the hunter said. "I apologize for the delay. I wouldn't have troubled you –"

"Threatened," the captain. "You said if I refused, you'd report me for interfering with transporting a prisoner."

"Can *you* do that?" Kase asked.

"Having a Creet on our world is serious," she said. "So are the laws of any Teck that interferes with catching one or helps one escape."

"My ship isn't equipped with a brig," the captain continued.

"I'll take an empty room," she said. "Somewhere away from the passengers."

"Mr. Alcot," the captain growled. "have two cots prepared in the stern equipment locker."

"Yes, sir," Alcot said, saluting before heading off.

"Bringing this... Teck onto my ship puts my passengers and crew in danger," the captain said.

"You won't see him again until we reach port," the hunter said. "I've got him under control."

"Says the hunter with a bloody nose," the hooded figure scoffed.

Brell stiffened, drawing a glance from Kase, but she didn't say anything.

The captain left, and Brell moved away from the railing, gesturing Kase to join her.

"We have to break him out," she said.

"This isn't our problem," Kase said. "Isn't that what you're always telling me? Well, for once you're right."

"He's a Teck," Brell said.

"Trespassing in the Creet world," Kase added. "If we get involved and caught, it would be a short trial and a quick death."

"I'll do it myself," she said. "Just stay out of my way."

"Even if we did," he said, "we're in the middle of the sky. There's only so many places to hide him."

"One thing at a time," she said. "I'm working on it."

They went back to the rail as the argument between the captain and hunter ended.

"We're going to our room," the hunter said, glaring at her prisoner. "No trouble between here and there. I have a spell that will literally wipe your mouth off your face that I'm dying to try out."

"Why are you being so harsh?" the prisoner asked. "Are you trying to conceal your true feelings for me?"

The two remaining crew grinned at the jibe, but their smiles vanished under the withering scowl of the hunter.

"Take us to my room," she growled.

Once the group was out of sight, Brell led Kase to the deck below.

"I have to find out where her room is," Brell said.

They went down the hallway and hurried to the next intersection of corridors. From there, they peeked around the corner in time to see the hunter shove the prisoner into another corridor.

Staying at a careful distance, they followed the group to the far end of the ship. Off limits to all but the crew, the corridor opened on to closets, supply, and utility rooms.

With a rattle of keys, one of the crew unlocked the equipment locker and handed the key to the hunter.

Kase and Brell hurried back the way they'd come as the crewmen turned and left the hunter with her prisoner.

Returning to the lounge, Brell and Kase found a corner table and pulled their chairs close together.

"Now that we know where they're staying," Brell said, "it makes our job easier."

"They're in a locked room. At the end of a hallway with only one way in or out. How is that easier?"

"She won't stay in there for the rest of the flight," Brell said. "We can get in there when she comes out to eat."

"How do you know she won't eat in her room?" he asked.

"Did you see the daggers in her eyes?" Brell said. "She'd kill that guy if there wasn't a reward for him. She won't stay locked up in that room with him more than necessary."

"All right," Kase said. "She leaves the room, then what?"

"We have to know what our options are," she said. "We'll break into the room and see if there's any other way in there: air ducts, freight hatch, that kind of thing."

"We have a couple days before reaching port," Kase said. "Will you have a plan by then?"

"I don't have a choice," she said.

They spent the evening in the dining area, but the bounty hunter never appeared.

"She must have thicker skin than I gave her credit for," said Brell the next day.

"We only have tonight left," said Kase. "What if she doesn't show up?"

"Then we'll use plan B."

"You have a plan B?" he asked.

"Not yet," said Brell.

That evening, they went into the dining area early and waited for the hunter to show up.

Minutes turned into hours as the evening wore on with no sign of her.

"She's not coming," Kase said. "Maybe she'll show up for breakfast."

Brell was about to answer when the dining room door slammed open and the hunter waded into the room like a glowering storm front. Waves of anger radiated off her as she sat down. She put her hands on the table, clenching them into two white fists.

Across the room, two waiters argued out of the corner of their mouths over whose job it was to serve her.

Brell looked at her, a smile spreading across her face as Kase ogled in amazement.

"I have annoyed a lot of people," he said, "but I've never made anyone that mad."

"Only a professional creep knows how to hit the right nerve like that," she said.

"Are we still doing this?" Kase asked.

"Look at her," she said. "She's not going back to her room until she's finished off four or five bottles."

Kase wasn't feeling as confident as Brell, but she did have a point.

They moved through the corridors as quickly as possible without drawing attention, until they reached the door for restricted to ship's crew.

If the hunter turned the corner now, they could make up an excuse for being here, but she would remember their faces.

Then when the prisoner disappeared, all fingers of suspicion would point directly at them.

They slipped through the door and hurried to the equipment locker.

"I have something to pick the lock," Brell said, reaching into her belt.

Kase tried the doorknob and it turned.

"Unlocked," he said, surprised. "How mad did she have to be to forget that?"

They went inside, closing the door behind them.

Inside, the walls were lined with shelves full of tools, and the air smelled of grease. Pieces of machinery, lengths of hose, cleaning supplies, and boxes had been shoved out of the way for two cots.

In the middle of the room sat the lone figure of the prisoner tied to a metal chair.

Still hooded, the prisoner turned his head, listening to Brell and Kase as they searched the room, looking to see if there were other ways to sneak in.

Their search ended quickly; except for the door, there was no other way in or out.

"Who's there?" the prisoner asked.

"Hi," Kase said.

Brell gasped and tried to stop Kase from removing the hood, but she was too late.

"We're going to break –" Kase began.

"Brell?" the prisoner said with a huge grin.

"Hanover," she groaned. "I was hoping I was wrong."

The prisoner shook his head, his tousled blond hair swaying until it settled neatly in place. He gazed at Kase with deep blue eyes and a dazzling white smile.

"You know him?" Kase asked.

"Oh, sure," Hanover said. "Me and her go way back. Don't we, angel?"

"Angel?" Kase said, glancing at Brell.

"What are you doing in Creet?" Brell asked, frowning and crossing her arms across her chest.

"I took a contract to cook a rogue bot," Hanover said. "A real psycho."

"You better not say Ethan Five Seven," Brell said, raising her eyebrows.

"Ethan Five Seven," Hanover said, his handsome face lighting up. "They hired some loser who botched the job. Never heard from them again. Amateur, probably got themselves killed. Total rookie move."

"That's me," she said. "And I didn't botch the job."

"No kidding?" Hanover said. "They gave you a contract too?"

"She means she's the rookie," Kase said.

Brell glared at Kase, who shrugged an apology.

"You?" Hanover said, looking up at her. "And here I am, cleaning up your mess. Well, this is awkward, am I right?"

"Something like that," she said, grinding her words through clenched teeth.

"It's nothing personal," Hanover said. "I don't ask questions. I just take the jobs. I have a great idea. Let me make it up to you by taking you out to dinner."

"What?" Kase said.

"Oh." Hanover frowned at him. "You don't mind, do you, guy? You two aren't..."

"No!" Brell said, flushing red.

"Great," Hanover said. "How's the food on this bucket?"

"You've been arrested for trespassing on the Creet world," Kase said. "There's a furious bounty hunter in the dining room who wants to see you hang."

"I'm not following you," Hanover said, his brow knitting together.

"You're a prisoner," Kase said.

"I was until sweetness here showed up."

Nobody moved. Puzzled, he glanced back and forth between Kase and Brell. "What am I missing?"

"As soon as you go missing," Brell said, "the hunter will take this ship apart to find you."

"No problem," Hanover said. "I'll wait behind the door. When she comes in I'll snap her neck like a twig and throw her body overboard.

Then it's dinner and drinks on me. Which reminds me, can I borrow some money?"

"Whoa!" Kase said. "You can't murder her."

"Too much?" Hanover asked.

"You stay here," Brell said. "We're going to search the ship for a place to hide you until we reach port. Then we'll pay off a couple of crew members to smuggle you off."

"Brains and beauty," Hanover said. "Maybe we should give it a second chance. Imagine what our babies would look like."

"There was never a first chance," Brell said.

"She's got fire, doesn't she?" he asked Kase.

"Yes, she does," Kase said.

"Did she give you that shiner," Hanover said. "I thought that looked like her work. A little advice. Don't go for the direct approach with this one."

"Knock it off," said Brell, smacking the back of Hanover's head. She grabbed the hood and roughly yanked it back into place.

"See what I mean?" Hanover muffled through the hood. "She gets all flustered when you're nice to her. So... I'll see you guys around soon?"

They left him, and Brell resisted the urge to slam the door.

"I see it now," Kase said. "You have the same murderous look the hunter did."

"I keep hoping someone will kill him," Brell said.

"We can leave him there," Kase offered. He wouldn't admit it but part of him was tempted to. His instincts told him Hanover caused problems wherever he went.

"I'm tempted," she said as they went through the utility door and into the passenger area. "But knowing I was responsible would take some of the enjoyment out of it."

They passed through a couple of corridors, and Brell noticed Kase kept glancing at her.

"What?" she said.

"The way he talked about you," Kase said. "Did you and him...?"

"Think very carefully about how you finish that question," she said, glaring at him.

"So tomorrow morning we start looking for a place to hide him," he said.

"If we time it right, we'll break him out a couple of hours before we dock. That way there won't be enough time to search the entire ship, and we can sneak him off."

They reached their cabins and stopped in the hallway. Brell looked at him, her eyes serious. "It's all right if you don't want to be a part of this."

He looked at her for a moment, weighing a decision that could mean the rest of his life in prison.

"I'll see you in the morning," he said. "I need to think about it."

She nodded somberly and went in her room.

Alone for the first time all day, Kase stared at the long empty corridor, letting his thoughts unravel until a yawn pushed itself out. A wave of fatigue washed over him, and he went into his cabin.

Moonlight streamed through the portal as he dumped his clothes on the floor in the same place he'd found them that morning.

Squirming into his bunk, he pulled the blanket close around him. As soon as he closed his eyes, he felt his body relax and sink into a dreamless sleep.

Something slammed into the cabin wall, jolting Kase out of his sleep. He sat up quickly, forgetting the low ceiling of the bunk and smacked his head.

Bright dots exploded behind his eyes, and he rubbed his head, swearing as he rolled out of bed.

As the ringing in his head subsided, he heard Brell yelling from her cabin.

She's in trouble!

Kase threw on his pants and pulled on his spiritbridge as he charged out of his room and barreled into hers, ready to fight.

What he saw brought him to a standstill.

"What are you doing here?" he demanded.

"I got bored," shrugged Hanover. "Did you see how small that room was? Not even a window. I thought I'd see if you guys found me a hiding spot, get the lay of the land... like that."

Brell glared at him, angry and disheveled. A new red mark on Hanover's jaw and a dent in the cabin wall explained what had woken Kase.

"You snuck into my room while I was asleep," Brell spat.

"Did you know you snore?" he said. "But on you it's cute."

"You were watching me sleep?" Her fist balled up for another swing.

"I think what everyone's missing here is how amazing I am that I tracked you to your room. Am I right?"

"Where's the hunter?" Kase asked.

"She's asleep."

"Get back there before she finds out you're gone," yelled Kase.

"Relax," Hanover said, smiling dismissively. "I used an old bounty hunter trick to make it look like I'm still in my cot."

"You idiot," Brell hissed. "Did it occur to you that *she's* a bounty hunter too?" Suddenly, the room was filled with the blare of alarms.

"Oh, yeah," Hanover said.

Kase stuck his head out the door, seeing several groggy faces looking out from other cabins.

"This is the captain," boomed the voice over the loudspeaker. "Due to an emergency, everyone is confined to their cabins. "There's nothing to be concerned about. The ship is running perfectly safe. Remain in your cabins until further instructed."

"They'll be sending out search parties soon." Brell said.

"We have to disguise him."

"I can't pass for Creet," Hanover scoffed. "I look too evolved."

Kase pushed past him to look out the porthole. The sky was clear, and he could see they were over land. He pressed his face to the glass but couldn't see the port.

"We can't hide him," Kase said. "The port's hours away."

"They'll be able to scour the ship with time to spare," Brell said.

"He's got to get off the ship."

"We're miles up in the air," she said.

Kase thought back to the platform on the rudder. Logi, the ship's engineer, might let Hanover hide down there. It would be the last place anyone would think to look.

He shook his head, instantly seeing the flaw in his plan. Once they docked, Hanover would be easily spotted. Then he remembered the lifeboats.

"The ship's got lifeboats," he said. "If we can stay ahead of the search parties, we can get him on one. Get ready." Kase glanced at his naked chest. "I'll be back in a second."

He dashed out and into his room, scooping up his two day old clothes. A moment later, he shouldered Brell's door open, pulling on his last boot.

Brell's face was lined with tension. Hanover looked mildly amused.

"Let's go," Kase said.

The three of them headed out of her cabin and moved quickly down the corridor, toward the stern deck of the ship.

Despite the corridors being empty, Kase's nerves were stretched thin. A door could fly open at any moment with a search party pouring through.

They'd just turned a corner when the door at the other end slammed open. The three of them sprang back the way they'd come.

Someone in the search party barked orders, directing smaller groups down different corridors. The sound of their footsteps faded, but one set grew louder.

Kase tried to think of what to do next when Hanover's big hand landed on his shoulder, and he winked at him with a smile.

"No," Kase hissed.

He didn't know what Hanover was going to do, but Kase knew it was a terrible idea.

Hanover went to the nearest cabin door and tried the handle.

Locked.

He pressed his shoulder against it, then bumped into it. The door opened with a soft crack, and Hanover slipped inside.

Kase glanced at Brell, who cocked her head at the door and followed. Kase moved in behind her, and Hanover silently closed the door.

He held his finger to his lips and pointed at the two snoring figures bundled up in their bunks. The small table was crowded with empty bottles, and the inside of the room smelled of stale alcohol and sweat.

Across the hall they heard the search party rapping on a cabin door.

"Now what?" Kase whispered. "The moment they knock here, those two will wake up and we'll be surrounded."

Hanover was listening at the door as Brell rummaged for something in her belt and swore.

"I left my gear in my room," she said.

"Calm down," Hanover said, giving her a wink. "I'll protect you."

"You'll what?" Kase sputtered. "We're protecting you."

"Sure you are." Hanover nodded. "And you're doing a great job. Isn't he?" he asked, grinning at Brell. "Now get behind me. The grown-ups are working."

Too stunned to object, Kase moved aside as Hanover moved in front of him and put his hand on the doorknob with his ear to the door.

Outside, the voices stopped talking and a door closed. Hanover paused a beat, then flung open the door. Two crewmen froze in place as they ogled up at the big bounty hunter filling the doorway. Together, their mouths fell open.

Hanover reached out, grabbing the sides of their heads, and banged them together with a *clack*. Their eyes rolled back, and he caught them as their knees buckled, easing them to the floor.

He glanced up and down the empty corridor, then waved Brell and Kase through the door. Hanover dragged the unconscious men into the room and quietly closed the door as he stepped outside.

Kase could only stare at him, openly impressed by his audacity.

"You're doing great," Hanover said, giving Kase a friendly pat. "What next?"

Speechless, Kase cocked his head for them to follow.

He peeked around the corner and saw the corridor was empty. They quickly reached the opposite door, which opened onto the rear deck.

He cracked it open and saw the deck was empty. The chill morning air gripped them the moment they stepped outside. Shivering, they cautiously crossed the deck until they came to one of the stairways leading down to the lifeboats.

Kase led them down the stairs until they came to a steel mesh security door. Kase's hands were red with cold as he tried the frigid metal handle. It didn't budge.

"What are you lot doing here?" a voice snapped.

Kase looked up in surprise at a gruff face peering at them from the other side of the mesh door. The man was wrapped in a thick coat and wore a ship's cap. It was instantly clear that the captain had been thinking two steps ahead and had ordered the lifeboats locked off and guarded.

"Uh..." Brell said.

"You should be searching the upper deck," the guard said.

"We did," Kase said, jumping in. "They sent us here to search the boats."

"Already been searched," the crewmen grumbled. "I don't need anyone checking up on me."

He eyed them up and down and Kase saw the change in the guard's expression from resentment to suspicion.

"You ain't part of the crew," he said.

"There's not enough to cover the entire ship," Brell said. "We volunteered to help."

"You got a captain's authorization?" he asked.

The three of them glanced at each other without an answer.

The guard was quickly coming to the conclusion that he was looking at the ones everyone was searching for.

"Yes!" Kase said. "I put it somewhere."

He turned his back to the guard and opened his gloved hand. He closed his eyes and focused his mind on an image of a piece of paper. He pictured bold but hurriedly scribbled words and a signature underneath.

His body shook from the nagging cold, and his mind was pulled away by the sound of his chattering teeth.

He could feel the eyes of the guard boring into his back. With a shuddering breath, he yanked his focus under control and imagined the captain's note. Here it came, the wall of potential magic. It pressed on him. Wanting to overwhelm and surge through him. He carefully opened himself to only a small pinprick of it. He felt it trickle through and something form in his hand.

He opened his eyes and there was a written note in his hand.

"Here it is," Kase said, turning around.

He held it up, and the guard glared at it, trying to read it through the metal mesh. Kase watched as the guard's eye flicked between the note and the group until he made up his mind.

"Alright," he said, working the locked door. "But I'm telling you, there's nobody here, but me."

He swung open the door and lead them onto the narrow deck where they saw a string of lifeboats, each hooked to their own davits.

"You dummies are gonna freeze before you search them all," chuckled the guard. "I got some coffee over…"

Kase and Brell heard a thump and spun around to see Hanover standing over the guard as he crumpled to the deck.

They glared at the big man with frustration and annoyance.

"So he wouldn't struggle," said Hanover, picking up the unconscious guard.

They watched, unsure of what he was doing until he carried the guard to the railing.

"Whoa. Whoa. Whoa!" yelled Kase as he and Brell charged him.

They grabbed the guard and pulled him out of Hanover's hands then laid him on the deck.

"You were going to throw him off the ship?" stammered Kase. "Like it was nothing?"

"Sure," said Hanover, looking genuinely perplexed. "He saw your faces. As soon as he wakes up he'll turn you in. So, problem solved." He turned to Brell. "Do you have to explain everything to this guy? Where'd you find him?"

"You're not killing this man," said Kase. "If he goes over the side, you're going next."

"Really," said Hanover, a dark smile slinking across his face. He turned, facing Kase with a predatory gleam in his eye.

"If one more ounce of stupidity spills out of your mouth," growled Brell, "I'll kill you, myself."

Hanover relaxed, raising his hands and leaned against the rail, smiling at her.

"You know," he said, "I love your style of pillow talk."

"Get in the boat," she ordered.

Hanover sighed, raising his eyebrows at her. "Alone?"

"No," she said. "Take the guard with you."

"And...?"

"Put him safely on the ground when you land," Kase said.

Hanover shrugged and pulled back the canvas tarp, covering the boat.

He put the limp guard in it, then hopped over the rail, joining him.

"It's been great seeing you again," he said, eyeing Brell.

Kase and Brell unhooked the boat from the railing and went to release the safety catch on the davit. She thumbed the catch, and the small thrusters on the boat quickly moved it away.

Sensing it wasn't near the airship, a magical auto-pilot came to life. It took a moment, adjusting to its location and determining the nearest place to land. Short wings extended from the sides of the boat, and the pilot headed for solid ground far below.

"I'll call you." Hanover waved as he disappeared through the clouds.

12

LIMBORN

Kase and Brell hurried back inside the ship, desperately rubbing their arms for warmth. Retracing their steps back to their cabins, they nearly ran into a search party. They changed direction and detoured, taking a longer route that led them all the way to the front of the ship.

They picked up their pace when another party came through the door far behind them. It looked like they just might make it back to their room unseen when the door ahead opened and they came face to face with another party.

Each group stopped, surprised to see each other.

"We just finished checking these cabins," Kase said, flashing his captain's note at them.

The other group hesitated, confused by who these two strangers were.

"All right," Kase said, trying to sound annoyed. "Check them for yourself. We're going to search the engine room unless you want to deal with Logi."

Hearing a name they were familiar with, added to their credibility and the crew members moved out of the way.

"No thanks," one of the search party said. "The guy's got sea bats on the brain."

Looking like they had a job to do, Kase and Brell strode away, heading into the next corridor and out of sight.

They made it to their cabins without encountering anyone else. Kase joined Brell in her room, looking at her with a grin as she packed up her bag.

She moved around her room curiously silent, but Kase knew why.

"He'll call you?" Kase grinned.

"I don't want to talk about it," she said, shoving her gloves into her bag.

"Did you used to date?"

Brell roughly stuffed a shirt into her bag, venting her annoyance on it.

"I'm not judging you."

"Good," Brell snapped, turning her back on him as she checked for anything she might have overlooked.

"But I have to wonder," he began.

"Oh come on!" she said exasperated. "Yes, okay? I was going through a bad time in my life and was lonely. We had a couple of dinners together."

"I'm sorry," Kase said. "It sounds like you were hurting."

"I was," she said, pausing as memories of the time flitted through her mind.

The room went quiet and she went back to picking up the last of her things.

"So only two dinners?" Kase asked. "Or did you...?"

"Get out," she said, throwing the bag at him.

Laughing, he ducked out of the way and scrambled into the hall, closing the door behind him.

An hour later, the ship filled with the sound of the captain's voice announcing everyone was free to leave their cabins.

He apologized for the inconvenience and said a brunch was being arranged in the dining area.

"I regret that it must be a short brunch," he said, "because we will be arriving in Limborn in forty minutes. Thank you for your patience."

A short while later, Kase found an empty table and sat down, eager to dig in. He had finally warmed up, but the cold and excitement had honed his appetite to a pinpoint.

He popped a forkful of scrambled eggs into his mouth and sighed, savoring the moment.

He looked over, hearing the scrape of a chair as Brell sat down with a plate of food.

The silverware clattered when she dumped it out and gave him a curt nod.

Kase grinned playfully, but she wasn't in the mood and stood, picking up her plate.

"I won't say another word about it," he said, waving her back. "I promise."

She stared at him until satisfied he was telling the truth and sat back down.

They ate in silence until the tension ebbed away and both were feeling better for having something in their stomachs.

Kase was eyeing the buffet table when the captain announced they were docking. Everyone was requested to disembark as soon as possible.

"Do you think they discovered the lifeboat is missing by now?" he asked. "It sounds like they're still looking for him."

"They might think he used it as a distraction," Brell said, "and he's going to pass himself off as a passenger instead."

They got up and went to their cabins to collect their bags.

There were crew members in every corridor, directing passengers to the forward deck where they would exit the ship.

Kase and Brell glanced at them out of the corner of their eyes, looking for any signs of suspicion or recognition. But nobody gave them a second look, and they were waved along with the rest of the passengers.

They came out onto the main deck under a brilliant sun and crystal clear sky.

"That's..." Kase began, fumbling for words.

"Something, isn't it?"

Across from the airship was a huge island… floating in the air.

"I'm seeing it," Kase said, awestruck, "but it's impossible.

Formed when the world had fractured, hunks of the planet had broken off and drifted high above. They'd lingered there ever since. The how and why to explain them had never been answered, yet they existed on both sides of the Rift.

Kase had seen their hazy shapes from far away while traveling with his mother, but he had never been this close.

A long bridge connected the ship and the island, where passengers waited their turn to cross over.

"Take my advice and don't look down when you're on the bridge," Brell said.

The line of passengers shrank as they inched closer, giving Kase a better view of the underside of the island.

From what he could see, the island was shaped like a funnel, widest at the top and narrowing toward the bottom. Plants and trees grew from the sides, and as he looked closer, he could see homes built into the sides.

He imagined what it would feel like to live in a house suspended over a cliff. Looking down on the sheer drop made him feel wobbly inside.

He focused on the top of the island and scanned the broad plain before him, which spread out for miles.

"Hey," said Brell, nodding, showing him it was their turn to cross the bridge.

Until now, he hadn't thought anything about crossing the empty expanse between the ship and the island. But when he stepped onto the bridge, he felt his gut clench. With each step, his heart thudded louder in his ears.

"How are you doing?" Brell called over her shoulder as she led the way.

"Good," he said, locking his eyes on to the back of her head.

He refused to let himself look at anything else.

Wind hummed through the flexing cables of the bridge, teasingly reminding him of his precarious position.

As they neared the other end, he saw the red haired bounty hunter standing at the exit. She was looking at everyone coming off. Then he saw there was a group of Creet soldiers with her.

They stood behind her, waiting for her to identify her missing prisoner. Not even Hanover would be able to fight off five soldiers armed with swords.

Kase hadn't been this close to her before and couldn't help but stare.

She watched the passengers with clear bright-orange eyes, catching every detail. Her long hair was fire red and ruffled around her like a living thing in the wind. He liked her face. It was crafted by sun and rough weather, giving her a look of resilience. He toyed with the idea of saying something to her, maybe something clever to make her laugh. He considered what his opening line should be...

Having been lost in his own thoughts, Kase twitched when he realized she was looking directly at him.

A flush of embarrassment climbed up his neck and colored his face a proper hue of red.

He was about to pass her when she put out her arm, blocking him.

He looked at it puzzled, then at her. He noticed the soldiers had become alert and were looking at him intently.

"What happened to your eye?" the hunter asked, her voice flat and direct.

Brell turned, quickly taking in the situation. The hunter glanced at her, and Brell forced herself to appear calm. She knew any hunter that could capture Hanover would see the telltale signs of someone preparing to fight.

"A couple of men were being too familiar with her," Kase said, cocking an eye at Brell.

The hunter gave Brell another look.

"They weren't happy when I told them to leave," he said. "One of them got in a lucky punch before I put both of them in the hospital."

Brell nodded at the hunter, who dropped her arm.

"I would have done a lot worse if they'd tried that with me," the hunter said.

"Nobody would try if I was with you. I'm Kase," he said with a smile.

"You're done," the hunter said and went back to watching the people coming off the bridge.

Brell waited until they had merged into the busy crowd before she started snickering. "What was that?" she asked.

"I was distracting her with my natural charm."

Brell's eyes bulged, and she laughed until her eyes watered. Kase walked alongside her unfazed.

"You're laughing," he said, "but here we are free. The facts speak for themselves."

Her chuckling died off as they followed the crowd away from the docks.

The dock area branched off into several streets, leading deeper into the city.

It looked like any other city to Kase, and he kept reminding himself that he and everything around him was floating thousands of feet in the air.

"How do we get down to the surface?" he asked.

"We're meeting my contact tonight," she said. "He's got a couple of ways off the island.

"There's a lot of soldiers here."

Everywhere he looked were men and women in uniform – shopping in stores, chatting on street corners, and generally going about their normal lives.

"There's a military base on Limborn," Brell said. "Most of the major islands have them. It gives them the best vantage point to see across the Rift."

"For what?"

"Invasion," she said. "We don't trust you, and you don't trust us. Each side accuses the other of what they're most afraid of."

"Do you think Teck would invade?" he asked.

"I don't think so," she said. "But my world is made up of a lot of different countries. It's possible some of them have thought about it, but the Central Union wouldn't support it."

"I don't know what that is."

"It's a governing body of countries in my world," she said. "It was formed after the Rift. You can't find it in any history book, but I think the reason they made it was to decide what to do about the Creet. Nobody had declared peace back then. The Rift made it impossible to keep fighting, but that didn't mean everyone stopped hating each other. All the politicians and military leaders practically lived there for a while. Some augured we should attack; wipe the Creet out. Others said it was too risky and we should set up defenses. In the end, nobody did anything and after a while they began using the Union to air each countries differences with the others. I think the whole thing is useless. Once in a while someone new comes to power in a country and wants to make an impression. They talked about invading into Creet, but the other ambassadors shut that down pretty fast."

"We don't see individual countries," said Kase. "We just see Tecks. If one of your countries attacked us we would see the entire Teck world guilty of the aggression."

"And nobody wants to get sucked into a world war," said Brell.

"A world war?" scoffed Kase. "There's not that much hate."

She felt different and thought about saying something, but decided to let him have his rosy illusion of the world

"Follow me," she said, turning onto another street. Curiosity piqued, he followed, wondering what was happening.

They came to the end of the street, at a guardrail, only a few steps away from the edge of the island.

Kase's breath stopped as he tried to comprehend the enormity of what he was seeing.

He was standing above the worlds. Below, he saw huge land masses, broad carpets of forest, mountain ranges, an ocean; all of it abruptly ended at the jagged, black void of the Rift.

An ocean spilled over the edge in an immense boiling cloud of spray. He stared expecting to see it utterly drain in moments, yet the sparkling field of blue remained unchanged.

"I bet you don't see that every day," grinned Brell.

"It's too big to look at, at one time," said Kase. "The Rift is staggering and terrifying at the same time. And the ocean..."

He paused, too dumbstruck to find the words.

"It should be a desert," he said.

"Nothing about the Rift makes sense."

"I can't take my eyes off of it." He stared at the raw cliffs, imagining if he fell into it. "It's endless."

"It's a long way to fall."

"I read about people trying to discover what's down there," he said. "The Shade makes it impossible to see anything."

The Rift was filled with a swirling black mist that was impossible to see through. Scientists had created entire studies trying to understand the Rift, but it refused to give up its secrets. Everyone and everything that ever delved too deep into the Shade were never seen again.

"I can't wait to get a closer look," Kase said.

"You might feel different once you're hanging over it."

"What is it like?" he asked excitedly.

"Not fun," she said, frowning.

Night crept over the island, and Brell led him to a bridge at the edge of the city. Kase discovered that Limborn was the largest of three islands all connected with heavy, strong cables. The bridges were built with thick ropes of steel securely anchored at both ends. But no matter how strong they were, they still swung and wobbled unnervingly in the wind.

Kase wasn't looking forward to crossing another bridge, especially in the dark, yet he was pleasantly surprised when he found that not being able to see made it easier.

As he set foot onto the smaller island, he noticed a distinct change in the atmosphere.

Shadowy figures huddled together near the weak pools of light emitting from the streetlights. Gruff voices murmured from the shadows of alleys with only the glowing ember of a pipe or cigar to mark their presence.

Brell scanned the street around them from under her hood, as she walked confidently, with her hand resting on the fighting knife under her cloak.

Kase flexed his gloved hand, weighing the usefulness of the few spells he knew, dissatisfied with all of them.

She turned into a bar under the sign 'Knuckle & Bone' with Kase close behind.

This was not a bar for people to get drunk. There was no music, no singer, or stage. The only lights were the torchstones above the bar and a single stone in the center of each table.

The bartender watched the strangers approach through a poker face, giving nothing away. The overhead light threw long shadows over his face, carving deep lines across his forehead.

"Chamchak," Brell said.

The bartender stared at her stone faced for a long moment before subtly tilting his head toward the back of the room.

As they crossed the room, a few heads looked up from other tables, glowering eyes following them before returning to their dark and secretive business.

A lone table occupied the back of the bar in a private alcove. A small torchstone sat in the middle of the table, hardly enough to illuminate its stained and blemished surface. Beyond that was darkness. All they could see in the impenetrable shadows were a pair of glittering eyes. They observed Brell from the other side of the table as she sat down. A hand slid into the light of the torchstone and stubby fingers closed around a shot glass.

Brell remained quiet as the hand withdrew, taking the captive glass with it.

"You are not alone," a strangely high and wheezy voice said.

"Neither are you," Brell said.

Kase blinked twice in confusion when he saw three other eyes appear further back in the darkness, standing behind the seated figure.

"I have a poor habit of collecting more enemies than friends," the voice whined. "A little protection calms my nerves. We may speak openly around my companion."

The stubby hand pushed the glass into the light and poured another drink.

Kase could see the pair of eyes creeping over him before returning to Brell.

"I don't know that one," the voice said.

"I do," said Brell. "That's enough."

Something that was supposed to sound like a laugh squeezed out of the shadow.

Brell put a small pouch on the table and pushed it next to the glass. "He has to come with me across the Rift. There's twice the amount you want in the bag."

"Brellll," the voice said, sounding like an icepick dragging over glass. "I don't have to count it to tell you that is not enough."

"How much do you want?" Kase said.

He saw Brell stiffen. Kase realized he was in a world he knew nothing about. Trust was as tenuous as a strand of spider silk.

"Chamchak –" Brell began.

"He speaks," Chamchak said.

The three eyes behind him took on a sinister gleam.

"There are two kinds of people I move across the Rift," Chamchak said. "The kind that reaches the other side...and you."

Brell pushed away from the table, reaching for her knife. Kase only knew it was time to act and raised his gloved hand to cast.

"Hold," a voice spat from the three eyes.

Brell and Kase froze in place. The thing behind Chamchak was a mage.

Chamchak chuckled, making Kase's skin crawl.

"I thought you were smarter than bringing someone new here," he said. "You were dead the moment you landed."

"He's safe," she said. "You know my word is good."

"Until it isn't," Chamchak said. "I hate killing you. It cuts down on the income. I have to answer to someone over me, and he's not a tolerant man."

"Your boss," Kase said, something tickling at the back of his mind. "Does he have pointy teeth?"

Chamchak's only reply was a wheezing gasp. It wasn't much confirmation, but Kase took it as a yes.

"He wouldn't blink twice about having your limbs chopped off for a small annoyance," Kase said. "But oooooh, imagine what he'd do for killing his friend."

"He knows about the Squire," the voice in the back whispered.

"A ploy to save his life. The Squire doesn't have friends," Chamchak said, yet his voice had picked up a tremble.

"He didn't until yours truly saved his life," he said. "And you're the one holding him in a freeze spell," Kase said, tsking.

Chamchak's glittering eyes flicked back and forth as the numberless ways he'd be tortured rattled through his mind.

"Release them!" he said.

The hold on Brell and Kase disappeared.

"It was a mistake of ignorance," Chamchak said pleadingly. "Take back your money."

He reached into the light and pushed the bag of coins back to Brell. "I'm sure the Squire would understand."

"Why would he understand? Are you saying the Squire makes mistakes?" he asked.

"No!" Chamchak stammered. "I meant that someone as wise as he is... He could easily understand how... and you hadn't been introduced to me, so how could I..."

"I should kill you here and now," Kase said. "I can't stand the idea of the Squire dirtying his hands with your blood."

Brell's hand slid out from under her cloak and softly closed around Kase's wrist, giving him a gentle squeeze.

You made your point.

Kase understood and made a show of calming himself down.

"Make your plans," he said to Brell.

"We'll be at the bottom ledge at Limborn tomorrow night," she said.

"My man will be there," Chamchak said, happy to change the subject. "He'll see that you make it across safely. You have my word."

Brell nodded and stepped away from the table.

"You'll tell the Squire I was helpful, won't you?" Chamchak asked. "I did it for free out of respect for his friend. You'll tell him?"

"I will," Kase said.

"Thank you."

The hand slid into the light. The trembling fingers closed around the glass and dragged it into the shadows, rattling across the table as it went.

13

A LITTLE PRACTICE

"Is it always like that?" Kase asked, sitting down across from Brell.

"Last night?" she said, sipping her brew. "No. Most of the time everyone gets along. They have to, or the whole system falls apart."

"Has that ever happened?" he asked.

She shielded her eyes from the bright morning sun and looked out over the sweeping vista.

They were having breakfast at a restaurant known for the best view of the Rift. Below was the Creet side – rich greens of land and sea blues ending sharply at the ten mile wide chasm.

"I never noticed that before," she said. "The way the two halves rotate back and forth."

She pointed to a structure on the Teck side.

"Yesterday, that building was parallel from the mountain on this side," she said. "Now it's to the right, by..." She held her thumb out in front of her eye, judging the distance.

"I read that the distance they shift changes during the year," Kase said. "It's one of the reasons they never tried to bridge the Rift."

"That and it's illegal."

"Do you think we'll have any trouble because of last night?" Kase asked.

"What? Chamchak will want revenge?" she said. "No. The Earl –"

"Squire," Kase said.

"Yeah, that one," she said, watching the steam rising out of her cup. "The Squire must carry a lot of power to rattle the scummy worm."

"You really don't like him." Kase chuckled.

"I don't, but that wasn't an insult," she said. "He's a worm."

Kase stared at her, his mouth hanging open.

"The Edgers found a whole civilization of them when they tunneled into a cavern or something like that," she said. "There was a city and everything."

"Worm people," Kase said, shifting in his seat. "That would be something to see."

"Before you ask," Brell said. "No. I don't even know where it is. They didn't want to be disturbed, and the Edgers left them alone. They closed up the tunnel behind them."

"But Chamchak?" Kase said.

"A few of them were curious and left," she said. "They like the dark, so if they move around, it's at night." She took another sip. "He's not going to be a problem."

"Will there be other *problems*?" he asked.

"Just keep your eyes open," she said casually. "After a while, you get a sense for it."

The answer did little to fill Kase with confidence.

"I couldn't live like you," he said. "Never knowing what's happening next or who to trust."

Brell chuckled, swirling the brew in her cup.

"You already *are* living like me," she said.

They weren't making the crossing to the Teck side until later that night, leaving Kase with a lot of time on his hands.

Brell was content to find a quiet corner in the city and mind her own business, but Kase wasn't about to pass up the first chance he got to go off the beaten path and explore the island.

The edge of the island held a lot of unanswered questions for Kase, and he went exploring, hoping to find some answers.

Where there wasn't a building or other large structure barring access to the edge, there were low fences acting as safety barriers. The guard rails were mostly symbolic because anyone could straddle over them with no effort.

He wanted to be at the very edge and try some experiments about how the island stayed afloat in the air. He considered the various ways he would approach it, and eventually found a particularly promising spot.

One of the first hurdles was the strong gusts of wind. When he got closer to the edge, the gusts became strong enough to push him if he wasn't braced against something.

His stomach fluttered at the thought of being swept off the edge. He decided it made sense to lay on his belly and crawl forward until he could look over.

The part of his brain that tried to caution him and tell him this was a foolish plan was exhausting itself. With Kase, curiosity was king, and the temptation to explore meant the warnings fell on deaf ears.

Having made up his mind, he stepped over the low safety barrier and instantly felt the wind build in strength. Ahead of him was a small ledge that stuck a few feet out.

He knelt down and hammered the ground ahead with his fist, judging if it felt solid. He nodded, satisfied, and stretched his body out.

His nostrils filled with the scent of dirt and grass, and he paused a moment to enjoy the feel of the warm ground radiating against his body.

He turned, looking at the short distance to the ledge and smiled, anticipating the amazing view.

"What the gurn are you doing, boy?" a voice shouted behind him.

Kase jolted with a gasp, quickly looking back.

A small old woman holding a sack of groceries, was staring at him, her eyes filled with astonishment.

"I was – uh," he stammered. Now that he had to put it into words, it sounded like something an idiot would say. "I was going to look over the side?"

"Are you stupid or something?" she snapped.

"Uh," he stammered, knowing he couldn't refute the answer.

"Well, don't let me stop you," she said. "There'd be a lot less idiots if people like you didn't have children."

Kase scooted away from the edge and stood up, brushing himself off. He looked at her, wilting under her inescapable, withering glare.

"Come here," she snapped.

He walked over, feeling like a child about to be scolded.

"Take this," she said, stuffing an orange into his hand.

"Thank you?" he said, confused why she had given it to him.

Is this a reward for not killing myself?

"It's not for eating, nitwit," she growled. "Toss it onto the ground just before the edge."

She demonstrated by swinging her arm underhanded. "And don't miss. I'm not wasting another on you."

Kase tossed the orange up into the air. It came down right where he wanted. To his horror, the patch of ground he had been crawling toward collapsed like brittle glass and fell away.

"The islands been dropping out from under us since before I was a little girl." Her sharp expression softened a bit, amused by the pale color washing over Kase's face.

"You want to go exploring," she said, "I got an attic that hasn't been touched in generations. You can explore that while you clean it out for me."

"Clean your attic?" he said, trying to figure out how he'd gone from lying on the grass to doing her chores.

"You can pay me back for throwing my orange away," she said.

"But you gave it to me."

"Come on," she said, hobbling away. "My feet are getting tired."

Kase glanced between the back of the tiny old woman and the ledge. He looked around, hoping someone would come to his defense, but there was no help to be found.

They walked another couple of blocks before turning up the path of her house. It was a charming, if not an older house with a high peaked roof and arched windows. Yellow and blue flowers grew in a well-tended flagstone planter next to the porch.

An ancient tree towered over the house and front yard, casting a wide blanket of dappled shade. Strong gnarled roots grew out of the ground, looking like the humps of a small sea serpent in a pond of green grass.

The lawn was tidy, and the edges were trim and straight.

Kase wondered if that was the old woman's work or if she had pressed another unsuspecting stranger into service.

She pushed the bags of groceries into his arms and pulled open the screen door. Then she jangled a charm bracelet next to the lock, and the door opened with a click.

She led him into the kitchen and gestured to the table with her whiskered chin to put down the bag.

It was only then that he realized he didn't know her name.

"My name's Kase." He smiled.

"Floy, if you have to know," she said. "Up the stairs, at the back of the hall, there's a trap door. Pull the rope and a ladder comes down. Try not to bang yourself on the head."

"Mrs. Floy," he said, "what exactly do you want me to do?"

She tilted her wrinkled face, staring at him as if she were looking into the vacant eyes of a cow.

"Air it out," she said. "Sweep. Dust. I think something died up there, maybe ten years ago. Brush out the cobwebs, but don't tangle with any big spiders if you see them. I suspect that's what happed to whatever died up there."

Spiders?

To say he didn't like them was an understatement. In his opinion, they were evil and loved nothing better than to terrorize him. He hated them with the flames of a thousand fires, and it had all started from an encounter he'd had as a small boy.

"How big?" he asked, looking up at the ceiling. He could imagine the vile creatures listening in and rubbing their creaky legs together with anticipation.

"Spider size." She piffed. "Tell me when you're done. I got supper to prepare, so go on."

She pushed a broom into his hand, and with that, she turned her attention to emptying out the grocery bag.

Making his way up the stairs, he passed a lifetime of photographs and paintings on the wall. At the top, the landing went off to the left and right.

The right ended with a closed door, and he guessed that was the master bedroom. To the left, the hallway extended all the way to a window that looked outside. Just in front of it hung the rope for the ladder.

He covered the distance in a few strides and looked up to see a square panel in the ceiling. He walked up to it, about to pull the attic door open, but then changed his mind.

He wasn't keen to surprise what was up there. Using the handle of the broom, he gently tapped the ceiling.

"I'm coming up," he said tentatively.

He stopped and listened but heard nothing. Kase couldn't decide if that made him feel better or worse. Had he given the *things* up there a polite chance to find somewhere to hide or an advanced notice to arrange an ambush?

He took hold of the rope and pulled. The panel slowly swung down with a grumble of old hinges followed by a sliding ladder that extended down in front of his feet.

Just in case.

He reached into his back pocket and pulled on his spiritbridge. He looked up into the dark attic, not knowing what to expect, but the glove gave him the confidence to go up.

"I'm coming up now," he said. "I mean you no harm."

He stopped, rolling his eyes.

You sound like an idiot. No harm. He scoffed.

Kase climbed to the top of the ladder. Poking his head through the opening, he quickly glanced around. Windows were positioned at each end of the attic, but their heavy curtains allowed only a meager stream of sunlight to come through.

Satisfied there were no signs of a spider ambush he climbed the rest of the way up and hurried to the nearest window, pulling the curtain aside.

The room was silent, and more importantly, he didn't detect any signs of spiders.

Thick dust laid on the floor, and it was comforting to see the only tracks were his.

Above him, large timbers arched overhead, supporting the peaked roof.

The walls were lined with boxes, cases, a few steamer trunks, old furniture, and tarps draped over who knew what.

There was a taste in the air that took him back to the ancient ruins he had explored as a boy. The familiarity made him feel like he was more in his element.

It took some pulling, but he eventually pried the jammed window open, letting in welcomed fresh air. The curtain billowed and curled in the breeze, and he walked to the other end of the room and worked open the window facing onto the backyard.

With that, fresh air was able to flow freely through the attic. It already felt like a different place.

He began sweeping, and it wasn't long before he had created a respectable mound of dust. Glancing around, he realized there was nowhere to put it.

The last thing he wanted to do was ask the old woman... anything.

He poked around until he found a box. Inside were a few books, some buttons, a brush, and loose papers.

He wondered what the books might tell him about the people who lived here. He brushed them off and examined their covers, but any hope of an interesting discovery was quickly snuffed out.

One was a reference to fresh water fish and another a romance book. The others were equally uninteresting and left him feeling bored and disappointed. He emptied the box, putting everything neatly aside, then brushed the dust into the box.

He had to sweep the attic twice before it was cleaned to his satisfaction.

He stood with his hands on his hips, wondering what he was supposed to do with everything else.

With a groan, he only just realized his mistake. Everything stacked against the walls were covered with dust too.

Cleaning all of it would end up getting dust all over the floor again.

This is why I hate cleaning.

He listened for the old woman, weighing his odds of sneaking out of the house without being caught.

And then what? Be chased down the street with her screaming behind me?

Still, the alternative was starting over. He tapped his finger on his chin, turning it over in his mind when his eyes drifted to his glove.

Could I?

The number of spells he knew made a sad short list, and if he was honest with himself, he hadn't practiced enough to master any of them.

But he was comfortable with his *push* spell. He nodded to himself, deciding to use it.

I can use it on a single thing... Well, isn't dust a thing? Sure... if I want it to be... right?

He shrugged and walked over to an empty hat rack. He looked at it, studying its shape, the dark brown color of the wood, and finally, the grey frosting of dust.

He thought only of the dust, imagining it suspended in air but still in the shape of the hat-rack. He turned his mind to the magic, which swelled up to meet him. He let in a tiny bit, focusing only on the dust.

Suddenly, the dust whipped away, leaving the hat-rack untouched and more importantly, clean. He watched as it bloomed and settled to the floor.

Kase grinned, rubbing his hands together.

I am the dust mage.

Working his way around the attic, he quickly whisked away ages of dust from the jumbled collection of objects until there wasn't a speck on anything...except the floor.

Once that was done, he turned back to the disappointing task of sweeping the floor for the third time. With a sigh, he picked up the broom.

What am I doing?

He leaned the broom against the wall and focused on a small area of the floor. He cast his push spell and the dust rolled back in a powdery wave.

It wasn't long before he had worked his way from the front of the attic to the back. The floor was spotless, but now there was a sizable heap of dust piled under the rear window, higher than his knees.

He looked outside for the first time in hours. The sun was taking on a golden cast as afternoon was turning into evening. He only had a couple of hours before meeting up with Brell.

Kase made a rough guess how long it would take for him to get back to his hotel room, get his gear, clean up, and travel across the city to meet Brell. He wasn't going to be late, but he would be cutting it close.

He roughed out that using his box, it would take him four or five trips to dump all of it...

Unless.

He eyed the window with a smile spreading across his face.

"I'm getting good at this," he said.

"Knowing *what* you're doing with a spell," Alwyn said, "is as important as knowing how to use it."

"What does that mean?"

"If I gave you the answer to every question," he said, "how would you learn to think these things through for yourself?"

"Why do you have to make it sound complicated?" he asked. "Look, dust." He pointed. "Window. It couldn't be more simple."

He sensed Alwyn wasn't going to say anything else.

Kase slid the curtain to the side as far as it would go and draped it out of the way. He settled his shoulders and glanced between the pile and the open window. He cast his spell.

Suddenly, an invisible force lifted the large mound of dust and blew it through the window in a swirling thick column.

Grinning, he folded his arms across his chest, admiring his achievement.

"See?" Kase said. "Simple."

Suddenly, a yowling squawk bellowed from outside.

"What the damnable gurn?" Floy cried. "My garden! My laundry!"

The color drained from Kase's face as he leaned out and saw the old woman and most of her backyard frosted with dust.

"You!" she said, locking eyes on him, pointing a crooked finger.

Sputtering curses and dark oaths, she angrily hobbled toward the house.

Panic jolted through Kase, electrifying his legs as he dashed to the attic ladder. He hit the second floor, hardly touching a single rung and flew down the stairs.

He passed the kitchen at a flat out run, catching only a fleeting glimpse of the old woman picking up a butcher knife.

His feet never touched the porch as he dashed out of the house and down the sidewalk.

He kept running until he thought his heart would explode and, even then, made a point of dodging down side streets on the wild chance the old lady was still hot on his trail.

"What happened to you," Brell asked as he shuffled into their room, ragged and streaked with sweat.

"I don't want to talk about it," he said. "The sooner we're off this rock, the better."

An hour later, Kase had showered and changed.

They checked out, ready for dinner. Kase insisted they find an out-of-the-way place to eat as the sun sunk below the horizon.

They had just finished when Brell wiped her hands and got up.

"It's time," she said. "I hope you have your legs back."

"Why?" he asked, glancing at her suspiciously.

"You'll see," she said and headed out the door.

Kase followed her out and onto the street which gradually sloped down.

They turned down several streets, soon passing old factories and abandoned buildings.

She turned up a weed choked street that ended at the foot of an old brick building. She turned on her flashlight, and Kase took out his torchstone before pushing past the large rusted steel door.

Inside the building was empty, stripped of whatever equipment it had once held. They crossed the long concrete floor to a pair of heavy rusty steel basement doors.

The fat corroded hinges groaned in protest as they lifted it out of the way and stepped down onto the broad stairs.

Closing it behind them, they couldn't see anything beyond the reach of their lights. They followed the stairs, which switched back twice more before they reached the basement floor.

"Here we go," Brell said and disappeared.

Kase's eyes flew open, and he swept his light back and forth, but she was gone.

"Hey," she said, appearing from the middle of the wall. "This way."

She slipped back out of sight. Kase felt along the wall until his hand disappeared.

False wall.

He stepped through and suddenly felt his head swim in a wave of vertigo.

They stood on a small platform jutting out from the side of a cliff, suspended hundreds of feet high. Walkways branched out to the left and right of the platform, hugging a wall of rock as they circled far around to the other side.

"Welcome to the inside of the island," Brell said.

Kase looked at the hollowed out interior of the island. Clinging to the sides was a network of catwalks, platforms, girders, and struts.

Torchstones lit the passages that spiraled down out of sight until Kase couldn't make out their details. It looked like a hive of fireflies.

"I shouldn't have sprung that on you," she said, looking Kase in the eyes. "You feeling steady now?"

"Yes," he said, feeling his heart and stomach settle in their proper places.

They began the long walk down, Brell's boots clashing on the metal plating with every step.

High above, Kase heard the tramp of others and bits of conversation echoing down to them.

Along the way, they passed several closed doors and locked grates, but none of those were their destination.

Kase glanced down and saw there were still several rings of catwalks below them. He inwardly sighed but kept his complaints to himself.

They went around twice more before Brell abruptly stopped next to a door. It looked like all the others, but she knew this was the one.

"We're going outside now," she said to him. "Hold on to the railing and do what I do."

She opened it, and they hunched against the chill wind as they pushed through it to the outside.

They stopped on a similar platform as those inside.

The moons were cresting the horizon, their lights winking off the sea below like diamonds on a blanket of dark velvet.

Bright stars filled the sky with sharp clarity.

"There you are," a voice said from the darkness.

A head floated up from alongside the platform as their smuggler steered an air-skiff close enough for them to step in.

Kase watched Brell hold on to the handles in front of her, and he did the same.

"This is the part where you hang on tight." Brell grinned.

The smuggler pitched the nose of the skiff forward, and they plunged into the night.

Kase felt his spirit race as they lanced downward toward the city below.

I have to get one of these.

14

CROSSING THE SHADE

The cold painfully pinched his nose and ears, but his pounding heart and the giddy thrill made him oblivious to it.

"Hang on," the smuggler called. "This is the tricky part."

Kase looked ahead, seeing nothing, but wisely tightened his grip.

The skiff straightened out, came to a standstill, then dropped like a stone. Kase felt his rear come off the seat. Brell's eyes twinkled with excitement.

With a sudden jolt, the skiff stopped cold.

"Right on target." The smuggler smiled.

Brell motioned to Kase, and they got out on a wide ledge.

"Where are we?" he asked.

"Inside the Rift," the smuggler said.

"That's the Edger city," said Brell, pointing up to the lights above the cliff.

"So we're back on solid ground again?"

"Enjoy it while it lasts," she said.

"That's not encouraging," he said as she headed off the platform and into a tunnel.

The tunnel was wide enough for three people abreast and was well lit with smooth walls.

"Where now?"

"We're officially in Creet Edger territory," Brell said.

"Why do you say it that way?" Kase asked. "Is there a Teck Edger territory?"

"Yes," she said. "Don't mix them up. They get touchy about the difference."

Kase shrugged, unsurprised. Edger or not, it was an insult to refer to a Creet as a Teck. It only made sense Tecks would feel the same about it.

They turned into a side tunnel, then another that dropped steeply. The tunnel narrowed, and the walls became roughly hewed.

They heard laughing and boisterous voices echoing up the tunnel, then saw bright light ahead.

The tunnel opened into a large natural cavern. The walls arched high overhead before disappearing into the shadows. In the center of the irregular cathedral was a single building carved from the floor of the cavern. Warm yellow light poured out of the windows and open door, reminding Kase of McLennon's tavern. He felt a twinge of homesickness, but it quickly passed as they entered the cheerful room.

"Odd place for a tavern," Kase said.

"Not if you're an Edger, I guess," Brell said. She cocked her head toward an open table. "We wait there for our contact."

They didn't have to wait long. A few minutes after they'd sat down, a woman had taken a seat across from them.

She was dressed in clothing similar to most of the other Edgers. Tough boots, overalls, and a harness with straps around the legs, waist, and arms. A pair of work gloves hung from her belt, next to a small utility case.

She silently looked at Kase and Brell, her face difficult to judge between the smudges of dirt and shadows cast by the lights behind her.

"That seat's taken," Brell said. "We're waiting for our friend."

"He's not coming," she said. "I'm your friend now."

"That friend was going to do us a favor."

"I know," the Edger said. "He asked me to take care of it for him."

Whatever Brell was thinking, she kept it hidden behind a mask of stone.

The Edger shifted in her chair and glanced over her shoulder before leaning closer across the table.

"I'm the one taking you across the Rift," she said. "Are you interested or not?"

"What happened to Atem?" Brell asked. "I know him. I don't know you."

"Like I told you," the Edger said, speaking slowly as if Brell didn't speak the language. "He told me. How else would I know to meet you here?"

Brell consider her options for a moment.

"Who are you?" she asked.

"Winno. You want to get going, or do we sit here gabbing and painting each other's nails?"

"All right," Brell said.

Winno pushed herself away from the table and led the two of them out of the tavern. They walked around the back of the building where she picked up an extra light and a coil of rope.

Behind the tavern, there were three tunnels. Winno picked the one on the right and walked in. Kase was following Brell and could tell by the way she carried herself that she wasn't happy about the unexpected change. He didn't sense any danger coming off her, but she was definitely more alert.

Unlike the smooth tunnels before, this one was rough. The floor was uneven with hunks of fallen stone jutting out of it. The ceiling quickly lowered, making it necessary to crouch low to get through.

Winno glimpsed Brell looking over her shoulder. "Don't worry. We're alone. Nobody uses this tunnel. All of the rock around here is unstable."

Kase grinned ironically to himself.

What's to worry about?

"Be careful here," Winno said as they came into a wide chamber. She pointed down where the floor of the cave stopped. Beyond the ledge was empty blackness and a deep pit.

Winno unwound the rope and attached a piece of wood to it. Kase frowned, knowing he'd seen something like this before but couldn't place it. She swung the rope in a tight circle and let it fly.

She watched the end of the rope as it sailed out over the chasm until it began to fall. "Branch!" Winno shouted.

The rope and piece of wood fell into the dark pit, and Winno reeled it back in.

Now Kase remembered why it looked familiar.

Winno started spinning the rope for another throw when Kase interrupted. "Try saying stick," he said.

"Yeah," Winno said, with a curt nod. "I'm always getting it wrong."

Kase gave Brell a dubious glance, shaking his head. He didn't believe Winno.

How can she always get it wrong? You only have to look at it to know the spell word is stick.

Winno spun the rope and let go, watching until the rope had reached its high point.

"Stick," she yelled.

The wood abruptly stopped, hanging motionless in the air. Winno tugged on the rope, testing it, but the wood didn't budge.

She glanced at Kase before handing the rope to Brell.

"There's another shelf on the other side," said Winno. "Swing the rope back over once you get there."

Brell took the rope and gave it a sharp tug. She ignored the annoyed frown from the Edger.

Kase had the sudden thought that Winno might release the stick while Brell was halfway across.

Kase watched her like a hawk as Brell tucked in her knees and swung, but Winno only watched, and Brell made it to the far side of the chasm.

"Come back," she yelled, her voice echoing off the rock walls.

A moment later, the rope appeared, and Winno grabbed it before it could swing out of reach. She passed it on to Kase.

He wrapped the rope around his wrist and swung off the shelf. He fought the urge to look up at the suspended piece of wood that was keeping him alive.

I know magic works. I know magic works.

Ahead was Brell, who reached for him. Using his momentum, Kase leapt off the rope and landed squarely on the rock shelf.

Soon, everyone was on the other side.

"Stick," she cried.

The wood dropped, and she pulled it back in. Slipping her arm through the coil of rope, she led them on for several minutes. The tunnel quickly widened, and they came to a stop.

The way was barred by a stout metal gate. The hinges had strong springs that kept the gate closed. Next to it were the remains of a mechanism used to hold it open, but it had long since rusted away.

"I have to use a token to open it," Winno said but didn't move.

"Go on," Brell said.

"They're expensive," hinted the Edger.

"That's not my problem," Brell said. "I already paid to get across."

"If you want to get through it'll cost extra."

"I said I already paid," Brell growled.

"Okay," Winno said. "We'll go back."

"Hang on," said Brell, stopping her. Fuming, Brell reached into her bag and shoved extra money into Winno's hand.

She glanced nervously between Brell and Kase as she put the coins in her pocket. She took a small silver star from the top pocket of her overalls and dropped it in the gate's lock.

The gate slowly opened as the sound of the creaking hinges echoed off the walls.

They passed through and onto a ledge where a strange plate-shaped object was tied to the wall.

"This is our way across," Brell said.

The plate was big enough for five or six people to stand on. In the center was a pole with rings holding several safety lines and control levers to fly it.

As Winno stepped onto it, Kase saw it slightly rock, which made him wonder if this thing could tip over like a boat. Winno clipped a safety line onto her harness. Now he was convinced it would do just that.

Brell and Kase followed, each looping a safety line around their waists and clipping in. Winno untied the anchor line and steered them away from the rock shelf.

Out of everything they had done this night, this was the most stressful moment for Kase. In spite of all his excitement to see the Rift up close, he would have given anything to be anywhere else.

All of his anxiety evaporated when he looked down and saw a faint ethereal light deep in the Shade.

"It's glowing," Kase said, captivated.

"Yeah," Winno said. "Everyone thinks it's entirely black, but at night, if you get close, it does that. Not everyone sees it."

"It only shows itself if you get close," she murmured. "Then you see..."

Her voice trailed off as she gazed, unblinking, into the swirling mist. As Winno stared into the Shade, the platform began to slip into the mist. Wispy tendrils of black smoke lapped at the platform and began curling around their boots.

"Hey!" Brell snapped. "Pay attention."

Winno snapped out of her daze, seeing Brell glaring at her. She rapidly moved one of the levers, and the platform rose again. The dark smoke slipped over the sides and was gone.

Kase looked over his shoulder, seeing the cliff face of his Creet world disappear into the night.

That's my world I'm leaving. I'm not ready for this.

Doubts welled up in his mind; pulling him to go back. To return to what he knew, the familiar.

He knew nothing of this place.

My only way back to Creet!

If anything happened to Brell... If they were separated...

What if I get lost?

He would be alone in a land where he was an outcast, an enemy, and hunted.

No one would help him. He'd never see home again.

He stared back at the void, desperately hoping to catch a glimpse of home. It was gone.

Turning back, he saw Brell looking at him, into him. There was recognition in her eyes.

"You'll come back," she said. "I'll make sure of it."

It was a rare and unexpected thing for her to say, and the sureness in her voice was like a tonic to his confidence, spreading through his limbs and giving him strength.

He smiled and nodded at her, but she was already looking toward their destination.

They traveled for several miles. They were in a hole of darkness, nothing ahead or behind. The only light were the sharp points of stars high above.

"It doesn't feel like we're moving," Kase said.

"We are," Winno said.

He saw her glance at the controls as if to reassure herself that they really were and she hadn't slipped into another dream.

"How much further to the other side?" Brell asked.

"About nine miles."

Brell was about to say something else when everyone tensed. Nobody spoke, but they all looked at each other, searching for confirmation.

"What was that?" Kase asked.

"You heard it too," said Brell.

"It sounded like... words?" said Kase, unsure.

"No," Brell said. "I only heard a sound."

"What's down there?" Kase asked, looking at Winno.

"Nothing," she said. "It's the vapor. Breathing it can make you hear things."

"But we're not near it," Kase said.

"If you breathe it too long, it will make you insane. Some Edgers went missing in the Shade. Rescue parties went looking for them. Some they found, others..." She trailed off for a moment before picking up her thoughts again. "Their minds were gone. They talked about things, visions. They were never right in the head after that."

Kase looked down into the Shade and tightened his grip on the handrail.

"Did they say what they saw?" he asked.

"Whatever crazy people see," she said. "Monsters. Gods. It's only stories their heads made up. I live in the real world."

After that, Kase listened closely but didn't hear anything more.

He could tell Brell was getting impatient. She shifted from one foot to the other and pressing her lips together.

Her mind was complaining, but she wasn't going to give it a voice. He tried to think of something they could talk about to take her mind off the monotony, but then he glanced at Winno.

Knowing Brell, the less a stranger, like this Edger, knew about them or their business, the better she liked it.

Huh. I'm thinking like a bounty hunter.

The thought made him grin.

"There!" Winno said, pointing.

Out of the murky darkness emerged several dim spots of light. They grew brighter with every moment until they finally came into sharp focus.

They had reached the other side and were looking at work and navigation lights.

Brell was used to being on her own, but she couldn't deny the deeply embedded need for human contact. Seeing other people dusted away the cobwebs of isolation and lifted her spirits.

Solid ground was just in sight, and Kase was eager to feel it under his boots when Winno veered away to the left.

"What are you doing?" he said between frustration and confusion.

"We come flying out of the middle of the Shade," she said "and what do you think it looks like? Nobody's going to asks questions? As soon as you open your mouth, everyone will know you aren't an Edger."

Kase looked at the Edger overalls he was wearing and didn't see anything different between him and Winno, but saying anything would only annoy her.

She steered them to a deserted rock shelf.

Unhooking from her safety line, she hopped off and anchored the platform to a sturdy ringbolt buried in the wall.

Stepping onto the rock shelf, Kase stamped his feet, smiling at the feel of solid ground under him.

Winno scrunched her face, mocking him, but Kase didn't care.

"Come on," Winno said.

"No," said Brell. "I know where to go from here," Brell said.

Winno cocked an eyebrow and shrugged. "Okay. I already got paid. If you get caught, I don't know you."

"That works both ways," Brell said. "You don't talk to anyone about us."

Winno hesitated suspiciously, making Kase wonder if she was considering the benefit of turning them in.

An image appeared in his mind's eye of him and Brell walking through the Edger city, suddenly surrounded by grim police. And pointing them out was Winno.

He realized their freedom, maybe their lives, depended on a girl who could easily be bought.

"Just a moment," he said, making a show of raising his gloved hand toward her. She didn't know what he was doing, but she didn't like it.

Before she could protest, Kase cast a gentle *push* spell at her. She rocked on her feet as her hair blew back.

"What was that?" she demanded, blinking in surprise.

"I've put a curse on you," Kase said, knitting his brow and glaring at her.

Brell looked at him, both confused and amused.

"Filthy mage," Winno said, reaching for her knife.

"You are safe for the moment," Kase said dramatically. "But if you speak to anyone about us, even a single word, they'll watch in horror as you melt like a candle before their eyes."

"I'm not going to tell anyone," she said. "Take it off me."

"Why?" Kase said. "If you keep our secret, then you have nothing to worry about, right?" he said, turning to Brell.

"He's got a point," she said.

Winno frowned, then let her hand drop from her knife.

"The curse will lift in five days," Kase said with a wave of his hand.

Brell pursed her lips, forcing herself from laughing. "We need to go," she said, losing her grip on a snicker.

She gave Kase a gentle push to get him moving before she broke out laughing in front of Winno.

They walked through the tunnel a short way before Brell sputtered into laughter.

"I curse you" she said, waving her hands.

"It just came to me," Kase said, taken up by her laughter.

"Melt like a candle?" She sniggered.

"I liked the imagery."

"I'm never going to forget the look on her face."

They followed the tunnel to a set of stairs cut into the rock and climbed until they came to a small chamber.

Crates and parts of equipment were stacked up against the far wall, next to a door.

Through the door, they came into a major concourse buzzing with activity. The change from the dim roughly chiseled chamber to the bright and modern surroundings was like night and day.

Carts of miners, small trucks, and trollies rolled along the paved streets bordered with stores, eateries, and bars catering to any Edger with coins burning a hole in their pockets.

In spite of being in a tunnel under tons of rock, the avenue was lit like midday. The sounds of activity were lively and boisterous.

Brell led the way off the main thoroughfare and down a smaller street into a series of alleys.

The farther they went, the bleaker their surroundings became.

People glanced at them, suspicious and secretive, out of the corner of their eyes. They spoke in hushed voices, guarding their conversations from prying ears.

The road was older and narrower. All the shops wore a fine vale of grime, looking tired and worn. Nearly every door had a large rough looking man leaning next to it.

"Keep your eyes ahead and don't stare," Brell said quietly. "People here don't react well to curiosity."

Kase tried to follow her instructions...

But I'm in the Teck world!

Even in this grungy corner of the Edger city, Kase could see one thing after another he wanted to look at more closely.

What's that on his wrist? What's she have in her ear? What does that switch do? What's inside the street light?

Everything was equally unknown yet familiar.

A stranger nodded at Brell, who returned the gesture without a word.

"You know him?" Kase asked.

"Only when I need to," she said cryptically.

"By the way everyone's looking at us," Kase said, "the feeling is mutual."

"Edgers aren't shy about making outsiders feel unwelcome," she said. "They do the hard work of supplying the rest of the world with important materials but get treated like the ugly stepson of society. They know they hold all the cards, and once in a while, they'll go on strike to remind everyone the dog wags the tail, not the other way around."

"I imagine that doesn't improve their status in everyone's eyes."

"If you mean it creates a million extra metric tons of resentment," she said, "you're right. Back before my time, a governor or something like that decided he'd show everyone who was boss. He sent bureaucrats and inspectors into the Edger cities and slapped them with fines, penalties, you know, the usual petty junk politicians do to feel superior."

Kase nodded, keeping his smirk to himself. Her dislike of anyone associated with politics was one of the few things Brell made no bones about concealing. She didn't need anyone to argue with her about politics. She could get angry just talking about it.

"His minions didn't waste a minute citing violations and notice of closures," she said.

"I'm guessing the Edgers did not react well to that."

"They rounded up all of the intruders and marooned them in the middle of the Rift." She snorted. "It may have escalated a little from there. The governor got the army involved. Personally, I don't think they wanted to touch that mess, but he pushed them into it. They rolled up with all kinds of fire power, demanding the release of the hostages. The spokesman for the Edgers said they didn't know anything about hostages. The bureaucrats had gone out for a sightseeing tour of the Rift and didn't return. In front of the news cameras, they opened the way and invited the army to go into the Rift for themselves and look for the missing people. That's where the governor's plan kicked him in the rear. The army wasn't going in there. The Rift is the Edger's back yard. No one knows it like them. The army backed down and left. The governor tried to spin it, saying the Edgers had started this mess, but he was choosing peace. I don't think if fooled anyone."

"But they *found* the bureaucrats?" Kase asked.

"Yeah," Brell said. "I wouldn't have. We'd all be better off without scum like that."

"Scum?" a voice behind them said.

They turned as two big men came out of the shadows of an alley.

"Anyone we know?" another voice from their backs said.

They turned around again, seeing a hulking brute of a man. His Edger overalls strained across his thick arms and barrel chest, giving the impression he was one deep breath away from exploding out of his clothing.

Next to him was a woman with pale skin and black eyes. Compared to the brute, she looked small but menace dripped off her like venom.

The four strangers formed a loose ring, blocking them in, glaring down with contempt.

Kase thought about casting a spell, but Brell caught the subtle flinch of his arm and put her hand on his wrist, cautioning him.

She recognized the thugs and met their hard stares with an indifferent smile, trying not to let them see her sweat.

She cursed herself for not bringing a back-up power source for her gun.

The thugs moved aside as another Edger walked through.

"There's a shark swimming in our pond," he said. "You wouldn't be looking to collect a bounty on me, would you?"

"Novecky," she said. "If I was, I'd show you the respect of warning you first."

He sighed, pulling his jacket around his large gut and lacing his fingers together. He tucked his chin against his chest and looked at her through salt and pepper eyebrows.

"I told myself the same thing," Novecky said, "but after what you did to Letto." He spread his hands and shrugged. "It's so hard to know these days."

"We've known each other for years. It's worked for both of us."

"Is it still working for you, Brell?" he asked. "Is there anything I should know about, like who you're escorting through my city?"

"He's small time," she said.

"He must be." Novecky chuckled, scratching his graying hair. "I've never seen him."

"I wouldn't have wasted my time on him either," she said, "but I'm returning a favor."

Novecky took an optical scanner out of his pocket and aimed it at Kase's face. Orange brackets formed on the scanner and framed his face. A small dash began blinking.

Kase fidgeted under the stares of everyone around him. He tried not to fixate on the big glass eyed device Novecky pointed at him and casually glanced anywhere there wasn't a face looking at him.

Novecky looked out from behind the scanner, giving him a reproachful grimace.

"If you don't mind," he said to Kase. "It helps if you don't move."

Kase nodded and Novecky returned to the scanner for a few moments.

He put it back in his pocket and rubbed his stubbled chin.

"Unknown?" he said, looking quizzically at Kase. "Where are you from?"

Kase glanced at Brell, who kept her eyes on the grizzled crime boss.

"Answer the question," one of the thugs said, dumping his thick hand on Kase's shoulder.

"Hey," Brell said, grabbing the guy's hands. "Don't touch my property."

The thug's fat lips spread into a wide smile as he leered over Brell.

She stared into his eyes, watching the gleam of malice turn into confusion and then to pain. Something cracked as she squeezed harder, and his fingers lost their color.

The others tensed, and weapons appeared in their hands. Brell didn't break eye contact with the thug. His face was screwed up with pain, but he bore it in silence.

"That's enough!" Novecky barked. "Everyone settle down."

Brell released the thug's hand who yanked it back, glaring darkly at her, then examined it. One of his fingers was pointing in an unnatural direction.

"That temper of yours." Novecky chuckled, pointing a finger at Brell.

"I'm on a schedule," she said.

"Yeah, sure," he said, lacing his fingers in front of him again. "Look me up next time you're here. I need work doing and it's tailor made for you."

"I will," she said. "Nice seeing you again."

"Always is," he said, nodding to his thugs.

They stepped out of the way. Brell took Kase by the arm and led him down the street.

"Is there anyone you know who isn't doing something illegal?" he asked.

"Lots of people," she said, glancing over her shoulder. "They aren't as useful in my line of work."

They turned down another street and eventually came to an elevator terminal, where they waited with some other people.

The grungy tiled platform offered five shafts, depending on where you wanted to go.

A red light above the second shaft began strobing, and a moment later, an elevator came to a stop.

"Levels seven through four," a robotic voice said.

A couple of people shuffled in and waited with a look of weary boredom. The red light flashed, and the platform rose out of sight.

"How deep are we?" Kase asked.

"Maybe a mile."

"Underground?"

A new red light began flashing.

"That reminds me," Brell said, watching another platform stop in front of them.

"Levels two, one, and surface," the automated voice said.

"Here." She handed him a small piece of gum.

"What's this for?" he asked as they stepped onto the platform.

"So your eardrums don't explode," she said as the platform began to rise.

Kase looked curiously at the small square she'd given him.

"You might want to get started on that," she said. "This thing picks up speed pretty fast."

Kase popped the cube into this mouth and screwed up his face at the gritty texture as he began chewing.

Brell took the wrapper off hers before putting the cube into her mouth. She dangled the paper in front of Kase. "It tastes better without this."

15

TECK CITY

Kase was still picking paper out of his teeth when their elevator came to a halt at the central terminal.

As Brell led the way, Kase took in the ultra-modern surroundings.

"This is a lot different from home," he said.

"You mean better."

Gleaming gray floors stretched off to multiple platforms. Light emanated from seemingly everywhere: the ceiling, walls, and floors. Kase tried to make a shadow, but it was impossible.

"Yes," Kase said. "If you like bleak."

An automated voice gave non-stop information about train times and directions to the platforms.

Brell had taken off her Edger overalls but told Kase to keep his on.

"Now," she said with satisfaction, "you're the one that sticks out. I'll get you some real clothes when we get home."

"You're enjoying yourself, aren't you?"

"A little bit." She grinned. "Yeah."

Kase studied the people rushing by without giving him a second look.

They turned the corner and came to the train that would take them to Brell's city.

He had trains and elevators on Creet, some powered by fuel,

others by magic. The concepts weren't new, but the designs were more polished. He was impressed but wasn't about to give Brell the satisfaction of telling her.

The train was sleek with a long tapered nose. Its polished skin reflected the overhead lights down the length of its body like a giant opal serpent.

"It looks fast," Kase said, unable to hold it in.

"It's a little over four hundred miles to Suhun city," she said. "We'll be there in an hour."

"That's amazing," he said.

Brell smiled, enjoying the chance to show Kase the superiority of technology.

"Not as fast as teleporting," he said. "But for a machine, very respectable."

"Tele...? You're making that up," she scoffed. "Stop being a child and admit technology is better than..." She looked around, confirming nobody was close enough to hear her. "Magic."

"Teleporting is real," Kase said. "But rare."

"I knew it," she said. "Anyone can use this train."

"Are *all* of your trains this fast?" he asked.

The doors slid open on silent rails, and she stepped in without answering.

"I didn't get that," Kase said, cupping his hand to his ear. "How many?"

"Just this," Brell snarled. "They're expensive to make. The track has to be certified twice a year to make sure it stays aligned."

"Hmmmm," Kase said, nodding sympathetically. "That's a lot for just one train."

"Are you going to be this annoying the entire trip?" Because I'm already regretting my decision to let you come."

"I have an idea," Kase said. It wasn't solely her idea that he come and she knew it, but he felt that pointing it out would only make her more irritable. "I won't keep poking holes in your technology if you stop using it to criticize magic."

She frowned at him for a moment before sitting down.

"All right," she said. "But no cracks about my world."

"That's fair," Kase said, holding out his hand. "Deal."

"What's that for?" she asked.

"Shaking hands," he said hesitantly. "It's how people show they agree –"

"Put it down," she said, glancing around. "We don't do that here."

Kase sat down next to her, shifting in his seat as he settled in. "When we first met, I thought you were grumpy because you didn't like being in my world."

She said nothing as the train gave a gentle tug, slowly moving away from the platform.

"But you're just as grumpy here." He grinned.

The train came out of the terminal, and sunlight streamed through the windows.

After a few moments of adjusting to the brightness, Kase leaned forward to look past her for a better view.

Brell sighed and glanced at the ceiling. The seats around them were empty.

"There's an empty seat next to the window right there," she said, pointing.

"I know, but I thought you might miss me."

He moved to the seat across from her and smiled out the window.

She could feel her hackles up, expecting him to say something else annoying at any moment, but the quiet continued as the minutes ticked by, and she calmed down.

The passing landscape drew her gaze, and she stared at it, getting lost in her thoughts.

She was very worried Kase would accidentally use his magic or give himself away some other way. It would mean instant life in prison for the both of them.

People in Suhun city weren't like Kase. They were brisk, preoccupied, and didn't trust strangers. Kase was the opposite of all of that.

He was open and inquisitive. He found people interesting.

Brell rolled her eyes at the thought. There was nothing interesting about people.

He would talk to anyone. Simply strike up a conversation with a complete stranger.

Her eyes widened at the thought of him doing that on a street corner.

What have I gotten myself into?

She had work to do and needed to get it done fast, but how would that happen if she spent all of her time protecting Kase from himself?

Get a hold of yourself, Brell.

She ran down the list of the most dangerous people she had collected bounties on. Stone cold killers, every one of them.

They all wanted to kill me the first chance they got. If I could transport them and stay in one piece, I can manage a couple of days with Kase.

She nodded to herself, feeling it wasn't unreasonable to achieve both goals. Closing her eyes, she leaned back in her seat, feeling more confident as she sank into the plush cushion.

She woke up as the train gently bumped to a stop. Outside the windows was a sign proclaiming they were in Suhun city.

Kase stood in the aisle next to her, looking eager to explore. That was the opposite of her plans.

"First thing," she said, getting up. "New clothes."

And the sooner the better.

As they stepped off the train, people stared, wondering why an Edger was in their city.

Okay, not as bad as thinking he's a Creet, thought Brell.

"Keep moving," she said, walking ahead of him.

The last thing they needed was to run into a cop with an Edger chip on their shoulder.

The underground terminal was its own city with stores to meet every need. Groceries, appliances, clothing, jewelry, gyms, and entertainment.

"Do people ever go up to the surface?" Kase asked.

"Of course."

"What's up there?"

"The same as down here."

"I don't understand," he said. "What's the point of having two of everything?"

"Because..." she started but realized the question had never occurred to her before. "Mole people. The sun hurts their eyes."

"Where?" he asked, glancing excitedly around. "I don't see... Oh, that was a joke."

"Sure," she said. "Let's call it that."

They spotted a clothing store and went in.

"Look at all of this," he said, marveling at the endless rows of clothes. "Why is there so much?"

"People like clothes," Brell said, filling his arms with his new wardrobe.

She steered Kase to the nearest changing room and sent him inside.

The next thirty minutes was a process of trial and error. He came out modeling something new, only to be sent back to try something else. It was all the same to him, and with each return to the changing room, he looked at her quizzically.

It wasn't that Brell didn't like the clothes; they were fine. It was that Teck fashion looked strange on Kase.

He came out again, awaiting her judgement. It still didn't look right on him, but now that she understood her bias, she knew it was pointless to look any further.

"It'll do," she said.

"Great," he said, glad to be done with the large store and chemical smells.

"Where now?" he asked as they left the store.

"My place," she said, looking at the map on the wall.

They took the nearest stairs up to street level, and Kase got his first sight of Suhun city.

He expected to be dazzled and overwhelmed, but for all its glass and steel high rises, he felt a cold trickle of dread run down his spine.

"What's wrong?"

She couldn't miss the expression on his face.

"I've seen cities like this before," Kase said, hypnotically staring up at the giant buildings. "When I was a boy."

"But you haven't been here before," she said, confused.

"Not here," he said, lost in memory. "In Creet, but it was just like this, only... it was dead. The buildings were overgrown and crumbling. Silent." He paused, listening to the activity of traffic and people around him. "Looking at this is like..." He paused, searching for the right words. "Like I've gone back in time."

"I was expecting a lot of reactions," she said, "but that wasn't one of them."

"Sorry," he said, staring around him. "I mean, this is fantastic to see, but I can't help feeling that I've looked into the future and seen this city's death."

Kase gave her a lopsided smile by way of apology.

Brell glanced at the thriving city around her. She remembered the ruins where they had found Billy in the robot research building. At the time, it hadn't meant anything to her. It was just another place, empty of significance, but now that Kase explained it, she saw it too.

They were surrounded by millions of people coursing through this huge metropolis. It was impossible to believe it could die... except she had seen it with her own eyes.

It was disquieting.

Brell wasn't much for daydreaming, and she shook off the imagery, bringing her attention back to the here and now.

Kase had done the same and was oddly stamping his feet on the ground.

"Stop doing that," she said, catching the judging glances of passersby.

"I can't help it," Kase said. "I can't feel the ground through these boots."

"Why would you want to do that?" she asked.

"How do I know what I'm walking on?"

"Look that way," she said, pointing down the street. "Now look that way." She pointed down the street behind them. "What do you see?"

"Concrete."

"Mystery solved," she said. "No matter where you walk in the city, you'll be on concrete."

"How do you not get bored with all the sameness?"

She didn't respond.

They continued through the city as evening set in. The tall buildings brought an early chill to the people milling under the reach of their long shadows.

"Aren't you cold?" she asked Kase, seeing he was wearing his new coat open.

"A little," he said. "I should have picked a coat with buttons."

She nodded, realizing how easy it was to overlook the things she took for granted but were entirely new to Kase.

"It doesn't need buttons," she said. "Just close it."

"Oh?" He wrapped the folds of the coat around him. They stayed in place.

He opened his coat and closed it again, the flaps once more staying where he'd put them.

"It's like magic," he said.

"But it's not. I'm hungry," she said, wanting to quickly change the subject.

"That sounds good. How far is your home?"

"We're here," she said, turning into a set of large double glass doors.

They crossed the short lobby to the elevators, with Kase clomping awkwardly in his boots.

"Do you have to do that?" she asked.

"I don't *have* to, but I'm not trying," he said. "It's like walking with planks tied to my feet.

"Try to tolerate it just long enough for me to get a new gun," she said, waving her security card in front of the sensor. "Before you know it, we'll be back on the Creet side, and you can wear all the dead animals you want."

Kase looked around the elevator as the doors closed. The small space was filled with light, but there was no visible source. He thought about it for a few minutes and decided he didn't like it. Like other things here, it went against his senses and made him feel disconnected with the natural world.

He recoiled, jolting out of his thoughts when a large face appeared in front of the doors.

"Welcome back, Brell," the face said.

"Who's that?" Kase asked, feeling uncomfortable so near the big set of eyes in front of him.

"I told them to turn that off," she said, rolling her eyes. "It's part of the service that comes with the building."

"You have had zero visitors since you were last here," the face said.

Kase moved from one side of the elevator to the other, watching how the eyes followed him.

"It's like being a bug in a jar," he said.

"Pretty much." She grimaced.

"And Tecks like this?" he asked, waving his hand in front of the face.

She shrugged as the face blinked out and the doors opened.

"Is that going to happen anywhere else?" he asked, glancing nervously over his shoulder.

"No," she said. "Maybe."

They passed several doors before stopping at hers, where she put her hand on it.

A moment later they heard the lock click open and they went inside.

After his small exposure to the Teck world, Kase had been expecting everything to be clean, polished, with straight lines. Sterile.

That may have described this place at one time, but this was Brell's home, and it reflected her personality.

It was an organized mess. The style of clutter of someone busily working on several things at once.

All Kase needed to feel at home was a pair of dirty socks on the floor.

It wasn't a big space, but it was comfortable, providing you could find somewhere to sit.

Looking around him, Kase could see a bed and a desk with a chair.

"Don't touch anything," was all she said as she crossed the room, tossing her cloak and tactical belt onto the bed. She sat down at the desk, and the four monitors on the wall came to life as she began typing on the keyboard.

The wall by the bed was one large window looking out onto the city. Nearly the entire view was other buildings with their own big windows and lots of lights.

To see the night sky, he pressed his cheek against the glass and looked up. He finally saw a few of the brighter stars that could compete with the glare of the city, but the view wasn't worth the crimp in his neck.

Strolling to the other side of the room brought him to a short dark hallway. He paused, peering at a still figure in the shadows. "What is that?"

"Hallway," Brell said without taking her eyes off the screens.

The hallway lit up, revealing a suit of combat body armor hanging from the wall. He recognized the combat plating from a similar set of armor his uncle had.

"Don't mess with it," she called from the other room.

"All right," Kase said as he ran his fingers over the armor, feeling the faintly pebbled surface. It was the same as the plating on his spiritbridge.

It had seen a fair share of use, judging by the gouges and dents. The helmet and chest were pockmarked with scars, and the left arm was missing entirely.

Hanging next to it was a shadowbox containing ribbons and medals. He studied them with fascination even though he had no idea of their significance.

"Was your father in the...?" he began.

"Busy," Brell said, cutting him off.

Kase walked back into the room that now had the addition of a low wide table. A hum from his left caught his attention, and he saw a panel of the wall closing.

He glanced at the other walls, wondering what else was hidden out of sight.

Among the clutter on the table were a couple of stacks of books, some empty bottles, and a strangely shaped stick. Laying next to several small tools was the partially dissembled left arm from the suit in the hallway. Parts of the armor were badly mangled and scorched.

A partially exposed newspaper caught his eye. He moved a mug with something dried at the bottom of it, thinking his original impression of messy over sloppy might bear a second thought. He picked up the paper and scanned the banner for the date.

It was a few months old, but he shrugged it off, thinking that even if it was old news, it would all be new to him.

He sat on the bed and started to read.

"If you don't mind," Brell said. "Sit on the couch."

Kase looked around the room, seeing nothing.

Brell stopped typing and looked at him with open exasperation.

"Just say what you want," she said, then turned back to the monitors.

"Couch?" Kase said tentatively.

The wall next to the low table opened and a couch folded out with a *whirr* of motors.

He crossed the room and sat down, testing the cushions before settling in and reading the paper.

One of the first things he discovered was how uninteresting the news was in the Teck world. The names and places were different, but the stories were very similar to the kinds of goings on in his world.

Weather, crime, politics – it was all there and none of it was holding his interest.

He put the paper down and went over to see what Brell was doing.

One screen appeared to be a list of messages. Another displayed several graphs, updating in real time with bars and lines rising and falling.

Brell was focused on the main screen, where she was scrolling through page after page of intelligible information.

She stopped, aware he was looking over her shoulder and sighed loudly, giving him a sidelong glance.

"It looks like there's a lot of things going on." Kase smiled.

"There is," she said, keeping her voice flat. "That's why I need to concentrate."

"What's that?" he asked, pointing at the graphs.

"Those are open bounties," she said. "They're tracking the values and what's being bid on them."

"And that?" he asked, pointing to the left display.

"Messages from friends and clients."

"Who would send you one with a row of little..." Kase leaned over Brell's shoulder to look closer at the tiny icons, then snickered as he stood up. "Kittens?"

"That's my mother," she grumbled.

"It's from months ago." Kase smiled. "Aren't you going to open it?"

"I've been gone for a while," Brell said, getting annoyed. "There's a lot to catch up on, but at the moment, I'm trying to find any records of Ethan Five Seven accessing the network, which is high on my priority list *because* it might help narrow down where he is instead of me having to search your entire world!"

She glared at Kase, her jaw muscles flexing as she subconsciously clenched her teeth, waiting for him to take the hint.

Kase glanced between her and the display for a moment.

"But it's your mother," he said. "Do you really want to make her wait? She could be worried..."

"I'm opening it," Brell said, stabbing the keyboard. "All right?"

The display changed and an image of an older woman appeared. Kase could immediately tell this was Brell's mother from the striking similarities.

They shared the same nose, mouth, and cheeks. Their eyes were the most telling, although her mother had the sort of crinkles at the corner that came from someone who smiled a lot. Brell did not have those lines.

"Hello, Jelly Brelly," her mother said. "It's Mom. Let me know when you're back home. Even though you didn't want to tell me about your bounty, I could see in your face it was going to be dangerous. I know my girl is up to the challenge." Her mother smiled, but there was a hint of it being forced, and it didn't hide the worry in her eyes. "I noticed your place was a bit messy; you always were as a little girl. Before you left, I sent you a new cleaning bot. It's the latest version. Did you ever get it?"

Kase followed Brell's gaze as she looked at a corner of the room. He saw a boxy robot with several throwing knives lodged in it.

"Oh, are you still seeing what's-his-name?"

"Alden," Brell groaned, looking at the floor.

"Alden," her mother said, finally remembering it. "He was nice. Give him a chance before you scare him off."

"Alden?" Kase asked.

"Shut it," Brell hissed.

"Let's get together for breakfast soon. Kisses, bye."

The recording ended, and Brell kept her eyes down, avoiding Kase's stare. Whatever he was going to say, she was certain it was going to irritate her.

"Where's the bathroom?" Kase asked, catching her off guard.

"Uh, the other end of the hall," she said.

"Thanks," Kase said, disappearing around the corner. "Jelly Brelly."

"I have a *lot* more throwing knives!" she yelled.

Stepping back into the hallway, Kase noticed a panel with a grid of green lights next to a bank of small switches and a handle. He threw a sly glance toward the living room. Hearing the soft taps of Brell on the keyboard he lifted the handle, and a door slid to the side. Kase jumped back, seeing a face contorted in surprise right in front of him. He knocked into the wall behind him and raised his hand, ready to cast, but his attacker didn't move.

It took a moment for his heart to slow down. The figure hadn't budged. He realized the person was, as near as he could tell, frozen.

His fingernail clicked when he tapped their face, and saw they were encased in a hard clear shell.

"Brell?"

"I am *not* showing you how the toilet works," she called.

"There's a body in your closet," Kase called.

"And?"

"I thought I'd mention it in case you might not have known," he said. "Or is this common in Teck houses?"

"He broke into my place, and the security system caught him," she said. "Thanks for reminding me. I forgot he was there."

"You forgot?" he asked, walking back to her desk. "How long has he been in there?"

"He's fine," she said glancing at another monitor then typed something. It displayed the same grid of lights he'd seen in the hallway. "Yeah, he's fine. I'll call the police to have him picked up."

Kase blinked, trying to comprehend how bizarre it all was.

"Doesn't it bother you having a stranger staring at you every time you go to the bathroom?" he asked.

"Sure it does," she said. "That's why he's behind a door."

16

FAMILY

Thunder rumbled in the distance as Naz kept his dark gaze fixed ahead, looking through the tall white gates in front of him. The guards on the other side stood with their backs to him. An insult he would remember.

He was accompanied by three of his acolytes wearing the dark crimson robes and hoods of his sect.

They stood silent, ever watchful and protective of their master. It was a loyalty he demanded, though their protection was only symbolic. The master mage's stark frame belied a powerful dark magic at his command.

Naz glowered, looking through the gates at the approaching royal chamberlain. The man made no effort to hurry as he crossed the large courtyard. He was sending an unspoken message about who was in command here, and he wasn't going to be intimidated.

Naz boiled with impatience but forced his hands from balling into fists. He was an open book to no one.

The chamberlain reached the gate and met the menacing gaze of the master mage with an unflinching stare of granite.

He nodded to the sentries, who then turned and pulled the levers. The large gates slowly opened, softly murmuring on their ancient hinges.

As he stepped forward, the chamberlain thrust out his hand.

"Your fanatics stay outside," he commanded.

The acolytes' faces were hidden behind bone white masks, but all three tensed, prepared for Naz's command to attack. Instead, he waved his hand, gesturing for them to wait.

No sooner had he stepped through than the sentries closed the gates.

"Follow me," the chamberlain said.

"I know the way."

"You'll do as it was agreed," he said, moving his hand to the hilt of his sword.

Naz stopped, a smile snaking across his face as he lowered his shoulders.

"I can think of few things I would enjoy more, Gramath," he said, eyeing the sword. "Do me the kindness; draw it. By the time your sentries reach us, I'll have made you cut out your own heart."

Gramath looked at him with flint hard eyes.

"You have become the very thing I warned you of," he said. "You've only proven to me that your exile was justified."

"Exile," Naz scoffed. "I left because I was sickened by this city's ignorance and your blindness. Believe what you want, but you will not live long enough to rewrite history."

"Look around you," he said.

Naz's eyes roved around, looking at the hundreds of guards lining the courtyard and its walls. All of them were staring at him, tense and eager to be the first one to cut him down.

"Your threats are meaningless here," he said. "Save your prophecies for your lunatic followers."

They reached the tall doors of the great house and climbed the wide steps to the tall ornate doors of the main house.

"I am here for one thing," he said, looking around the courtyard a final time. "Once I pass through these doors, I will adhere to our agreement." His eyes flamed with a glowering heat as he stared into Gramath's eyes. "But I warn you. If a single whisper of discourtesy passes over your lips, I will paint these walls with your blood."

Naz stepped over the threshold. The menace had disappeared from his face, and he offered the chamberlain a courteous smile.

"Chamberlain, would you be kind enough to accompany me?"

"My duty to the lady requires it," he said and stepped inside.

Their footfalls softly echoed as they entered the white marbled grand lobby.

Portraits of men and women, each with an air of nobility and benevolence, hung from the walls as a visual history of lineage of past rulers.

Royal guards joined them when they started up the grand staircase.

Naz softly grinned at the clink and jingle of the guards' armor as they climbed the stairs behind them.

The top of the stairs opened onto a generous mezzanine, where they were met with another pair of royal guards who stood rigidly at the entrance to a wide hallway with an arched ceiling.

Naz and Gramath walked in complete silence, yet the space between them crackled with angry static energy.

Passing into the hall, they stepped onto a carpet of rich deep blue. Their boots sank into the thick plush, muffling their footsteps. The carpet was trimmed with intertwining swirls of red and gold, stretching down its full length.

The walls were decorated with tapestries and portraits between carved busts and large ornate vases. As they walked past a painting of a very round man with a narrow beard and long hair, Naz glanced at the baseboard, where he saw two small letters carved into it.

His glowering eyes softened, and the lines of his grimace faded while his gaze lingered on the marks, but all too quickly, they were lost from sight and his scowl returned.

They stopped outside a set of double doors with two sets of guards in full ceremonial armor on either side.

Naz stepped up to the blond wood doors with Gramath at his side. "Per the arrangement," said Naz, "you wait out here."

Gramath pursed his lips into a thin bloodless line, frowning in disapproval but said nothing.

His protests had been heard when the terms of the agreement

had been formed. Most of his demands had been included but not all. He would honor the agreement no matter how foolish he thought it was.

Naz rolled his shoulders and forced his hands to relax. His palms bore the marks of his fingernails.

The doors opened from inside, revealing a spacious but simple bedroom.

A clutch of nervous men were conversing in hushed tones as Naz walked in. They glanced at him with open disapproval, their murmurings becoming clipped and darker.

Tall windows, open to the fresh breeze, reached up to the ceiling. Their long gauzy curtains flowed and billowed like willowy spirits.

Naz softened his motion as he walked across the polished floor to the large bed.

"Leave us," he hissed to the men without looking their way.

They recoiled as if slapped and, gathering what dignity they could, scurried out of the room.

He looked down onto the soft, frail features of the woman lying on top of the quilted satin blanket.

His entire countenance changed as her hazy pale green eyes drifted from the nearby window and settled on his.

Gentle, warm affection filled his face, but the weight of his sorrow was too heavy for his smile to reach his eyes.

He felt the weight of sorrow, like a stone hung around his heart as he looked at the whisper of the once proud, vibrant, and powerful woman lying before him.

"Hello," she said, hardly above a hush.

"Altrese," he said, laying a trembling hand on her cheek.

Her eyes cleared, and she smiled up at him, taking his hand in hers.

"Naz," she said. "You can't know how happy it makes me to see you. Why has it been so long?"

The question stung him. The answer hurt even deeper, tapping into an anger that even in this moment would not be denied.

"The selfishness of our people remains the chasm between us as it always has," he said.

"Please, brother," she said. "It pains me that these old wounds have not healed even after all these years."

"As long as they reject me," he said, "they can never heal."

"That painful decision was mine," she said. "The protection of our city fell to both of us."

"And the amount of magic we expended keeping our people safe was slowly draining our lives," he said. "It's the only reason I advocated for... other methods."

"Dark magic," she said.

"Using it to maintain our people's safety would have cost us an ounce of the energy of natural magic."

"Dark magic brings other debts that must be paid."

"It was the answer to your dilemma,"

"It was wrong," she said. "When we worked together, our magic –"

"Still wasn't enough," he said. "Not without dark magic. Using it, I could have taken the burden from your shoulders. I could have enchanted armies of guardians, not just a meager handful. I could've created powerful illusions driving off outsiders. And you... would not be here. Like this."

"I know," she said. Her eyes fluttered closed, heavy with fatigue.

Naz looked at her intently, afraid to breathe in her direction for fear of blowing her out like a candle.

Thunder rolled into the room like the distant crash of waves, and she opened her eyes.

"Our laws have always rejected dark magic," she said.

"We had the power, the right, to change them."

"It's not our way." she said.

"It's not *their* way," he said, glancing at the door. "They drove me out, leaving the burden of protecting this city to fall on your shoulders. They knew what it would do to you. They didn't care."

"Come back," she said. "I'm going to die soon. It's only right my brother should take his place once more."

"No," he said gently, brushing strands of hair out of her face. "You're too young to die. I passed the doctors on the way in. They told me..."

"Do you think I'm so weak that I don't see through their lies?" She smiled. "It's time you came back."

The room lit with a soft flash of purple light, and thunder echoed. Neither of them seemed to notice.

"I will come back," Naz said, "but not while you're alive. I couldn't bear to see the hurt in your eyes if you saw what I will do to this city."

"Naz," she said, softly scolding him. "Revenge is beneath you."

"It's not revenge I'm after," he said, holding out a small bracelet. Dangling from it was a bird carved out of a yellow stone. "This," he said, showing her the bird. "This stone, Kendium, is everywhere under our feet. We saw it only as a semi-precious stone. Good for simple adornment. But my years of exile have not been wasted."

He gently put the charm in her hand.

"It has unique properties," he said. "Powerful properties."

Altrese gazed at the bird, frowning.

"With weapons of this stone," he said, "I will rain ruin down on the Teck. When I do, they'll turn to their god, technology, to deliver them, but their god won't be there."

"You would reveal our people to the Teck?" she asked, her pale brow furrowing. "Our people won't willingly give you a means to wage war on the Teck."

"I know," he said, softness returning to his voice. "Out of respect and love for you, I'll wait. After you are gone, I will return and raze this kingdom to the ground. Then I'll strip away what's left, exposing the Kendium."

"This is our city," she said, rallying strength. Her eyes became a deeper green, her spirit returning in defense of the city she loved.

"This city is what has brought you to your death bed," he said. "They've taken and taken until there's nothing left of you. After you are gone, I will return the act a thousand fold."

"All you have are the few misguided fanatics who follow you," she said. "You have no army. Brother, I fear you are going to get yourself killed."

"I'm aware of your spies," he said. "They only see what I show them."

Her hand groped for his, and he lovingly scooped it up. He

frowned looking down at it; it was akin to holding a feather. There had been a time when great magic had flowed from these hands. She was magnificent. He'd loved her then even though he'd felt his own powers were pale in comparison to hers. He loved her still.

"If I could stop you," she said, "I would."

"I wish you could," he said. "Then I'd die knowing you were still full of life."

Another flash of purple was followed by a soft rumble.

"I saw our initials are still in the hall," he said.

He remembered when Altrese had used the first spell she had ever learned to carve her initial into the baseboard. Naz had tried to do the same, but the spell had been clumsy, and it showed in the carving of his initial.

"You sound surprised I didn't have them removed."

"A part of me is," he said, smiling.

They were quiet for a while. He glanced around the room, remembering how gigantic it had seemed to him as a boy. The games they'd played, racing circles around the room.

"Do you remember," he started but caught himself when he saw her eyes were closed.

Worry stitched his forehead, and he looked at her chest, watching intently until he detected the subtle rise and fall of her breathing.

Relief washed through him, and he carefully laid her hand on the bed.

He studied her face for a long time, transcribing every line and nuance in his mind, to this, his last memory of her.

He would not see her again. The thought squeezed his heart, and his eyes welled up with tears.

He leaned over and kissed her gently on the forehead.

Naz stood up and turned around. He wiped his eyes dry and brushed his clothing free of wrinkles. Quietly crossing the room, he paused at the doors and pulled his hood over his head.

He knew the people on the other side of the door would be looking at him, hoping he would reveal a moment of weakness. Give something away about what he had been doing over the years since his exile. More importantly still, perhaps a clue into what plans he had for the future.

He would give them nothing. They deserved nothing...

Except my contempt.

Gramath was not comfortable standing still and had been pacing the hallway, frequently checking the time.

All eyes turned toward the door as Naz stepped through.

The small mob of doctors wanted to return to their patient, but they stayed back, avoiding eye contact for fear of provoking a terrible consequence.

Naz did not possess the same reluctance.

He held the doctors in his stare until they squirmed under his relentless gaze.

"Exhaust yourselves for her care," he said. "No sacrifice is too great. Understand?"

One of the doctors straightened, indignation flushing, rosy red, up his neck.

"Every man and woman here has devoted their..."

"Your devotion means nothing," he sneered. "She bought your safety with her life. Return the debt by spending what's left of yours to save her. I will know if you fail me," Naz said, acid dripping off every word.

The gaggle of heads bobbed in horrified understanding.

He turned and headed down the hall. Gramath quickly caught up, and they retraced their steps in silence.

The sky was a gray cast as they reached the palace gates, and Naz was pleased to see that his acolytes had not budged from where he had left them.

No words were exchanged between the mage and chamberlain as the gates were opened and he passed outside the royal walls.

Naz never looked back as he strode away with his acolytes following at a respectful distance.

They continued down the royal avenue and stopped where it reached the main thoroughfare. To his left, the road led into the city. From here he could see the landscape of buildings making up the city center. Further away than he could see were the farmlands that provided everything these people needed.

He glanced up the road to the city gates. Strong, imposing, and thousands of years old.

"Take a side path until you're certain you're not followed," he said to his followers. "Then change out of your robes and return to the city."

The three of them nodded obediently.

"Watch for my sign," he said. "I will have need of you soon enough. You must be ready to act quickly. Remember, my disciples, we light the path for the return of the fallen."

"Return of the fallen," they repeated, bowing, and left him.

As he neared the gates, a curious sensation rippled through him, and he cocked an eyebrow. In the past, these brute-like fortifications had inspired a trickle of fear in him. High and imposing, they towered over his insignificant, frail body. But things were about to change. The next time he saw these mighty gates, they would be piles of rubble at his feet.

And the people who lived behind them? Dead or slaves.

17

THE BOUNTY AGENT

Kase was excited about taking the exterior elevator when he saw how tall it was but forgot about the view the moment a synth-bot walked on at the thirty-second floor.

It wore shoes, pants, and a shirt over its poly-tone skin. A new variation on the bare metal and white carbon shell models. The color wasn't meant to be identical to flesh color. The aim was to give the bot a warmer hue, less sterile.

Brell didn't like it, but she wasn't a fan of bots in general.

She was busy reading something on her arm terminal and didn't look up when it walked on.

Kase, on the other hand, couldn't stop staring at it. He cleared his throat, trying to get her attention without success.

"What – uh," he said. "What are we doing after this?"

"Depends on what the bounty agent says," she replied, focused on her terminal.

He casually moved closer and bumped her with his elbow.

"What?" she said, looking at him.

Kase tilted his head in the direction of the bot and nodded at her.

"I know," she said. "I've seen them before."

"Shhhh, oh never mind," he said.

"Why are you being so strange?" she asked. "They don't care."

"I didn't want to be rude to it."

"You wanted to melt Billy because it was a bot," she said. "This one's a bot. What's the difference?"

"This one looks... domesticated."

"You're kidding," she said. "You know it's all about programming, don't you? Hey, bot."

The synth-bot turned its head, looking at her without expression.

"Can I help you?" it asked.

"Why did you do that?" Kase said, feeling uncomfortable under the robot's gaze.

"What would you do if I aimed a gun at you?" she asked.

"Nothing," the bot said flatly.

"What would you do if I told you to kill this guy next to me?" she asked.

Kase's jaw dropped, and he backed away from the bot.

"Are you insane?" he said. "We're trapped in a glass box with this thing, and you're provoking it?"

"I would not comply," the bot said as impassively as if she had asked it about the weather. "It is impossible for me to inflict harm. If you persist in trying to instigate violence, I will notify the authorities. Is there anything else I can do for you?"

"No, that's all," she said, smiling at Kase. "See? It's just a machine doing what it's programmed to do."

The elevator came to a stop, and they walked off followed, by the bot.

Kase paused in the lobby, watching the bot as it passed them, turned into the left hallway, and walked out of sight.

"Which way is your bounty agent?" he asked.

"Hemmel's office is that way," she said, pointing right. "Will you relax?"

"I was until you tried picking a fight with the robot," he said.

Brell muttered something under her breath and started down the grey carpeted hall.

The walls were paneled in a honey brown wood grain, as were the office doors they passed, each with names and numbers on a small plaque.

"Remember..." she began.

"I heard you the first time," he said. "Try not to be me."

She nodded, satisfied, and opened the door.

They walked into an office where a young girl sat behind a wide desk. She glanced at the two of them with a pleasant smile and picked up the phone.

"Brell is here," she said and hung up.

"Hi," Kase said, grinning at her.

"Hello," the receptionist said before going back to work.

"I'm Kase," he said. He was about to stick out his hand when he remembered that wasn't a Teck custom and stopped himself.

"Hi, Kase," she said. "Are you with Brell?"

"Yes," he said. "That is, yes and no. We're together, working. Not together, together."

Brell looked at him with a hard stare, wishing he would stop talking.

"You're a bounty hunter?" the receptionist asked.

"In training," interrupted Brell. "And currently *failing*."

The receptionist politely smiled and nodded, then turned her attention back to her work.

The door next to the reception desk opened and a big man in a rumpled suit stuck his head out.

"Come in," he said and disappeared back inside.

Kase followed Brell, giving the receptionist a final glance. She did not return the gesture.

They stepped inside a large office with a broad window overlooking the cityscape. One wall was covered with an array of monitors, several of which had graphs similar to the ones Kase had seen on Brell's computer at home. Other displays had an ever changing collage of pictures of men and women.

Three of the displays had maps rendered in blue and white grids with small icons marked with a name and number beside them.

"Business looks good, Hemmel," Brell said, scanning the displays.

"It's keeping food on the table," he said. "Did you wrap up the contract with... hang on."

A new picture appeared on the display with a flashing red border around it. Hemmel tapped something on his keyboard, and the screen on his desk lit up.

"I want that one," he said.

"You're too late," a voice said from the screen.

"Don't push my buttons," Hemmel barked. "I'm looking right at it. I have a hunter already lined up."

"The contract is promised to someone else," the voice said.

"Is it Orban?" Hemmel said heatedly. "It's Orban! What are you doing giving a contract like that to a small time?"

"He's turned in the last four ahead of estimated catch date."

"Four?" Hemmel asked, losing some of his steam. "All right, keep it."

He jabbed a button hard with his thick finger, and the screen went out.

Hemmel leaned back in his chair, running his fingers through his bristles of short hair looking at Brell.

"Where's the bot?" he asked.

"Funny thing," she said. I ran into Hanover. He was on the Creet side. Do you know anything about that?"

"He's a loose cannon," said Hemmel, waving off the question. "Who knows what he does."

"I do," she said, crossing her arms across her chest. "Before he got caught by a Creet bounty hunter, he was poaching my *exclusive* contract. The one you hired me for."

"Oh, that Hanover," he said. He wet his finger and rubbed out a ring of dried brew on his desk under Brell's stare. "Well... I thought you were dead," he said. "I was expecting you weeks ago. When you didn't show, I thought that psycho machine killed you."

"And you gave it to Hanover?" she said. "Do you know how insulting that is?"

"He's my second best hunter. Almost as good as you."

Kase gave an involuntary snort, and the conversation stopped as all eyes turned to him.

"Who's he?" Hemmel asked as if Kase had suddenly appeared out of thin air.

"Training," Kase said, feeling Brell looking at him with daggers in her eyes.

"You any good?" asked the agent, sizing him up.

"Well, I..." said Kase.

"It's not looking good at the moment," she said. "I want Hanover pulled from the contract."

"You know how it works." Hemmel spread his hands.

"Yes," she said, "I do, and you can't break an exclusive contract without proof of death."

"Be reasonable," he said. "You didn't contact me."

"I think E57 was monitoring combinations."

"It did that?" he asked, blowing out a breath of surprise. "Smart bot."

"Pull his contract," she said.

"I can't," Hemmel said, pleading.

"I want a thirty percent bonus on completion of the job."

"Out of the question." He sputtered like a leaking steam valve.

"Not after you read this," she said, tossing a small white wafer on his desk. "It's a full report of everything I learned about Ethan Five Seven."

He picked it up, glancing at it with curiosity.

"Give me the short version," he said.

"There's a massive synth-bot corporation that will remain unnamed, but they will pay a metric ton of money to keep what you're holding from seeing the light of day," she said.

His brows slid into each other as he looked at her suspiciously. "Are you saying there's a defective bot on the loose?"

Brell leaned over the desk with a sly grin.

"Not defective," she said above a whisper. "They didn't wipe its personality."

Hemmel's face went slack as he stared at the wafer, swearing under his breath.

"I'll give you an extra ten percent," he said.

"It's building other bots and downloading its own psychotic need to murder into them," she said slowly. "Thirty percent or I take this to someone else."

"It's yours!" Hemmel said.

"And a raise on all future contracts," she tagged on.

"Done, but this has got to check out," he said, looking down the finger he pointed at her. "And that includes putting E57's head on my desk. None of this means a thing without proof."

"And I'll get it," she said, "but I need an advance on my pay."

The grin of being a rich man fell from Hemmel's face, and he sat back in his chair.

"Why?" he asked.

From where Kase stood, the agent had already decided 'no.'

"I need a replacement for my gun," Brell said. "Mine overloaded."

"Get it fixed," the agent said. "It's cheaper."

"It doesn't have the punch to take down E57," she said. "It was right in front of me when I dumped five bolts into it. They didn't even slow it down."

Kase remembered that terrible night. The terrifying ferocity of the bot and the dead bodies it had left behind. He could smell the cooked air from Brell's gun. He squeezed his hand into a fist, breaking away from that night. He didn't want to think about it. Ever.

"I can't help you," Hemmel said.

"It's just an advance."

"On what?" he asked. "All I got is a data card and your stories."

"If you don't help me," she said, "that's all you'll have. I can't take it down without a better gun."

"I'm just as much a victim as you," he said, putting his hand on his heart. "The laws are strict about guns and bounty hunters. The military, sure. Cops, you bet. We're lucky they let hunters have them at all."

"They let us have guns so they don't get stuck with the ugly jobs," she said. "We're an easy scapegoat when the bad guy isn't brought in fast enough."

"Hey," Hemmel said. "I'm taking heat all the time. Is that Aresh?"

He and Brell both looked at the screen on the wall. A picture of a reed thin man was framed in red.

Hemmel stabbed the button on his desk, and his display lit up.

"He's mine," Hemmel said.

The face on the other end of the call opened their mouth, but Hemmel interrupted.

"You owe me this one," he said, ending the call.

He looked up, seeing Brell staring at him, determined not to take no for an answer.

"I can't do it directly," Hemmel said. "But I know someone."

"Good."

"He doesn't like attention, if you get my meaning," he said.

"Yeah, he's underground. What's new."

"He's very underground," Hemmel said, looking serious. "Be careful with him. He's tied up in all kinds of things. He'll want to get his hands on someone with your skills, and you don't want to get mixed up with his business."

"Thanks for the warning," she said.

"Here's his information," said Hemmel, typing on his keyboard.

Brell checked her wrist terminal, nodding when she saw his message appear.

"I know I don't have to say it," he said.

"Then don't."

"Don't mention anything about the bot to him," he said, undeterred.

"Anything useful I should know?" she asked, heading to the door.

"Where's Hanover?" he asked.

"I don't know," Brell said. "Last time I saw him, he was drifting in an airship lifeboat with the Creet army looking for him. But I wouldn't worry. He's *almost* as good as me."

Brell reviewed her new contact as they walked out of Hemmel's office.

"Rast," she said.

"What?" Kase asked.

"I've heard about him before." She smiled. "He'll have what I need."

"That's good."

"I think so," she said.

Kase cocked an eyebrow in an unspoken question.

"Hemmel's right," she said. "This guy's involved with serious players."

"Players?"

"He's doing business with very dangerous people," she said patiently. "Rast doesn't hire talent. He leverages it."

They got off the train at the last stop and were the only ones on the platform.

Instead of taking the stairs to street level, Brell led the way to a maintenance door at the end of the platform.

She punched in the code Hemmel had given her, and the door unlocked with a growling buzz.

The transition from the well lit, clean, and polished platform to grimy dull and gray walls and pipes was strikingly sudden. They walked down a narrow corridor to a set of stairs leading down. The landing emptied into a simple room with two large doors on opposite ends.

One was marked with Service Operations Servers. The other was a bare gray metal door.

Kase was mildly surprised when Brell walked over to the server door and opened it.

Stepping inside, the air was filled with the hum of row after row of processors, each one reporting their status with rows of indicator lights.

Brell went to the end of the room and stopped at a door. Kase couldn't see any hinges or a handle on it.

"You're one of Hemmel's, aren't you," a voice said from above.

"I need a gun," Brell said.

"That can be arranged," said the voice. A moment later, the door slid open with a greasy hiss.

In front of them was total darkness. Not even the ambient light illuminated the space ahead.

It was disturbing, and the first thought that came to Kase's mind was a deep empty shaft.

"Take two steps forward," the voice instructed.

Brell put her hand through the threshold and it disappeared.

"It's a null-light field," she said, dropping her hand. "It disrupts light waves."

"Is there a floor on the other side?" he asked.

"I guess we're about to find out." She grinned.

Kase was filled with questions but knew he'd have to wait for a better time and place.

Brell walked in, utterly vanishing from sight. Even though she had explained it, it didn't make him feel any better. The question remained in his mind.

What if we're walking into nothing?

"Hurry up." came Brell's voice out of the dark.

He walked in, counting off two steps, and stopped.

Behind them, they heard the door close.

Kase had never experienced such total and complete darkness. He rocked his feet, feeling the floor just to keep a sense that he wasn't falling.

They winced as the null field was turned off and they saw they were standing in a small box. It was barely wide enough to hold the two of them. There were no seams or gaps anywhere and no sign that there was a door behind them.

"Face the scanner," the same voice said.

A panel opened at eye level, revealing a set of different sized lenses. Hair fine beams of light criss-crossed over Brell, starting at her head and working down to her boots.

The lights went off.

"Now you," the voice said.

Kase glanced at Brell, who nodded, and he moved in front of the device. The beams of light reappeared and scanned over him head to toe, then turned off and the panel closed.

"Put your weapons in here," said the voice as a drawer slid out from a side wall.

Kase had left his assassin's dagger at Brell's apartment, so he stepped back as Brell reached across him and put her knife in the drawer.

It receded into the wall, leaving no signs.

Every second they waited in the confined space felt like minutes. Kase glanced at Brell out of the corner of his eye and saw the muscles in her neck flex. He was glad to know he wasn't the only one feeling the growing urge to get out of here.

They heard a hum, and to their relief, the right wall of the box swung open. Walking out, they entered a tastefully furnished reception room.

"Hello, Brell," a synth-bot said, nodding its head in greeting. It wore a suit and tie, holding its hands behind its back. "I don't have a record of your companion."

"I can vouch for him," Brell said.

The bot paused, its expression frozen on its face as the bot sought direction from an outside source.

"Mr. Rast is not comfortable with strangers," the bot said. It reached under its jacket. Suddenly, it was pointing a gun at Kase's head.

"Hold on," Brell said, putting her arm in front of Kase. "You know me. You're probably looking at my profile right now. Look at my history. Am I someone who would work for the police? I swear he's clean."

The bot paused a moment, its unwavering aim pointing at Kase's head. He fought every urge to move out of the way, but he instinctively knew that if he flinched one inch in any direction, he'd be dead before hitting the floor.

The bot returned the gun under its jacket and gestured to the wall where a door slid open.

"Mr. Rast will see you now."

They walked into an office that was surprisingly similar to Hemmel's. Displays and monitors covered two of the four walls. Behind the far desk, the wall appeared to be a huge window looking out across the city.

We're underground... aren't we?

He couldn't tell if it was a real window or a giant display screen. He pondered if it was possible that the pitch dark box was also a very fast elevator. It was another question to ask Brell later.

"Have a seat," the man behind the desk said.

They crossed the room, and two comfortable chairs swiveled to face them.

They turned back to face Mr. Rast after Brell and Kase sat down.

"You're looking for a gun," he said plainly. "I carry a lot of inventory. Can you narrow down what you need?"

There was something peculiar about Rast, but Kase couldn't put his finger on it. The man was average height and thin but not frail.

Kase caught himself staring at Rast and pulled his eyes away to let his gaze wander distractedly around the room.

"I need something small," Brell said. "Portable and light. Easy to carry and keep out of sight."

"That sounds like any number of pistols you can have registered to you from the government."

"It has to be capable of burning through molly carbonate steel," she said.

Rast nodded, smiling.

"Well, that does change the discussion. I have four pistols with that capability. You are looking for a pistol, correct?"

"Yes," she said.

"Molly carbonate steel," he said as if tasting the words. "It's not my venue, but isn't it rare to have a bounty on a synth-bot?"

"I imagine it is," Brell said, keeping her face a mask of stone. "Do you have the pistols here? I'm on a deadline."

"This way." Rast tapped a button on his desk.

Two doors swung open, and they saw lights come on within the next room.

Rast came out from behind his desk and led the way through the doors.

Kase had no sense for how far back the room went as they passed one aisle after another. He saw rows of dark gray chunky cases stacked twenty feet high. Other rows had similar colored cases but of different shapes and sizes.

Next, came racks of weapons. Long rifles of multiple variations: two barrels, four barrels, some fixed, and others rotating.

"Here's what you're looking for," said Rast, turning down a row.

Resting on wall mounts were twelve pistols, each slightly different from the next.

"My *unregulated* handheld stock," said Rast. "All of them have been wiped of any ballistic signatures. Untraceable and *highly illegal*."

"I need a gun with a short cycle cool down," Brell said, clearly in her element. "Intuitive aim and high capacity."

Rast smiled, creating creases around the corners of his mouth as he scanned the wall of guns.

"This will fit your needs," he said, taking down a weapon and handing it to her.

"Positive grip," said Rast. "Counter recoil. Auto-correcting optics based on distance to your target. Selective power ballistics from humane to lethal, thanks to a military grade mag-rail accelerator for guaranteed penetration every time."

The gun had a short serpentine handle supporting the main body. Kase couldn't tell what parts he was looking at, except for the barrel, which was unmistakable.

He didn't understand anything they were talking about, but just by looking at the gun, he could tell it was a thing of lethality.

Brell turned it over in her hand. Aiming it, she inspected whatever people inspected. Kase had no idea.

"Perfect," said Brell.

"I knew it was the right match for you," said Rast, "the moment you walked in the door."

'What is it about him I'm missing?'

"Are you asking me?" Alwyn said.

'Sorry. I wasn't paying attention to my thoughts.'

"It's all right," Alwyn said. "I've been enjoying seeing so many familiar sights. This city is how I remember the world before I died."

'It was like this even in Creet?'

"Before the Rift," the mage said, "there was no Creet. There was no Teck. There was just people. These two cultures began forming over the years even before the end of the war. Naturally, the Rift made the division all the more easier."

'Are these guns like those used when you were... when you had a body?'

"Similar," he said. "I see they've made advancements. It's really very impressive."

'It's troubling.'

"How?"

'We don't have weapons like this. How can we stand up to a Teck attack with this arsenal?'

"I understand how you could see it like that," he said. "But your doubts are founded in your inexperience with magic. Consider the effect of an illusion spell on just one Teck soldier. One moment he's among his fellow soldiers, the next, he believes he's surrounded by the enemy and opens fire."

'I hadn't thought of that.'

"What would happen if the spell were used on a general looking at a battle map?" Alwyn said. "You could make him blind to the actual location of enemy forces while having them appear on the map where his flank is or deep behind his own lines. Suddenly, he's scattering his soldiers, chasing phantoms, leaving himself wide open to attack."

'All of that from a single mage.'

"Now do you understand why the Creet are so mistrusted and hated?" he asked. "The Teck understand guns. They make every man and woman equal to the next, but magic…"

18

JUST OUT OF REACH

Kase looked at his hands, imagining the magic he would master one day. Growing up, surrounded by it, he had never fully considered what weaponized magic could do in the hands of an experienced mage. He realized there would come a day that mage would be him. The power to create and utterly destroy would flow through him.

He involuntarily shook his hands. The idea frightened him.

'It's too much power for one person.'

"There are always checks and balances," Alwyn said. "That you're scared of having that much power is a good sign. Magic isn't about being great or having strength. At least, that's true for natural magic."

'Dark magic isn't natural?'

"No," he said. "In its twisted form, dark magic can do things natural magic can't. But it only brings suffering. You have a good heart. I don't think you'd ever try it."

'Thank you.'

"And if you did," he said, "the other mages would eventually kill you. Like I said, checks and balances."

Kase felt eyes on him, and he looked up to see Brell staring at him.

"I said let's go," she said.

He followed her back into Rast's office. He was already in his chair, the new pistol on his desk.

They sat across from him, and Brell made a point of not giving the weapon a second look. She didn't want him to think she was too interested in it and have him use that as leverage against her.

"My favorite part," Rast said with a smile. "The negotiations."

He sat forward, resting his elbows on the desk.

Brell started to speak, but he held up his hand, stopping her.

"I will make this short in your case," he said. "Let's not pretend you can afford this. You can't."

"I can trade," she said.

"I know everything you own. Of value, that is. I know what's in your bank account, and I know all of your debts. You're practically broke. Your mother, on the other hand…"

"She's not a part of this," Brell said firmly.

"Are you sure?" he asked, smiling. "She is a woman of considerable finances."

Kase looked at Brell, struggling to conceal his surprise.

Brell remained silent while Rast looked at her a long moment, giving her time to reconsider.

"Then our business is concluded," he said with false disappointment.

Kase stood up, but Brell didn't move.

"I'll give you my time for the gun," she said.

"You were holding that option in your pocket, weren't you?" Rast smiled. "I didn't give you enough credit for this game."

Brell remained behind her poker face.

"I do have several activities needing my attention," he said, "but I would be wasting your collection of rare talents on things so mundane. There is a particular situation I'm keenly invested in. I can't think of anyone better suited for the task."

"Details?"

"Not long ago, a harvester was destroyed."

"I saw the news," she said.

"Contrary to the reports, I was informed by a reliable source that it was attacked." He nodded, seeing the brief flash of surprise on her face. "Yes, I thought the same thing. Who and what?"

"The news said there was a breach in one of the Gramite containment cases. The harvester was destroyed by the explosion," said Brell.

"A lie to placate the public," Rast said. "I'd like you to find out who did it and recover at least three of the crystals."

"That's an oddly specific number," she said. "That's how many were supposed to have been smuggled to you."

"You are a natural at this sort of thing," grinned Rast.

"There's a lot of government agencies that will be looking into what happened to the harvester," she said, thinking it over. "And if the Gramite's containment is breached... that'll make them very dangerous to handle. You're asking a lot."

"It's a lot of gun," Rast countered. "And it's my only offer."

"All right," she said, putting her hand on the gun.

Rast put his on top of hers. She frowned at him, taking her hand back.

"This is your payment for the finished job," he said.

"Whatever I'm going up against, I'm not doing it empty handed."

"My bot will provide you with a choice of weapons that should be sufficient," he said.

Brell was not happy, and the dark look in her eyes made that clear. But she knew taking the job was her only option. Nobody else in the city had the kind of inventory Rast had, and if they did, they certainly wouldn't let a gun like that go on a trade.

"How long do I have?" she asked.

"As long as you need," he said. "But sooner rather than later."

"I'll need a way to contact you," she said.

Kase cocked an eyebrow as Rast stretched his hand across the desk.

"Your terminal?" he said.

Brell held out her arm and pulled back the sleeve, exposing her arm terminal. Kase's mouth went slack as the fingernail of Rast's thumb opened and a short ribbon extended from it. The interface blinked with tiny dots of light as he held it over Brell's terminal. A moment later, it retracted into his thumb, and the nail moved back into place.

"That's my secure line," Rast said. "No one will answer it except me."

The door out of the office opened, and the bot walked in.

"I'll show you the way out," it said.

Brell glanced at the gun on the desk, grinding her teeth before heading out the door.

The office door closed and sealed behind them as they followed the bot to the reception desk.

On it was a rugged gray case which the bot opened, revealing four pistols.

"Is this a joke?" scoffed Brell, looking at the weapons.

"I don't understand," the bot said.

"These are junk," she said, pointing at them. "That's practically an antique. This one," she said, picking it up and examining it. "See that? The shielding is paper thin. It could explode in my hand the first time I shoot it."

She flung it into the box.

"These are perfectly capable," the bot said.

After a moment, Brell picked the least objectionable of the four.

She turned it over in her hand, swearing under her breath.

"All of them have new crystals and are fully functional," said the bot.

"Functional?" she said. "Has this one been tested?"

"If you want to fire it," said the bot, "I can provide you with..."

Crack!

The bot stumbled back with a scorched hole in its suit.

"Test over," she said.

Smoke curled up in a hazy ribbon as the final embers on its jacket died out.

"Let us out of here before I test this again."

The bot and Kase traded looks, then it pressed a button on the desk and the exit opened.

As they entered Brell's apartment, she stopped short, glaring at the room which was considerably cleaner than it had been when they'd left.

Kase looked over at the tied up cleaning bot, but it was obvious it hadn't moved.

"My mother," she fumed.

"That was nice of her," he said.

"She doesn't do her own cleaning," she said. "That's what she hires other people to do, which means strangers were in my home. *My* home."

Kase could practically feel the waves of heat radiating off her. He had seen her fighting monsters and killer bots, but he was witnessing an entirely new depth of anger.

"Don't be hard on her," he said. "You're lucky to have a moth..."

"It's gone!" she yelled, looking at a clean spot on the coffee table. "My tools, the parts. I had it all laid out in the order I'd disassembled it. Where'd they put it? Never mind. I'll deal with this when I get back."

She marched across the room and flung open another hidden closet. Kase's first impressions of her home had been that it was comfortable but compact. With every revelation of new closet space, pantries, and fold-out furniture, he realized it was functionally much larger that it appeared.

She pushed her way in between the hanging clothes and returned with a backpack. She pulled a couple of pants and shirts off their hangers and stuffed the wad into her bag.

"You should be packing what you need," she grumbled to Kase.

"I'm pretty much wearing it," he smiled, holding out his arms.

She went over to the wall of monitors and displays and typed something on the keyboard. Part of the wall swung away to reveal several weapons mounted on a rack. She picked through a row of knives and stuffed some small marble-looking objects into one of the compartments on her backpack.

Kase sat down with his bag between his knees and took out his soft boots. He had given the Teck-style boots a fair try, but they were awful.

It took some pulling, but he was able to free his feet of the stiff clunky things and stood them by the couch.

"What are you doing?" she asked even though he was in plain sight of her.

"I'll wear everything else but not these," he said, dropping the new boots to the side.

She stared at him a moment, then grumbled under her breath and went back to her packing.

He had figured she was too annoyed with her mother to bother with him, and he was right.

"When are we leaving?" he asked.

"First thing in the morning. We're going to the storm fields, and I need to review my files. I might have a useful contact around that area."

"Storm fields?" Kase said. "I want to see those lightning storms up close."

"Not too close," she said. She made the sound of an explosion.

"Do you know anywhere that isn't dangerous?" he asked.

"Kase," she said, glancing at him. "Nothing interesting ever happens where it's safe."

The sun was an hour from cresting the horizon when Brell and Kase walked into the underground parking structure. Kase had noticed there was a lot of traffic but not many parked automobiles. Seeing the big concrete cavern under her apartment building explained a lot.

He marveled at the rows upon rows of actual still-working automobiles. The few he'd seen in Creet had been decayed hulks, hardly giving a hint of how their modern counterparts looked.

The underground parking had a cave-like feel, enhanced by the echo of Brell's boots on the concrete floor.

Although he had never seen it before, Kase glanced around, trying to see if he could guess which one was hers before they reached it.

Of all the low, sleek and sporty vehicles, there was one that stood out. There was nothing about it that cared about aerodynamics or styling.

"That's yours," he said, gesturing to it.

"Is it that obvious?" She smiled, enjoying that her truck was distinctive.

The truck looked like a predator hunching on four rugged tires, ready to charge at its prey.

Tapping on her arm terminal, the walls reverberated with the purring thrum of the truck's engine. She opened the driver side door and tossed her bag behind the seat. Kase followed her example and eagerly got inside.

The seat fit like a glove, comfortable with ample leg room. The windows were jet black, but sitting inside, Kase could see outside as if there was no glass at all.

The doors closed with a solid thud.

Brell watched as Kase adjusted the seat and rolled the window down and up. She headed him off as he reached for the instrument panel.

"My first car ride." He grinned.

"You won't be disappointed," she said with barely concealed pride.

The truck rolled smoothly out of its slot to the ramp leading outside. A moment later, they were driving through the dawn-lit city. Kase watched how Brell operated the truck, what buttons she pressed and how she managed the acceleration and stopping.

Morning sun had broken over the horizon by the time Brell turned onto the main highway. The stranglehold of traffic slowed them down to a stop and go, sapping the anticipation of adventure out of Kase.

"We don't have these problems on Creet," he said, fidgeting with the door controls as they crawled along.

"You're not telling me that a wagon is better than this," Brell said, glancing at him from under her eyebrows. "Compared to a wagon, this is…"

"Not going anywhere," he said.

"When it's cold, I turn on the heater."

"I put on a coat," he answered back.

"When it's hot..."

"I take the coat off," grinned Kase.

"What about this?" Brell pressed a button. The roof slid back, revealing a view of the sky.

"We have that too," Kase said. "It's called looking up."

"Never mind," she frowned, closing the roof. "I can't expect a Creet to appreciate technology."

"That's not true," he said, smiling. "I never said I didn't appreciate this. I only pointed out that you can do all the same things in a simple wagon. But the moment technology can do something better, let me know."

Brell twisted her mouth, muttering something under her breath, and Kase sat back in the comfortable seat, humming to himself.

Eventually, they worked themselves free of city traffic, and the horizon changed from tall buildings to distant mountains.

After another hour, the highway was their own. The only cars they saw were far ahead and behind.

The purr of the truck rose as she sped up. Brell glanced over at Kase. A sly smile curled the corner of her lips, and she tightened her grip on the steering wheel.

"Hey," she said.

"Huh?" said Kase blinked out of a haze.

"Can a wagon do this?" she asked, flicking a switch.

The truck went from a purr to a roar. It launched forward, throwing Kase into his seat. He looked ahead with wide eyes.

The road became a blur, and Kase could feel the growl of the engine vibrating in his chest. Road signs whipped by as the truck rocketed down the road.

A whoop of excitement jumped out of Kase, who was thrilled and terrified at the same time.

"Okay," he laughed. "You win."

Chuckling, Brell slowed down, and the engine settled to a soft purr.

"Who's a good girl, huh?" she said, patting the truck's dashboard.

"You have to tell me how this all works," Kase said with renewed interest.

She spent a few minutes explaining what each of the instruments did.

"This runs on the same crystal as your gun?" he asked, imagining the burnt disk she had showed him on the airship.

"It's the same crystal, but the size and shape is different," she said. "That's one of the challenges of using them. Every time they engineer a new type of motor, they have to experiment with different cuts of Gramite."

"The shape decides the amount of power a crystal has?" he asked.

"Something like that." She shrugged.

The miles and landscape rolled by. In the distance, a mountain range rose on the horizon, and he wondered what he would find if he explored them. He was sure somewhere out there were undiscovered temples and mysterious chambers that had not existed before the Rift. And maybe one of them held the secret to where magic came from.

He pondered that question often. The Nac' Aura was the portal that brought magic into the world.

What's on the other side? What would I see there?

The question made him consider what he had seen here, in this forbidden world of Teck.

Kase searched the countryside, expecting to see something that was drastically different from his world, but it was all the same.

Grass, trees, hills.

Of course it is. It's the same planet.

He'd grown up hearing talk about how Creet and Teck were so different. Yes, there were differences, he admitted to himself, but his expectations had been that the Teck were verging on something entirely alien.

After all if the prevailing belief was true, it was the Teck's reckless pursuit of technology that had led to the Rift. The fact that they wouldn't admit to it and, in fact, blamed the Creet for it stirred up mistrust. He didn't feel good about it, but even he carried some of that distrustfulness.

It clashed with his opinion of Brell. After his experiences with her, she didn't feel like 'one of them.'

He wiggled his toes, enjoying the freedom of movement in his trusty, familiar boots. Yet, looking at them, he was reminded that it didn't matter what he thought of the Teck. No. What mattered was he was, essentially, the enemy trespassing on foreign soil.

He doubted they would bother with the philosophical values that they all shared the same roots.

Suddenly, home felt very far away, indeed. Glancing out the window, he reflected that these were not his trees, not his grass. It was not his land.

It was several hours since the sun had set when they pulled into a small town sitting near the foothills to the mountain range beyond. There was one main street, and everything was closed up for the night, with one exception.

The lit sign over a lone corner diner was the only sign of life. Light spilled through its large dusty windows onto the street, and Brell slowed down, sizing up the patrons inside.

"I need real food," Kase said. "If I have to eat one more of your snack bars, I'm going to be sick."

"Me too," she said. "All right, let's go in."

She turned around and pulled into the empty parking lot.

"Ahhh," Kase said, stepping out of the truck and wincing. "A little stiff."

"Are you going to be okay?" Brell smirked.

"In a minute," he said, rubbing his neglected thighs.

Two old men looked over their cups of brew and out the window at the strangers. Neither man spoke but communicated with a nod and a lingering raise of an eyebrow. It was the language of small town folk who knew each other like the back of their own hand. A simple gesture said more than a sentence.

Sensors opened the cafe door, and Kase and Brell walked in where an old model bot greeted them.

"Thank you for coming," it said.

"Anywhere?" asked Brell.

"That will be fine," said the bot.

Brell led Kase to a table near the kitchen door. The smell of food instantly inspired grumbling from both of their stomachs.

The door swung open and a tired waitress came out. Everything from the food stains on her dated uniform to the limp curls in her hair said it had been a long day. She walked over to their table with an aura of thinly concealed disdain.

"The kitchen's getting ready to close," she said.

"Then we got here just in time," Brell said, undaunted.

The waitress stood next to their table, staring down at the two of them, wanting them to take the hint.

"Hi, Nella," Kase said, reading the name tag on her uniform. "This looks like an interesting town. Have you lived here very long?"

"I'll get your menus," she said, sighing loudly and disappearing through the doors.

A few moments later, she returned and unceremoniously dropped two plastic-coated flex pads on the table.

"Call me when you're ready," she said, turning to leave.

"I'm ready now," Kase said.

"Same," said Brell.

Kase watched Brell tap the flex pad, and a green checkmark appeared next to her selection. Kase did the same and handed it back to the waitress.

She frowned at the menus, muttering something under her breath, and left, pushing through the kitchen doors.

"A number five and eleven," she hollered.

Kase and Brell didn't have to wait long before she reappeared with their food. She put down their plates and carelessly dumped their utensils next to them.

The sight of real food set fire to their appetites, and they didn't speak again until there wasn't enough room for another bite.

"Ugh," Kase groaned, putting down his fork. "I can't move. All I want to do is stretch out and sleep here."

"I know what..." began Brell.

"No sleeping in the diner," Nella called out from inside the kitchen. "We got rooms upstairs if you want to rent one."

Neither of them were looking forward to a cramped night sleeping in the truck, and they happily rented two rooms.

They were old but hardly used. Apparently, the town did not see many people passing through since the underground highway had been completed forty years earlier.

It was five-thirty, and Kase and Brell hugged themselves against the bite of the morning chill while they stood outside the closed diner.

They could see Nella inside, making ready to open for business. When she caught sight of them, they could swear she slowed down.

It was only a couple of minutes past when she unlocked the doors, but they were sure she'd delayed it on purpose.

"Sit anywhere," she said as they walked in, appreciating the warmth.

They paused, seeing the two old men at the same table from the night before.

The diner had been empty before the waitress had opened the doors; yet, there they were.

They shrugged off the curiosity and took two seats at the counter. Their motives were twofold. One, being the waitress would appreciate she didn't have to walk the extra steps to a table, and two, they'd get their food faster.

She put down two cups and poured them a fresh brew.

"You're an angel," Kase said, gratefully wrapping his cold hands around the cup.

Nella paused, giving him a sidelong look.

"Are you being cute with me?" she said, her penciled eyebrows frowning.

"You started it," said Kase, giving her a sly grin.

She flushed as she headed back into the kitchen but not before he saw her smile.

"Stop doing that," Brell said. "She's old enough to be your mother."

"It's my natural charm," he said. "It's a force beyond my control."

"It's obnoxious," she said. "You know she sees right through your..."

Nella came through the kitchen doors and placed a plate of pie in front of him.

"The cook just took the first one out of the oven," she said. "I thought it might go nicely with your brew."

"Thank you," Kase said. "It's almost as warm as your smile."

Kase wanted to do something nice for her and thought about casting an illusion of flowers but instantly came to his senses and dismissed the foolish idea.

Brell looked open mouthed between his pie and her empty plate while the waitress beamed at him.

"You ready to order?" clipped Nella.

"Uh... number eight?" Brell said.

"How about you?" she asked, turning to Kase with a smile.

"What goes good with this amazing pie?" he asked. "Besides your cheerful company."

She laughed, waving off the compliment.

"I know just the thing," she said and left for the kitchen.

"I'm going to be sick," Brell said.

"It doesn't hurt to be friendly." said Kase, popping a piece of pie into his mouth. "Mmmm."

Kase couldn't eat another bite by the time they left the diner. The waitress had brought him one sample plate after another, nudging Brell's plate out of the way to make room for them all.

Brell ate in sullen silence, guarding her plate from further incursion.

When they left, Nella pushed a bag of extra food in his hands "for later" and gave him a hug.

"You remind me of my Lyan," she said. "You both have the same cheek."

Brell muttered under her breath as she trudged next to Kase back to the truck.

"This is for both of us," he said, trying to make her feel better.

"Don't spill that on my truck," she grumbled, getting in.

"Cheer up," he said. "We have enough real food for lunch and dinner."

She started the truck and pulled away from the diner.

Kase took a last look, seeing the two old men hunched over their morning cup of brew. The regulars watched the truck pull away and looked at each other, each passing judgement with a grunt and a raised eyebrow.

19

MONSTERS

No sooner was the town out of sight than the road began its climb high into the mountains.

The road hugged the mountainside, snaking in and out of its folds. The truck swayed with every curve, which was beginning to make Kase feel queasy. He rolled down his window and was instantly struck by the bracing pine-scented air.

They broke out of the tree line and were treated to a bird's eye view of the world below. Evergreens carpeted the lower valleys where a lake sparkled in the late morning sun.

After several miles, the main road swung north, following the contour of the mountain, but Brell turned east onto a side road of packed dirt.

"This will take us to the storm fields," she said to Kase when his eyebrows rose in an unspoken question. "This way will bypass the refinery and their security."

"Why would they care if we want to examine the harvester?" he asked.

"That's a good question," she said. "But I want to ask it *after* we see it for ourselves. If someone there is involved, they probably won't be happy with us prying."

The unpaved road wasn't meant for street cars and made no apologies for its ruts, loose gravel, and bumpy ride.

But Brell's truck was in its element, and the chunky tires ate up the road. Kase held on with a desperate grip as Brell raced over the runnels and potholes.

The road was an uneven track of dirt and loose rock. It was only wide enough for one car, and the original builders hadn't bothered with guardrails. The road widened and narrowed depending on how much the rains had washed away from the edge, which dropped away with a heart-stopping sheer fall hundreds of feet to a rocky gully below.

Brell's eyes glittered as she slewed around curves with the tires snarling as they clawed for grip.

Kase's stomach didn't know if it wanted to drop or leap as he looked out his window and watched the side of the truck glide toward the edge of the road and the long drop beyond.

"Too close," he said anxiously. "Brell!"

Brell pulled back a small lever on the console, and the truck sank as it grabbed the road and shot forward.

Finally, to Kase's relief, Brell slowed to a less death-defying speed as the road began to angle down.

She looked over at Kase, her face pink with a huge smile and shining eyes.

"We have to do that on the way back," she said, excitement coursing through her.

"No," Kase said, trembling. "We really don't."

The road leveled off as they came out of the mountains and followed it through rolling meadows. Here and there, side roads occasionally branched off, and Kase looked down their straight path, wondering what he would find at the other end.

Blue water filled the horizon as they crested the last of the hills, and the land narrowed to a wide causeway. Two large lakes bordered the road for several miles.

Wind swept across them, buffeting and stirring up short, choppy waves, making them look more like oceans. The waves rolled to shore like lines of charging cavalry, crashing against the sand in long bands of foam.

Kase looked in open amazement when he caught sight of a single boat in the distance.

"They might be in trouble," he said.

Brell glanced out his window and shrugged, unconcerned.

"If they live around here, they know what they're doing," she said. "These are the largest lakes in the region. They have their own weather systems."

"How deep are they?"

"Don't know. They say that way down deep, they connect."

"Has anyone ever seen...?"

"A lake monster?" she chuckled. "If they did, it's on someone's wall by now. Don't forget, you're in Teck now. Nobody tolerates magic. Nobody."

Kase watched the boat dip and rise on the waves, stubbornly riding the worst the lake could throw at it. Eventually, he lost sight of it as they moved farther away.

Miles later, the other shore of the lakes were heralded by a thread of yellow land on the horizon.

The end of the causeway brought a dramatic change from lively blue to flat dry desert. The ground was broken by patches of cracked dark-red rock exposed by the ever-shifting winds, only to be buried again in time. Tough stringy bushels of yellow-tipped scrub clustered together, offering pools of shade for small animals...

Or whatever else calls this place home...

They followed the road as it curved around a string of sharply carved mesas. Kase wondered at the multi-colored streaks running through them and was reminded of an archaeology dig with his mother. They'd found a hidden chamber in a place very much like this one.

But, this new territory wasn't finished showing off its wonders. As they rounded the mesa, Kase gasped when he saw the surrealistic landscape ahead.

"You don't see that every day," chuckled Brell.

"It doesn't look real."

Dark jagged mountains ran from horizon to horizon, crowned with boiling clouds of black and deep purple. The clouds were in constant movement – parting, revealing the raw rock teeth of the sharp mountains, then rolling back together, swirling in an angry churning of tidal forces.

As they got closer, he caught glimpses of jagged splinters of light flashing between the folds of the clouds. The mountains, which at first appeared solid black, began to reveal a craggy relief of blade-thin spines and plunging cliffs.

Scattered within them, pockets of red glowed, and the hellish landscape ignited the imagination to wonder if a giant or ancient beast was slumbering, passing the millennia within the folds of the mountains.

The ride turned rougher as Brell swerved off the dirt road and drove across the open plains, making a straight line for the storm fields.

She looked at a map on one of the dashboard displays and nodded with satisfaction, pointing to a location ahead.

"The harvester is up there," she said.

"I can't wait to see this up close," Kase said, gazing out the window. "The clouds never drift away from the mountains?"

"They're attracted to the element in the ground," she said. "Sometimes they drift outside of the fields, but they dissipate quickly. Lucky for us. Think what a storm like that would do to a city."

He could. The destruction would be horrifying.

Brell slowed the truck to a stop where the ground changed from yellow to gray.

"Welcome to desolation," she said, getting out.

Opening the door, Kase caught the strong smell of ozone in the air. The ground was ash gray and brittle under his feet.

"It's warm," he said, feeling heat through the bottom of his boots.

"There's the harvester," she said, pointing ahead.

"That?" His wide eyes sparked with an eagerness to explore.

Although it was still a several minute walk the machine, it stood out like the remains of an enormous prehistoric beetle – hunched backed and motionless in the vast field of scorched ground.

He walked a little closer until he felt the hair on his arms stand up.

"This is as far as we go," she said.

The sky rumbled as if it were growling a warning at them. A thick streak of light lanced across the clouds, and Kase could see strands of Brell's hair lift.

"That's it," she said, heading back to the truck. "There's a storm coming, and trust me, you don't want to be in the middle of that show."

Kase turned to follow, and a bolt of lightning shot down, hitting the ground two hundred yards away. The loud crack made him jump as it rang in his ears. It was more than enough to make him run for the truck.

They both dove in and slammed the doors behind them, looking at each other with wide eyes and pounding hearts.

"My hands are shaking," said Kase, staring at them.

Brell raised hers, which were trembling too.

They sputtered into laughter at the expressions on each other's face.

"You should have seen yourself jump," she said, tears running down her face.

"Your eyes were as big as dishes," he sniggered.

They laughed off their nervous energy and sat back, glad to be inside.

Catching his breath, Kase wiped his nose and glanced around the inside of the truck.

"Are we safe inside here?" he asked.

"Yeah," she said, brushing the tears off her face.

"Look over there," he said, pointing out her window. "Someone's coming."

Brell's expression became serious and she sat straighter in her seat as she looked at the distant truck approaching them.

"Security," she said. "They must have seen our dust cloud."

"Do you think they will tell us about the harvester?" he asked.

"Not a chance," she said. "We don't belong here."

Kase glanced between the closing truck and the harvester, furrowing his brow.

"Maybe we do," he said.

"What?" she said. "I don't know..."

She stopped, seeing his eyes were closed as he murmured to himself, holding his palm open.

She glanced between the coming security truck and Kase. Whatever he was doing wasn't happening fast enough. Her foot hovered over the accelerator, ready to tear out of there.

The security truck slowed and turned a short ways from them before stopping. The driver peered at her from their truck before getting out.

She turned away, avoiding eye contact. Brell clenched her jaw, holding back her words of urgency, hoping Kase would speed up.

Her head snapped around as someone tapped on her window. A heavyset man with a big gut was bent over, trying to see through the opaque windows.

"Step outside the truck," he said.

Brell rolled her eyes in frustration. If they sped off now, the guard would plaster the description of her truck up and down the storm fields, alerting every refinery guard post and cop in the area. She reached for the door, trying to think how to explain what they were doing there.

Before she moved, she heard Kase's door open, and she looked over in time to see him heading around the front of the truck.

Brell scrambled to get out, desperate to stop whatever was happening. Whatever it was, she was convinced it was bad.

"Officer... Mudem," said Kase, leaning close to read the security card clipped to the guard's shirt. The guard scrunched his chin into his neck to peer down at his own ID card.

Brell got out of the truck as Kase handed him a card.

"We've been hired to investigate the destruction of the harvester," Kase said.

"Property Investigations?" Mudem read doubtfully.

"Insurance, Mudem," Brell said. "That machine cost a lot of money, and the company is looking for who's going to pay the bill."

"Huh?"

"This is serious," Brell said. "Allegations of negligence. Destruction of company property. Maybe even sabotage."

Kase took back the card as the guard looked them up and down, frowning in confusion.

"You don't look like you're from the company."

"What are you trying to say, Mudem?" Kase said. "Would it make you feel better if we wore our suits and ties... in the middle of the desert?"

"No," he said. "I meant..."

"Our job is to interview everyone who played a part in that," Kase snapped, thrusting his finger at the harvester. "Did you happen to be on duty that night?"

"Me?" stumbled Mudem.

"Are you still drinking on the job?" Kase asked grimly. "Are you willing to swear to an official statement?"

"No!" Mudem said. "I mean I wasn't."

"This was an inside job," said Brell. "Were you working the night the crystals were stolen?"

"Which employees have complained that they're underpaid?" Kase asked.

"Are you happy with your job?" Brell asked.

"Everyone just hold on a minute," said Mudem. "I need to see some real identification."

"He's hiding something," Brell said. "Send a message to the VP of Operations that security might be a part of it."

The guard blanched and took a step back.

"You need to speak to the head of the refinery," he said, backing toward his security truck. "I'm not at liberty to talk about an ongoing case, so uh... follow me back to the shop."

"After you escort us in, confine yourself to your office," Kase said. "If you talk to anyone about us, I'll report that you're interfering with our investigation. Is that clear?"

Kase didn't wait for an answer and strode back to the truck, sharply closing the door behind him.

Brell left the guard muttering to himself and joined Kase.

"Where did that come from?" she said, looking wide-eyed at Kase.

"My father and uncle were both officers in the army," he said. "I saw them chew up plenty of soldiers, and it might have happened to me once or twice."

"And that part about the company?" She grinned.

"I dunno." He shrugged. "I figured a big machine like that costs a lot, and the company is looking for a scapegoat to fire over it."

They looked up in time to see the guard's truck's tires spit out dust as he turned around and headed for the refinery.

"Hang on to your magic card," she said, following the guard. "We'll need that when we get to the plant."

"Too late," he said. "It's already gone. I'm still learning about illusions. They don't last long."

"We're going to be there in a few minutes." Brell frowned. "Better get busy magicking up some new ones."

"I'll try," he said as the truck jostled him.

"And make us scary important," she said.

"I don't know what that looks like."

"Use your imagination," she pressed.

Kase shrugged and closed his eyes, trying to concentrate.

"Never mind," she said, taking his arm. "Knowing you, that's a bad idea. Just make us official."

Kase went back to focusing and tried to imagine what he could create that would demand the most respect.

The security truck went through the main gate and turned into the huge refinery yard. To their left was a building with high square walls. Behind it were four silos and large pipes that ran to house-sized cooling fans.

They drove on for another half mile past smaller outbuildings until they stopped at a huge double hanger.

Brell stopped alongside the guard's truck and got out.

"I'll take you to the mining operations manager," he said, leading the way toward the open hanger doors.

"Operations manager," said Brell pointedly to Kase.

She hoped whatever credentials he'd made would be enough to keep the manger from getting too nosey.

Walking inside, they saw two harvesters, broad and squat, with workers crawling over them.

Further inside was an open room with a row of consoles. Each one had their own main display screen with smaller ones arranged below.

Five people were sitting in a huddle, glancing at Brell and Kase.

Their anxious looks made it clear Mudem had radioed ahead and told everyone they were coming.

"I'm Mike Durrel," a man said, walking toward them. "Operations manager."

"Kase and Brell," Kase said, flinching as he remembered at the last minute to avoid shaking hands.

"We're here to inspect the harvester."

Durrel looked at them, with politely masked skepticism.

"Officer Mudem says you're from the main office?" he asked.

"We are an outside agency hired by the office," Kase said. "We've been given full authority to act in their name. They don't want to involve their own people until we know if this was sabotage..."

"What?" Durrel said. "My people..."

"Or an accident," continued Kase, "or someone got sloppy."

"We're relying on your cooperation," Brell said, "to make this process go smoothly."

"This is the first I've heard about anyone coming to my plant," Durrel said. "I was on a conference call with the director of this region, a man I've known for years. He would have told me if the company was sending you."

He wasn't buying their story.

"Show him our authorization," Brell said, hoping Kase had come up with something.

Kase reached under his jacket and took out a brown, thin wallet. He glanced around, looking for prying eyes. Satisfied, he opened the flap, revealing an ID card and badge.

Durrel's eyes flew open in surprise and confusion.

"Bounty hunters?" he said, keeping his voice hushed.

"Show him," Kase said, glancing at Brell.

Reluctantly, she took out her license and showed it to the manager.

"I thought you guys were investigators," he said.

"So did I," mumbled Brell under her breath.

"There's suspicion the Creet might be involved," Kase said.

"Here?" gasped Mudem.

"This is your... our main source of... uh –," said Kase.

"Gramite," Brell said.

"What would happen if that supply was interrupted?" asked Kase.

"But Creet? Here?" Durrel said.

"Don't say a word about this to anyone," Brell said. "It could cause widespread panic."

"Right. Right," he said. "That means you too, Mudem."

The guard bobbed his head up and down in agreement.

"We want to look at the harvester," Brell said.

"Sure," said the manager. "I'll get you geared up. Galin!"

A head popped up from the huddled employees.

"Make sure we have a tractor prepped," Durrel called. "I want you to take these two out to the harvester."

"Me?" Galin said, looking pale.

"Yeah, you," Durrel said, staring fixedly at Galin. "Five minutes."

In spite of the bulk of their shielded suits, Kase and Brell sat comfortably in the rear seats of the tractor as Galin drove over the desert terrain.

"That was quick thinking," whispered Brell near Kase's ear.

"I couldn't think of a better lie than the truth," Kase said.

"Something's going on with this guy." Brell gestured to the driver.

He hadn't spoken since they'd left and was becoming more anxious as they neared the edge of the field.

He looked out each window every few seconds as if searching for something.

Brell noticed the way he was squeezing the steering wheel. Eventually, he caught himself and opened his hands, relaxing them. But it wasn't long before he was looking out the windows again, craning his head in every direction. His hands would tighten around the wheel again.

At first, Brell thought he was nervously watching for a storm forming, but there were early warning sensors on the dashboard made specifically for that. All of them were in the green.

The longer she watched him, the more she realized that whatever he was looking for, it wasn't in the storm fields. His attention had turned to the wide expanse of desert, and it scared him.

"What do you do?" Kase asked.

"Uh," Galin said. "I'm a harvester pilot."

"Have you ever seen lightening destroy a harvester before?" Brell asked.

"It can't," he said. "The shielding is too thick. Is that why you're here? To find out what happened?"

"Yes," Kase said.

"But I told them about..." started Galin, then went quiet.

"About?" Brell asked.

"Nothing. I thought they already knew. Uh, put your helmets on. We're going into the storm field."

"Isn't the tractor shielded?" Brell asked.

"Yes," he said, flipping switches on the console. "It can take a lightning strike. But it doesn't have its own environmental system. If a bolt hits close enough, it will super heat the air and cook your lungs."

Brell and Kase quickly put on their helmets and clicked them into place.

"Tap the blue panel on your arm," Galin said. "That's your air supply."

Both of them activated their air. Brell looked at Kase, feeling mounting misgivings.

"How are you doing?" she asked Kase.

Kase grinned at her, enjoying the novelty of the suit, examining its construction and the engineering of the tractor.

They covered the uneven ground and soon were approaching the undamaged side of the harvester. Surrounding it was a field of debris.

"See that," pointed Brell. "It definitely looks like an explosion."

"We're not there yet," Galin said as he steered around, exposing the breached hull of the machine.

"It looks like something took a bite out of it," Kase said.

Galin stopped the tractor and checked the sensor data.

"It's safe to get out. There's no spike in storm activity."

They got out of their seats, checking that their helmets were in place.

"I'm staying here," Galin said, glancing behind them, to the open desert. "Keeping an eye on the storm readings. Oh, and don't step on any big crystals."

"Those will kill us too," Kase said.

"Pretty quick," said Galin.

They kept their eyes on where they stepped as their thick soled boots crunched over the brittle ground.

"Galin," Brell said. "We're switching to a private channel, but break in if you need us."

"Will do," came the static reply.

Brell showed Kase how to change their communication channel, and he nodded once they could hear each other.

"I take it back," said Brell, looking at the harvester's ripped up shell. "This had nothing to do with an explosion."

"Then what?" Kase said. "If we were in Creet, my first guess would be…"

"A monster, I know," she chuckled. "But there's nothing that big. And besides," she said, cutting him off before he could object, "we don't have those here. No magic. No monsters. No whoo-hooo of any kind."

"Yet, I'm here," he grinned. "All right, for the sake of discussion, what do you think did this?"

"No idea," she said, "Yet."

She switched on the suit's flashlight and stepped up onto the exposed interior deck-plate. Kase shined his light into the rear of the harvester where the crystal locker had once existed.

"There's no question it was after anything else," she said. "It wanted the crystals."

"Now we know it wasn't lightning," said Kase, "or a random attack."

Brell moved deeper into the belly of the machine, pushing pieces of wreckage out of the way.

Kase moved closer to examine a smudge on the harvester's shell that had been peeled back into a jagged roll.

"Brell?" Kase said. "Remember what you said about monsters?"

"That's the problem with Creets," she said, grunting to climb back to him. "The moment you don't understand something, you blame it on spells and witches or... whatever. Is there even one science book in your world?"

He didn't say anything, but waited for her to join him.

"All right," she said, blowing strands of hair out of her face. "What am I supposed to be looking at?"

He pointed at the hull, next to the ripped up shell.

"It's a big dent," she said with a glance.

"Look again," he said, shining his light on it.

He angled the beam across the dent until shadows defined its true shape.

Kase heard the sound of her gasp over his headset. The shadows revealed an enormous handprint deeply embedded into the reinforced steel. Brell put her hand on it; hers was tiny in comparison.

"On what page in your science book does it explain giants?" asked Kase.

20

STITCHERS

Brell's eyes grew wide as the reality of what she was looking at came into sharp focus.

She swore, running her hand over the huge print.

The size of the thing made it easy to not see it for what it was. The print was as tall as Kase.

"Monster," Kase said.

"Stop saying that," she said. "There's got to be another answer. Security drones patrol these regions."

"What are drones?"

"Flying bots," she said.

"They can fly?" he asked, shocked.

"It's a different kind of bot," she said. "They're small." She made a fist.

She could see the relief on Kase's face through his visor.

"Nothing big enough to make that print could roam around here without being spotted... unless..." She trailed off, staring at the distant mountains.

"What is it?" Kase prodded, following her gaze. He didn't like the look of those mountains either, and the dread he saw in Brell's eyes deepened his disquiet.

"Nobody knows what's beyond there," Brell said.

"You just said you have drones," said Kase holding up a fist. "With all of your technology, how is that possible you don't know every nook and cranny of your world?"

"It's a dead zone," she said. "Tech doesn't work there. Nothing does."

"Hasn't anyone ever gone into the mountains?" asked Kase. "Seen what's on the other side?"

"They've tried," she said. "Several times. The ones that come back say it's impenetrable. There's active volcanos up and down the entire range. Exploring parties have been trapped, surrounded by lava flows, and disappeared into sink holes. Strange things happen in there. Entire parties have blacked out. When they come to, they are miles away with no memory of how they got there. Some scientists think there's random vortexes of energy that affect the brain."

"They could have blindly wandered into a lava pit," Kase said, shuddering at the thought.

"The whole place is a maze of gullies," she said. "They might be a dead end, or they might circle back on themselves. Geologists think the Rift created fractures that ran deep into an unknown type of bedrock. It pushed them to the surface, creating these mountains."

"Sounds like the perfect place for a monster to hide," said Kase.

Their headsets buzzed when Galin broke in.

"You guys need to wrap it up," he said. "It's getting dark soon."

"Thank you," Kase said, "but our torchsto…"

Brell frowned at him, shaking her head.

"Flash lights," corrected Kase. "Are working fine."

"We're not staying out here in the dark," Galin blurted, making it clear it was a declaration, not a request.

Kase and Brell traded looks.

"I mean," he said, forcing himself to sound calm, "it's getting close to quitting time."

"Sure, okay," Brell said, shrugging to Kase.

"Durrel is going to want to know what we found," Kase said, as they started back. "He wants an answer," said Brell, "but is that the answer we should give him?"

"How about that? I was thinking the same thing," said Kase.

"Telling him he has a monster on his hands will create a lot of activity out here."

"That's attention we don't need."

The tractor door opened as the reached it, and they worked their way back into their seats.

In contrast to the grim desolation of the barren storm fields, the desert was awash in pastels of pink, orange, and purple as the edge of the sun touched the far horizon.

The beauty was lost on Galin, who couldn't get out of here fast enough. Before Kase and Brell had strapped in, he pushed the accelerator to its limit.

Over the whine of the struggling engine, they could hear the driver muttering to himself. His eyes constantly scanned the landscape around them.

Kase rested his helmet on his knee and leaned in beside Galin.

"You look like you've seen a monster," said Kase.

Galin's face went slack, and his color drained as his foot slid off the accelerator pedal.

"Is that what happened to the harvester?" Kase asked.

Galin stammered something incoherent at first. "I didn't see anything," he said, getting the tractor moving again. "There was a storm. The lightning plays with your eyes."

"But you thought you saw something," Kase said. "We aren't your enemy or judges. We only want the truth."

"They deleted my report anyway," Galin said. "It was only a big piece of the harvester blown off by a lightning strike. That's what I saw."

"The harvester's cameras were destroyed," Brell said. "How could you see that from your terminal?"

"I was saving Hank," Galin said. "I drove out here to rescue my bot."

"And that's when the lightning hit?" she asked.

"Yeah. It blew off a big chunk. That big piece is what I mistook for..."

"You must have been close," she said.

"Too close." Galin chuckled nervously.

"If it was lightning," Kase said, "why didn't it cook your lungs?"

"I was..." Galin stammered. "Because I... There was..."

He stopped talking and stared straight ahead. He stayed that way for the rest of the trip back to the refinery.

The moment they pulled into the equipment lot, he turned off the tractor, got out, and left, leaving Kase and Brell still inside.

They went back to the hanger, and Durrel marched in with Galin in tow as they were getting out of their safety suits.

He glanced nervously at Kase and Brell over Durrel's shoulder.

"Did you see anything?" asked Durrel. "Was it Creets?"

"We'd like to talk to Galin before we leave," Brell said.

Durrel jerked his head at Galin, who hurried away.

"He's talked enough," said the manager. "I know what you're thinking, but you're wrong."

"What are we thinking?" she asked.

Durrel shook his head, waving off the question. "The ones who did this were Stitchers," he said. "They were after parts."

"Stitchers?" Kase said, wrinkling his nose in confusion.

"Stitchers don't have anything that could peel open a harvester like that," Brell said.

"Maybe not before," Said Durrel. His tone inspired Kase and Brell to look at him with curious anticipation. "Some of my people were relaxing at the local bar. Off hours," he added quickly, raising his hand. "When some of those freak Stitchers came in. You know how they're always making trouble. It wasn't long before they started mouthing off and... of course, my people weren't having it. They busted some heads, and the police showed up. They were taking a bunch of Stitchers away, and one of them started making threats. He said there's a war coming and they were going to crush us like bugs. I'm thinking they've made a weapon."

"And you think that's what attacked the harvester," Brell said.

"Maybe it was a test run," Durrel said. "But it fits with the threat."

"Tell me the truth," Brell said. "What did Galin write on his original report? The one that got deleted."

"Nobody's report got deleted," Durrel said, staring in her eyes. "The man saw Stitchers. End of story."

They drove out of the refinery yard under the angry glare of the operations manager.

"I'm confused," Kase said. "How did we go from Creet and magic to Stitchers?"

"I'd go back and ask him, but I don't think he'd be very talkative."

"I've been waiting to ask –" Kase said.

"What are Stitchers?"

He nodded.

"They're a radical group who want to break away from Teck laws and form their own society."

"Did you know that historically that's how a lot of societies began?"

"And probably how wars started," Brell said.

"That too," he said. "Why do they reject Teck culture?"

"They believe it's their right to self-augment," she said.

"Self-augment what?" Kase asked, glancing at her.

"Their bodies," she said, looking to see if he connected the dots.

He stared at her with a vacant expression, an empty hole in the puzzle he didn't have the piece for.

"With tech," she said. "They illegally replace their own organs and limbs with tech."

Kase muttered a long curse, recoiling at the idea.

"That's disgusting," he said. "They put... But it's unnatural!"

"I wasn't expecting that," she said, "but a lot of people feel the same way."

"What excuse could justify disfiguring themselves with... machines?" he asked.

"Some people don't have a choice," she said tersely. "They have a bad heart or some other organ. They get it replaced with a synth organ and go back to living a healthy life. What's wrong with that?"

"The body is a sacred thing," he said. "Cutting out a natural organ and shoving a soulless piece of clockwork into it... That doesn't sound unnatural to you?"

"What would you do, let them die?" Brell said. "Or mumble some nonsense and shake a rattle in their face? Hope they get better?"

"I wouldn't let anyone die," he snapped. "I would *heal* them. Not carve them up."

"What do Creet know about medicine?" she asked.

"Magic can heal people," he said. "A skilled mage knows how to cast spells or make potions..."

"Potions?" spat Brell. "Do you hear what you sound like?"

"Their bodies are healed," Kase said. "No tech. No artificial... *thing*. Natural organs."

"Organs age. Get damaged, diseased. That's only extending their suffering."

"Knowing that they're being whittled away one piece at a time." Kase grimaced. "That's not suffering?"

"It's called progress," she said.

"By the time their family buries them," he said, "it isn't even the person they knew. They're not burying a body. They're throwing away used parts."

"I don't expect someone living in the dark ages to understand," she said, staring straight ahead, her eyes hard as ice.

"How is someone full of tubes and gears any different than one of your robots?" said Kase. "They're not even a real person."

Brell slammed on the brakes, sending the truck into a howling slide. Kase clutched the dashboard as the tires clawed for grip. The truck shuddered to a stop, shrouded in cloud of dirt and grit.

She glared at Kase, jaw clenched and anger in her eyes. He stared unflinchingly.

Seconds ticked by; the cabin of the truck was deathly quiet.

"You should think carefully before you open your mouth," she said through clenched teeth.

He was about to reply when one of the instruments on the dashboard chimed. They stared at each other as the chime persisted, elbowing into the tension.

Brell's gaze shifted only a fraction, but it signaled the end of the argument.

She turned to the dashboard and pressed a button, shutting off the noise.

Kase turned forward and sat back in his seat. His face a mask of stone, he stared ahead with balled up fists on his thighs.

Brell restarted the truck and turned them around until they were heading in the right direction.

The air in the truck was brittle with tension. Neither spoke, their mouths clamped shut, their eyes fixed ahead, and their faces taunt, refusing to acknowledge the other.

The tires crunched over the unpaved road, and small pieces of chipped rock and sand pinged unusually loud off the fenders in the taut silence of the cabin.

Eventually, Kase's eyes drifted to look out his window and watch the barren landscape go by. He saw the skeletal remains of a structure and was about to ask about it when he remembered he was angry. He kept his mouth closed, squaring his shoulders.

Brell's lips were pressed into a thin line. The cords on her neck stood out and flexed as she ground her teeth.

Her eyes never left the road ahead except to check a display, which she did quickly, refusing to look his way.

The next hour ground by in frosty silence.

Both of them saw a smudge on the horizon but said nothing. Soon it became clear they were approaching a small town.

To Kase, it was similar to the previous town they had passed through, though this one felt tired and neglected.

Drab single-story buildings clung to the edges of the main street like worn-out survivors to a life boat. Their windows were covered with a film of dust.

One building was set back from the street with a dirt lot in front of it. A long wide sign hung on the front of the building. Juiced Bar and Grill.

The only feature of the squat building was a dented dark-red front door. There were no windows, and the walls were littered with graffiti.

As they pulled in, Brell slowed down, paying close attention to painted scrawls.

Kase glanced over the beat-up trucks parked in front. Hoses and bundles of thin cables stuck out from the front and sides, running to the rear and underneath. Whatever their use, it was lost on Kase.

Satisfied, she turned off the truck and caught Kase looking at her from the corner of her eye.

"I spoke too harshly. I'm sorry for that," he said, pushing his words through his ill temper. "There are things about your world I don't understand."

"That's clear," she snapped.

"All right," he said. "But we can accept that we disagree and still get along?"

She opened the door and got out, immediately feeling the dusty heat fall on her. Kase did the same, and they started for the bar.

"Maybe," she allowed, grudgingly.

"The best thing is to drop the subject completely," he said, waving his hands as though sweeping the words away. "What do you say? No more talk about Stitchers."

"Good luck with that," she said, walking through the door and into the bar.

Kase followed her inside and stopped as several eyes turned to look at him, some organic and others artificial. He tried not to stare as his mind fumbled to make sense of the men and women sitting around tables and standing at the bar, most of them only part human. Some had artificial hands or entire arms. Other's had one or both eyes replaced. They shone orange, blue, and red.

Foreign, loud music pumped through the room that smelled of tobacco and sweat.

A girl passed by, bumping him with her shoulder. The floor clunked as her metal feet landed. She glanced at him over her shoulder with a frosty smile.

Brell was leaning across the bar, talking with the bartender.

The guy next to her was staring at Kase. What at first looked like a tattoo glinted, and he saw it was a device grafted into his skull.

He wore black pants, boots, and a sleeveless T-shirt. His head was shaved and...

He doesn't have ears.

The Stitcher picked up his beer can and tilted back his head, finishing it off. He faced Kase and peeled back his lips, exposing pointed steel teeth.

"If ya gonna stare," he said to Kase, "come closer for a better look."

He bit into the can, neatly cutting a chunk out of it. He snapped his teeth at him. Small sparks arced into the air, and he sniggered at him before turning back to order another drink.

A hand landed on his shoulder, breaking the spell. Startled, he spun to find Brell looking at him.

She leaned in to be heard over the loud music.

"The Freedom Clan is at the table over there," she said, cocking her head. "I know these people. Last time... last couple of times we crossed paths, it got a little bumpy."

"Tell me we're not going to get into a tavern fight," he said.

"Nah, I'm pretty sure they're over it by now."

"Pretty sure?" he asked, glancing at the far table.

The people around the table looked rough. Their faces and limbs were disfigured with tech, replacing what once had been there.

"Uh... mostly sure," she said, loosening the gun in her holster.

Kase pressed his coat against his back, feeling the reassuring bulge of his dagger.

He wasn't planning on stabbing anyone, but its ability to teleport him short distances made for a reassuring escape plan.

They walked over, stopping a respectful distance from the table.

"This the Freedom Clan?" asked Brell.

"Yeah," said a girl, getting out of her chair. "And you don't belong here, meat pie."

The others at the table snorted and chuckled, but Brell looked at her without reaction.

"Is your clan still by the old wreck?" she asked.

"Don't even think about going there," said the girl. "We believe in the individual's rights to self-augment. Anyone thinks they can stop us..." She raised her synth hand, briefly wiggling her fingers. Suddenly, her hand spun, the fingers folding away as other pieces locked into place, forming a gun.

Brell looked at the gun with thinly veiled boredom.

"Nice party trick" she said. "You try that in a real gun fight, your little toy will still be unfolding when the other guy puts one in your head."

"Are you threatening me?" hissed the girl. A glance at all her friends at the table fed her confidence and she leaned close to Brell's face with a grin.

Other people around the bar had picked up on the tension and were watching to see what happened next.

Kase eased a step to the side, wanting a clear view of the people around the table if a fight broke out. He wasn't a fighting mage, and the three spells he knew were painfully basic, but if push came to shove, he would wade into the brawl to help his friend.

"Get out of my face, wind-up," Brell said and head-butted the girl, making a terrible thud.

The girl's eyes rolled up, and she dropped to the floor.

The rest of her friends watched with open mouths as Brell sat down in her chair.

"Everyone calm down. I'm not your enemy," she said, glancing at the unconscious girl. "I hope she wasn't the smartest one of the group, or this is going to be a long day."

The irony of the prostrate girl at her feet wasn't lost on Kase.

"I have bona fides with your leader," she said. "We've done business in the past."

"So?" one of them said.

"So," Brell said, "I want you to arrange a meet-up with them."

The clan members traded looks of surprise and skepticism.

"How do you know our leader?" one of them asked.

"I did a favor for Enoch a few years ago," Brell said. "Tell him I want to see him."

Nobody moved.

"Who else do I have to put on the floor before one of you call him up?"

"Give me a minute," one of them said, standing up.

Brell leaned back in her chair as the clan member went outside.

The girl at her feet groaned, her legs slowly moving as she regained consciousness.

"You guys still out by the old ship?" Brell asked.

One of them nodded wordlessly.

"I remember Enoch had big plans for that place," Brell said. "He wanted it to be the capital for his future country. Well," she said, sitting forward and waving her hand dismissively. "Those were early days. He hardly had enough followers for a tent city. I expect a lot more have flocked to his banner by now."

"Together, we can make our voices heard," one of them said. "We can break the hold the big companies have on augmentation."

"I understand," said Brell. "Making prosthetics a subscription service was a pretty underhanded thing to do. It was just a matter of time before hackers started cracking the digital rights to the operating software."

"See?" said a Stitcher, "she understands what we're fighting for."

"I understand," said Brell. "That doesn't mean I support breaking the law."

"I couldn't afford it after they inflated their prices," another said. "They turned off my leg when I couldn't make the payments. All they care about is money."

"How did you lose your leg?" Kase asked, thinking the horrible stories about Teck culture could be true.

The person cocked their head in confusion as he looked at Kase.

"I didn't lose it," they scoffed. "I cut off."

"On purpose?" he asked, openly shocked.

"Are you trying to say something?" They glowered.

"Ignore my friend," Brell said. "So what happened?"

"I had a down payment on the second one when the company changed to their pay-to-play system. They forced me into a subscription. I couldn't afford to buy my second leg. The only thing I can do now is scrap and hope I find one."

Kase was about to ask what that meant when the clan member returned.

The girl on the floor pushed herself up onto her hands and knees. The clan member helped her up and walked her to his chair.

She flopped down, glaring at Brell through unfocused eyes. Brell pretended not to pay attention, but she put her hand on the butt of her gun under the concealment of the table.

"You got your meet." The clan member grinned. "Let's go."

They all walked out of the bar, wincing under the brilliant sun.

"I'm Ning," the leader of the group said.

"Sure," said Brell nodding in reply. She saw a dark filter slide over his eyeballs, shielding him from the harsh sunlight. "You and him are with me," he said, gesturing to Kase. "Huejax will drive your truck."

"No one drives it but me," said Brell.

"Stay here then," he shrugged and headed to his car, leaving her behind.

Kase glanced between Brell and Ning as he and the other Stitchers got in their cars.

Ning stopped next to her and leaned out the window.

"Last chance," he said. "The president said he couldn't wait to see you."

"President?" she scoffed. "That's what he's calling himself?"

"Is that a no?" he asked.

"Do we have time for another option?" Kase asked. "We still have to find E57, and it's not waiting for us."

Brell tapped on her arm terminal, and the lights on her truck flashed.

"There's not enough replacement parts in the world that can fix what I'll do to you if someone messes up my truck," she said.

Ning grinned as Brell opened the rear door and got in. She moved over, making room for Kase as Huejax got out and jogged over to Brell's truck.

They rolled out of the parking lot and raced down the main street, looking defiantly out the windows for anyone willing to complain.

Outside of town, Ning steered off the paved road, onto one of hard ground and dead weeds.

The Stitcher next to Ning leaned over and whispered something to him while glancing at them. Kase felt a ripple of unease when the

Stitcher sat back and smirked at him, like someone who was in on a joke the other person didn't know.

It wasn't long before Kase saw they were driving between two lakes, but on second look he realized these were not the same they'd traveled past before. The causeway was narrow, and the water was tinged with a greenish yellow that spoke more of marsh.

Reaching the other side, they turned away from the rich red-brown and green of the pine forest and grassy pastures.

The ground became a mix of limp pale stalks of grass and muddy pools. They followed the road between dense stands of moss-covered trees, and the air became thick and pungent.

Eventually, the trees thinned out, and they drove into the open. Over Ning's shoulder, Kase saw what looked like a town made up of large metal cargo containers. Hundreds of them formed multi-story buildings, modified with windows and doors.

Beside the road leading into the city was a large sign with Freedom City painted on it.

"This feels like a mistake," Kase said in Brell's ear.

"I've been thinking the same thing," she said.

21

JAIL

The tires grumbled over the streets of crushed rock as Ning drove them through the center of the makeshift town.

Kase began to appreciate the true size of the population as he gazed down the numerous side streets of improvised homes.

The road ended at the edge of a large brackish swamp, and just as Kase was beginning to wonder where the president lived, Ning turned to follow the swamp and stopped next to a towering wall of steel that rose up and up.

Kase leaned against his window and looked up, following the wall as it sloped outward, ending at a wide balcony.

He boggled over how he hadn't seen this monstrous structure from town, but much of it was covered with ropes of thick vines, curtains of moss, and trellises of hanging plants.

Ning turned onto a stone jetty which took them deeper into the swamp and stopped next to a long ramp. Stepping out of the car, Kase instantly realized he was looking at an ancient warship from before the Rift.

Its size and lines were very similar to the Waveforger back home.

Ning led them up a long ramp that ended at a hatch in the side of the ship.

Stepping inside, Kase expected the same cramped warren of

confusing hallways as in the Waveforger, a place he had explored every time the ship came in to port.

It was entirely the opposite. The deck was a gigantic cavern that ran the full length, from bow to stern. Hulks of machines cluttered the far end, nothing more than metal skeletons. Picked clean over the centuries, their original shape and purpose had been entirely lost to time.

Ning led them to the edge of the ship and stopped on a large platform jutting out over the open landscape.

Brell and Kase flinched as the platform jerked before slowly rising with the deep whine of unseen motors.

Soon their heads became level with the top deck of the ship. Four burley men waited for them, looking down on the approaching platform.

Brell grunted unhappily and Kase looked over the side, trying to gauge if the swamp water far below was better suited to escape or suicide.

The top deck was completely flat except for a tall steel fortress on the other side of the ship.

A small crowd of people shaded their eyes, peering at them from under a large awning next to the fortress.

As they were escorted across the patchwork deck, Brell squinted in the bright light, looking for a familiar face under the awning.

Surrounded by the four half-machine thugs, Kase was feeling like they were walking to their own execution. His eyes flicked left and right, looking for danger as his instincts sounded alarms in his head. Yet, he couldn't see any threat or reason to be worried.

Strike now while you still have time to run.

He balled his hand into a fist, trying to exert common sense, but he couldn't quell the warnings in his mind. He opened his hand and turned his mind to conjuring a fire. If he set the awning ablaze, they could escape in the confusion.

He felt the magic spill into his mind, and... Brell swore under her breath and Kase paused.

"Brell," a women said, standing up from her chair. "They said you wanted to speak to the president."

They know each other.

It was enough of a distraction that Kase abandoned his spell.

"I said I wanted to talk to Enoch," Brell said.

"You can talk to me."

"Lynnder," Brell sighed. "I didn't come here to speak to his adviser. Can we drop the grudge this time? Just get Enoch so I can ask him a couple of questions and then I'll be gone."

A man stepped up next to Lynnder and whispered in her ear. Kase's jaw fell open. He looked like a nightmarish doll more than a human being.

His eyes swiveled independently of each other from metal sockets. His ears were missing, and in their place were wide flat disks. But the real shock was when he turned away. He had an artificial eye in the back of his head.

Kase was at a complete loss why someone would willingly mutilate themselves.

It's looking at me!

As the man whispered in Lynnder's ear, one eye swiveled unnaturally to the side, locking on to Kase. All he wanted in that moment was for that *thing* to stop looking at him.

Brell sighed loudly at the interruption, shifting on her feet.

The strange-looking man took a step back, and Lynnder's expression hardened.

"Why do you think we should help you with anything?" she asked. "You've done more to hurt our cause than help it."

"That wasn't personal. I had a contract to fulfill," Bell said. "I would have taken the guy to jail even if he wasn't a Stitcher."

Lynnder seemed to consider this until the man leaned in to whisper to her again.

"Now what?" Brell said, her eyes narrowing in annoyance.

His eyes swiveled, looking at both Brell and Kase as he whispered his case. Lynnder's hardening expression made it evident he was stirring up resentment in her.

"Hey!" snapped Brell. The man yelped, and covered his augmented ears. "This is a conversation between Lynnder and me. She can think for herself."

The man's reaction confirmed Kase's suspicions; not only could he see everything around him, but his hearing was designed to eavesdrop on others.

"What is that disgusting thing crawling up his arm?" Kase said so quietly he couldn't hear himself speak.

A look of shock overcame the man, and he frantically swatted at his arms. He quickly realized there was nothing on him. He glowered at Kase with lidless eyes.

"What's happened to you, Lynnder?" Brell asked. "We don't get along, but I always respected that you had your own mind. What's this worm got to do with anything?"

"This is Otash," Lynnder said. "He's my adviser."

"I get it," Brell said, doing little to hide her sneer of contempt. "I bet the moment you took over from Enoch, this guy appeared at your side with all the answers. And since we're on the subject, what happened to Enoch?"

"He suffered a meltdown," Otash said. "It was a surprise to all of us. And regrettable, of course."

"He was too smart for that," she said. "Don't lie to me."

Otash recoiled, and the four big Stitchers took a step toward Brell. Kase tensed, seeing her hand disappear under her coat.

It looked like everything was about to go wrong very fast. If there was any hope of learning about what happened to the harvester, it wasn't going to be at the end of a gun.

"With respect," Kase said, stepping into the middle of the potential battle, "I am not familiar with your ways. What does meltdown mean?"

Brell looked at him, her face a mix of surprise and protest.

Lynnder turned to him, glowering at the interruption, but the respect and sincerity in his voice extinguished her anger.

"Each time someone augments themselves," she said, "it adds millions of additional lines of programming. Everyone in Freedom has deep-core nan-ramenan-ramdd processor grafted into their brainstem. It's how we're able to use multiple augmentations."

Kase listened, keeping his personal disgust from showing on his face.

"If an augmentation is defective or the organic coding is flawed, the processor's safety protocols are supposed to shut it down," Lynnder said. "Sometimes that doesn't happen. The flaw self-replicates faster than the protocol can correct it. The processor is overwhelmed and melts from the inside, eventually burning through the brainstem."

Her eyes shimmered with the painful memory and fear it could happen at any time.

"That is a horrible death," said Kase. "And a terrible price to pay for your people."

Lynnder looked at Kase, deeply and unexpectedly moved by his empathy. Brell was utterly confused but kept her thoughts to herself.

"Thank you," she said.

"He would still be alive today," Otash interrupted, his voice grating and harsh, "if we weren't rejected and treated like criminals. Your sympathy costs you nothing. If you want to make a difference, come back with a real doctor."

"Otash," Lynnder said, gesturing with her hand for quiet. "Please."

"They made us outcasts, then blame the system to numb their responsibility for our suffering. Just like her," Otash said, pointing at Brell. "She hung the tragedy of the clinic around your neck, but what happened wasn't her fault. She was only a tool of the system."

"You mean the law?" Brell said. "Lynnder was running an underground augment clinic."

"Judged illegal by those who think they're better than us," snarled Otash, stepping in front of Lynnder in a show of shielding her. "She was the only help those people had."

"You can't be part of a society and pick and choose what laws you will and won't obey," Brell said. "She was augmenting without a medical license." Brell leaned in, pointing a finger in Otash's face. "You know what happens when you play doctor? You put an implant in a psychopath."

"I was helping people," snapped Lynnder.

"You helped that animal mangle a train full of people," said Brell. "With the augmentation *you* just implanted."

"That doesn't outweigh all the good she's done," said Otash.

"She broke the law!" spat Brell.

"Outsiders' law!" Otash shrilled. "Our people are watching. Are you going to allow these intruders to mock you and stain the sacrifices you've made to help our people?"

"Madam President," Kase said. "we are not intruders. We are here with your permission. The only reason…"

"Forget it, Kase," Brell said. "I'm done with this clown show."

She started to leave, but Otash waved to the four guards. They moved in front of Brell, glowering down on her.

"You orthotic mouth breathers, get out of my way," she snarled at them, "before I start breaking things they don't make parts for."

"Otash?" Lynnder said, wanting an explanation.

"Before we let them go," he said, "wouldn't it be wise to know they aren't spying on us?"

"Is your whole world a conspiracy story?" Brell asked.

"She'll work for anyone with money," Otash said. "You know the New Border clan has been trying to create conflict among our people. How do we know she's not here to find a weakness or make people question your authority?"

"I'm a bounty hunter, not a spy."

But doubt and distrust flickered in Lynnder's eyes.

"I need time to think," she said. "Put them below, under guard."

Brell must have been expecting this. Before the guards moved, she pulled her gun and squeezed the trigger four times in lightning speed.

Everyone recoiled and the guards flinched, but Brell's gun never fired a shot.

"Piece of junk!" swore Brell, throwing down her gun.

"Take them!" screamed Otash. "Before she tries anything else."

Kase glanced at Brell as two of the big guards latched onto her. She signaled to not resist. He relaxed as the other two crowded him, and he held his hands up.

"I'm not a fighter," he said.

Lynnder watched, trouble clouding her brow.

"This could cause us trouble in the future," she said.

Otash was standing behind her, smiling as the two outsiders were taken away.

"At the most," he said, "when you release them, they will have learned a healthy respect for your authority."

The guards took them down deck after deck, deeper into the dim humid bowels of the ship. They passed through a hatch marked "Brig" and marched them into a cell.

The room was small and square with two foldaway cots attached to the wall. The guards searched them for weapons, taking Brell's belt and knife and Kase's dagger.

Kase glimpsed at the door, looking for weak spots. It was a solid steel door with a small thick round window no bigger than his fist. It swung closed on heavy hinges and locked with the sound of a vault.

"I didn't see today going this way," Brell said, sitting on a cot.

"Were you really prepared to shoot all four of those guards?" Kase asked.

"I pulled the trigger, didn't I?" she said. "Nobody was going to die. I was aiming for flesh wounds. Big guys like that, they'd walk it off in a day or two."

"Why did you change your mind?" he asked.

"Huh?" she said. "Oh, you mean..."

"When you told me not to fight."

"We could have," she said. "I have other things in my belt I could have used, but then we'd be back where we started. Lots of questions about a giant and no answers."

"After all of this, do you still think Lynnder will tell us anything?" asked Kase.

"Once we explain why we're here, maybe," she said. "I think Lynnder would be eager to clear up any suspicion they're behind a marauding giant."

"This ship is big enough to hide one," Kase said.

"The Freedoms aren't a radical clan. That much, I got from seeing how they're trying to build a community for themselves." She leaned back in the bottom bunk and grinned at him. "What I want to know is when did you suddenly get so sympathetic about Stitchers? When she talked about meltdowns, I thought you were going to hug her."

"What they do is revolting," he said, "but they're still people."

Kase looked at her, feeling Brell's eyes on him him.

"Why are you looking at me like that?" he asked.

"So that's what enlightenment looks like." She grinned. "Since we met, I felt like I was the one always wearing it."

"That's funny," he said, trying to sound serious, but couldn't hide his smile.

"It looks good on you," she said, framing his face with her outstretched fingers. "Kind of a natural fit."

"For someone trapped in a steel box, you're having a remarkably good time."

"I've been through this kind of thing before. You need something, but the other guy has a bone to pick, so they make you work for it. Once they feel like they showed you who's boss, they let you go. You get some or all of the information you needed, and you're on your way."

"Except it wasn't Lynnder who threw us in here," he said.

"Huh," she said, sitting up. "I didn't think about that."

"My mother let me keep a book we found during one of our archeology trips," he said. "It was the history of great civilization and how it all collapsed when the royal advisor overthrew the king."

"How?" Brell asked.

"Over time, the advisor used the king's authority for his own agenda," Kase said. "He formed alliances, bought favors, and threw suspicion on the king's supporters, removing them from positions of power. It didn't take long before everyone knew who was really in power."

"And it wasn't the king," Brell said.

"What I just saw was history repeating itself. Otash is the one in charge."

"Not a chance," she scoffed. "He's a spineless coward. He's got no power."

"Did you notice how Lynnder did everything he told her?" he asked.

Brell tilted her head, considering it, then waved off the idea. "You're seeing things that aren't there."

"Am I the only one who saw him giving orders to her guards?" he asked. "He didn't ask her permission. And the guards followed his orders. They never looked to her to make sure she approved."

"Hmmmm," she said, thinking it over. "Okay, so?"

"What if he tells the guards that Lynnder wants us to disappear?" he said.

"How did we suddenly end up at murder?"

"Do you honestly believe he suspects us of being spies?"

"No," said Brell.

"Me neither," Kase said. "It would be much less trouble kicking us out of the city. Instead, he makes up an excuse to keep us here."

"That's what doesn't make sense," Brell said.

"It does if you believe he's trying to pull Lynnder's throne out from under her. He wants to use our being here to further his plans."

"What plans?" she asked.

"He instructs the guard to report they overheard us talking about spying for another clan for a sneak attack," he said. "He tells others he knew it all along, but Lynnder didn't want to believe it. She's turning a blind eye to the safety of her people. She can't even keep them safe from two unarmed spies escaping prison. Lynnder's indecision and refusal to see what's going on is exposing the people to terrible danger. The people lose confidence in her, and they start looking for a new leader. Otash."

Brell stared at him for several moments, gaping in surprise.

"When did you start being so suspicious?"

"You're rubbing off on me." He shrugged.

"Is that how I think?" she asked.

"It's a little disturbing for me too," he said.

"I'm not saying you're wrong," she said, getting up. "The more I think about it, the more I think that's what's going to happen."

"Really?" Kase said, looking disappointed. "I was hoping you were going to tell me to stop being so pessimistic."

"Maybe later," Brell said. "I think Otash is going to send a couple of those wind-up toys down here to kill us. We need to get out of here. Right now."

"All right," Kase said, looking at her expectantly.

"Why are you looking at me?" she said. "They took all of my gear."

"They took my dagger. I can't jump to the other side of the door."

She looked at his right hand, seeing he was wearing the spiritbridge.

"You have that," she said, pointing to it. "Do something. Throw a spell at the door. Turn it into paper or a tiny bug."

"I don't know any spells like that," he said.

His mind zipped through the few spells he knew. None of them applied to this situation.

Using his *push* or *pull* spell on the door would need more power than he could control.

The illusion spell?

He had used it to create a fake note and some other things, but he couldn't think of anything useful.

"Is there another way out?"

Except for a small vent in the ceiling, the room was a solid box.

"What have you got?" Brell pressed.

"Nothing!" Kase snapped. "I can do a couple of illusions but nothing big."

"Like what?" she asked.

"Uh..." stammered Kase. "This," he said, creating a small puff of smoke. "I can do this."

She frowned, waving it out of her face. Then her expression changed, and she told him to do it again.

Kase cast the spell, and a small cloud of smoke hung in the air.

"How many times can you do that?" she asked.

Kase shrugged, shaking his head.

"Do it again," she told him.

An instant later, he produced another puff of smoke. The hand-sized illusion swirled, mingling with the first.

"More," she said.

"How many?" Kase asked at a complete loss.

"Enough to fill the room."

The corner of Kase's mouth curled down as he puzzled over it. Then suddenly, he understood what she had in mind.

Small billows of smoke popped into existence as he summoned the illusions. As quickly as he could cast, another appeared.

With all this practice, his confidence grew and he began experimenting, casting larger, thicker clouds of smoke.

He was hoping for huge billowing smoke, but the best ones he could do were a quarter of the size. Still, it was better than nothing.

As the room filled, Brell urged him on, but he began to have doubts about this plan as he felt an acrid sting at the back of his throat.

"Keep going," coughed Brell.

"We're going to run out of air," he said. "What if the guards don't come? We could suffocate."

"What do you mean, if?" Brell asked, looking worried. "You were the one who said they were coming to kill us."

"I said it was possible," he said. "I didn't say it was guaranteed."

"You got me all wound up in your story," she said. "Now you're saying they won't come? Stop making smoke."

It didn't matter that he stopped. The room was filled with gray churning smoke that stung their eyes.

The back of Kase's throat burned as he noticed the ceiling light. Either it was dimming, or he was about to pass out.

He saw a narrow thread of light coming from the bottom of the cell door. Racked with coughing, he laid on the floor and put his face to the crack.

A meager draft of fresh air thinned the smoke enough to make it breathable.

I have to get Brell.

He had lost sight of her.

Just as he was about to push himself up, the door flung open. Spots of light exploded in his eyes when a boot hit him in the face.

Something heavy fell across his back with a grunt, and he pushed up, getting to his feet.

He leapt into the fresh air of the hallway and sucked in a huge gulp.

The smoke thinned to reveal a confused guard inches from his face. He glanced at the smoky cell apprehensively. His companion had disappeared inside there, and he wasn't keen on finding out what had happened to him first hand.

He looked at Kase and smiled. The guard liked his odds against the smaller prisoner.

Kase did the first thing that came to mind and punched him. His fist connected with the guard's metal jaw, and the blow came to a bone-jarring stop. The punch did nothing but amuse the guard, who grinned at the pain on Kase's face. He lunged, throwing Kase against the wall.

Through the smoke, Kase saw his dagger tucked into the guard's belt and grasped for it. He glanced at the guard when he raised his other hand, which Kase saw was made entirely of steel. He balled it into a fist and reared back for a smashing blow.

Kase realized the guard was about to crush his skull.

Straining madly against the guard's vice-like grip, Kase clutched at the dagger tauntingly out of reach. His fingertips just brushed the dagger's hilt.

No good.

He furiously struggled to break free when the guard's hand loosened. The hulking brute slumped against him and tumbled to the floor.

Brell's smiling face appeared out of the gloom, and she patted him on the shoulder.

"It worked!" she said, pleased with herself.

"It did?" he said, still baffled. "All I know is I got kicked in the face."

"Win, win," chuckled Brell. "Let's go."

They raced down the corridor and turned at the first chance they got, then stopped.

"I don't know where to go," he said.

"This way," she said, pushing past him and took off. Kase followed as he strapped his dagger to his belt.

She started up the third set of stairs, and Kase paused.

"Are you sure this is right?" he asked. "I don't remember three flights of stairs."

"Did you count your steps? I did," she said, not waiting for an answer.

"I didn't think of that," he said.

"Feel better now?" she said. "You don't think exactly like me after all."

Their feet rattled off the stairs and down the corridors until a short time later, they came out on the deck next to the awning.

"Great work," Kase said, starting for the platform at the other side.

"Hang on," Brell said, calling him back. "I still have questions for Lynnder."

"Those guards are going to be here any moment," Kase said. "We don't have time to climb through this ship, looking for her."

"You forgot I've been here before. She'll be in Enoch's old rooms."

She ran along the side of the metal tower until they came to another hatch.

She pulled it open and slipped inside with Kase right behind. They raced up the first set of stairs, which emptied into a landing next to another set going up.

Breathing hard, they ran up the next three flights, turning sharply at the landing and heading down the corridor.

Kase was running behind her when she suddenly threw her shoulder into a door and charged in.

22

TRAITOR

Kase had no idea what he was charging into, but he wasn't letting Brell face it alone.

He ran in, ready to throw himself into the fight but stopped short at the nearly comical looks of shock on the faces of Lynnder and Otash.

Brell had her gun pointed at them, breathing hard and angry.

"One word comes out of your cake hole," Brell said, aiming at Otash, "and you're a dead man."

"How dare..." seethed Otash.

"Brell. No!" shouted Kase.

CRACK!

Otash fell to his knees, clutching his arm and howling in pain.

"I was aiming for his head," Brell sputtered. "Piece of junk."

She shoved it in her holster and crossed the room to Lynnder.

"You'll die for that," Lynnder bristled.

"You can thank me later," Brell said.

Lynnder's mouth opened in raw confusion.

"Madam President," Kase said, racing up to her. "In just a moment, two guards are going to come running in here. If they're loyal to you, they're going to tell you Otash ordered them to murder us."

"See how they're trying to turn us on each other?" Otash said.

Brell whipped out her gun and stuck it in his face. "Want to bet I don't miss from here?"

Otash threw up his hands, desperately trying to shield himself.

"The reason we came here was to ask you what you knew about the busted harvester," Brell said. "We heard a crazy story…"

They heard the approaching thumps of the running guards a moment before they charged in.

Their eyes quickly took in the scene and stared at the miserable Otash on the floor.

"Explain yourselves!" Lynnder demanded. The guards looked at the advisor, reluctant to speak. Fury swelled in Lynnder as she realized they were looking to Otash for instructions.

"Don't look at him!" she snapped. "I gave you an order. The truth. Now."

"He said you ordered us to kill the prisoners," a guard said.

"I told him," the other said, nodding his head at the first guard, "this isn't right. We should check with you first."

"No, you didn't," the other growled. "You always do what he says."

"What else has Otash told you to do?" she asked.

"They were mundane functions," Otash said. "I was only lightening your burden."

"What *burdens* were those?" she asked the guards.

The guards confessed everything they knew. A little at a time, Otash had used Lynnder's authority for his own gains – undermining her position and even meeting secretly with other clans to support his eventual takeover.

Contrite and embarrassed, the guards pled for forgiveness.

"I'll decide what to do about you later," said Lynnder. "Use what little time you have to show me I can trust you. Put Otash in jail then return for my next orders."

The guards practically lifted Otash off his feet in their eagerness to please her.

Otash went quietly, without protest, which Kase hadn't expected and found a little troubling.

Lynnder called her senior head of security and instructed him to gather the clans' leadership.

"Yes, ma'am," he said.

"Arrest anyone who refuses," she said coolly.

He saluted and left, leaving only the three of them in the room.

This started a string of people coming in as orders were given and questions asked. Brell and Kase knew it would be some time before Lynnder was ready for them. They made their way to the galley, where they were lucky enough to catch the cook before she finished making lunches.

When they returned hours later, Lynnder was alone in her office with the exception of a carpenter repairing the door.

"If someone told me that you were going to help save my clan," she said.

"Me neither," Brell said. "It's a funny world."

"All right," she said. "It's obvious you're not interested in small talk."

"No offense," said Brell.

"It's fine," she said, looking at the time. "I have another meeting in..."

"A harvester got attacked," Brell said, unwilling to wait any longer. "Did you do it?"

"Attacked?" she sputtered, taken aback. "No! Why would I?"

"The crystals were taken," Kase said. "You could use those."

"And refine them with what?" Lynnder asked. "When you came through my city, did you see any infrastructure or factories?"

"I didn't think it was you, but I had to ask," said Brell by way of apology.

"Because Stitchers are the first ones when you think of for vandalism and stealing," Lynnder said bitterly. "I don't understand you, Brell. You help my clan but look at us like criminals. You should go now."

"Right," Brell said.

They had burned this bridge, and they weren't going to learn anything more. She turned to leave.

"I saw a hand print," Kase said, "on the side of the harvester."

Lynnder looked at him, confused but curious.

"It was enormous. The thing that left it would have been sixty feet tall."

"A giant," Lynnder said hardly above a whisper.

"A guy from the refinery said that's what he saw," Brell said, sensing Lynnder's interest had shifted.

"Come with me."

They went into the hall where several people were waiting to talk with Lynnder.

"Wait in my office," she told the group, ignoring their questions.

Brell and Kase followed her down the stairs and out to the large deck.

"Some people come here because their minds can't accept the augmentations," she said, leading them across the large platform. "The best I can do is give them a place where they can't hurt themselves or others."

They retraced their steps from earlier in the day and were soon crossing the gangplank back to shore.

"Their mental illness takes different forms," she said. "Depression, anger, confusion. And sometimes, hallucinations."

Kase and Brell traded looks, suspecting they were on the track of another clue.

They came to a narrow spit of land that crossed the swamp and opened to a wide island. It appeared to be a small version of the city with homes and gardens.

Several of the people smiled when they saw Lynnder and started to approach but stopped in their tracks when they saw the two strangers with her. Some faces were fearful, others filled with distrust. They hurried away, into their homes.

"This is the Farm," Lynnder said. "It's a safe place for them, where we can treat or, at the very least, make their lives easier."

"Wouldn't their lives be easier if they didn't put artificial things in their bodies?" Kase asked.

"What he means," Brell began.

"I know what he means," Lynnder said, stopping and turning on Kase. "What do you do when you can't get the job you want because your eyes are too weak to see or your other senses don't work? You can't drive or fly. What if you can't speak, or you feel like you're going to die because after a few steps, your lungs give out? Most of these people just want a normal life but can't afford the surgery."

"He doesn't mean to be insulting," Brell said, glaring at him. "He's just... you know. Stupid."

Kase flushed, pursing his lips but didn't say anything more.

It was enough to satisfy Lynnder, who led them to a small home, neat but stark.

"Jatus," she said, knocking on the door. "Are you there?"

Kase prepared himself for whatever self-imposed disfigurement was about to appear.

The door opened, and Kase flushed pink as an attractive girl appeared.

"Hi," she said, brushing her long blonde hair out of her face. The light caught the flecks of blue in her walnut-colored eyes as they swept over Brell and Kase. She glanced at Lynnder in an unspoken question.

"This is Brell and Kase," Lynnder said. "They are safe. We'd like to come in."

"Okay." She frowned but stood back, allowing them to enter in spite of her misgivings.

Much like the outside, the interior was simple, bordering on barren. The few pieces of furniture she had gave the impression they only existed to convince the occasional visitor that she was normal, like them.

Jatus sat with her hands under her legs and looked everywhere but at her guests.

Kase, on the other hand, couldn't keep his eyes off her.

Her shoulder-length blonde hair was tied back in a ponytail, but a few strands had slipped out and framed her gentle features. The flecks in her eyes reminded him of snowflakes at dusk.

"How have you been?" Lynnder asked.

"Good!" Jatus said maybe a little too brightly. "No nightmares for a while. I think I'm getting better. That's a good sign, isn't it?"

She looked at Lynnder, searching for a sign of hope.

"That's why we're here," Lynnder said.

"My hallucinations?" she asked, anxiously. "Who are they?"

"They want to hear about the graveyard," she said.

Jatus paled, suddenly looking terribly frail and vulnerable. Kase's chest unexpectedly ached and felt an overwhelming urge to comfort her.

A wave of cold water crashed onto his emotions as Jatus pulled off her flesh-colored glove and picked up a handkerchief to blow her nose.

Her hand was entirely mechanical. Tubes and wires ran across the back of her hand, protected with a clear covering ensuring nothing could be snagged or damaged with normal use. The palm and fingers were highly polished and clearly several steps above the other augmentation Kase had seen so far.

"I don't understand," she said. "Everyone knows it was all in my head.

"I can better explain afterward," Lynnder said. "Do this for me, please."

Jatus paused and breathed deeply as she called up a terrible memory.

"Me and four others, we were scavenging at the graveyard," she began, her hands fidgeting.

"A graveyard?" Kase said a little too loudly.

"Not that kind," Brell said. "It's a big landfill where broken tech used to be dumped."

"Oh," Kase said, feeling awkward under the girl's stare.

"You can find anything there," Jatus said. "The deeper you dig, the further you go back in time."

"I'd like to go exploring there," Kase said to Brell.

She ignored him, keeping her gaze on Lynnder.

"I had the best salvage crew." She smiled. "They could find a glass filament in a square mile of junk. Once, we were..."

"Can you tell us about the last time you were there?" Brell asked.

The smile faded from Jatus's face, and she stared at the floor.

"We were looking for small things," she said. "Power cleaners, actuators, but it's dangerous there. Predator synths have built warrens under the junk. They go for miles. You have to keep your eyes open. They can come at you from any direction."

"Predator...*synths*?" Kase said, staring at Brell.

"I'll tell you about it later," she said with a dismissive wave.

"We shot at a couple of them to make them keep their distance. But we knew they were watching us. You could hear the strange way they cackle, coming from their hiding places. Then everything changed. They started yipping and howling. You could hear them running, like, scattering. A couple of them ran right past me. No attack, nothing."

She looked at them with a brittle smile.

"Kenzmen said he's got something good but needed help pulling it free. The others joined him. Whatever he found, it was deep. Really deep. They had to squeeze their way in. It can get crazy claustrophobic," she said, nodding. "Not everyone can do it, but hey, it's for a good cause." She nodded to Lynnder, tears beginning to shimmer under her eyes. "Isn't it?"

"Yes," Lynnder said. "The best one any of us can do."

"Then I hear a strange hum from deep inside the mound of scrap. I thought, you know, my hearing was acting up. Except Kenzmen says he hears the same thing."

Jatus nodded to herself, muttering. "He heard it. It wasn't just in my head. That's when everything started moving," she said, looking for understanding in their eyes. "I mean, the whole mountain of scrap, okay?" She held her arms apart, nodding. "I'm thinking, um, they triggered a cave in. I called them, but all I heard on my comms was yelling."

Her shoulders hitched, and her bottom lip trembled.

"Calling my name," she stammered. "Pleading for me to save them."

Kase was doing everything he could from going to her side and comforting her. He couldn't understand how Brell could see this poor girl come apart in front of her and not do something. He glanced at her and saw Brell's face was tight and pale. Though she was sitting ramrod straight and had her hands folded neatly in her lap, her knuckles were white.

"I was climbing my way to them as fast as I could when the top of the mountain... blew. There were hunks of giant scrap dropping down around me like boulders. One of them must have hit me because that's all I can remember."

Brell and Kase looked at Lynnder in confusion.

"Jatus," she said. "That's not all you remember, is it?"

"Yes," she said. "Everything else was a delusion. Things my mind made up... to deal with the guilt."

"I believe it was real," Kase said.

"Wh..." stammered the girl, glancing at Lynnder. "What?"

"The mountain of scrap," said Brell. "What did you see?"

"The mountain grew like a volcano. The top kind of blew open; stuff flying everywhere. This... thing climbed out. The night sky was behind it. It was hard to see details." She stopped and took a shuddering breath, steadying herself. "There were eyes. Towering over me, glowing in the dark. Whatever it was, it must have crushed a junked power core because there was an explosion as it climbed out of the pile. There was light and sparks everywhere. It was beautiful and horrible at the same time."

"You saw a giant," Kase said, "didn't you?"

"Yes," she said hardly above a whisper. "It was real?"

"The same thing ripped the guts out of a harvester," Brell said. "Could you tell if it was organic or tech?"

"Tech," she said, trying to accept that she wasn't insane after all.

"What happened after that?"

"We found her," Lynnder said. "She was wandering out in the wastelands."

"None of my crew ever came back," she said.

"We couldn't make sense of her story," Lynnder said. "We thought it was augmentation dementia."

"If someone else saw it," Jatus said, "then... I'm not... crazy?"

"No," smiled Lynnder. "Did you find out what you wanted?" she asked Brell.

"Enough."

"Thank you for ..." Jatus said.

"Yeah," Brell said, standing up. "You're welcome." She turned to Lynnder. "We have to go."

"I'm going to stay with her," she said. "I appreciate the risk you took coming here."

"Good luck with your clan," Brell said, heading for the door. "And Jatus, believe in yourself more than others. It'll save you a lot of grief."

"There you are!" grinned Brell, as her truck came into view. "They didn't hurt you, did they?"

Kase stood by, feeling awkward as Brell took her time inspecting the truck for signs of damage.

She lovingly patted the hood before climbing inside.

"I told you no one would touch it." Ning frowned. "What will you do now?"

"I'm going giant hunting," Brell said, chuckling. "That'll look good on my resume."

"We're going to the graveyard?" Kase asked. "Don't you think we're a little under equipped?"

"Do you have a better idea?" Brell asked, getting in the truck. "Someone's got the crystals, and they're standing between me and my new gear."

"What about the predator synths?" Kase asked, climbing in.

"They're nothing," Brell said. "I'll tell you on the drive there."

"They sound like something to me," mumbled Kase to himself.

She put the truck into gear and rolled smoothly out of Freedom City.

Brell looked up through the windshield at the lowering sun, clicking her tongue.

"A whole day wasted," she said. "Let's see if we can't make up a little time."

Before Kase could brace himself, she put her foot down on the accelerator, and the truck leapt forward.

"Are you sure that's what she said?" Otash asked, listening through the jail door.

The guard on the other side spoke quietly, his mouth near the doorjamb.

"Yes," he said. "The girl told them about the giant and everything."

"Send a message," Otash said. "Tell him they'll be coming."

"I will," the guard said. "And the girl's doctor?"

"Tell him to leave her alone," he said. "I don't want him to cause suspicion."

"What about Lynnder?" the guard asked. "I can let you out and take care of her before the sun comes up."

"No," Otash said. "She'll let me out soon. I have more to do before the time is right."

"I'll be ready," the guard said. "Say the word."

"Good man," grinned Otash.

The sun was down by the time they passed the Stitcher bar, but both agreed they'd be better off stopping for the night somewhere far away and off the road.

Their headlights swung off the packed road, to a rolling landscape of scrub and rugged trees. They drove for a mile before she was satisfied they wouldn't be seen from the road and stopped to camp. Kase was already tired, and the rough ride had rattled away the energy he'd had left.

The compartment inside the truck bed had the bare essentials for a single camper. Luckily, she had enough blankets to make a passible pad for Kase to sleep on, even though his feet hung off the end of the truck bed.

Brell set up her sleeping bag near the truck and climbed in for the night.

It was a rare moonless night, and Kase had a grand vista of the sky. The great canopy of stars spread from horizon to horizon in pinpoint clarity of the desert air. Sweeping the eastern sky was a wispy band of white and orange clouds studded with dense stars belonging to the Fritag Galaxy.

The ancient disk of stars had been slowly spinning across the night sky since recorded history. Kase felt his thoughts drifting when...

Zip!

The truck bed briefly lit with a blue light.

He sat up as the light disappeared and peered over the side of the truck at Brell, who was sound asleep.

I didn't imagine that.

He waited and watched for the light but nothing happened.

I'm too tired for this.

He was about to lie down when a tiny ray of blue light lanced out from the small lantern next to Brell.

The light hit something crawling, which curled up on its back and stopped moving.

"Only one to a sleeping bag," Brell mumbled and rolled over.

Kase glanced around the desert encircling their camp and all the crawling, slithering things it held. Suddenly, he didn't mind the unforgiving floor of the truck bed.

The first thing Kase noticed before opening his eyes was his body's complete and utter refusal to move. Between the hard truck bed and the chill desert night, every muscle and joint had locked up. Every movement brought new protests from somewhere in his body.

Brell handed him a cup of brew, which he thankfully warmed his hands around.

Judging from the bags under her eyes and disheveled hair, she hadn't been awake very long either.

"Was it any better on the ground?" he asked, looking over the side.

His eyebrows rose as he saw a ring of electrocuted insects around her bag.

She murmured something into her cup as she took a long pull on her steaming brew.

She waved at him to make room on the tailgate of the truck and then sat next to him as they watched the distant horizon fade from dark blues and purples to oranges and pinks.

The quiet around them was only disturbed by the occasional breeze rustling through the scrub.

Kase imaged what he would see if he was in this place hundreds of years before.

It would have looked exactly the same. Completely undisturbed.

He pictured explorers finding their way through here. He was looking at the same things they saw. His imagination took him further back, the years blurring until there were wetlands. The land was green and soggy, populated with countless insects and wildlife.

Going back further, the wetlands became ponds, then lakes until the water level rose. Kase looked up, imagining standing on the bottom of the ocean, looking up at the rippling surface hundreds of feet above. The tips of the distant mountains had once been islands.

And what was before that?

"Are you going to drink it or marry it?" Brell smiled.

Kase blinked out of his haze, looking at his cup hovering just in front of his lips.

"Well," she said, sliding off the tailgate and putting down her cup. "I'm going to find a bush and then we can figure out what to do about the graveyard."

After she came back, she took her seat on the tailgate again.

"I was thinking about that," Kase said.

"The graveyard?"

"The giant," he said.

"I'm not convinced there is one," she said, surprising him. "They saw something, but eyewitnesses aren't always reliable."

"The history of our world is based on eyewitnesses." Kase scoffed.

"What can I say?" She shrugged. "People are fallible."

"Whatever they saw," Kase said, "it was big."

"Oh, yeah."

"Do you have a plan in case we run into it?" he asked, glancing around the truck bed.

"Run away," she smiled, patting the truck. "Really fast. Besides, the giant – or whatever it is isn't my target."

"It's whoever has the crystals."

"Right," she said. "We find them, get the crystals, and get out."

"I think whoever attacked the harvester is hiding the giant in the graveyard," he said.

"It makes sense," said Brell, grinning at him. "The graveyard is secluded in the middle of the desert, and has plenty of room to stash the thing under a layer of junk."

"I'm curious to see this place," said Kase, sliding off the tailgate.

"Oh, okay." She grinned. "Looks like we're heading out."

A short time later, they had packed up and were pulling onto the dirt road. As the miles ticked by, the landscape became more desolate. Islands of craggy mountains broke the flat horizon, and the patches of scrub disappeared until there was just sand and rock.

Nothing grew out here.

23

THE GRAVEYARD

"Are there any towns around here?" he asked.

"No," she said, glancing at the map on the dashboard. "It's miles and miles of empty wasteland. That's why they picked it for the graveyard. It's not safe to be around old tech once it starts to degrade. The old fashioned power cells would eventually leak. It mixed with other tech, and, yeah, it made a mess."

"Huh."

"Huh, what?"

"Magic doesn't have toxic waste," grinned Kase.

"No," she said. "Just curses, monsters, and demons."

"Which reminds me," he said. "Predator synths?"

"Oh, yeah," she said, shifting in her seat. "Once they started making bots intelligent enough to perform simple tasks autonomously – that means without a person..."

"I know what it means," said Kase.

"Someone came up with the idea of using them for protection," she said. "Military sites, personal protection, things like that."

"They gave guns to robots?" Kase asked, astonished.

"See, that," Brell said, "It's that kind of thinking that gets in the way of real progress."

Kase could see the chasm sized argument that had just opened in front of his feet. Any other time, he might have felt like challenging her but not today.

"So they didn't arm them?" he asked, ignoring her jab.

"No," she said. "They could only trust bots so much. But they still wanted some form of autonomous protection. The next thing off the drawing table was the first generation predator synth. Kind of a four legged shark that can walk and run on its hind legs or on all four."

"That doesn't sound like a mistake waiting to happen at all." He smirked.

"There's always bugs that have to be worked out," she said. "But they eventually worked out the kinks."

"How many of those kinks killed people?" he asked.

"Hardly any. They were used in remote, highly sensitive locations. If anyone was killed, chances were they had broken into a place they didn't belong. The funny thing was, though, every now and then, one of them would go missing."

"Do you mean like they got lost?"

"Lost. Wandered off. Chased a squirrel, who knows," she said. "It didn't occur to the boneheads in development that when they embedded bits of animal behavior like, loyalty, obedience, things like that, they also included a pack mentality. If there wasn't a well-defined pack leader, they'd go looking for one or become one themselves."

"And you end up with wild synths," he said, "roving the countryside, staking their territories, and protecting them against intruders."

"Something like that," she said. "But they seem to be happy staying away from human populations."

"So what you're saying is these, what did you call them – walking sharks?" he said. "They gathered in desolate areas."

"Yeah," she said.

"Far out here, as an example."

"Now you're getting it."

"And your gun isn't working."

"That could be a problem," she said. "But they're not aggressive. They were programmed to protect property, but outside of that, they have a very limited response pattern. It makes them easier to anticipate how they'll respond if we encounter them."

"In other words," he said, "avoid at all costs."

Hours later, they hit a very wide, well-worn road, and Brell turned off to follow it.

"This is the old road the waste trucks took to the graveyard," she said.

"If someone is hiding something in the graveyard, wouldn't they be watching the most obvious routes to it?"

Brell abruptly veered off the road, the truck jolting over the rugged terrain.

"Maybe," she said.

Kase grinned but kept looking ahead.

They took a long sweeping path for several miles until Brell came to a stop.

"We're here," she said, turning off the truck.

Kase looked around but saw nothing other than the same flat landscape as the past few hours.

"Come on," she said, getting out and walking ahead.

Happy for the leg stretch, he climbed out of the truck and trotted up next to her.

They came to a stop, and Kase gasped at the epic sight in front of him. A few feet from the tips of his boots, the ground abruptly dropped hundreds of feet into a massive gorge that spanned for miles to his left and right. Straining his eyes, he peered into the distance, seeing the multi-colored, banded canyon walls far, far away.

The late afternoon sun threw the bottom of the gorge into dark shadow, giving the sense they were standing on the brink of a bottomless pit.

"It's almost like a second Rift," he said, stunned by its size and beauty.

"Except this one is natural," said Brell.

"Has anyone explored it?"

"I don't know," she said. "Probably, but then they turned it into a landfill."

"Which part?" he asked, frowning.

"All of it," she said, sweeping her arm from one side to the other. "Everything down there is junk."

"How many miles of it is trash?"

"All of it."

Kase gawked in disbelief. "It's impossible to fill something this huge."

"Generations of use," said Brell. "No one's proud of it. All that junk had to go somewhere. It was only in the last two hundred years that the technology to recycle every piece of tech was developed. Nothing is thrown away anymore. That's why no one comes here. Plus, the toxic levels are off the charts but don't worry. We won't be there long enough to get sick."

"Where do we begin?" asked Kase. Scanning the huge chain of canyons, he judged it could take a few lifetimes to sift through it all.

"The same place the Stitchers saw their monster," Brell said. She showed him a map on her arm terminal. "They would have to carry out whatever they'd found. Here's the closest natural passage down there. It's steep, but we can walk it."

"What's that?" he asked, tapping the display.

The 3D image zoomed in to a large structure with a series of smaller outer buildings.

"An old processing plant," she said.

"That looks like the perfect place to start," he said. "This ridgeline should give us a good vantage point." He circled his finger over the map. "Once it's dark, we can watch for lights, signs of movement, something like that."

"It sounds like you have everything worked out," she smiled.

"I've spent half my life sneaking into ancient sites," he said. "It's what I do."

"Did your ancient sites have rampaging giants?"

"And that's what you do," grinned Kase. Brell rolled her eyes as an ironic smile turned the corners of her mouth.

They got back in the truck and followed the edge of the gorge at a respectful distance. Several times, they had to turn sharply away when they came up on an arm of the canyon jaggedly carving away from the main abyss.

The sun made its final flare of light, sinking out of sight, as they found the narrow passage that angled steeply down into the canyon.

Brell drove at a crawl after a couple of near crashes when the truck lost all traction. The truck slid on a sheet of loose pebbles and dirt, toward the rocky walls before finally coming to a stop. After several tense minutes, they made it to the canyon floor.

She backed the truck out of sight, between the folds of canyon walls, where they left it and headed out on foot.

Softer stone had eroded away, creating a natural shelf they used to climb to their vantage point.

Below, they could make out the large bulk of the processing plant. It looked as ancient and derelict as everything else.

"Larcast, I see someone – no, two people on the ledge," a figure said, clothed in robes.

"It's them," another said.

"We should kill them now," a third said.

"No," hissed Larcast. "The master wants to question them. They'll come, and we'll let them. Have your spells ready."

"Return of the fallen," they chanted, tensing in anticipation.

"I haven't seen anything move," Kase said, "and my rear's getting sore."

"It looks dead to me too."

"Maybe the giant was moved after the Stitchers discovered it?"

"This job is starting to feel like a no-win situation," she said, getting up.

"On the other hand," he said, "I wouldn't call running into a giant a success."

They carefully followed the rock shelf to the canyon floor, then made their way to the processing plant, staying to the canyon walls to hide their approach.

The robed figures silently moved through the shadows, finding vantage points among the debris. They began slowing their breaths and focusing their minds. Their spells training had taught them how to resist the ever present tidal force of magic before committing themselves to casting their spells.

Larcast stiffened, hearing a footstep crunch on rock.

They're close!

"This place really is dead," whispered Kase. "There's no birds, or insects."

"Hang on," Brell said, tapping on her arm terminal. "Let's see if I can pick up any energy readings. The range on this isn't much, but… Yeah, I'm not seeing anything."

They made their way to a pathway running between the canyon wall and a high mound of debris.

The robed figures stayed completely still, ignoring the tickle of sweat and their cramping muscles. Their heartbeats quickened as the two intruders came to the mouth of the passage.

The trap was about to close on them.

Larcast tensed in anticipation. He blinked the sweat out of his eyes, and they were gone. He stared, thinking the dark was playing tricks on him.

The shadowy figures were gone.

Risking giving himself away, he inched his head up and peered over the jumbled edge of junk.

Where are they?

His brothers were already in place, hidden and silent.

How do I tell them? What if they confuse me with them and cast?

A moment ago, he had felt strong – part of many and able to overwhelm the two intruders. But now that he was on his own, doubt made a quick meal of his confidence.

The glory of single-handedly bringing his master both of them made him smile. Yet, he didn't think he could win against both. He pulled his knife from under his robes. *One will have to be enough to satisfy Master.*

Larcast slipped from the shadows and crept along the edge of the debris to where the figures had disappeared.

They chose the other passage.

Only one path led to the processing plant, and that was where the ambush had been set. The other path meandered along for miles to nowhere.

He flexed his grip on his knife and quietly gave chase.

Larcast smiled, imagining the look of surprise on the intruders' faces when he slid his knife between their ribs. Before the other knew what was happening, he'd cast a paralyzing spell on them.

What a trophy... and my first kill.

A sound!

He froze, squinting into the darkness ahead.

Kase looked up the endless path, wondering how far it went.

"We could be doing this all night," he whispered quietly.

A voice!

Larcast prowled closer, trying to find the shadow swimming in shadows. Were there two? More? It was too dark to tell.

His soft boots hushed over the arid ground, and he moved his hand, finding the favorable angle for the killing thrust. He changed again, unsure where flesh ended and shadow began.

With his next step he lashed out with his dagger. His hand whipped back then plunged, expecting to feel the warmth of spilled blood.

Pain exploded through Larcast's body. His limbs locked, and every muscle bunched and shuddered. Lights exploded in his eyes, and he toppled forward with a wheezing groan.

Brell stepped out behind him and holstered her gun.

"At least stun works," she said.

The first thing Kase saw when he turned around was a wickedly sharp knife at his feet.

"You were right about the ambush," he said, picking it up.

"A lucky guess," she said. "That's where I would set up guards."

"And he hasn't returned?" Naz asked.

"No, Master," the acolyte said.

"Find the intruders," he ordered.

The acolyte bowed and left.

Naz dropped his chin, pondering his next move.

The room was filled with a low hum he felt through his bones. It was a reminder of the great destruction at his fingertips, but that temptation was also a distraction.

"Doctor Katrell, is it ready?" he asked.

"No," said Katrell, squinting at the bank of displays. "Some of the systems aren't responding."

"You must hurry," he said.

"If they power up out of cycle," she said, "they're almost certain to overload and rip themselves apart."

"How long?" asked Naz, his eyes closed.

"These warbots are archaic machines," she said. "Their degraded condition makes them unpredictable."

Naz stretched out his hand toward her. Red mist began swirling around it.

"How long?" he repeated.

"I'll do what I can," she gasped, her wide eyes fixed on the mist.

He dropped his hand, the mist vanishing.

"Master," an anxious voice crackled from the overhead speaker. "Two more followers are missing."

"There must be more than two intruders," Naz said. His eyes roamed the room as he rapidly decided his next move. "Gather my remaining acolytes. I'm coming." He turned to Katrell with a disturbing smile wriggling across his face.

"Power it up in five minutes," he said. "Kill all of them."

"B...but," she said pleadingly, gesturing to the systems board. Several of the status displays were still red.

"I know you will do your best." He pulled his cloak around him and left the control room, working his way through the plant to the exit.

He stepped outside and strode down the pathway to his waiting followers.

They looked at him with trembling anticipation as he considered them with a benevolent smile.

"I am Naz," he said, raising his hands. "The worthy receive this rebirth."

"We receive," they said, their eyes shimmering with joy.

Naz's face tensed as he fought to master the flow of magic. The air around his hands rippled. Translucent waves of energy spiraled out, enveloping four of his followers. Naz turned his will on the magic, twisting it, tapping into the darkness that waited to be called on.

The others watched between horror and envy as the four spasmed, their eyes rolling back in their heads. Their mouths gaped open in silent screams of agony. Under their robes, bones snapped, flesh ripped and reformed.

Deep lines carved into Naz's face as he grimaced. His teeth clenched, and cords of muscle stood out on his neck.

An acolyte's hand appeared from his sleeve, their fingers cracking backward as flesh bunched, pulled, and thickened.

Their hunched shoulders widened as he grew taller.

His agony faded, and his spasms came to an end.

Naz smiled up into the impenetrable darkness within their hoods. Smoldering yellow eyes glared down on him.

"You are now vassals of the Fallen One," Naz said.

The remaining untouched shuffled away from them as the four uttered a chilling, hollow moan.

"Spend yourselves in his cause," Naz said.

"*Chu magreht ronah*," they answered with voices not meant to be heard among the living.

The hulking misshapen Vassals turned and left down the path.

Naz breathed deeply, wiping the sweat from his face.

"Return to the city," he said. "Continue seeking out new followers."

"Master." They bowed and left in a swirl of robes.

Unsteady at first, he went back up the path and into the control room.

"And you say Stitchers are abnormal?" hissed Brell, ogling at Kase. "Did you see what that Naz guy just did?"

They were lying on top of a scrap pile overlooking where Naz had just left, squeezed into the shadows.

"Magic," he said grimly. "Very dark magic."

He felt a tickle at the back of his mind.

"What did he say his name was?" he asked.

"Naz."

"That's the same mage Gamion was hunting," said Kase. "Remember?"

"No."

"We need to follow him," Kase said, ignoring Brell.

"Didn't you just see him turn those people into... things?" Brell said. "There's something seriously wrong with you people."

They heard the thud of heavy feet coming up the path. It was one of the yellow eyed creatures.

It stopped at the base of the scrap pile, slowly turning.

They could hear it sniffing the air.

Kase glanced at Brell as she quietly eased her gun from the holster.

Its eyes came into view as it looked in their direction, but its gaze passed by.

Brell aimed and squeezed the trigger.

The gun bucked in her hand, and the creature instantly leapt. The energy bolt smacked harmlessly into the dirt.

"Where is it?" she asked.

The steel above them sank with a thud as the creature landed behind them.

"Ba gee yash!" it wailed. A thorny tentacle lanced out from its robes, sinking its hooks into the thick metal sheet, and flung it tumbling into the air.

Brell rolled onto her back. There was no time to worry if the gun would work and she flipped the setting to full power, and fired.

Her gun bucked three times, fast. The crackling bolts tore into the creature, punching scorched holes into its robes. The bolts flew out of its back and kept going.

The air filled with the stench of burnt decay, but the creature didn't even flinch.

A second tentacle shot out; the creature grabbed for both of them. Kase cast a *push* spell, knocking it off its feet. Garbage clattered and banged as the thing plunged helplessly out of sight.

"Go. Go. Go!" shouted Kase, but Brell was already scrambling to the path below. He landed and pointed to a pocket of deep shadow. "There!"

They raced inside as they heard the bang of the monster landing above them. Kase felt ahead with his hands, fearing at any moment to run against a dead-end, but it didn't come.

"It's a warren," he said over his shoulder.

"How do we kill it?" asked Brell, right behind Kase.

"Everything has a weakness," he said. "Fire? I don't know."

The warren echoed with a chilling scream from behind them.

"It's coming. I hope your theory is right."

"What theory?" Kase barked. "It could be anything."

Angry footsteps hammered through the uneven warren, closing on them with frightening speed.

Brell's stomach knotted as yellow eyes appeared from the darkness.

Sparks jumped from its barbs as the thing scraped them across the walls.

She pulled out a small soft triangle from her belt and flung it into its path. Thumbing the switch on her gun, she aimed and fired.

A field of stunning electricity crackled down the warren. The static field reached the object, stabbing it with needles of energy. The triangle erupted into a ball of fire. Air whooshed past Brell as the conflagration sucked it in with a howl.

The monster threw itself against the walls, blindly running for escape. Ribbons of flames lanced through it, but to Brell's shock, the creature gathered its strength. Struggling, it began to march out of the flames toward her.

Brell turned, her boots scrambling for traction, and collided into Kase coming the other way.

"What's hap..." The words caught in her throat.

Out of the darkness appeared the metallic, snarling face of a predator synth. Ice-blue eyes scanned them above rows of carbon alloy teeth.

"Brell!" stammered Kase as the predator reached out with its hybrid-fingered paw and grabbed him.

"It's ready," Katrell said.

"Wake it!" Naz hissed. "And attack."

Katrell sent the commands, activating the drive and reviving the long dead power source.

Buried deep under generations of garbage, a relic of ancient war awoke.

Like everything else in the graveyard, it had been cast aside when its usefulness was over. The terror and destruction it had rained down, wiping out entire cities, was now a faded memory. But its memory had not been erased. Naz had learned of these titans of war. He'd sought them out, sending his acolytes crawling through the graveyard, and he'd found them.

Hundreds of them!

Reviving all of them would take time. Arming them with his specialized weapon would take even longer, but once complete, he would use the Teck's own unnatural machines to wipe them out. All of them.

Anyone would laugh at the ravings of this madman, but the sobering, horrific truth was he could do it.

Unknowingly, Brell and Kase were about to see it for themselves.

Power surged through the giant's limbs. Banks of processors fired off billions of commands a second. Some systems, too far degraded, sizzled and fried.

"Eighty-three percent response," she said. "Drives engaged. Artificial awareness and optics are working. Spatial…"

"Enough!" said Naz uninterested in the meaningless words. "Does the thing work?"

"Yes," Katrell said.

"Then kill them."

The predator synth froze as the world around them began to hum.

It let go of Kase and ran.

"I feel it too," Kase to Brell said.

"We can't go back," she said.

Regardless of its determination, the fire had gravely injured it, slowing it down.

"This way," said Kase, fast crawling on his hands and knees.

They'd gone mere feet when the floor beneath them heaved, pinning them to the ceiling.

The floor dropped, and the two raced to reach the other end of the warren. The floor heaved again with a crushing roar of thunder.

"Why hasn't the warbot moved?" demanded Naz.

"I don't know," Katrell said, searching the readouts for an answer. "Maybe we underestimated the weight of debris? It can't push out?"

"Give it more energy," Naz said.

"Any more and the power core could detonate. It could vaporize..."

Naz glared at her, his face twisting with anger. She paled and turned back to the control board; her fingers tapped over the displays. Several of the indicators turned red. One began flashing a warning.

"I see light," Kase said, speeding up.

The freshening air on this face was like an elixir of promise that they would soon be free.

They jumped into the open and ran, hoping it was the quickest way out of the graveyard. They charged through the weaving path, their chests heaving for breath. Rounding another curve, they skidded to a stop.

A few feet away laid the shredded carcass of the predator synth. Standing over it was one of the robed vassals. It looked up at them, and its yellow eyes flamed with renewed malice.

Kase cast a *push* spell as barbed tentacles snaked from its robe, but the creature hardly moved.

Brell fired over and over, each bolt sizzled through it with no effect. Bunching its shoulders, the monster flung the synth's wreckage out of its way and stepped toward them.

All of them flinched as steel and debris crashed together as the mound of trash rose next to them.

In an ear-splitting avalanche, a giant erupted out of the mound of junk.

Kase yanked Brell into a pocket of the canyon wall as the vassal screeched before disappearing under tons of garbage.

All thoughts of the creature vanished as they craned their heads up, gawking at the enormity of the giant.

They could hear the angry whine of motors as it fought to free itself from the mound of junk.

"It's snagged on something," Brell said.

"Fascinating," Kase snapped, nudging her towards the pile of scrap in their way. "You can tell me all about it while we run for our lives!"

Shaking off her daze, Brell scrambled over the junk with Kase right behind her.

They raced out of the graveyard, stumbling over loose rock, and ran for the hidden truck.

With massive effort, the giant strained and finally pulled free.

"It's coming," panted Kase.

24

HUNTED

Kase didn't have to tell her. Brell could feel the impact of the giant's footfalls.

They quickly slipped into the fold of the canyon wall and dove into the truck.

Brell punched the power, and the truck came to life.

"Hang on," she said.

The truck lurched forward, then violently stopped, throwing Kase into the dashboard.

A huge foot crashed into the ground just in front of them.

They looked up through the windscreen at the warbot. Its head turned as it searched for them.

"It doesn't see us," Brell whispered between gulps of air.

The age of the warbot was visible. The outer shell of its leg had large corroded holes exposing the motors inside.

"Can you see a way to cripple it?" Kase asked.

"I don't have anything that big," she said.

The giant rocked on its feet, then turned, moving its foot out of the way.

Brell didn't waste a second.

She punched her foot onto the accelerator, and the tires dug in. Dirt and rock kicked up, pinging off the truck's body as it shot out of its hiding place in a trail of dust. The giant's head snapped around and zeroed in on them.

A wrecking ball of a metal fist crashed into the ground just behind them, launching the rear wheels into the air.

Spinning wildly, the tires came back down, and the truck shot off in a plume of dirt.

"We can't outrace its reach," shouted Kase above the howl of the truck.

Brell yanked and spun the steering wheel, throwing the truck in erratic turns.

"Faster!" Naz yelled.

"Several systems are overheating," said Katrell.

Naz's face darkened. He wanted to see death, and the longer he had to wait, the less discrimination he'd use when deciding who to punish for the delay.

"The path!" shouted Kase, pointing to the narrow ramp they'd taken to the canyon floor.

In a fraction of a second, the warbot calculated the truck's speed and direction. Then it determined its most likely evasive maneuver and punched down.

Brell saw the stars blotted out of the sky above, instantly understanding why.

Her hand flew to a covered switch next to her seat. She flipped the cover out of the way. She cringed in anticipation as she flicked the switch.

Jets of white flame blew out from the rear of the truck. Their bodies were savagely slammed against their seats as the truck catapulted forward.

The giants crushing blow thundered inches behind them,

throwing the truck off course, sending them flying at a jagged canyon wall.

Brell turned off the switch cutting off the jets and grabbed the wheel with a death grip, wrestling the truck into a sharp turn. The truck swayed sickeningly, and Kase braced himself as the right side tires came off the ground.

"You're going to miss!" Kase yelled.

Brell jerked the wheel, and the truck slammed down, fishtailing toward the ramp.

They flinched as the truck glanced off the ramp's rock wall, sheering off the fender. They skittered to the other side, but Brell fought it under control and straightened out. The truck flew up the gully, desperate to escape the warbot's reach. Shards of rock banged off the truck as the giant smashed into the narrowing gap, making a final grab for them.

Brell gripped the wheel with both hands, her face drawn and tight as she tried to steer them up the winding path, around hairpin turns.

They slid sideways, smacking the wall, the spinning tires whined, blowing plumes of burnt rubber into the air.

"We're out," Kase said, rubbing his head where it had hit the window. "It can't reach us in here."

"Can it climb?" she said through gritted teeth. "It got out of the canyon before."

Kase's stomach churned at the thought of seeing the giant appear at the canyon's edge.

The rock walls fell away as they reached the top of the canyon. Wide open sky and flat terrain stretched before them.

"Let's not wait around to learn the answer to that question," he said.

They both craned their heads around, fearing to see the giant's head rise into view as it climbed out of the canyon, but it didn't appear.

Brell slowed. Not by much but enough to have full control over the truck.

By the time they reached the dirt road, the truck was making a terrible noise and parts of the body were rattling in the wind.

"They got away?" Naz said, trying to keep his temper under control.

"The autonomous systems were never designed to attack small objects," she said.

"Bring it back," he said. "I'll send for one of my pilots. He'll finish the job."

"You're sending the warbot after them?" she asked, typing the return command to the giant.

"We're too close to the day of our attack to be discovered," he said. "Those weren't Stitchers. Someone will listen to them. I cannot afford being exposed. Not now."

He went out the door and climbed the stairs until he reached the roof of the building. He walked over to a long table on the far side and stood, looking down on several drones. Many were in the process of being cobbled back together from what parts could be found in the graveyard.

They had small bodies and wings that spanned out two feet. A metal polymer flexible sheet spanned between each rib of the wings, giving the drones a bat-like quality.

He moved to the few which were already repaired and held his hands over them, closing his eyes in concentration. He began murmuring and casting. An ethereal light formed over the silver bats and seeped into them. One after another, they picked themselves up and looked at him with their camera eyes.

"You know what I'm looking for," Naz said, having completed his enchantment. "Find them. Go now," he said, sweeping his arm.

Each of the drones beat their wings, climbing into the night sky. Naz reached out his mind to each of them, seeing what they saw.

The bats spread out in every direction according to Naz's orders and began their search.

"We have to warn the people at the refinery," Kase said.

"What about the Stitchers?" Brell winced as a piece of the fender flew off the truck, tumbling behind and lost to sight in their dust.

"They aren't the ones in danger," Kase said. "The giant went after the Gramite. The miners need to know what they're up against."

"It's a warbot," said Brell. "An old one."

"Why would you bury a war machine in a dump?" Kase asked, amazed.

"It wasn't like that," Brell said, pausing as she tried to think how to explain it to him. "Okay, it was a little like that. But this was a hundred and thirty...thirty-eight years ago. It was at the end of the war with the Reliance Union. The bots were supposed to be decommissioned. Weapons stripped, dismantled, systems gutted."

"That did not look gutted to me," Kase said.

"I know," said Brell, gazing at her mangled truck. "I was there."

"Wait, *bots*?" Kase said, suddenly realizing that she'd said plural. "How many of those things were buried there?"

"A lot." She could feel Kase staring at her, expecting a better answer. "Hundreds."

Kase blew out a long breath as he visualized legions of giant machines. "You people are insane."

The sun was still an hour away from cresting the horizon, but the sky was taking on a lighter shade of blue.

Brell ignored him and she ran her hand lovingly over the dashboard, murmuring something to it.

"I don't understand why anyone would go to the trouble of resurrecting one," she said. "It's an antique compared to modern weapons."

"Sure," Kase said, looking at his shaking hands. "Practically harmless."

"Nobody makes parts for them," Brell continued. "Their power systems are completely outdated."

"The armor had holes in it."

"They wouldn't last ten minutes against current military weapons. They're no threat to anyone."

"Except the harvester," Kase said.

"And the Gramite," she said.

A new knocking sound came from somewhere in the truck and Brell brought the truck to a stop.

They got out, and she circled her pride and joy, assessing the damage.

"Will it get us out of here?" Kase asked.

Brell climbed underneath and disappeared with only her feet sticking out. Kase couldn't resist seeing what was under there. Lying on his back he wriggled over the warm ground until he was next to her.

"What are you doing?" Brell asked, scrunching her face as she waved at the added dust.

"I'm looking at the belly of your truck," he said as his eyes roved the engineering mystery of cables, hoses and composite steel.

They laid under the truck in silence for a few moments as she watched him survey the machine.

"It's fascinating," said Kase.

"You don't even know what you're looking at," she scoffed.

"Why should that matter? Someone turned an idea into all of these moving parts that can carry us hundreds of miles without stopping." Kase looked at her, grinning. "Doesn't that amaze you."

"When you put it that way," she said.

"What are we looking for?" he asked.

"*I* am looking to see if anything's broken."

"And?" he asked.

"It looks like it'll hold together," she said, and squirmed back out.

Kase followed her and dusted himself off as she peered up at the sky

"What?" he asked.

"Funny," she said. "I saw something shiny."

He searched the sky but only saw a blue field of dimming stars.

She shrugged it off and got up, dusting off her pants as she went to the bed of the truck.

"I have to remove this fender before it gets sucked under the axel," she said, pulling out the toolbox. "Or else we'll be in for a long walk."

High above, the small metallic bat sent out a signal as it wobbled in the air, looking down on Brell and Kase.

"Found them." smiled Naz. "Is the pilot in the warbot?"

"Yes," she said.

"They're not heading to the city," he said, puzzling a moment. "They're going to... the storm fields. The refinery!" he said. "Tell the pilot where to find them."

"And then?" she asked.

"Kill them, of course. Destroy every trace they were there," he said. "I don't want a single clue about what they saw here, getting out."

Inside the cockpit of the warbot, the pilot lowered the optics visor over his eyes, allowing him to see through the warbot's optics.

He walked the big war machine to the end of the canyon, where the wide mouth sloped up to the surface.

He switched the warbot into track-mode. Ancient hydraulics disengaged the bot's joints and folding in limbs. Four huge tires pivoted into place as the bot turned into a large armored transport. The pilot engaged the drive and drove the warbot up the incline and out of the canyon. He headed to the dirt road which ultimately led to the storm fields.

Hours later, Brell turned off the road, which curved away from the fields.

"Keep your eyes open for miners," she said.

Kase nodded, looking out onto the blasted landscape. Only a few minutes ago, they had been basking in the late-morning sun with a spotless blue sky overhead. Now they were in a land of perpetual dusk with thick dark storm clouds roiling overhead.

"There's a truck out there," he said, pointing.

She looked, seeing a maintenance tractor similar to the one they had ridden in.

"Hang on," she said and steered into the field.

Kase gripped the dash, watching for small dangerous craters.

"It's okay," she said. "The tires will insulate us from the crystals... I think."

They quickly reached the tractor and were met by a confused crew.

"You want me to tell the ops manager what?" the miner asked, holding the comms link.

"We are investigating what happened to the harvester," Kase said. "Did you hear about what Galin saw?"

The miner snorted. "Oh, the monster. The guy's paranoid."

"We think it's on its way here," Kase said.

The miner's grin disappeared, and he glanced over their shoulders at the broad void of the desert landscape.

"Here?" he asked. "Now?"

"You saw it?" another asked.

"You need to clear everyone out of here," Brell said.

The miner radioed for the operations manager, who instantly lost his temper.

"... you tell them if they aren't gone when I get there, I'm going ..."

The miner held the radio away from his ear until the manager's voice lowered.

"You better go," the miner said, hanging up the comms.

Kase was studying the sky, noting it was slowly becoming darker. He could feel the hair on his arms bristle.

"Tell everyone in the field to get back to the refinery," Brell said, climbing back into her truck.

"If you're still here when that thing shows up, it'll kill you." Kase got in, and Brell pulled away as he fought to close the dented door.

The miner watched them leave, sniggering under his breath. But his eyes drifted out to the wide spread of desert. The thought of how little of the wasteland had been explored began to scratch at the back of his mind. He peered into the distance. Far off objects shimmered in the waves of heat...

Or are they moving on their own?

He picked up the comms.

"This is Coomy," he said. "The, er, tractor is acting up, and I'm bringing it in."

He tossed the mic on the far seat and got in to the surprise of the rest of the crew.

"If anyone wants to leave," Coomy said, "this is your chance."

Their eyes filled with apprehension as they glanced between their boss and the empty desert.

"Are you say'n you believe a monster's coming?" asked one of them.

"I'm not saying anything," Coomy said, starting the engine.

The others hesitated until the tractor's lights blazed to life and the crew quickly piled in. With a final glance at the desert, Coomy turned the tractor in a tight circle until he was pointed at the refinery and sped up.

"There's a harvester out there," Kase said.

Brell glanced out his window and saw another of the big machines deep in the storm field. Shepherding alongside it was another tractor.

The clouds were moving faster, and Kase was sure he saw a flash of purple light deep within their belly.

They turned into the field, and the truck began being pelted with dust as the wind gathered strength.

"I don't like this," Kase said. "We don't have suits."

"That idiot manager isn't going to recall the crew," she said.

Kase was starting to smell the strong metallic scent of lightning. It was a warning sign, but it wouldn't do any good to tell Brell they were going in the wrong direction.

As they passed the wreck of the harvester, Kase stared at it, visualizing the giant tearing into it.

Brell tried to avoid the small craters and spare the truck further abuse, but the wind was making it hard to see. She kept her eyes on the tractor ahead.

Moments later, they pulled up and waved the tractor crew down.

"You can't be out here without a suit," one of the miners said. "Are you trying to get yourselves killed?"

They told the miners about the warbot, warning them to get away. The miners laughed off their story.

"It's true," Kase said.

"Look," one of them said, "I don't know and I don't care. I got a tight schedule to keep. In case you didn't notice, there's a storm building. You two morons get out of here because I'm not stinking up my tractor with your smoldering corpses."

"He's right," Kase yelled over the gusting wind. "We have to get out of here."

Even Brell couldn't ignore the angry clouds overhead and the gusting wind.

They climbed in, feeling the buffeted truck rock.

"I hope we're wrong," she said, turning the truck.

A short way ahead, they saw the dark silhouette of a vehicle coming their way.

"I didn't think the manager would really come out here," she said.

"He'll arrest us this time."

"No he won't," she said. "I know his type. A lot of chest pounding and threats. We'll be out of here..."

"Why is he stopping way over there?" said Kase.

They squinted, watching as the distant vehicle came to a halt, its headlights stabbing through the gusts of dirt.

"I don't know," said Brell, and slowed down as they got closer.

A curtain of grit and sand swept in front of them, obscuring their vision. The headlights went off, and the vehicle appeared to lose its shape, but it was hard to tell what was happening through the sheets of flying debris.

"Are you seeing..." began Brell, when huge arms extended from its sides.

"Go!" Kase yelled as the object pushed itself off the ground.

The huge warbot stood to its full height, towering over them.

Brell grunted as she threw the truck into reverse. The tires spewed funnels of dirt as the truck backed up.

Kase watched as the bot's head followed their movement and swept its hand at them.

She turned the wheel and hammered her boot onto the accelerator when the warbot hit the side of the truck with a bone-jarring blow, sending it spinning into the air.

Safety pads deployed in the truck's cab, cocooning them in place just before it landed. The truck flipped end over end, sending the rear axle cartwheeling away.

They came to a stop upside down as the pads released them.

Inside the warbot's cockpit, the pilot tried to find them through the blinding wind, unwittingly giving them time to drunkenly crawl out of the wreckage.

Brell was bleeding from a gash on her head, and Kase couldn't use his left arm. A short distance away, they saw the carcass of the harvester and stumbled for it.

The wind eased, and the warbot pilot saw the truck. He hurriedly lumbered over to it and, without pause, drove his fist down, pile-driving into the truck, crushing it to a wafer.

"We can't stay here," said Kase. "Maybe we can run..."

A lightning bolt slammed down outside the harvester, shattering the air.

The concussion wave punched their bodies, knocking them back.

Groaning for breath, they crawled deeper into the harvester, desperate for shelter.

"No chance of hiding here," Brell said. "It'll open up the rest of this thing and find us."

"We have to run," said Kase.

"Out there?" she said. Beads of sweat ran down her face, following the creases of fear.

"We can either die in here," said Kase, "which is a certainty, or out there, which is nearly but not entirely certain."

A shadow moved in front of the gaping hole, and they sunk their heads down as the warbot stooped down.

It craned its head, peering into the front compartment, moving objects out of the way with its finger.

"Get ready to run," Kase said.

Brell squeezed his shoulder, and he concentrated on an illusion. He felt like he had had his eyes closed for ages, but it was only for a few seconds.

They watched the great armored head turn toward them. Kase waited for only a moment more, then leapt forward, casting a shower of sparks into the warbot's face.

The pilot's inexperience showed as the optics flared bright white in his eyes, and he jumped back. The warbot's motion tracking followed the pilot's movements, and it stumbled back, losing its balance. It fell back, hitting the ground with a crash.

Brell and Kase raced out into the open and scanned for their best escape.

To their left was the open desert. To their right, the Nightcrag mountains.

"The mountains!" yelled Brell. "The bot can't work in the dead zone."

It was their only chance.

The wind had reduced to random gusts as they pumped their legs, ignoring the choking grit in their noses and mouths.

Angry and bruised, the pilot pushed himself up and kicked the harvester, crushing its middle and sending it rolling over. He was about to rain blows down on it when...

"They're running away," Naz said, watching through the system' monitor.

The pilot looked up and saw the two small figures weaving through the field.

They felt the impact vibrate through their boots and knew the warbot was running up behind them.

They searched ahead, but the mountains were too far.

Suddenly, Brell grabbed Kase's arm and yanked him over. She held onto him, guiding him around a large crater. She glanced over her shoulder at the closing warbot and stopped.

"What are you doing?" he yelled, scared she had given up. He looked into the empty crater, perplexed about what was happening.

He tried pulling away, but her vice-like grip would not break.

Wham!

The warbot's foot landed making the ground under Kase tremble. Fear dug its icy claws into him, rooting him in place and locking his limbs.

The pilot paused, expecting them to run. Before, his target had been an object, a machine. It had been easy when it had just been a thing, but now he was looking at people. He had never thought about killing anyone before. The reality of it shook him. He feared how it would change him.

"What's wrong?" growled Naz.

"Master, I..." stammered the pilot.

"Your worthiness to be *my* acolyte is on trial," Naz said. "Kill them, and I will know you are ready to ascend. You will become an arch prefect."

The pilot gasped, unprepared for such a high honor. It was within his grasp, the authority and power, second only to Naz himself.

In his mind, the two figures below him transformed from being living people to obstacles, literally standing in his way of exaltation.

He attacked.

The warbot came at Brell and Kase. Intent on snuffing out their lives, it stepped forward.

Brell threw Kase to the ground, landing next to him.

"Cover your eyes!" she screamed.

Kase's face smacked into the acrid ground, and he looked up in time to see the wind gust through the crater, exposing a sliver of purple crystal.

He shoved his hands against his eyes and buried his face in the ground as the bot stepped into the crater.

The thinly armored foot of the bot came down, crushing the gem and releasing its energy.

Blinding light flared in a funnel of searing heat and energy. The bottom of the crater liquified. The warbot's foot took the brunt of the scorching blast; the escaping heat singed Brell and Kase.

The crystals' massive energy crackled up the body of the warbot, leaping past its insulated systems and shooting into the cockpit. Forks of energy stabbed into the pilot, instantly turning him to ash.

Naz winced under the bright flare of the monitor. It returned to normal, and he blinked the spots out of his eyes to see the charred remains of his follower.

"Fool," he hissed. "Switch auto pilot on," he shouted to Katrell.

Katrell bent over the command board. "Autonomous systems coming on."

Kase and Brell spit the dirt out of their mouths as they got up and stared at the warbot. They forgot the storm for a moment as they watched smoke funnel out of the bot's chest. It was completely still except for its gentle sway in the strong winds.

"Fifty credits says it falls to the right." Brell grinned, her teeth shining brightly in her dirt-caked face.

"I say left." Kase chuckled. "And it catches fire."

Fingers of ice-cold dread closed around them as they heard a deep whine from within the warbot. They looked up in horror as its head turned and looked down at them.

"Are you joking?" said Kase.

"Run," Brell yelled, but Kase was already ahead of her.

"Why is the soulless monstrosity not chasing them?" snarled Naz.

"The systems are badly damaged," said Katrell.

"They cannot be allowed to reach the mountains," he screamed. "Stop them at any cost."

Katrell scanned her controls, her face stretched with tension as she tried to make sense of a system she had only begun to learn.

She saw something flash on the screen.

Override.

She pressed the screen, and new system data began scrolling.

Wham!

The vibration of the warbot's footstep radiated out, and they knew without looking that the giant wasn't dead and, instead, coming after them.

They covered the first hundred yards at full speed and quickly hit the limits of their bodies. Their breaths came in ragged drags, and their lungs burned.

Kase's legs felt like bags of sand, but he wouldn't give up. Not with the mountains just ahead.

Somewhere behind him was Brell, but it was taking all his concentration not to trip over the rough terrain. If he fell, he knew he didn't have the energy to pick himself up.

He reached the low spine of the mountain and instantly smelled the sulfur of burning lava. He didn't know where it was coming from, but he could feel intense heat radiating off the rock.

The spine rose sharply as he turned, running deeper into a gully. The rocky path turned and wound like a snake, taking him deeper into the mountains.

"It's too late," Naz said. "We can't follow them into the mountains. Call off the machine."

"It's not responding to my commands," the woman said, trying the controls.

"No!" Naz roared, pushing her out of the way. He rained his fists down on the controls. "They can't know what I'm doing."

25

OUTSIDERS

Where's Brell?

The question rang in Kase's head with mounting urgency. He risked a glance behind him. The relief gave him new strength when he saw her close behind.

Brell gave him a thumbs up as she caught up to him.

"We're safe now," she said, panting. "It can't work in the dead zone."

Shards of rock exploded behind them, and the warbot pushed its way into the gully.

Brell stumbled, and Kase grabbed her as she groaned in pain.

"My arm is..." she grunted. "I think something hit me."

Her arm hung limply at her side. He threw her good arm over his shoulder and they ran.

"After this," he wheezed, "we're going to a nice, boring place where nothing ever happens."

Brell snorted, and he felt her pace quicken.

The ragged walls of obsidian rose around them as they raced deeper into the cleft of the mountains, leaving the struggling warbot behind.

"At this rate," Kase said, "it will soon be too tight for that thing to follow us."

They rounded a sharp bend and felt their hearts sink.

A dead end.

Chests heaving for breath, they searched for another way; a foothold to climb, a cranny to squeeze through, or a boulder to tunnel under – anything to escape.

"We're trapped," Brell said. "We literally have to climb over that bot to get out of here."

"All right." Kase gasped changing tactics. "When I cast my spell, you –"

"Even if we get past it and make it to the storm field, then what?" she said. "There's miles of open desert. It will catch us."

Before Kase could protest, a huge metal hand appeared, reaching out and grabbing a wall of rock.

Their ears filled with the shriek of metal as the warbot forced its way between the jagged rock.

Exhausted, Kase's face creased into a snarl as its head came into view. It turned and fixed its lifeless eyes on them.

Kase flexed the fingers in his hand, and he willed the magic to come.

All of it.

He knew what that meant. At least this way, Brell had a chance.

The warbot didn't pause to gloat or ponder. It went for the killing blow.

He only had a moment, and he squeezed his eyes closed, but before he could focus, the ground violently shook, knocking him and Brell off their feet.

Dust and stone showered down from the ravine walls as they watched, riveted with shock, as two gargantuan rock figures stepped out of the walls.

They charged the warbot, stopping it in its tracks as they attacked with staggering ferocity.

Brell and Kase scrambled out of the way, grimacing as enormous rock fists landed with ear splitting thunder claps. Metal screamed, twisting under the massive fists of the giants.

One of them swiped at the warbot, ripping away its arm in a spray of metal, gears, and hydraulics.

The warbot recovered its balance and attacked, locking its fingers together and drove its spear-like hand at the other giant.

It crashed into the giant's chest in an explosion of sparks and stone. The giant lost shape and stones tumbled apart. But in the same instant, the other giant swung its fists together, trapping the warbot's head between them. The rock walls trembled with the shockwave as the warbot's head was pulverized. It wobbled on its feet, and the stone giant hammered it in the chest, lifting tons of warbot off its feet.

The remains of mangled steel collapsed to the ground.

Brell and Kase gawked at the stone monster as it turned toward them.

"Halt!" a voice said behind them.

Kase and Brell spun around, seeing five people behind them.

"Who…" began Kase

One of the strangers stepped forward, wearing a talisman similar to something Gamion wore. Frowning, the stranger swept their hand at Brell and Kase, in a wide arc. They fell over and everything went black.

Woozy and confused, they opened their eyes discovering a crowd of unfriendly faces around them. Some were more curious than angry. Others brimmed with loathing and resentment.

"Your names," one of them demanded.

His dark eyes matched the rest of his features. He was dressed in a high collared shirt, pants, and brown boots with decorative emblems on the side of the leg.

Through his fog, Kase's brow knitted, recognizing a sword was hanging from the man's belt.

"Names!" he barked.

"Kase," he said, wincing. The man's voice wasn't simply loud. It was like nothing he had experienced before, piercing through his will to resist speaking or avoid the truth.

Brell grunted, scowling at him.

Kase could see it was having the same effect on her.

"Brell," she answered, blinking the grit out of her eyes. "Shout at me like that again and I'll beat you into next week."

"I'll speak as I wish. You brought your machine to attack our borders," he said. "You're fortunate you are still breathing."

"That wasn't our machine," Kase said. "It was chasing us."

"They are lying," a woman accused. "They brought tech to break through our defenses, to kill or spy on us.

"Spies? Are you joking?" Brell scoffed. "That thing was trying to kill us."

The man held up Brell's belt and gun.

"Are you going to deny you're Teck as well?" he asked.

Brell looked around the large room for the first time. They were seated in ornate chairs, unable to move, but she couldn't see any bindings.

The large room was cool and still, a jarring change from the past day and a half's experience.

Warm, richly carved wood accented the marble room. The walls rose high up, curving into an arched ceiling.

The polished floor was covered with a large rug of deep blues with a red and gold border.

Kase's gaze wandered from the large windows to the tapestry hanging on the opposite wall. His foggy mind tried to make sense of the hanging as the scenery was impossibly undulated. He glanced at the windows again, thinking the wind was the cause, but they were closed.

Blinking, he looked more closely and realized the tapestry was alive with motion.

The embroidered figures, trees, and animals were all moving, endlessly acting out a moment in time.

"You're Creet?" he blurted.

"We are," said the man, holding out Kase's spiritbridge. "But your trophy hunting is over."

"Chamberlain, I've seen enough," someone else said. "They're spies and killers for Naz."

"He's right," someone else said. "Execute them now."

A stern mage stepped forward and raised both of his hands. "My pleasure."

"I'm Creet!" Kase said. "That glove is mine."

The mage stopped, glancing between Kase and the man wearing the sword.

"You are a mage?" asked the man. "Release his hand so he can prove it."

"You cannot be serious, Gramath!" the mage said.

"If not, then he will trap himself in his own lie," said Gramath.

"And what if he unleashes…"

"Are you afraid the boy can outmatch your power?" he asked. "Do it."

Kase's hand was freed, and the man stepped up, roughly shoving the glove onto his hand.

"This is reckless," another protested. "What if he's a mage for Naz?"

"Naz only accepts naturals," Gramath said, holding up his hand and stopping further complaints. "Go on." He smiled. "Show us."

Kase thought of what he could cast. A *push* or *pull* at any of the people standing in judgement of him would instantly be seen as an attack, and the old mage would snuff out his life like a guttering candle.

He could feel the weight of their eyes on him as he searched for a way to demonstrate his magic without being seen as a fraud or threat.

"Where are we?" Alwyn asked.

'*I don't know. We're in Teck, but these are Creet.*'

"They don't look happy with you," he said. "What did you do?"

'*It's a long story, and I don't know how much of it I even understand.*'

"Why are they looking at us like that?"

'*They want me to use magic and prove I'm Creet, but I'm nervous. What do I do?*'

"Tell them you're Creet," Alwyn said.

'*That's what I'm trying to do.*'

"I mean *spell it out* for them," he said.

'*Oh. I understand.*'

Kase closed his eyes, shutting out everything around him.

My leg hurts. Did I ... Focus! Spell it out. Spell it out.

His ears rang from the terrific crashes and explosions of the lightning and giant's brawl.

Focus!

He tried again, clearing his mind and centered only on his spell.

"He's making a fool of us," the mage griped.

Gramath ignored him, watching Kase.

Kase's breathing slowed, and he let go of the tension. His mind became centered as he visualized his spell.

The crowd gasped and murmured among themselves as letters took shape above Kase's head and formed into the words, 'I'm Creet.'

The older mage gaped at him and turned to the man with the sword. *He's one of us. I know it.*

Gramath nodded in agreement.

"Set him free," he said.

With a nod, the mage released Kase from his invisible bindings.

Brell tried to move too, but she was still secured in place.

"Hey," she said. "Any time now."

"Explain why you are with this... Teck," Gramath demanded.

"First tell me who you are," Kase said, feeling more confident.

"This is Salta Dyrin, the sovereign and rightful land of Creet. I'm the First and the Royal Chamberlain. I serve our princess Altrese. If that satisfies your question, we will return to why you brought a Teck into our lands. The same is true if it does not satisfy your question."

"Not to split hairs," Brell said, "but we were *outside* your land. You were the ones that brought us in."

"She makes a good point," Kase said. "We didn't know any of this existed. We were trying to escape the machine."

"I don't trust her," the mage said. "And I don't trust her excuse for being here."

"If it makes you feel any better," Brell said, "I'm just as unhappy about being here as you."

"Our being here is entirely by chance," said Kase.

"Anyway," said Brell, puffing an annoying strand of hair out of her face. "I vote you let me go. I'll be out of here, and everyone will be happy."

"We're wasting time when we should be examining the machine our guardians destroyed," the woman said. "Mal'Beck, kill her so we can turn our attention to the important work."

The mage glanced between the woman and Gramath.

"She's my friend," Kase said, stepping in front of the old mage. "She's not a threat to anyone here or any Creet."

The group threw sidelong glances at Kase, and he could feel the shift in opinion turning against him.

"You have her weapons and my word," Kase said. "On my honor, she is trustworthy."

Mal'Beck glanced at Gramath, who nodded in return. Brell's bindings vanished, and she moved and rocked her shoulders, working out the soreness.

"She was hurt during our run from the warbot," Kase said, seeing her arm was still limp.

"I can try to heal her," the mage said.

"No," said Brell, holding out her hand. "No offense, but I don't want anyone using that inter-dimensional woohoo stuff on me. I'll be fine, thanks."

"You don't look fine," Kase said.

"Don't worry about it," she said, rubbing her arm. "It's an old injury. I'm used to it acting up." She held her hand out to Gramath. "My belt if you don't mind."

"I do," Gramath said.

Kase's attention had wandered back to the tapestry, reading the story it told.

"This city has been here a long time," he said.

"Longer than long," Gramath said. "Since before the Rift."

"Why didn't you return to Creet?" Kase asked.

"This is our land. Generations of Creet have lived and died here. We weren't going to surrender it to be defiled by the Teck."

"Both Teck and Creet had to evacuate their lands and return to their own worlds," Kase said.

"We're aware of the agreement," Gramath said. "Those were promises made without our consent."

"Consent or not," Brell said, "the pact was made. You shouldn't be here."

"What did you do when the Teck told you to leave?" Kase asked.

"They never have," he said. "They don't know we're here."

"The forces that created the Rift also worked to conceal us," the mage said.

"You're kidding," Brell said. "Now it's playing favorites? The Rift swallowed millions of people when it formed, but you it decided to spare?"

Gramath glanced darkly at her before going on.

"Everything you saw outside our kingdom didn't exist before the Rift," he said. "The storm fields and mountains formed during the upheaval when the world fractured. It created a natural barrier that has protected and kept us hidden for centuries since."

"Even the very ground you stand on defeats your prized technology," the mage said.

"You might want to rethink that," Brell said. "That warbot had no trouble walking up to your front door."

"That was not lost on us," Gramath said. "It appears your people have created a new technology that resists our protection."

"There's nothing new about that warbot." Brell scoffed. "It's outdated by more than a hundred years. Secondly, and you're going to love this one, but it wasn't *my* people that sent that warbot after us."

Everyone glanced between Brell and Kase, their faces a mix of confusion.

"The machine was under the control of Naz," Kase said.

"Impossible!" Mal'Beck said. "Even he would not stoop so low."

"I think he would do anything to achieve his own goals," Gramath said.

"Who is Naz?" Kase asked.

"A prince... once," said Gramath. "Now an exile and a stain on our people's history. He and Altrese ruled our people together. But he began exploring dark magic."

"A disgraceful act for any mage," the old mage said. "It wasn't enough that he began practicing it; he created a secret sect of followers loyal only to him."

"Our laws forbid dark magic in all its forms," Gramath said. "He knew if he persisted, we would have no other choice but to exile him. He dared us to try."

"That's when we discovered he had been anticipating this day," the woman said. "His followers have been secretly working their way into positions of power and influence. Judges, lawmakers, military leaders, and senators."

"Once in place, those followers sowed the seeds of division with accusations that we, the sworn servants of our kingdom, had been plotting to overthrow the throne," the mage said. "Their lies gathered strength and influence until it drove us to the edge of a civil war."

"And that would have been our fate, except his sister, the one voice he would listen to, became very ill," Mal'Beck said. "For once, he blamed himself, believing the chaos had broken her spirit, and he was right. The only thing he thought could save her was if he could mend the damage he had caused. But the fire had been set and was out of his control. Swords were drawn. Spells were readied. But it all came to a shocking halt when word spread that Naz had suddenly left."

"To save his sister, he finally accepted the judgement of the law and exiled himself," Gramath said. "With him gone, there was nothing to fight about. Like removing the flame under a boiling pot, heads cooled and people saw reason. We returned to peace."

"For a short while," the mage said. "The burden of knowing what he had done to his sister gnawed at him. I believe he couldn't bear the pain. Eventually, he twisted the truth, turning the blame on to us. He offered to return, ease the burden of the kingdom from her shoulders. But he would not reject his use of dark magic. We denied his return. He accused us of choosing our own selfish wants at the cost of his sister's health. He said we turned our backs to the terrible burden that was leaching the life out of Altrese."

"In his mind, we are to blame," the woman said. "He swore he would take vengeance on us in her name."

"Not long ago, he came to see her," Gramath said. "He said he would be returning, and when he did, he would destroy everything, kill or enslave everyone."

"We've rooted out most of his followers, but the few remaining could hurt us," the mage said. "But not fatally."

"No," said Gramath. "And not enough to overcome the protection of Altrese."

"Not yet," said the woman, looking grave. Although the meaning was lost on Kase and Brell, everyone else in the room suddenly looked like a wave of sadness had swept through.

"Our princess has been taxing her great magical strength to protect our borders," said another. "She's enchanted guardians like the ones you encountered today, as well as crafted illusions to confuse and distract anyone trying to venture beyond the mountains surrounding our lands."

"But her time is almost over," said Gramath. "Even combining the mages in our city, we can't maintain the strength of magic that is needed to maintain our protection. When she dies, so will our defenses."

"I get it now," said Brell. "Naz figured out that the dead zone doesn't have any effect on the antique technology of the warbots. With them, he doesn't need thousands of followers."

"How many of those machines could your army face?" asked Kase.

"And win?" said Gramath. "Perhaps eight. Maybe ten."

"After the war –" Brell shook her head slowly. "They dumped hundreds of those warbots in the graveyard."

"You saw how massive they are," said Kase. "With only a small group of followers, he can't have dug up many of them. Not to mention, he's got to get them into running order."

"Yeah," Brell said, cocking an eyebrow. "That knocks down the number but not enough to make a difference."

"We shouldn't be talking about this in front of the Teck," the mage said.

"She's a trusted friend," Kase said.

"What better way to worm her way into our kingdom than by duping you into believing that?" the mage pressed.

"I can't be trusted?" Brell said. "I'm not the one ignoring peace pacts, squatting in someone else's country without permission or using magic to make monsters."

"Brell," Kase said, trying to slow her down.

"What happens if one of those rock giants decides it wants to get a little air and strolls into a Teck city?" she said. "People will panic. Someone's going to take a shot at it, and how will your monster react? 'Oh, sorry for the inconvenience,' and leave? You use magic without giving it a second thought, and if it goes on a rampage, well, they're just Teck."

"Brell!" Kase snapped.

She stopped talking, but her smoldering eyes spoke volumes.

"Put her under arrest," said Gramath.

She backed up a few steps and lowered her shoulders.

"Come at me and see what happens," she growled.

"Everyone wait a moment," Kase said, putting out his hands.

The old mage flicked his hand, and Brell suddenly went ridged.

She wheezed, her swearing hardly audible. Two sentries appeared and took her by the arms, dragging her out of the room as Kase protested, but his words could not change years of bias.

Brell struggled to free herself, refusing to accept that the magical bonds paralyzing her were stronger than her tenacious will power.

She fought until beads of sweat ran down her red flushed face. She couldn't even spit on the two jerks dragging her out like a piece of old furniture.

She was aware of everything around her but helpless to do anything about it.

The guards took her across a small courtyard and through a strong iron-bound gate. Ahead was a long barracks for the royal guard. Next to it was a single-story bungalow of gray stone. Barred windows were inset in its walls which left little doubt that this was her destination.

The door to the building was solid wood with black iron bands to reinforce it. The guard rapped on it, and an inquisitive eye appeared through the peephole.

It peered at each guard in turn before coming to rest on Brell.

With a rattle of keys, the door unlocked and swung open.

"Welcome," the jailer said. A broad smile stretched across his face as he swept his arm, inviting them in.

Brell immediately hated his grinning rat-like face and wanted nothing more than to punch it.

He scurried ahead, leading them to an open cell.

"Oh! She looks like a Teck," he said, delighted. "Am I wrong? I'm a very good judge of character."

"You're right again, Oako," one of the guards said.

"Ha!" he said, clapping his hands. "I knew it."

They shoved her into her cell, and Oako closed and locked the door.

"Will she be here long?" he asked the guards. "I should think we'll make great friends."

"That depends on the Royal Host," the guard said. "But if you heard how disrespectful she was, I'd guess she's going to be here a long time."

Oako's smile pushed into his cheeks, reducing his eyes to mere slits. His braided ponytail bounced from shoulder to shoulder as he nodded happily.

"Thanks for coming," he said, patting the guards on the back, simultaneously escorting and spurring them out.

He closed and locked the front door behind them, then watched the last of them through the peephole.

Once he was sure they were gone, he practically skipped back to Brell's cell.

She stood, frozen and helpless, locked behind stone and steel at the mercy of her jailer. Brell wanted to scream but even that was robbed of her.

"I'm Oako," he said. "What's your name?" His eyes got wide, and he made a small O with his mouth. "Sorry. I forgot about the spell. That'll go away in a moment," he said, waving a circle in the air. "Be

333

careful you don't move too quickly when it ends. Muscle cramps. The more you've been fighting it, the more it will hurt."

He winced, mimicking a painful arm and nodded sympathetically. Without warning, the spell ended and all of the pent-up energy Brell had used trying to break free exploded through her body. Just as the jailer had warned, cramps erupted all over her.

Gasping, she pushed her fist into her thigh, working out the worse of the two cramps.

"Thanks for the warning," she said, feeling the pain subside.

He watched her limp over to her cot and sit down.

"Has it been a rough day?" he asked.

"What gave it away?" she said.

"I heard Packral – she's our cook, was making up her famous fish stew. I'll bet that would make you feel better."

Brell hated fish. The odor was nauseating, and the taste wasn't much better. But she couldn't search for a way out with the jailer camped outside her cell.

"Sounds great," she said, forcing a smile out of the corner of her mouth.

"I knew it," said Oako, drumming his fingers on the cell bars. His expression of delight abruptly fell into a contrite frown. "It's not ready yet. I shouldn't have teased you only to make you wait."

"It's fine," she said. "Waiting for it will make it taste better."

"That's right!" he said. "I have to tell Packral I have a Teck visiting me. She'll be so jealous," he said over his shoulder as he unlocked the front door. "It'll be a few minutes before it's finished."

"Take your time," smiled Brell. "I'm not going anywhere..." He left, closing the door behind him. "... for the moment."

The door locked with a heavy snap, and Brell quickly began searching her cell for a weak spot.

Her head popped up from looking under the cot when she heard someone chuckle from the next cell.

26

PLANS WITHIN PLANS

The jail windows allowed for a generous amount of sunlight, yet the hooded figure in the next cell had somehow found a shadow to nest in.

"Did I say something funny?" said Brell, not in the mood.

"You're wasting your time," said the figure.

"It's my time to waste,"

The figure looked up, their eyes gleaming from the shadow of their hood.

"He said you are a Teck?"

"You're not as stupid as you look," Brell said, examining how the bars fitted into the window.

The figure got up and came over to the adjoining bars, peering at Brell.

"Your tech won't save you."

"Yeah, yeah. I've heard it all before," she said, continuing to search her cell. "Tech is bad. Magic's all powerful."

The figure chuckled, mumbling something to himself.

"That's what everyone in this city believes," he said, "but soon they'll all be on their knees, begging for mercy and then they'll know how wrong they were."

Brell yanked on a bar, which shifted just slightly, but it was clear she wouldn't be able to work it free without tools.

"Good luck with that," she said, distracted.

"The destruction will not end here," the figure said. "When this city falls, it will mark the coming death of your technology."

"What is it with you people?" said Brell. "You pull a rabbit out of your ear and suddenly you think you can wipe out an entire population?" She gave the figure a second glance and recognized they were wearing the same robes as the acolytes had in the graveyard. "Oh. I get it now. You're one of Naz's nut jobs."

The acolyte stiffened a moment, then squared his shoulders proudly.

"I have been chosen by Naz himself. I will be there when..." He paused, then smiled knowingly but didn't speak more.

"You mean the warbots?" she said. "That's old news, bathrobe boy."

The smile under the acolyte's hood faltered a moment before returning.

"We will storm this city," he said with growing excitement. "Their feeble magic won't stop them. Neither will the mysterious dead zone."

Brell kept her expression blank as the acolyte dropped a large piece of the missing puzzle into place.

"I'm with you there," she said. "These mages can wave their hands around casting spells until their arms fall off."

"Naz *will* make this land his," the follower said.

"Okay." She chuckled, rolling her eyes, unimpressed.

"You mock out of ignorance," he growled. "He'll slap that expression off your face when he comes for your cities."

Brell wondered if she was listening to empty threats or if he had just dangled a hint to something bigger going on.

Regardless of what she thought about Naz, he was resourceful and clever. Resurrecting the warbots proved he had embraced technology.

Yet, he had to know those relics were no match against current tech.

He's out of his mind! Or he knows something I don't.

"Attack a Teck city?" She laughed, goading him. "With those pieces of junk? A couple of pissed off old ladies with guns will turn your army back into a scrap heap."

"The day Naz unleashes his super weapon will be the end of your prized technology. All of it. Forever. Your technology will be wiped from the face of the planet."

"I saw Naz, you know," she said. The acolyte physically started. "Yeah, at his base. I was almost as close to him as I am to you. The way all of you morons talk about him, I was expecting something special. All I saw was a psycho do a couple of magic tricks and a rusty old bot. If he had a super weapon, I would have seen it."

The acolyte sputtered into a humorless, malevolent laugh.

"You have," he said. "Your godlike tech doesn't work here."

"Yeah, old news," she said. "Everyone knows the storm fields mess with tech."

"Look around you!" the follower shouted. "Do you see any storms? Any clouds or crystals?"

Something scratched at the back of Brell's mind. She glanced out the window, squinting in the ray of sunlight. She tilted her head, seeing wide open blue sky.

Something's not making sense.

The follower searched her eyes, looking for realization.

"Ahhhh," he said, gloating in the moment. "There it is. You almost understand, but you're missing the last piece."

She looked at him, waiting, hoping he wouldn't pluck away the clue dangling just out of her reach.

"You are standing on it," he whispered.

She stopped her eyes from involuntarily glancing down and held him in her gaze, willing him to reveal everything.

"Naz discovered it," he said. "It's been here from the beginning." He took out a small charm of polished yellow stone he wore around his neck. "This worthless rock is Kendium. It's everywhere in the ground, and it snuffs out the power that runs your technology like water on a match. But don't believe me. Wait until the first bombs explode over your cities, raining flakes of yellow. Legions of your armies, their guns good for nothing but clubs. Your machines, dead piles of useless hulks."

"All because of that?" asked Brell, her voice quivering. "It... it can't be possible."

He stepped close, holding it in front of her mockingly.

"Now." He laughed darkly. "You know what real fear..."

Brell's hand shot through the bars and grabbed the acolyte by his robe. His eyes flew wide as she leaned back and pulled. The bars rang as his head collided into the steel.

She caught the necklace as he slumped to the floor.

A moment later Oako walked in with a tray of sloshing bowls.

"I think she's outdone herself this time," he said, sniffing the steam coming off them. "I hope you're hun..."

He stopped, gawking at the acolyte spread eagle on the ground, then at Brell grinning at him through the bars.

"Open this stinking door," she said. "And tell your bosses I have something they're going to want to hear."

The table was surrounded with expressions of doubt, fear, anger, and grim determination.

"We can't wait until Naz has collected enough of his weapons," the general said. "We must attack. Right now, with everything we have."

To see the general on the street, some would assume by his round face and double chin that he lived an easy life of abundance. Yet, his outward appearance belied his flint-hard, warrior spirit and courage.

"I agree," one of the Host said.

"But you'll leave the city without any defenses," Kase said.

"We don't know how many machines he has," the general said. "If we piecemeal our attack, it may not be enough to beat him."

"What of our mages?" asked another member. "Surely, Calon, you can add them to your forces."

The general looked down at the table, doubtful.

"Most of our mages have spent their lives using magic for

everyday life," Mal'Beck said. "There may be only a handful who have experience with combat spells."

"We haven't fought a war ..." began another.

"In generations," another said. "Not since we drove the Hakwell from the deep lands."

"These mages are willing to put their lives out there to fight," said Mal'Beck.

"I'm not doubting their resolve," Calon said, "but it's easy to stoke a fire in a man's heart while he sits in the comfort of his own home. Those delusions disappear quickly in the face of bloody combat."

"They will do," a hushed voice said.

All eyes turned to see Princess Altrese looking at them with a weak. but gentle smile.

"I agree with the general," she said. "There's little left of me but breath. I cannot help defend the city if Naz comes to our gates."

No one spoke, but they bowed their heads in obedience. Altrese had led her people with unselfish wisdom her entire life. While they might not agree with her rulings, they trusted her decision.

"It will be done," Calon said with a curt nod.

Brell had remained quiet, feeling she had no voice in the discussion, but she could read Kase's expression and knew he was troubled by the whole thing.

He was an explorer, a traveler. The idea of being in a battle, even for the right cause, was unsettling.

The princess turned away, supported by her attendants, and shuffled out of the room.

"Gather the mages," the general said. "Assemble all of our guardians. We will leave before sunset. Not a word to anyone outside this room."

The people left to put the plan into motion... except one. The lone figure quickly stepped into an anteroom and took out a pad of paper. This was a magic pad and linked to another just like it. The words written on one pad would appear on the other.

The figure began to write. *My master...*

"How many does it say?" Naz asked.

The woman looked at the writing pad before speaking. "All of them," she said.

Naz grumbled in annoyance and took the pen from her. He scrawled on the pad.

Give me the number of guardians.

They waited, staring at the blank page until the answer appeared.

Eight.

"That's too many," the woman said.

"Nonsense," he scoffed. "It's hardly worth my effort. Thank them for the warning. Their devotion will be rewarded."

Miles away, the spy sat alone in their quarters, basking in Naz's praise.

The mighty stone guardians had never been seen together in such numbers before. Even Brell was moved to admit it was awe inspiring.

The mages guided them into a single file line as they lumbered through one of the secret city gates which opened near a spur of canyon.

The huge stone brutes looked as though they were sinking into the ground as they proceeded down to the canyon floor.

Kase and Brell followed near the back. The general had organized their marching order to keep the "least needed" of the assault force out of the way.

The tedium of the march built with each hour they walked. Anoux was rising over their heads, in the night sky. Its icy silver-blue light washed over them, casting long deep shadows in the rocky folds of the canyon walls.

The guardians strode on, their footfalls pounding the ground, shaking loose small funnels of dirt and rock from of the sides of the canyon.

They had traveled for several miles and had many more to go before they reached the graveyard. There, they would catch Naz by surprise. He would not escape alive.

Deep in the shadows, eyes watched as the army marched by.

Naz observed from a safe distance, gauging the moment of greatest destruction.

He waited until the last guardian had its back to his warbots.

"Now," he hissed.

The Creet turned their heads, hearing a hum suddenly mingle with the rumbling cadence of the guardians.

Two warbots appeared at the rear of the guardians' line and charged.

"Turn them," shouted the general.

The mages sent new commands to the stone giants, who turned as one to meet the attack.

The warbots collided with two of the giants with a deafening crash. The giants were caught off guard and off balance as the warbots rammed them into the ground.

The remaining giants closed on the attackers, swinging their powerful fists. One warbot was caught in the shoulder, and its arm was shattered from its body. The other warbot tried to dodge but was hit in the side, caving it in and bending it over.

"Now the rest," said Naz.

More warbots appeared behind the giants, attacking with massive clubs of rolled steel.

"Behind them!" shouted the general, but the mages had seen the machines at the same time and were commanding the guardians to turn toward the new threat.

The warbots swung their clubs from overhead, crushing the closest two guardians. Dust and rock exploded, and the giants fractured into piles of rubble.

"The mages are in reach," one of the warbot pilots reported.

"Leave them," Naz said.

"But..." protested the lead pilot.

"The guardians are the fangs," said Naz. "Without them, these wolves become dogs."

Naz watched the pilot's monitor as he turned away from the mages.

What was that?

His eyes went wide, and he leaned in close to the screen.

"Turn back," he ordered.

The pilot obeyed, showing the chaos and terrified faces of the Creet as they tried to rally their forces.

"Those two," Naz said, jabbing the screen.

Looking up at the warbot, Naz saw the faces of Kase and Brell. He had missed his chance to kill them the first time, but he wouldn't make the same mistake again.

"Kill those two," Naz said.

"I serve," the pilot said.

"I think that warbot is looking at us," Kase said.

"You're seeing things," she said. "We're not even in the fight."

"Look," he said, pointing.

She looked across the canyon to the other side of the battle. Kase was right. One of the warbots did seem to be looking right at them.

"Uh..." she said.

Then it started walking toward them, ignoring everything and everyone around it.

"Run!" Brell said.

They ran into a cleft in the canyon that sloped steeply up.

"We have to reach the top," she yelled as they were forced to scramble upward on their hands and feet.

A moment later, the warbot had crossed the canyon. It couldn't see into the narrow cleft but knew they were in there. The pilot blindly drove the bot's hand in between the rock, trying to reach them.

Kase and Brell came to a narrow shelf as the bot's hand battered into the rock wall again and again. The shelf was hardly as wide as their own feet. But it led them farther from the bot, and that was good enough.

They ran along it, their feet slipping on the loose gravel.

The pilot looked up and saw them, instantly realizing they were about to escape out of his reach. He charged at them, throwing the bot at the wall to reach them.

The side of the canyon shook violently, and the shelf fell away as Kase stepped down. Gasping, he dug his fingers into the rock wall, clinging high above the canyon floor.

"I can't go any farther!" he yelled.

"Up," shouted Brell. "We're almost there."

He glanced up, seeing the edge of the canyon just out of reach.

The pilot saw Kase hanging by his fingers and threw himself at the wall again.

Kase and Brell cringed as the huge steel machine came at them like a wrecking ball.

Desperate, Kase jumped across to the other ledge, not knowing if it would crumble when he landed or if he'd slip off.

He came down with a jolt on hard rock and ran as Brell landed at his heels.

The warbot hit, sending curtains of dirt and rock down on them as they scrambled for cover.

The warbot grabbed for them, spraying Brell's back with sparks as the bot's fingers hit just behind her, gouging scars into the wall.

They slipped out of sight and were gone.

Naz swore with rage, launching spells, melting holes in the steel and concrete wall of the control room.

"Kill everyone!" he roared. "No one lives. *No* one escapes."

The rock ledge angled up, and Kase's fingers closed over the top edge of the canyon.

"I'll climb up and... ahhh!"

Brell gasped in surprise as Kase flew up and disappeared over the top of the canyon.

A moment later, Hanover's smiling face appeared over the edge.

"Hi, gorgeous," he said. "Small world, am I right?"

He reached down and pulled her up with ease.

"Hanover?" she said, astonished.

"You have a knack for getting into scrapes," he said. "Lucky for you, I was in the neighborhood."

Brell frowned, looking out over the wide flat landscape. There wasn't anything for hundreds of miles.

"What neighborhood?" she asked.

Something felt wrong, and she noticed the fugitive cage on the back of Hanover's truck was open.

"We have to help those people," Kase said.

"Yeah," sighed Hanover, glancing at the chaos and destruction in the canyon. "Trust me. You don't want to be a part of that mess."

Hanover drew his gun and shot Kase. Kase's eyes flew open as the stunning charge paralyzed him, and he dropped to the ground like a felled tree.

"What are you doing?" she yelled, going for her gun.

Hanover pivoted lightning fast and shot her. She went rigid, dropping her gun.

He sighed, glancing at his fingernails as he waited for the stun charge to drop her to the ground.

He walked over and scooped up Kase, and eased him into the cage. Then he did the same with Brell.

He went back and picked up her gun, frowning at the worn-out weapon as he dusted it off.

"Look at this junk," he said to himself. "It's sad when the goods ones hit bottom."

Returning to the truck, he tossed it in the back seat, then locked the cage before climbing behind the wheel.

The stun effects were wearing off, and Kase shook his head to clear it. All that could be seen of the battle were clouds of dust billowing up from the unseen clash between warbots and guardians.

Naz gripped the edges of the table, his knuckles bone white.

"We've lost a third warbot," the woman said.

"They only have one guardian left," he said, breathing heavily. "I want all of those Creet rounded up and executed. I want their bodies burned. I want them to..."

He froze. Katrell looked at him with growing alarm as the color drained from his face and eyes filled with dread.

"What's wrong?" she asked, frightened at his sudden change. "Naz?"

He vacantly gazed ahead, his eyes unfixed, staring at something far away.

He groaned as though a terrible, crushing burden had settled on his shoulders. His eyes swelled with tears, and he bent over the table.

"Stop," he said, his voice low and ragged.

"What did you...?"

"Enough," he said, not looking up. "The fight is over. Bring my machines back."

Katrell stared at him, completely baffled as he climbed the stairs to the exit like a man walking to the gallows.

Trembling hands gently lifted the edge of the gauzy white linen and laid it over the still face of Princess Altrese.

The honor guards next to her bed stood at ceremonial attention, tears streaming down their rugged faces.

The lyricist, who had been preparing her death song, tried to sing to her fallen princess, but her words were stifled in a flood of sorrow. She knelt by the bed and bent down, her body racked with sobbing.

Across the city, black flags had been kept near for many days with the grim knowledge they would be needed.

A shroud of grief fell over the city, and all felt its heavy weight as the flags unfurled, their sorrowful message plain for everyone to see.

"You guys have been busy." Hanover chuckled. "I've been racking up a lot of miles following you."

"How long have you been watching us?" Brell asked.

"Since you left the city."

"Why did you wait until now to take us?"

"I had to wait for the contracts on you guys to go live."

"You're making a huge mistake," she said. "Let me out."

"Ha, ha, no can do," he said, grinning into the rearview mirror. "The bounty on you is twice as big as his. I was suspicious of what you were doing with a Creet on the airship, but smuggling him into our world? Wow, that was gutsy even for you."

"You second rate..." she growled.

"Okay," Hanover said, pressing a button on the control panel. "Nap time."

The cage pulsed, knocking out Brell and Kase.

When they woke up, they were handcuffed and strapped to a wall. Hanover was humming to himself as he picked up a scanner.

He did a little dance move as he crossed over to them.

"Rise and shine," he said, holding up the device.

A narrow fan of light traveled over Brell and Kase, then turned off. Hanover looked at the display and saw their 3D images appear on the two contracts for their arrest.

"Once I send these in," he said, "I'll drop you guys at the local warrant office and collect a sweet chunk of money."

"Does a captured Creet pay a lot?" Kase asked.

"The live ones do. That's why you're still breathing. I got my eye on this beauty of a Tiliner III sports car, emperor red. Zero to blow your mind in one-point-three seconds, and you, little man, are the paycheck that's going to get it for me."

"It sounds amazing," said Kase.

"I'd love to show it to you, *buuuuuut*..." he said, giving him a sidelong look, "you won't be around."

"Settling for the three series?" Brell said. "It's okay. I heard the seven series makes it look like something your great grandmother would drive."

"Hey," said Hanover. "There's nothing wrong with the three."

"I know," she said. "That's why everyone and their dog drives them. You hardly see anyone driving a seven."

"But the three..." Hanover said, his face falling unhappily.

"I have inside info that will make enough to buy the seven with money to spare."

"With the sterling trim package?" he asked.

Brell nodded, smiling.

"How?" he asked.

"A master mage," Brell.

Hanover's mouth sagged open in surprise. The next instant, he dropped an eyebrow, looking at her suspiciously.

"You've lied to me before," he said. "I haven't forgotten Plantoria."

"She's telling you the truth," Kase said. "That's who we were going after when you grabbed us."

Hanover studied them as he pondered this new opportunity.

"He's got a cult," Brell said.

"How big a cult?" Hanover asked with growing interest.

"Twelve," Kase said. "Maybe more."

"Each one adds bonuses to the main bounty," she said.

Hanover frowned as he tried counting on his fingers but couldn't work it out and gave up.

"What's your cut?" he asked.

"It's all yours," Brell said.

He stared at Brell, trying to decide if he could believe her.

"Honest?"

She grinned, nodding her head.

"All you have to do is promise to keep a secret," she said.

"What secret?"

"Give me your word now," she said. "I'll tell you later."

Hanover smacked a button, and the straps and cuffs fell away.

"I'm in!" he announced, all smiles. "Just like old times, huh?" He wrapped an arm around each of them. "Bring it in," he said and squeezed them in a bear hug, smushing their faces into his broad chest.

They gasped for air as he let them go and began pacing the room.

"Okay," he said, clapping his hands. "How do we get this...guy?"

"Naz," Kase said.

"Sure," Hanover said. "How do we get him?"

"All we have to do is separate him from a few antique warbots."

"Warbots?" he said, squinting at her.

"They're old technology," said Kase. "Practically falling apart."

Hanover chuckled, rocking Kase with a friendly smack in the shoulder.

"I'm just messing with you," he said, throwing open a set of double cabinet doors. "I know what they are, and I got just the thing."

Brell's mouth fell open as she saw racks and shelves of all kinds of weapons.

"How?" she said.

"I don't turn in everything when I capture a bad guy. I save the good stuff for a rainy day, and baby... it's pouring."

Kase was rolling his eyes when Hanover stuffed an arm full of guns in his hands.

"No time to waste," he said. "I want to be driving my new car by tomorrow night."

"We need a plan," Brell said.

"Yeah," Hanover said. "Kick in the door. Hose the room with guns. Put what's left in a bag and cash it in. It's a great plan."

27

STONE AND STEEL

Hanover slung a rocket over his shoulder and walked out to his truck, leaving Kase and Brell staring at each other.

"This might have been a mistake," Kase said.

"If you have a better idea, I'm all ears," she said.

The truck's horn blasted twice as the headlights came on.

"You guys coming or what?" called Hanover.

"He's going to be mad when he finds out you lied about the number of warbots," Kase said.

"Do you really care?" she asked.

The horn blared impatiently.

"Not really," grinned Kase.

In spite of his complaints, they talked Hanover into taking a detour. He didn't know where they were going until they stopped at the end of the canyon. Set into the side of the mountain were the large city gates of Salta Dyrin.

"I've never seen this before," Hanover said. "What is it?"

"This is the secret you swore to keep," Brell said.

A moment later, the gates rumbled open and a contingent of sentries strode out to meet them.

"Your tech doesn't work here," Brell said, seeing Hanover's hand twitch to his weapon. "They're friends. Behave."

Two of the guards were battered, their armor scarred from the early attack. They had been left to watch for stragglers and remembered Kase and Brell.

It took some haggling to convince them to let Hanover come inside with them.

"This is a Creet kingdom," growled the sentry. "Creet land. It won't be stained by this Teck."

The other sentries glowered at Hanover, who was staring at a guard gripping his sword.

"Think you're good enough?" Hanover said with a wicked grin.

"Enough!" boomed a voice, startling everyone.

Mal'Beck waded into the crowd, anger flushing him red.

"Our princess is dead," he seethed. "We've lost too many in our failed attack. I will not stand further bloodshed on our doorstep!"

Hanover's arrogance evaporated under the mage's glare.

"I'm deeply pained to hear of the princess," Kase said.

"Thank you," the mage said, his anger deflating. "Why have you returned? We've been defeated. There's nothing more you can do here."

"Maybe," Kase said, glancing at the big bounty hunter,. "But we'd like to talk to the chamberlain."

Mal'Beck's tired eyes wandered over them before he shrugged and gestured for them to follow.

The little they had seen of the city on their first visit had drastically changed.

The streets were busy with people rushing in and out of their homes and shops. Teams of horses and carts were being hastily loaded with their possessions.

"What's happening?" Kase asked.

"Everyone is leaving," the mage said. "The chamberlain can answer your questions. I have other duties to see to."

Hanover craned his neck, looking at a city that wasn't supposed to exist, populated by a culture that didn't belong.

"Like fish in a barrel," he murmured, thinking of the money he'd make turning them in.

Brell gripped his arm and squeezed. "You gave your word," she said quietly.

"Don't get so worked up," he said. "I'll keep it. But you remember this the next time I need a favor."

Mal'Beck brought them into the palace, where they were met by most of the Royal Host.

They were murmuring over a map of the city and surrounding area.

One of them looked up in surprise. "We thought you were dead."

"Our... friend," Brell said, nodding to Hanover, "saved us."

"What's happening?" Kase asked.

"The surprise attack was a complete failure," Calon said.

"All but one of the guardians were destroyed," another member said.

"We have nothing left to protect the city," Calon said. Although he wore a fresh uniform, his face and hands bore the bruises and cuts of the earlier battle.

"Without our princess, we are defenseless."

"Everyone's evacuating before Naz can attack," another said.

"Is that the guy I'm... you know?" whispered Hanover to Brell, making a gun with his hand. "Pow."

She nodded and asked the member to continue.

"There has to be something," said Kase.

"If there was, we'd be doing it," growled the general. "Do you think we'd surrender our home so easily?"

"I apologize," Kase said, taken aback. "I didn't..."

"None's needed," interrupted the chamberlain. "All of us are feeling the strain. We must leave. The alternative is death or worse – punishing enslavement under Naz."

"Yeah," frowned Hanover. "Sounds tough. Well, good luck with that," he said, rubbing his hands together. "Let's get going."

Kase and Brell glared at him, but he didn't notice as he glanced around for the exit.

"He's right," one of the Host said. "There's nothing left to do here."

The door at the end of the room slammed open, and a dirt-smeared boy raced in. The sentries quickly grabbed him, and the boy struggled to break free.

"He's one of mine," Calon said, and the guards let him go.

"Naz," the boy said, his eyes filled with terror. "He's coming. All of his giants are marching with him."

"Where?" Calon demanded.

The boy pointed at the map. His small finger trembled over the same branch of canyon where they had been defeated.

"How much time do we have?" Gramath asked.

"How fast are they moving?" the general said, leaning over to the boy.

"At first, the machines were walking very fast," he said. "But I think it was too much for them. Two of the giants broke. They slowed down a little until another one stopped working. Now they're moving slow as syrup on ice."

The general looked down at the map, his brows knitted.

"At that speed," he said, "I'd estimate they'll be here sometime tomorrow morning."

The chamberlain looked at Mal'Beck, reading the dismay on his face.

"It's not enough time," the mage said. "He'll catch us with at least a third of our people still here."

"We have no choice," the general said, rapping the map with his fist. "We attack."

"With what?" protested one of the Host.

"Whatever I can scrape together," Calon said. "The only way to buy our people time is to intercept him before he gets here."

"Hey. Do you guys mind if I ride along?" Hanover asked, drawing a look of surprise from Brell and Kase. He grinned back at them, shrugging. "What? While they're busy knocking heads, Naz'll be out in the open. Easy pickings."

"Easy?" the general said, incredulous.

The boy yelped as Hanover easily picked him up and stood him on the map.

"Show me exactly where you saw him, kid," the bounty hunter said.

The boy knelt down and put his finger on a jagged length of canyon.

"He's coming up that draw," Hanover said, pointing to the smudge that had been left by the boy. "That means he's got to go through those kinks."

He tapped the map where the canyon narrowed to a twisting crinkle of choke points.

"He can't send more than a couple of his warbots through there at a time," he continued.

The general studied the map for a long time, playing out all the ways the fight could go.

"Agreed," he said. "Gather every mage, soldier, guard, and citizen willing to fight. We leave immediately."

Kase stood outside the city gate, watching the uninspiring ragtag string of men and women who had courageously volunteered.

Naz is going to brush them aside like crumbs on a table.

He knew the smart thing would be to leave. Go back home and leave these people to their fight. The brutal truth was he and Brell wouldn't make an ounce of difference in the outcome of this battle. They were going to lose.

He was shaken out of his thoughts when the ground vibrated under his boots.

They're here already?

Ice water raced through him, and his eyes flicked around, expecting a warbot to appear. He caught motion behind him and saw a huge stone head appear over the top of the city walls as a massive guardian strode out of the gates.

Others around him gasped, sharing his astonishment as another appeared; then two more.

The people cheered at the inspiring sight, sending their confidence soaring.

Calon and Mal'Beck came through the gates, and Kase ran over to them. "How?" he stammered, craning his neck as the towering brutes strode by.

"One of my mages was digging through the library basement and found the ancient spells," Mal'Beck said.

"They are much needed," the general said, "but I wish your fellow mages had worked harder to give us more of these."

"Mastering the spell to create these behemoths cost the lives of most of my mages," the mage bristled. "They knowingly gave their lives for these precious few. What more than that can we ask?"

The general dropped his chin to his chest.

"Forgive me," he said. "Worry consumes my thoughts about the coming battle. I was blinded to the heavy price that has already been paid."

Spurred on, the patchwork army pushed themselves throughout the night to reach the knots in the canyon where they would set up their defense.

Hanover drove the general, Brell, and Kase ahead to scout out their best position.

As the Creet arrived, Hanover gave a few of his heavy weapons to those who looked the least likely to blow off their own foot or kill everyone around them.

He gave one to Brell, whose face lit up like a kid on birthday morning.

"General Calon," Kase said, pacing anxiously. "What can I do to help?"

"I don't know," he said, sizing him up. "What can you do?"

Kase opened his mouth to answer, but the words stuck in his throat.

What can I do?

With his spells, he could push and pull objects but only small things. Nothing on the scale of a warbot. He could create small illusions – a new skill he was proud of, but they were nothing more than party tricks compared to the wave of giant war machines coming their way.

The general's heavy hand clasped his shoulder, and he looked at him kindly.

"I honor your heart," he said, "but there's no place for you in this fight."

"I have to do something," Kase said. "I couldn't live with myself knowing I walked away, leaving all these people to die."

"Stay then," he said. "You will die casting pebbles at a tidal wave with the rest of us."

"Hey, little guy," greeted Hanover, trotting up to them. "Well, general, everyone's in place for the surprise party. We'll knock down his tin toys and be back home in time for dinner."

"I wish I shared your confidence," Calon said, glancing doubtfully at Kase.

"I got my confidence right here," the bounty hunter said, patting his rocket launcher.

The general and Kase traded looks of skepticism as Hanover smiled, humming to himself.

"You were right," Katrell said, looking at Naz on her screen. She switched her view to the feed from the bat drone scouting ahead of his column of warbots. "The Creet are waiting for you."

Naz studied the display from inside his personal warbot before switching his radio channel and addressing his troops.

"Stop here," he said.

His pilots staggered their machines to a halt. He didn't have enough pilots for all of his warbots. Instead, each pilot was in command of three to five autonomous bots depending on the pilot's skill.

"Nowal," he said. "Take your group and attack."

"Master," the pilot acknowledged. He relayed the commands to the squadron under his control.

Looking at the canyon from the bat drone's feed, Naz fixed his gaze on an area in front of the hiding Creet. He beckoned the magic to come as he focused his mind and cast the spell.

The Creet had been waiting for hours, and with no sign of Naz, boredom had set in. The strain of staying alert for so long was exhausting, and eventually, many had found comfortable places to rest in the shade.

Kase climbed up to the top of the canyon. The ledge proved to be an excellent vantage point of the entrenched Creet below.

Brell sat cross-legged next to him, listlessly drumming her fingers on her rocket launcher.

They had run through the long list of Hanover's annoying attributes, and with nothing else they could think of, had fallen into silence.

Their eyes popped wide when they heard a shout echo up from the canyon. The cry sent a wave of adrenaline through the Creet as people jumped to their feet to see what was happening.

Looking down, Kase and Brell saw a smudge of gray smoke beginning to take form in front of the mouth of the choke point.

It grew larger and thicker until it stretched from one side of the canyon to the other. It was impossible to see past it, leaving only their imaginations and fears to guess what was coming.

They heard it. The stomp and rumble of heavy footfalls.

The general raised his hand. The Creet readied themselves. Doubt gnawed at some. They glanced out of the corner of their eyes at their comrades, hoping to draw strength from the more braver among them.

They steadied themselves while the veterans of battle stared into the smoke with hard faces chiseled with determination.

Out of the smoke came huge, gruesome fiends.

Gasps and cries rippled through the Creet lines as hellish demons splattered with blood broke through the smoke. Behind them were skeletal monsters with ghastly clawed hands.

The general was the first to see it. The warbots had been painted to make them more horrific.

"Hold!" he bellowed, his voice echoing off the canyon walls. "They are only machines."

At last, the Creet saw them for what they were, but there were new cracks in their courage.

Three warbots came through the smoke, and three more.

The general dropped his hand, signaling his troops.

Two of the massive guardians waded into the fray. The warbots were smaller, their heads only as high as a guardian's shoulders, but they outnumbered the stone titans. The bots charged, focusing their attack on a single guardian.

Mages on the ground melded their magic together, casting a net spell and sparing the guardian from the full brunt of the charge. Two warbots staggered as they were caught in the invisible barrier.

The other warbots hammered into the guardian. Weaker but faster, they smashed away great chunks of stone. The guardian swung its mighty fist, knocking away the crush of warbots. The other guardian swung low, ripping off a leg and sending it toppling end over end like a rag doll.

Leg in hand, it battered another robot. Armor plating and twisted parts sprayed across the canyon to the sound of thunder and screeching metal.

And then... it all went quiet. Dust fell like misty rain, revealing the carcasses of warbots shattered and broken.

Mages propped themselves up, breathing hard from the exertion.

A cheer sprouted from somewhere in the canyon and spread throughout the Creet, except for the general.

From his high ledge, he examined the carnage below, his brow furrowed and troubled.

"That's all?" Hanover said. "You guys made it sound like that Naz guy was unstoppable. Well," he said, holding out his arms, "mission accomplished, and... you're welcome."

"This isn't right," the general said. He looked across to Kase and Brell perched a hundred yards from him.

They looked equally confused.

"That can't be all," Kase said.

"Scouts?" Brell said.

"Send the next wave," commanded Naz.

Several more warbots began moving.

"Don't bunch up!" he snapped. An order easier said than done.

In spite of embracing technology, he'd turned a blind eye to its complexity. Meanwhile, his pilots frantically split their attention between steering multiple warbots while narrowly avoiding collisions.

Slowly, they mastered their movements, and the bots formed into ranks. Now moving smoothly as one unit, the pilots gave the command, and the warbots broke into a run, charging for the enemy.

The cheering stopped as ground under the Creet's boots trembled, building quickly to a thundering roar.

They stared at the wall of smoke with mounting dread, blind to what was coming.

The general filled his lungs and bellowed over the noise. "Guardians! Wall!"

The mages sprang to work, commanding the stone giants to stand side by side.

The slow moving mammoths had nearly formed up when a wave of warbots shot out of the smoke. Steel and rock crashed together in an ear-splitting thunderclap.

The impact sent a guardian staggering backward as terrified Creet tried to scramble out of the way.

Stone cracked and steel groaned as the guardians fought to hold the enemy back. With a heave, the guardians pushed, breaking the deadlock.

"Oh no," the general said as another wave of warbots tore through the smoke. Running at full speed, they rammed into the backs of the first bots, using them like battering rams.

"Fall back!" the general yelled.

His cry was taken up throughout the Creet line as the mages strained to control the guardians.

Many of the warbots in the first line were ruined or badly damaged under the crush of the second wave.

"What are they doing?" Kase asked, watching the chaos below.

Two of the second-wave warbots were ripping open the back of a bot in front.

"I don't know," Brell said, her brow furrowing.

One of the two drove its hand into the front bot and ripped out a large glowing blue cylinder. The front warbot fell over like a puppet with its strings cut.

With the cylinder in hand, it pushed forward until it couldn't get any closer to the stone giants.

Confused, they watched as the bot punched into the guardians' line, crushing the cylinder in its fist.

"Down!" screamed Brell, throwing herself into Kase.

A ball of searing blue-white energy exploded in the middle of combat, rocking the canyon with a bone jarring shockwave.

Shrapnel and molten steel blasted into the line of guardians, pulverizing the nearest two.

The canyon collapsed, burying the mound of wreckage and blocking the passage.

Choking on dust, the general could only wave for his army to fall back. The stunned Creet slowly picked themselves up and, without looking back, shambled to their next line of defense.

Their ears ringing, Kase and Brell watched in shock as the boiling column of churning dust rose high into the sky.

Pieces of rock and metal fell from above, raining down with thuds and clatters.

They pushed themselves to their feet and ran to Hanover's

truck. Shaking the fog out of her head, she drove to their new position and dashed to the edge, overlooking the second line of defense.

Hanover looked up, seeing Brell above him, and smiled as he dusted himself off.

"I'm beginning to think you lied to me about the number of bots this guy had," he said over his radio.

"I might have miscounted," Brell answered.

"We have to go down there and help," Kase said.

"With what?"

"I can't stay up here when those people are fighting for their lives."

"And do what?" the general asked, hearing Kase over the radio. "We only have two guardians left. That blast killed most of our mages. When Naz comes again, all we can do is slow him down."

"I can use one of the rockets," Kase said.

"One rocket. One less warbot," Brell said. "Who knows how many warbots he's got in reserve."

"I don't know!" snapped Kase, clenching his fists.

But her question rang in his head.

How many? Enough to sacrifice some in this battle... but not all of them.

This was only the first step in his plan. After this, he would set his sights on the Teck.

Reserve! He didn't bring all of them to this battle.

"We have to go!" he said, grabbing Brell's arm. "Come on."

She blinked in confusion as he took off, running for Hanover's truck. Utterly baffled, she ran after him.

He pulled open the driver's door of the truck and hesitated, looking at the controls.

"You drive," he said, racing around to the other side. "Hurry!"

Brell jumped in and started the truck without a clue to what they were doing.

"Where?" she asked.

"The graveyard," he said.

She swung the truck around and took off. The truck shrugged off the rough terrain with only a few squeaks and rattles.

Kase glanced at the map, making a rough estimate to the graveyard.

We'll be too late.

"We have to go faster!" he said.

Brell scanned the dashboard; the engine was still well within the green.

"Let's see what this thing can do," she said and floored the accelerator.

Under the hood, a secondary engine kicked in. Their heads were thrown against the seats as the truck shot forward.

Brell wrestled to control the truck as it bucked and went airborne with every bump it hit.

Naz sat in the open top hatch of his command warbot, gloating over the twenty steel bots waiting for his order to attack.

These machines were the result of years of back-breaking, unyielding determination. He had scoured miles and miles of the graveyard, endlessly searching for these forgotten corpses.

Enduring one agonizing failure after another, he'd attempted to breathe new life into them. Yet, no matter how many times he'd failed, he would not quit.

Now he stood at the threshold of his great plan. The Creet city was his for the taking. He would level Salta Dyrin and rip open its ground, striping it bare of Kendium.

With missiles and bombs infused with the yellow stone, he would blanket this world in a cloud of fine dust and kill every last soulless piece of technology.

He would bring the entire civilization to its knees and rule it under the mastery of his dark magic.

"We are ready, Naz," reported his lead pilot.

"Leave no one alive," Naz said as he lowered himself into the armored confines of his warbot.

The machines twitched as they came to life. Together, they turned and headed toward the tattered remains of the Creet defenders.

28

A CLASH OF MAGES

Hanover's truck sagged under the beating it had taken, but it brought Kase and Brell to the graveyard with astonishing speed.

Vaulting over piles of junk and wreckage, Kase and Brell ran past the mound they had seen the warbot emerge from the last time they'd been here.

Dashing up the path, they hit the stairs to the large reclamation building two at a time.

At the top, Kase threw his shoulder into the door. It swung open, slamming into the wall with a clang. The noise echoed throughout the dim cavernous building. Shafts of light pierced through the corroded ceiling as they spread out to search the building.

Piles of cannibalized mechs were heaped up around them.

"Got one!" Brell yelled.

Kase ran to her, and they looked up at the barrel-chested hulk of a war-mech.

"That's a warrior mech," she said, impressed. "They were the biggest bots ever made."

The huge bot was surrounded by scaffolding used by Naz's engineers for repairs and refitting.

"It would be a lot more impressive if it had a head," Kase said.

"It doesn't need it," she said. "There's a secondary cockpit in the chest."

Brell led the way as they clambered up the ladders. Thick cables were attached to each limb and four to the torso.

Kase got into the pilot's seat and gazed at the confusing panel of controls as Brell shimmied around the back.

"Why didn't they take this one?" he said, randomly pressing buttons. "It's bigger than all the others."

"Because it's an ancient piece of junk," grunted Brell, reappearing. "We have to find something else."

"There's nothing else here," Kase said. "We have to make this work."

"How?" she asked, frustrated. "My arm terminal has a hundred times more computing power in it than this thing."

"Then use that," Kase said.

"I can't just plug this in and..."

"How do you know if you don't try?" he pressed.

Brell glanced between Kase and the onboard interface.

"Okay," she shrugged. She extended the interface ribbon from her arm terminal and plugged it in. "Don't touch anything."

Kase raised his hands as she intently read and typed on her display.

He bit his lip, feeling every precious second tick by. He wanted to urge her on but knew she was doing everything she could.

"Fire!" yelled Hanover.

Warbots were massing at the avalanche of rock and dead mechs, trying to claw their way over.

Five trails of white smoke shot out from the Creet's hiding places as rockets twisted through the air.

One impacted uselessly into the rock wall in a plume of flame and shrapnel. Another punched into a mech's armor like parchment and exploded. Hunks of the blasted robot crashed into others next to it, knocking them back, but they shook it off. The other two were fired in panic and sailed pointlessly into the sky.

The machines returned to the barrier, trying to force their way through.

"Persistent," Hanover said, firing his next rocket.

It lanced out at the group of mechs, exploding into their center.

No sooner had the smoke cleared than five more mechs took their place.

There was only one guardian left, and it was trying to defend the barrier, but the repeated attacks by the mechs had shattered one arm and rendered the other nearly useless.

"We're almost through," Naz's lead pilot reported.

Naz smiled within his warbot.

"Yes!" Kase said as lights flickered across the control panel, then died. "Brell..."

"I know," she snapped. "This isn't as easy as it looks. It's an antique. It's not like I can...."

The control panel lit up; this time it stayed on.

"Oh, I get it now," she said. "I can't disconnect my terminal, or the thing shuts down."

The cockpit was designed with three stations: the driver, weapons control, and command. Brell was connected to the command panel and was too far to reach the driver's seat.

"You can't drive from over there." Kase smiled.

"Figured that out all by yourself?" she said. "You have to drive, but..."

"Done!" he said, belting himself in with a wide grin.

"Don't get carried away," she said.

He jammed his boots onto the foot pedals and grabbed the two arm controls.

"See?"

The war-mech's arms followed his motion, sending scaffolding flying in every direction.

"I have this figured out." He grinned, ignoring the clash of beams smashing to the floor. "Not bad for a Creet."

"Before you pull a muscle patting yourself on the back," Brell said, "you should know these were purposely made so anyone could drive them. You walk, it walks. You punch, it punches."

The obvious jab was wasted on the grinning Kase.

"Okay, let's go," Kase said, stepping the war-mech out of the wall harness.

"We have to disengage the exterior power cables before…"

The big cables tore away from the war-mech's limbs as it marched across the room to the hanger doors.

"Close the hatch!" Brell yelled, pointing to a lever next to his seat.

Kase pulled it, and two chest pieces pivoted from each side, closing in front and sealing them in just as they hit the hanger doors.

The big panels sheared off their hinges, and the warrior marched through without slowing down.

"Hang on," Kase said, breaking into a run.

Brell grabbed on as the cockpit rocked with each impact.

"I see them." Kase pointed at a monitor.

It showed the section of canyon where the battle was taking place. They could see symbols for the warbots.

"What does that mean?" asked Kase, pointing to a warbot with a stick figure symbol.

"I think it means it has a human pilot," Brell said.

Their radio crackled, and the cockpit filled with a harsh, seething voice.

"Ulmur. Send in your wave."

"Look," Kase said, pointing at the screen. "See that bot behind all the others? It lit up when we heard the radio."

"What are you thinking?" she asked.

"The same thing you are," he said. "That's Naz."

The last guardian fell as a wave of mechs smashed through. Many of the Creet had given up and ran long before. The remaining mages tried combining their powers, but the few of them left were too tired and hurt.

The warbots trampled over them without looking twice. They knew the city laid opened and undefended.

Inside his war-mech, Naz smiled, clenching his fists.

Soon he would cut off the escape of the refugees, the very same people who had demanded his exile.

They feared and despised him because of his dark magic.

"You were right to fear me," he chuckled.

Brell winced as the cockpit blared with alarms and strobing red lights.

"Stop running," she yelled, feeling like her bones and organs had been rattled loose. "The mech is shaking apart. If you don't slow down, we won't have anything left to fight with."

"If we slow down," he said, "there won't be anyone left to fight for."

Hanover stood out of reach at the top of the canyon, shooting down on the warbots with his rifle. It was an act of futility except for the lucky shot that pierced a robot, hitting the pilot.

The bot slumped, motionless.

"Warbot killer," he said to himself. "That's going on my business card."

A moment later, the auto pilot came online. The bot straightened up and joined the others.

"Ignore the one on the ridge," Naz said. "We will..."

A new blip appeared on his tactical screen. The curious thing was it was coming from behind him and moving fast.

He tapped the blip and connected to its radio.

"Who are you?" Naz said.

The mech kept coming but didn't answer.

"This is Lord Naz," he said. "I demand..."

"I heard you, you freak," Brell said. "You better call your army back because you're going to need all the protection you can get."

Naz glanced at the map. His warbots were too far to return in time, but he didn't need them.

Something told him he knew who was in the approaching mech.

"The two spies in the graveyard?" he said. "Are you... No. This is too rich. Are you coming to fight me?"

"Unless you want to surrender," she said.

Their cockpit echoed with Naz's laughter.

"You run like cowards," he said, "and only find courage once you're inside a metal machine."

"Look who's talking," Brell said.

"You feeble inhuman Teck! Come and see what real magic can do."

"I got a mage too," she said.

Kase's head snapped around, looking at her in shock.

"He's a master mage!" Kase said, aghast. "Compared to him, my spells are party tricks."

"You better pick your best one," she said, "because there he is."

Naz heard the rumble of the approaching mech and smiled as the brutish machine rounded the corner of the canyon and came into view.

An easy kill.

He breathed deeply, forming his spell, but the war-mech suddenly sped up, devouring the space between them. He hurried to cast before they collided.

Kase shot out his hand, the war-mech mirroring the motion, and made a fist an instant before reaching Naz.

Tons of charging battering ram smashed into Naz's bot with staggering force. Armor buckled and steel collapsed with a shriek as the warbot crashed into the canyon wall.

The padded pilot seat took most of the shock, but it didn't stop Naz from seeing stars.

"Great hit," Brell said.

"What now?" Kase asked.

"Hit him again," she said, scrambling for ideas.

"How many times?" he said, winding up for another strike.

"As many as it takes. The fights were over pretty fast when these had weapons."

Kase glanced around the cockpit. The weapons panel had been stripped when the mech had been decommissioned. Behind him radiated the blue glow of the war-mech's power core, and to the other side was Brell, anchored to the command panel.

"Not helpful," he said.

"Look out!" she screamed.

A swirling ball of crackling magical energy formed between the hands of Naz's warbot. Kase was too close to dodge.

Naz thrust out his hands and the orb shot out like a cannon ball. It slammed into the war-mech in a blast of sparks and color.

For a surreal moment, time slowed down and Brell and Kase were weightless as their mech fell back.

Auto action systems took over, reacting faster than Kase could have. The war-mech spun with amazing speed, catching itself from falling, nearly making Kase and Brell throw up.

Kase tried to clear his head as he scanned the controls for something to fight back with.

"Do something!" Brell said.

Kase glanced up as another spell crashed into the mech's right arm, staggering him.

He looked at the screen in time to see Naz casting huge darts at them. Naz fired one straight for the center of the war-mech's chest.

Kase flinched more than dodged, but it saved his life as the spike punched into the cockpit, scraping Kase's chair. Its jagged point buried itself in the empty weapons panel.

The war-mech shuddered as Naz rapid fired more spikes. Out of reflex, Kase raised his arm, shielding the cockpit.

"My turn," Kase said.

He ripped the spike out of his cockpit and threw his war-mech at Naz with all his strength. Power levels shot into the red as Kase stabbed into the head of Naz's warbot. Pulling out the spike, he tore at the ragged gash, peeling open the armored compartment.

He searched the screen, expecting to see Naz's terrified face looking back at him.

"Where is he?" Brell asked.

"In the chest," Kase said.

"What's he doing?"

Naz stepped back, his warbot making subtle moves with its hands.

"He's casting," Kase said.

"Cast back!"

His mind raced as he frantically grasped for a spell. The cockpit was a chaos of sounds and lights, screaming for his attention in every direction. He couldn't think of anything.

"Look out!" Brell shouted.

Kase's eyes flashed open as an enormous flaming spear erupted out of thin air in the hands of Naz's warbot.

"Where is your mage?" Naz taunted. "Still hiding? I'll find him myself."

Naz lunged.

The tip of the spear filled their display screen as Naz struck. The flaming weapon lanced through the war-mech's armor, crashing into the cockpit and blowing out its back. Kase and Brell shrank back from the terrible heat as Naz twisted and pulled the spear, trying to free it.

The war-mech jerked from side to side like a dog shaking a dead rat.

With a final pull, Naz wrenched out the spear, ripping open the containment shield holding the war-mech's power core and sheering off the cockpit doors.

Sun, smoke, and dust streamed through the gaping hole in front of Kase.

"If he hits that core," Brell screamed, "we're dead. We have to eject!"

Panting hard from the effort, Naz sneered with satisfaction at the devastating effects of his spells.

"You see what real magic can do?" he said, chuckling.

Without warning, the spear crumbled and vanished.

"What's happening?" he mumbled, confused and alarmed.

He began to cast a new spear when his legs buckled and he sunk into his chair, exhausted. "It has been too long," he said, realizing the strain of casting these enormous spells. "I must... *No!*"

Terror grabbed him as his strength faltered and with it, his control over magic. He felt the raw hunger of the magic as it raced at him, urging to break free into this world with all its power.

At the last instant, Naz gathered his mental will power and slammed the doors on the magical force.

He looked at the war-mech in front of him. Punched through with holes, armor shattered, smoke pouring through the jagged hole in the cockpit.

"What a fool's death that would have been," he wheezed. "This close to victory and die, idiot that I am."

He saw Kase in the pilot's seat. Vulnerable and afraid. Desperate to find anything to fight back with.

"You needn't be afraid much longer," he said, raggedly gulping for air.

Naz smiled, wiping the sweat out of his eyes and relished how he had destroyed the mighty tech of his enemy, leaving him stranded and helpless in front of him.

Kase glanced at the power core laying on the floor, looking terrifyingly fragile without its shielding. Its remaining attachments to the war-mech were six steel hoses.

I can cut them and kick that out before it explodes.

His hand fell to his assassin's dagger.

"Kase!" screamed Brell. "It's too late for party tricks now. Pull that red cord by your head."

He glanced doubtfully at the ejection cord.

"When you land, run for all your worth," she said.

"To where?" he asked. "He's got a bot and magic."

"It's better than being trapped in here," she said. "Go!"

Brell grabbed her red eject cable and pulled. Ceiling panels over her head blew off as a harness secured her to the chair. Hot light flashed in the cockpit as rockets blasted her up through the opening.

Kase stretched his face as he blinked away the spots in his eyes.

He reached for his ejection cord but stopped. He imagined Naz looking down on their tiny figures. Horribly exposed, they would make easy targets.

Brell needed more time to get away.

Congratulations, dummy. You just volunteered to do... what?

He couldn't match his magic, and Naz's warbot wasn't a smoldering wreck. Kase glanced out the hole at Naz's bot and then at the pulsing cylinder on the floor.

"One last party trick," he said and launched his mech at Naz.

His heart had finally stopped thudding in his chest when Naz glanced at the screen. The young mage was staring at him with a troubling look in his eyes.

"What is he..." Naz began.

He shrieked in alarm as Kase launched the war-mech at him. He clutched the chair, bracing himself just as the two giants crashed together.

Naz was thrown violently against his safety harness, knocking the air from his lungs. The cockpit was a chaos of warning buzzers and sparks.

Shaking off the stunning impact, Kase wrapped his war-mech's arms around the warbot, and locked the mech's powerful hands together in a death grip.

The cockpit was still madly rocking when Kase jumped out of his chair and pulled his dagger. With savage desperation, he started hacking at the power core's cables.

Flinching and ears ringing, Naz clutched his chair, expecting another stunning blow.

Dazed, he paused, trying to listen over the thudding of his heart.

Nothing is happening.

He was genuinely puzzled.

Did the fools kill themselves in the crash? No. A final desperate attempt.

Grunting, Kase chopped through the last of the cable's thick shielding.

Two left!

Naz knew they were beaten. They knew it.

So what game you are playing? What do you hope to...

As he turned off the alarms his eyebrows shot up in realization, and a wicked gleam edged his eyes.

They've abandoned their robot.

They were using their dead mech to bind him in place and buy time for their escape.

"Cowards!" he barked. His voice rang off the metal walls around him.

Using the controls, he pushed against the war-mech. The hum of motors climbed to a wail as Naz poured on the power, but he couldn't break free.

Ignoring the warning lights, he pushed harder.

The dagger slipped off the cable as the mech rocked under Kase's knees.

He froze for an instant, seeing the gap of sunlight between the mechs widened.

He's breaking free!

His hand cramped painfully around the dagger's handle, but Kase would not let go.

With a final swipe, the blade passed through the last cable. Grabbing the core, Kase dragged it to the ragged tear in the war-mech's chest.

The sunbaked armor of Naz's bot burned as Kase leaned against it.

He squeezed his eyes closed and clutched the core tight to his chest then raised the dagger over his head and…

Naz swore in frustration, burning several motors as he tried to break free.

His face froze in a twisted snarl as Kase, unbelievably, appeared in his cockpit.

Kase's eyes flashed around the cockpit until they settled on Naz.

The instant they saw each other, they cast spells at the same time. Kase hit Naz in the face with a fountain of dazzling sparks.

Naz swatted at his body, expecting gaping holes of fire burning through him, but he was confusingly free of wounds.

Furious and partially blinded, the mage cast a hail of white-hot darts across the room as Kase rapidly fired off a screen of smoke spells.

His shoulder exploded in pain as one of the sizzling darts knocked him back. He crouched, hissing through his teeth, and backed against the wall. He could hear the air begin to crackle as Naz created another swarm of darts.

Kase squeezed his eyes shut, trying to focus past his screaming shoulder and waiting for the right moment.

Not yet. Listen for it.

He trapped a ball of magic within him, trying to hold it in. It fought back, angrily protesting as it writhed and squirmed. His strength was draining fast, and he felt his hold beginning to slip.

Naz grunted as he flung the spell – the sound Kase was waiting for. The air cooked as darts flashed toward him.

Now!

With a guttural yell, Kase funneled the magic as he threw his *push* spell.

Naz jolted in shock as his own darts shot back at him from the smoke.

Panicking, he slapped his hands together, creating a magic shield. The air before him rippled as darts hit it, shattering into glowing embers.

He winced as three darts streaked through his shield; one hit the corner of the chair, another singed a nick in his ear, and the third shot through his outstretched hand.

Kase grinned as the cockpit reverberated with a wail of pain and fury.

"You have to do better than that," he goaded.

White and trembling with rage, Naz glared at his charred hand. Sputtering words of healing the scorched, cracked wound blurred as it closed up, leaving no trace or scar.

Naz flung off his safety harness and came to his feet, snarling a string of jabbering curses.

He reared back, throwing up his hands. The air between them burst into a churning ball of liquid fire. Heat rippled outwards as the surrounding metal walls began to glow.

"I'm going to sear the flesh off your body," hissed Naz, "and watch your bones turn to ash!"

Naz spread his arms and heaved the spell. The ball of fire flew at Kase, cooking the air as it came.

Kase grabbed his dagger and disappeared, leaving the pulsing power core behind.

Kase appeared in the war-mech's cockpit and scrambled for the pilot's chair. Without belting in, he reached up and yanked the red cord to eject.

Nothing happened. The ancient mechanism didn't work.

The chest of the warbot flashed red as the horrific fire ball hit.

Kase's eyes were transfixed with terror, knowing the last thing he'd see would be a flare of blue energy.

His fingernails bit into his palm as he clutched the red cord for one last...

The seat brutally punched into his body with a bang. The rockets shot him up, knocking the wind out of his lungs and shoving him into the chair.

Hot air washed over him as he raced like a bullet high above the two bots.

Above the roar of wind, thunder clapped in his ears as a blue-white flash erupted from Naz's warbot. His lungs vibrated from the explosion, and the bots disappeared in a blinding nova of energy and magic.

Scorched chunks whistled out in every direction.

Before he realized what was happening, the momentum holding him in his chair disappeared when the rockets sputtered out.

The pilot's chair fell out from underneath him.

Kase swiped at the air, catching one of the harness belts. His wounded shoulder stabbed with pain as he looped his arm through the straps.

He heard a pop, and a stream of fabric rustled up from the chair.

The parachute snapped open, abruptly slowing the chair, nearly breaking Kase's grip.

Except for his pounding heart, everything was quiet. Gentle wind sung through the cords of the parachute as he hung high in the air. The rich blue sky faded to a hazy silver where it reached the curved horizon.

The entirety of the canyon was displayed below in all of its grandeur. Off in the distance, he could see the faded shadows of the dark mountains bordering the storm fields.

He floated for what felt like a lifetime, but the ground was coming up to meet him and he wiggled, trying to steer to a landing spot.

"Hey!" yelled someone. He looked down to see Brell waving at him. "What did you do?"

"Party trick," he shouted back.

29

ONE LOOSE THREAD

Kase thought if Hanover's grin got any wider, the top of his head would fall off.

"Keep your calendar open," chuckled the big bounty hunter. "I'm taking you for a spin in my new series seven."

"That's okay," Kase said. "I..."

"Sorry, guy," he frowned. "It's a two seater if you know what I mean, and you're kind of a third wheel."

"A third wheel to what?"

"What do you say, babe?" said Hanover, smirking at Brell. "It is babe, isn't it? Sure it is."

A gust of desert wind played with Brell's hair, and she grinned. She had known Hanover long enough that these sorts of things didn't bother her anymore. He was arrogant and a pain in the neck, but somewhere, very, very deep down, he wasn't too horrible.

He propped himself against his truck and tapped the cage where Naz lay in a crumpled heap.

"Are you sure that's safe?" asked Kase.

He glanced over at the city gates of Salta Dyrin, where the chamberlain and Mal'Beck were still arguing the merits of releasing custody of the dark mage to Hanover.

"Oh, yeah," Hanover said with a dismissive wave. "I only get the best. This gives off enough cryostatic juice to scramble his melon for weeks. No more magic for him. I gotta say, Brell, when I saw that blast, I thought you were dead."

"And you lost your reward," Brell said.

"That too," he said. "When I opened his escape pod, I thought I was going to find a wet smear, but darned, Brell, if you didn't come through like a champ!"

"I was there too," Kase said.

"Sure, you're a hero too," he said. "So what do you say? You. Me. My brand new series seven and a quiet dinner?"

"I wish I could say I'm flattered," said Brell.

"No need. It's written all over your face."

"I'd like to write something on your face," muttered Kase under his breath.

"I'll have to take a rain check," Brell said. "A hard working girl like me, there's no time to play."

"Which reminds me," Hanover said. "Your gun? It's terrible."

"I know," Brell groaned.

"I'm a little embarrassed to be seen with you," he said.

"Thanks."

"So I want you to have this," he said, handing her a gun.

Brell couldn't keep the happiness from showing on her face and beamed as she examined the gleaming weapon in her hand.

"That's a custom Rex Peace Reaper," he said, smiling with admiration.

"Hanover." Brell gasped. "I... don't know what to say."

"You're the best bounty hunter I know," he said. "You can't do your job without the right tools."

The chamberlain and Mal'Beck joined them, glancing at the cage.

"I'd feel better," the chamberlain said, "seeing him at the end of a rope."

"In a way," Mal'Beck said, "the cage is worse than death for someone like him."

"Thank you all for your help," the chamberlain said. "I'm putting the lives of our people at stake, trusting you will not reveal our kingdom."

"You got my word on it," Hanover said. "But if any of your people start causing trouble, I'll be happy to take them off your hands. I'll even give you a finder's fee."

The chamberlain pursed his lips, choosing only to nod.

"You have already done so much for us, but our duty to our people compels us to ask more."

"Our librarians have been scouring the archives," Mal'Beck said, "and we've discovered that our princess has distant relations on Creet. We are sending a select few to search for them in the hopes they may possess the qualities to be our next leader."

"Take this." The chamberlain handed a sealed letter to Kase. "That contains all the information we have about this lost family."

Kase took the envelope with reluctance.

"I'm only asking that when you travel," said the chamberlain, "that you keep an open eye, nothing more."

A wave of guilty relief washed through Kase, and he nodded, putting the letter in his pocket.

"I hate to break up the party," Hanover said with a lopsided grin. He jabbed his thumb at the cage. "but you know…"

"We have a tireless list of work ahead of us as well," said the chamberlain. "Safe journeys."

It was a long way back, and Kase wasn't looking forward to spending the trip with Hanover, but he was all they had.

Happily, he slept most of the way, and by the time he woke up, the big bounty hunter had run out of stories to tell.

Brell and Kase shuffled into the lobby of her apartment, dusty, sore, and hungry.

"You can have first shower," she said, opening her front door. "I've got a ton of messages from my mom. If I don't call her soon, her head will explode."

Kase dumped his bag on the couch in a puff of dust and pulled off his boots. He wiggled his toes, basking in the glorious sensation and headed to the bathroom.

Brell scrolled through the endless messages from her mother and swiped them all to delete.

"How about we give ourselves a few days to rest," she called over her shoulder. "Then we'll go after Ethan…"

A scream shot out from the hallway, and Kase broke into a string of angry swearing.

"Sorry," she grinned. "I promise the burglar will get picked up tomorrow.

THE END

30

MEET ME IN MY READER GROUP

J oin my reader group and get a behind the scenes at upcoming books, exclusive content, and more. See you there.

31

YOUR REVIEW HELPS

Reviews are a huge support for a self published author, like yours truly. If you enjoyed this book, please leave a review and tell your friends about my books.

Thank you.

You can leave your review here

THE RIFT SERIES

Is your Rift library complete?

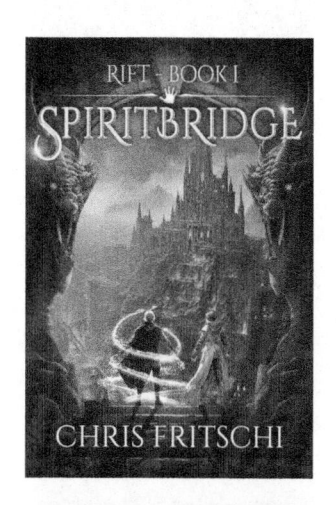

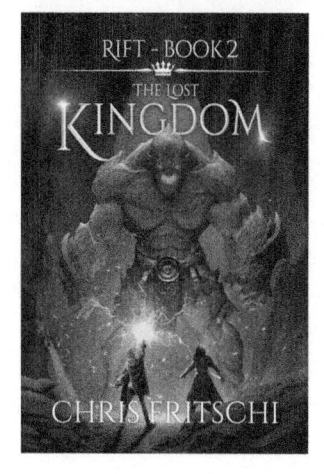

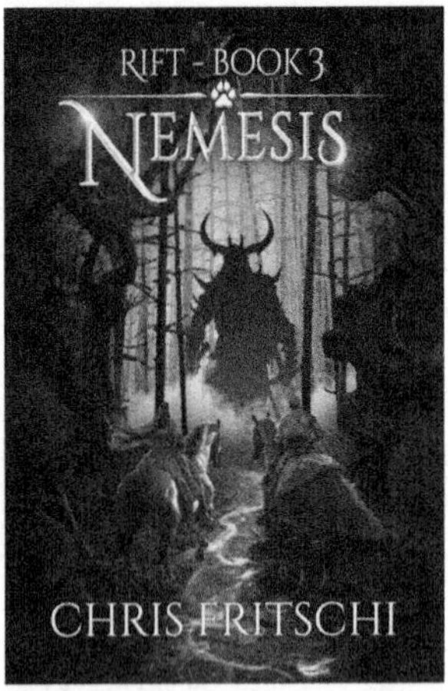
RIFT - BOOK 3
NEMESIS
CHRIS FRITSCHI

OTHER BOOKS FROM CHRIS

The Grave Diggers is a thrilling action/adventure that will keep you riveted to your seat.

A zombie invasion. A secret society. A plot to destroy the country. You're about to find out which is the most deadly.

The Grave Diggers

The Suicide King

Grave Mistakes

Deadly Relics

No Good Deed

Lethal Passage

Start your Grave Diggers library with this *free* book.

Hard Contact

ABOUT THE AUTHOR

Chris Fritschi is a best selling author with a talent for writing gripping stories, engaging characters and building worlds you can get lost in.

Whether fighting the undead with the Grave Diggers team or exploring an epic fantasy world of the Rift series readers are immersed in stories they can't put down.

website: chrisfritschi.com

Printed in Great Britain
by Amazon